PRAISE FOR HOLT MEDALLION WINNER VICTORIA CHANCELLOR'S PREVIOUS ROMANCES

ACROSS THE RAINBOW

"This charming and lovely little tale fits the bill for a good evening's fantasy."

—*Romantic Times*

MIRACLE OF LOVE

"Victoria Chancellor is a master of re-creating the magic and miracle of love. A heartwarming read. I loved it."

—Evelyn Rogers, bestselling author of *Golden Man*

"*Miracle of Love* is a beautiful, tender and touching story that is sure to delight fans of special author Victoria Chancellor. A wonderful reading experience."

—*Romantic Times*

BITTERROOT

"Victoria Chancellor wastes no time drawing the reader into this intriguing tale of love and treachery. *Bitterroot* is an absorbing time-travel . . ."

—Rosalyn Alsobrook, bestselling author of *Love's Image* and *The Perfect Stranger*

"Victoria Chancellor works magic with her clear, crisp prose, drawing the reader deeper and deeper into the story. She weaves history, past and present, together, making this a truly believable and heartwrenching tale."

—*Romantic Times*

FOREVER & A DAY

"A mesmerizing adventure with star-crossed lovers who will leave your heart pounding!"

—RITA award-winner Helen R. Meyers, author of *After That Night*

"Victoria Chancellor has penned an exciting, eerie and romantic tale of obsession, true love and sacrifice."

—*Romantic Times*

A TEST OF DESIRE

Jackson Durant looked unconvinced. "Do you always find excuses for inappropriate behavior?"

Randi's heart sped up; her breath caught in her throat. He was so close she could see his dark eyes and inhale his unique scent. He'd been out riding, she could tell, because the smell of horses and sunshine came with him to this shady garden spot. He seemed to be sensing her also, because his nostrils flared ever so slightly, and his eyes narrowed.

"Was it intentional?" she whispered, her gaze locked with his.

"What do you think?"

Think? How could she when he was so close? But she forced herself to look away, take a calming, deep breath, and focus.

As much as his dark good looks and off-limit status excited the woman in her, something told her this seduction scene wasn't genuine. He wouldn't have seemed so surprised and embarrassed if he'd meant to come on to her. He wouldn't have pulled away, then changed his mind. No, he was up to something, and the realization caused a sudden jolt of disappointment.

"I think," she said slowly, clearly, "that this is another one of your tests."

"Let me see if I can convince you otherwise," he whispered, before his lips descended to hers.

A Cry At Midnight

Victoria Chancellor

LOVE SPELL BOOKS ◆ NEW YORK CITY

LOVE SPELL®

March 1999

Published by

Dorchester Publishing Co., Inc.
276 Fifth Avenue
New York, NY 10001

ISBN 0-505-52300-0

The name "Love Spell" and its logo are trademarks of Dorchester
Publishing Co., Inc.

Printed in the United States of America.

A Cry At Midnight

Chapter One

Randi Galloway knew from experience that she wasn't good at waiting tables or flipping burgers. Resting her hand on the vacuum cleaner handle and looking around the silent, darkened museum, she really appreciated handling historic relics instead of pickle relish.

"Been there, done that," she murmured, recalling her disastrous two-week stint at Burger-Rama. The memory of that recent but short-lived job made dusting old furniture, polishing antique silver, and vacuuming fading carpets a bit more appealing.

She pushed a strand of short-cropped, blond-streaked hair off her forehead and reminded herself that she needed the money. Cleaning the Black Willow Grove Historical Museum was honest labor. She also had the advantage of working by herself, something she truly appreciated after her day job in a busy office.

However, just because she rather dust 'em up than dish 'em up didn't mean she was crazy about *all* her working conditions. The gift shop and library weren't

11

bad, but this part of the museum gave her the creeps. Not only was the lighting poor—especially with the inky darkness outside—but the long, narrow hallway led to a half-dozen small, unlit rooms. Each tall doorway appeared either a portal to another era, or a black void that hid all kinds of menacing creatures—depending on her mood that night.

And each of those rooms held personal items of a long-dead family—a creepy thought in itself. The smells of the past never changed, despite a hundred and fifty years. Stepping down the hall was like entering the ill-fated Durant family's mausoleum.

She placed her hand on her churning stomach. Something inside was giving her the willies, that was for sure. Something inside . . . but not in the empty place. Her palm drifted down, where she'd been round and full of life last winter. No longer. Now her stomach was as flat as ever.

With a shudder, she turned on the vacuum cleaner and attacked the threadbare carpet. No use thinking about what might have been. She'd just finish this one last section before getting into her car and driving home. If she kept herself really busy and dropped onto the mattress exhausted, she wouldn't have time to think about what she'd lost.

Burning the candle at both ends, that's what her mother called her schedule. Well, she'd only be working here for a short while. By this fall, her dreams would begin to come true and she'd pack all the bad memories away like artifacts in a dusty attic . . . or a museum.

The long carpet runner led to the newly completed replica of Black Willow Grove, illuminated by a single spotlight high overhead. She promised herself a quick look at the magnificent home before she left the building. She'd always wanted a fancy dollhouse, which is what the replica looked like to her. In her youth, she'd made do with painted and decorated shoe boxes, which were hardly the same as a real dollhouse.

The loud whine of the engine drowned out her thoughts, and dust temporarily blocked out the smell of aged linens, old books, and leather. No evil monsters lurked in the darkened doorways, and no ghosts of the past were going to jump out and frighten her.

With a last shove, Randi flipped off the heavy vacuum cleaner and paused, stretching her tired muscles. She sure wished the museum could buy one of those self-propelled, environmentally pure models. This old machine was killing her back. She felt twice as old as her twenty-five years.

Just as she grabbed the handle to push the vacuum back to the janitor's closet, she heard a faint, whimpering cry. She paused, listening, trying to locate the direction of the sound. Was there a kitten just outside the window? Or maybe in the attic? She cocked her head, stepping farther into the room, into the shaft of light that reflected off the replica.

Randi jumped as the clock in the parlor began to chime. Twelve times the reverberating chords echoed through the museum. Even after the clock fell silent, she still heard the chimes inside her head. *Bong! Bong, bong . . .*

Finally, the echoes faded away. She rubbed her temples, sure she'd imagined the sound of crying. Dead silence and the smells of the past surrounded her once more, reminding her it was time to go home. She took a step toward the waiting vacuum, then stopped.

There! The sound came again, this time stronger. Now it didn't sound like a kitten. No, this whimpering noise came from . . . a baby!

I'm hearing things, she told herself. There was no baby inside this museum. Maybe the wind, maybe some kind of animal. Randi tiptoed around the room, hugging her arms, listening intently. No matter where she turned, circling the Black Willow Grove replica and the sphere of light, she couldn't tell where the sound came from.

But the cries continued. Frustrated, she spun around, certain this was no trick of the wind. "Where are you?" she whispered.

She stood perfectly still, her heart thudding wildly in her chest, a rush of adrenaline making her forget she was tired and sore. She listened over the pounding in her veins, focusing on nothing but the faint, mewling cries.

The noise originated *inside* the light, not in some dark corner of the room, she realized with wonder. Inside the "dollhouse," not outside the museum's high, narrow windows.

On shaky legs, she stepped around the house, looking in each of the tiny windows. Of course there was no baby inside, even though she heard the crying grow louder. She paused, studying the six white columns holding up the roof and the second-floor balcony. Three doors opened onto a wide porch on the first floor, with duplicates on the second floor veranda. Three dormer windows jutted out from the roof, with chimneys between the dormers at the apex of the roof. The house was absolutely beautiful, from the tiny red bricks to the white painted wood trim.

Then she noticed the hinges on the panel.

With trembling fingers she unlatched the replica's front. The crying sound grated on her nerves, pushing her on. As the beautifully detailed facade of the plantation home swung away, she gasped. Inside, a fully decorated interior was protected by clear, rigid plastic.

Light slanted into the dollhouse, illuminating the mahogany dining room table and chairs, the miniature carpets, the tiny candelabras. Randi gazed in awe up the stairs, with the finely carved balustrade and landing, to the second floor. Rooms of beautiful detail, four-poster beds and ornate chests, more minute ornamentation than she'd ever seen before. Why, there was even a tiny riding crop and a pair of black boots resting against a cherry table on the second floor!

"Amazing," she whispered.

Finally, she looked into the top floor, with a large room on one side and a small, less elaborate bedroom and nursery on the other.

She pressed closer, her palms resting on the barrier, her breath feathering against the cool plastic. As with the rest of the house, the room was beautifully decorated, with tiny sprigged wallpaper and white woodwork. A folded quilt rested on a narrow iron bed, and a vase of flowers stood on a chest of drawers.

Within a fancy bassinet lay a tiny baby, the kind she'd played with as a child, the kind baked inside king cakes during Mardi Gras. Nothing special. Just pink plastic with human features, outstretched arms and legs, a "diaper" barely visible on the torso.

Not a real baby. Not a child who could cry.

Randi eased away from the house, her hands trembling. She must have imagined the sound of a baby's cries. She was simply exhausted, thinking about her own recent past, thinking . . . too much. So she'd imagined the sound. No baby had really cried inside the Black Willow Grove Museum. Her mind played cruel tricks on her.

She took a deep breath, closing the replica with great care. She didn't want to damage the beautiful piece. She'd never seen anything so delicate, so accurate in every detail. If she hadn't reminded herself that she was looking into a dollhouse, she would have thought the place was real. She could almost imagine a finely dressed couple strolling down the stairs, holding that tiny baby in their arms.

Except they would have been real. The baby wouldn't have been pink plastic. A real house deserved living occupants, not just a single little toy in the third-floor bassinet.

"Good grief," she mumbled, disgusted at herself for being so foolish. She was a cleaning lady, not a historian. What did she know about history, anyway? She hadn't learned much about Black Willow Grove in the three weeks she'd been working here. Maybe she should.

Her legs still shaky, Randi rolled the vacuum cleaner down the threadbare carpet to the janitor's closet. She heard no more crying, imagined no more ghouls lurking in the darkened rooms.

Before she locked up for the night, she took another look at the replica, then visited the gift shop and selected a really nice book on the plantation. They sold for twenty-two dollars, but she didn't have the money to buy it. She'd be careful with her borrowed book and return it the next day. Beside, shouldn't employees know about the place where they worked?

"Sounds good to me," she said as she cradled the book in her arms. With a last look down the long, narrow hallway, she fastened her fanny pack around her waist and slipped out into the night.

"Whatcha readin', Randi Mae?"

She looked up from the book she'd borrowed from the museum last night. "It's a history of Black Willow Grove plantation, Mom," she answered, ignoring the plate of pork chops and mashed potatoes her mother had placed beside her. Randi sure didn't want to mess up this book, because as interesting as it was, twenty-two dollars would dig a big hole in her wallet.

"Did you know the museum is built on the land where the plantation once stood?" she continued, looking over her shoulder at her mother.

"What happened to the house?"

"Destroyed in the flood of 1849. It's a really sad story.

The man and his daughter must have died in the flood, too. At least, that's what they think. The slaves and servants told the neighbors that he and the little girl vanished when the house was flooded."

"That water can be powerful," her mother added, nodding her gray-streaked, light brown–haired head. "You remember that time—"

"Don't remind me," Randi cut in, shuddering. "I'd rather not think on it." She and her brother Russell had built a raft out of driftwood. They'd both thought navigating the Mississippi like Huck Finn would be great fun. They just hadn't realized how fast and strong the current could be during the spring rains, or how flimsy their raft was.

Without Russell's help, Randi would have drowned in that muddy water. He probably still had half-moon shaped indentations in his shoulders where she'd clung to him, frightened out of her mind by the churning water that threatened to suck her under. Since then she never went in the river—wasn't real crazy about water of any kind. The thought of a father and daughter drowning in a flood made her shudder again.

"That's okay, honey," her mother said with a pat on Randi's shoulder. "It was a long time ago."

Randi wasn't sure whether her mother meant the family's death or her own near brush with drowning, but she wasn't about to talk about either subject. Thankful for the familiar smells of fried meat and fresh rolls, for the sound of her father in the living room, watching some sitcom on television, Randi pushed the memories out of her mind. Nothing was more comforting than the normalcy of home. Unlike a lot of twenty-somethings, she didn't mind moving back in with her parents to save money. They'd welcomed her with open arms, making her feel as if she'd never left the safety of childhood.

"I'm learning a lot from this book. Funny thing is,

there's no mention of the wife." Randi watched her mother walk to the kitchen counter and pour a glass of iced tea. "You'd think they'd mention what happened to her."

"There aren't any pictures?"

Randi shook her head as her mother placed the glass beside the warm plate of food. "That was before cameras, Mom."

"Oh, well, that *was* a long time ago."

Randi smiled, knowing her mother had an even worse grasp of history than she did. Her mother hadn't liked school, hadn't wanted to do anything but graduate and marry Curtis Galloway. Three babies had quickly followed, and her parents were happy with their lives.

Randi wanted more. She had goals she'd put off long enough.

"Food's gettin' cold, honey."

"I know. Let me just show you one more thing," Randi said, turning the pages back to a section earlier in the book. "See here, Mom? The reproduction of the house that they've just built is based on these sketches that a former slave donated, years after the flood. I wish the pictures in the book were bigger so I could see the detail. They look so wonderful, though, Mom."

Her mother leaned over and peered at the book. "Those are awful small, but look like they've got lots of detail."

"Imagine making drawings of a place from memory," Randi said, running her fingertips across the glossy paper as if she could absorb the talent into her own body. If a former slave, probably without a formal education, could do that, surely she could too. Right? After all, she had *some* training. Just not enough to get the job she wanted.

"You will, honey. You've got talent."

"I hope so, Mom. I really hope so."

Her mother gave her another pat on the shoulder before heading back into the kitchen. "The good Lord wouldn't have given you the will without givin' you the talent to go along with it."

Randi closed the book, then placed it across the table so she wouldn't splatter food or spill tea on it. With a sigh, thinking about drawings of a long-destroyed house and a long-dead family, she reached for her supper.

Later that night, after cleaning the restrooms and dusting the exhibits, she pulled the big vacuum out of the janitor's closet. Darn, but the thing was heavy! She unwound the cord, plugged it into the hall wall outlet, and tackled the long runner that led to the dollhouse.

She'd decided to call it a dollhouse. Somehow, that made the replica more friendly. After her overactive imagination last night, coupled with the haunting story of the family who had once lived right on this land, she needed all the normalcy she could get.

The loud whine of the engine drowned out her thoughts as she pushed and pulled her way toward the beam of light at the end of the hall. When she finished, she gratefully switched off the vacuum, resting her arm on the handle while she stared at the dollhouse.

"I didn't hear anything last night," she said aloud, trying to convince herself but not sounding too confident, either.

As though on cue, she heard the faint cries of a baby.

"Oh, no," Randi moaned. She put her hands over her ears, but couldn't block out the sound.

Unable to ignore the wailing, she opened the hinged front and looked inside. Quickly she took in the general layout, her gaze resting on the nursery upstairs.

The crying stopped.

"This is too weird," she mumbled.

The little pink plastic baby still lay inside her crib. The quilt was folded on the bed, the vase of flowers rested on top of the chest. Nothing had changed. Nothing was weird . . . except that darned crying. Was someone playing a trick on her? A sick trick to make her remember her loss? She didn't know anyone who could be that cruel.

Certainly not the only person who hadn't grieved over the loss, Cleve Sherwood. He hadn't wanted any responsibility, she reminded herself. She'd been such a fool—such a stupid, gullible, fool.

With a shake of her head, she reached for the panel to close the dollhouse when something caught her eye. She didn't know what it was for a moment. She scanned the rooms, the intricate detail and beautiful furniture. What was different? Then she realized—the riding boots and crop she'd noticed in the hall yesterday were gone. Her breath quick and hot against the plastic, she stared inside the depths of the house. Nothing. No boots, no crop.

With shaking hands and trembling legs, she looked all around the platform for extra wires, for signs of tampering, for anything that would explain why she was hearing a baby's cries and why things inside a sealed replica were moving. But she couldn't find any clues. No extra wires, no tape recorders, no broken seals on the clear plastic.

Damn.

Something strange had happened in that dollhouse. Tomorrow, she was going to find out what was going on.

"Ms. Williams, may I have a word with you?"

"Of course. Come in, Randi."

Randi entered the small, tastefully decorated curator's office.

"What can I do for you?"

"I noticed something kind of . . . odd last night, and I wanted to ask you about it."

The middle-aged, friendly woman cocked her head and folded her hands on her desk. "What kind of odd thing did you notice?"

"Well, you know the new replica?" *Of course she does, you ninny*, Randi scolded herself. This wasn't going well. She was too nervous. "Anyway, when I was cleaning, I looked inside two nights ago, right after y'all set it up."

"It's a wonderful reproduction. The artisan crafted it for years."

"Yes, it's a wonder. All that detail . . . But you see, I noticed a pair of black riding boots in the second-floor hallway that first night. Oh, and there was a riding crop on the table."

The curator frowned. "I don't recall those on the inventory."

This was getting weirder by the minute. "That's just the thing, Ms. Williams. I looked again last night, and the riding boots were gone. Did someone rearrange things?" *Or is someone trying to drive me crazy with the sound of a baby crying?* she wanted to ask.

"No one has touched the model since it was set up. Are you sure of what you saw, Randi? You could have been tired."

She started to shake her head, to tell the woman she knew what she'd seen, what she'd heard. But she wasn't ready to reveal the sounds. Seeing the riding boots one night and not the next was enough for now. "I'm pretty sure," she answered.

"Well, I'll check on the model later, before I go home." Ms. Williams glanced at her watch. "Which is just about now," she added, rising from her desk chair. "You came in early, didn't you?"

Randi shook her head. "I just stopped by on my way home from my day job to talk to you."

"You've been working awfully hard," the curator said, walking around the corner of her desk and smiling.

21

Randi knew the lady was being nice, but her words and actions seemed a bit patronizing. She knew she worked hard, but how else was she going to pay off her bills and save enough for this fall?

"Sure, Ms. Williams. Well, I'll be going. My mom is expecting me for dinner." She turned and stepped toward the door. "No one else has reported anything . . . odd about the replica, have they?"

"Odd?"

"Oh, like maybe noises or something. I just thought I heard a sound the other night."

"No, no one has said anything. The model was sealed by the man who created it. There shouldn't be any wind passing through, or anything like that." Ms. Williams looked at her, a hopeful expression warring with the concern etched on her face. She no doubt wanted Randi to say that she was just kidding.

She couldn't tell that big a lie. "I'm sure the sound came from somewhere else," she finally said, hoping that was enough.

"You're probably right." Ms. Williams released a sigh of relief.

Even though the curator seemed appeased, Randi knew she'd nearly stepped over the line. Now the woman thought she was a little weird, hearing things from inside a sealed-up model. The best thing to do was leave before she said anything else to worry her employer.

"You're doing a great job, Randi. I hope you're not working too hard." Ms. Williams followed her across the carpeted floor.

"No, of course not." *If you don't count that huge, heavy vacuum cleaner,* she felt like adding. She'd save that for another day, though. No sense making the curator think she was delusional and whining at the same time. Randi paused and smiled weakly.

"Thanks for mentioning the . . . situation. I'll go right now to check on the model."

"Thank you, Ms. Williams. Good night." Randi turned and stepped onto the wide plank flooring of the hall.

"Good night, Randi," the curator called from her doorway.

Randi frowned as she strolled slowly down the familiar hall toward the front door. A few tourists wandered toward the gift shop. The sound of paper bags rustling and people talking came from that direction. Familiar noises, along with the same smells of old furniture, books, and linens. Nothing strange.

She should take a clue from Ms. Williams and chalk this up to a mild case of exhaustion. The only problem was, Randi didn't feel too tired. As a matter of fact, she couldn't wait to finish reading the book she'd borrowed two nights ago. Surely there was a mention of the baby's mother somewhere in the darn thing. How could they have a "family" without a mother for the little girl who drowned in the flood?

She varied her routine that night, hoping she wouldn't hear the sounds that haunted her. First, she vacuumed, then dusted the display rooms, cleaned the restrooms, then headed for the gift shop.

She straightened the trinkets, postcard racks, and cleaned the glass counters. Then, with a regretful sigh, she placed the borrowed book back on the bottom of the stack. She'd enjoyed reading about Black Willow Grove, even if the book hadn't mentioned the baby's mother. It was almost as if she'd never existed, or if she'd simply vanished into thin air, erasing herself from everyone's memory.

Randi finished emptying the trash can from Ms. Williams's office, then returned to the janitor's closet for her fanny pack. Tonight, she wasn't going to be haunted by the sound of the baby's cries.

Nonsense. There were no cries. She'd imagined them. Plastic toy babies didn't cry.

Still, before she fished her keys out to lock up, she felt compelled to check. The end of the hallway beckoned, the light calling to her as insistently as the sound of a baby's wails. She closed her eyes, gritted her teeth, and clenched her fist around the zipper. She should leave right now. Walk out the door. Lock up. Drive home. Forget the dollhouse and the lonely baby in the third-floor nursery.

As she stood in the hall near the front door, the clock chimed midnight. The heavy tones reverberated through the museum, sending shivers down her spine. *Lonely?* Here was some concrete evidence she really was exhausted and delusional. There was no reason to place such a human emotion on a dab of plastic with human features. No reason at all.

Still, she couldn't leave. Not without checking.

Her tennis shoes felt like lead boots as she walked down the hall toward the "model," as Ms. Williams called the replica of Black Willow Grove. To Randi, it was simply a dollhouse. And inside, a little pink doll.

She brushed her bangs back from her forehead and advanced, already knowing what she'd hear, already sensing the faint cries as she neared the dollhouse. She didn't realized her eyes were full of tears until a drop ran down her cheek.

"What's going on?" she asked, resting her head against the wooden shingles of the roof. "Is someone playing a sick joke? Why is this happening to me?" She didn't know anyone who would want to make her think she was going crazy or torment her with her loss. No one hated her that much. Which left other explanations . . .

Only she wasn't exhausted. She wasn't hallucinating.

A CRY AT MIDNIGHT

She was angry.

With a moan, she dashed the tears on her cheeks, then flipped open the catch and looked inside the dollhouse. Her heart pounded so hard she couldn't tell if she still heard the baby's cries. All she knew was that she had to find out what was going on.

As usual, the interior looked . . . normal. No other figures inside the house, no boots in the hallway, a pink doll in the bassinet. The baby wasn't real, but she still heard the cries. This time, they seemed to come from inside her soul.

She couldn't stand this any longer. With an angry shriek, she pried the plastic away from the wooden frame, not caring that she might damage the valuable replica, not caring about anything but getting inside to discover why she kept hearing the baby cry. Why was *she* the only person who heard the sound?

The covering began to give. She managed to get two fingers between the plastic and the wood, then pulled harder. The dollhouse rocked despite its size and weight as the plastic pulled away from one side. Randi realized the miniature bassinet was tipping over. She couldn't let that happen! She had to catch that little plastic baby before it hit the floor of the nursery—just as if it were a real baby.

She reached inside the dollhouse, her hands cupped to catch the tiny infant before the bassinet pitched to its side. The only sensation she had was of warmth, as though the air inside the dollhouse was warmer than the rest of the museum. Along with the warmth came a burst of light. Then her fingers connected, and she felt lacy fabric against her outstretched fingertips.

The whole incident happened so fast she didn't know if she'd really kept the doll from falling for only a moment. Her mind spun blindly for a second. She closed her eyes, shook her head, and suddenly became aware of her surroundings once more.

Tiny sprigged wallpaper. An iron bedstead, a vase of flowers on a chest. A quilt draped across the bed. A fancy bassinet.

A real, crying baby lying in her outstretched arms.

For the third time in Randi Galloway's life, she screamed.

Chapter Two

Jackson heard a scream above the cries of his daughter. Damn Suzette for leaving Rose alone once again, he thought as he pounded up the steps to the third floor. How many times had he told her to stay with his daughter unless she napped, and to listen for her waking? He would have a proper governess soon, though, someone who would be with Rose constantly, someone to raise her as she should be raised. Until then, he vowed as he turned the corner of the stairs and strode into her room, he would . . .

"My God, who are you?" he roared.

The young woman who held his precious child turned panic-stricken eyes to him, extended her arms, and turned as white as Rose's crib hangings. He grabbed his daughter from the woman's hands, then watched in amazement as she sank to the floor in a dead faint.

Confused and angry, he held Rose at arm's length, inspecting her small body for damage caused by the hideous woman who was now passed out at his feet. If she'd harmed one hair on his daughter's head, he'd have her flogged. He'd lock her up for the authorities, or send her downriver so fast she wouldn't have time to scream.

"Rose, what did she do to you?" he asked the baby. She couldn't answer, of course. If only she could speak, perhaps he'd understand her more. Maybe he could tell what made her smile, or what caused her to cry so often. If only she had a mother. . . .

But she didn't. She had only him, and soon, a governess from New Orleans who could raise his daughter properly, dress her appropriately for a child of their social standing, teach her all the things young ladies needed to know.

All the things about which fathers had no knowledge.

He nudged the woman with his boot, but she didn't stir. She was damned odd-looking, with hair too short for most men, pants that were too tight for even a lad, and a strange, striped shirt that didn't appear to be any woven fabric he'd ever seen. Striding quickly to the stairwell, he called downstairs.

"Birdie, get up here right now!"

Rose began to fuss once more. Jackson noticed right away that her diaper was wet. He hoped that was the only reason his daughter was fretful. He felt constantly helpless around her.

He walked back into the nursery. The woman still lay on the floor, one hand outstretched, the other curled beneath her. Lashes too dark for her hair rested on pale, high cheeks. Except for her breasts—outlined by that strange, striped shirt—and the hips that flared below her small waist, she looked more like a young man than a female.

Why was she dressed so strangely? Why was she here?

"Yes, Mas'r Jackson?"

"Who is this woman?"

His short, heavy housekeeper peered around him and gasped. "I don' know, Mas'r Jackson."

"Well, find out. Have her carried out of the nursery, then have the floor scrubbed. Put her in an extra bedroom somewhere, and have Lebeau guard the door. I don't want her leaving."

"Yes, Mas'r Jackson."

"And have Suzette come up here right now. Better yet, take Rose downstairs to Suzette."

"Yes, Mas'r Jackson."

He pointed his finger at the nervous housekeeper. "Don't let my child be left alone again. I don't care if she's not your responsibility. Tell Suzette to stay with Rose, even when she's napping. I never want to enter a room and find her alone again. This," he said, pointing at the fainted woman, "is what happens when no one watches my daughter."

"Yes, Mas'r Jackson," Birdie said, her eyes wide as she took the fussing baby from his arms.

"Her diaper is wet," he said unnecessarily, peeling his dampened shirt away from his skin.

The woman nodded, then grabbed a fresh cloth from the stack before hurrying from the room. He watched her scurry down the stairs, her knees obviously stiff from years of walking up and down, of carrying too much weight on her slight frame.

For once, he'd like to be addressed as something besides "Mas'r Jackson." Maybe just Jackson, or maybe even . . .

No, he'd made his bed, and he'd live in it. Apparently alone, at least for the moment. As a small consolation, he thought with twisted irony, his bed *was* large and extremely comfortable.

The sound of Birdie's voice, calling out orders, summoning her troops, echoed through the house below. Her footsteps faded as she carried a now-quiet Rose through the rooms, no doubt searching for Suzette.

Rose needed a governess. Hell, *he* needed a governess.

He swore, nudging the fainted woman once more with the toe of his boot. "Who are you? *What* are you?"

Randi awoke with a start, struggling to sit even as she felt sucked into a soft void. Bright sunlight nearly blinded her; she couldn't tell where she was for a moment. Batting at the soft layers around her, fighting a sense of panic, she pushed herself up to a sitting position. Only then did she realize she'd been wrestling with a thick mattress—probably one of those feather beds she'd read about but never slept on. With a sigh, she leaned against a carved, ornate headboard pressed uncomfortably into her back. She frowned, then swept a pillow behind her. Her unease refused to go away even though she realized a fluffy marshmallow wasn't trying to swallow her.

Her unfocused eyes swept around the room. This wasn't the same place she remembered. No sprigged wallpaper, no white bassinet or iron bedstead. No real infant resting in her hands. She uncurled her fist, finding the tiny pink doll pressed into her palm.

Wow, had that been a dream or what! She must have passed out at the museum and hallucinated the whole incident. Her obsession with the replica of Black Willow Grove and the crying baby had affected her imagination more than she'd realized. But that didn't explain where she was right now, and what she'd been doing all night. She'd blacked out around midnight. From the look of the sunlight, at least twelve hours had passed. What had happened? She rubbed her forehead, then stuffed the little pink doll into her jeans pocket.

She had sure imagined a great-looking guy, who'd rushed into the room with righteous anger blazing in eyes as dark as his tall riding boots. She'd obviously even put that small detail into her dream, based on the dollhouse. His hair had appeared windblown, thick, and as black as coal. His white shirt had been open at the neck, revealing tan skin and silky chest hair. She hadn't gotten much lower than that in her dream, unfortunately. The last thing she remembered before passing out was the look of fury in those black, black eyes.

He hadn't been real, had he? Surely not. He was merely a figment of her imagination, like the crying baby. But she had torn open the replica to find where the noise was coming from.

Unfortunately, no one was around to answer her questions. As her eyes started to focus, one fact became obvious: She sure wasn't in a hospital. This room was filled with antiques, most of them cherry or mahogany, based on the items in the collection at the museum. However, this wasn't one of the rooms at the museum—unless they'd created one overnight. The place looked vaguely familiar, like the impression she'd gotten when visiting the homes of distant relatives she'd seen before, when she was very young.

Well, she wasn't going to get her questions answered in bed. Pushing toward the edge, letting her legs dangle over the side of the mattress, she fought the dizziness left over from her fainting incident.

She *never* fainted. Well, once, but that didn't count. The doctor had said she'd gone into shock. She didn't think something like that was happening to her now. And surely she wasn't tired any longer, since she'd been sleeping for at least twelve hours.

She'd just find someone to tell her where she was. Then she'd call her parents to come and get her. For some odd reason, she felt a strong desire to be home, surrounded by familiar items, family, and friends. Heck, even the tomblike atmosphere of the museum would be preferable to her unsure status in this sunlit bedroom.

She'd get up. As soon as her head quit swimming.

"So, you're finally awake."

The deep, chilling male voice snapped her head around. Standing just inside the doorway was the man she'd seen earlier. The man she'd *imagined* earlier, she reminded herself. He wore the same white shirt, riding breeches, black boots, and angry expression. And now he was gently slapping a riding crop against his thigh.

"I'm just imagining you," she said, looking into his angry eyes. "You're not real."

He looked at her like she was a ghastly vision from Hell. Sure, she must be a little messy. After all, she had been asleep for twelve hours. But he didn't have to stare as though she were repulsive, did he? Especially since she was just imagining him, anyway.

"Who are you?" he asked, eyes blazing, nostrils flared.

Damn, but he looked like the proverbial wild stallion. Her imagination was working overtime, she supposed. "Randi Galloway," she answered, watching him in wonder. "And who are you?" she asked, wondering what answer her overactive mind would come up with.

"I'll ask the questions in my own house. What were you doing in my daughter's room?" His voice seemed to push her back, away from his power and fury.

"She was crying?" Randi answered in a weak voice, scooting back against the pillows.

"Don't be insolent!" Each step brought him closer to the bed. "How did you get in? Why were you there?"

For the first time in her life, she felt intimidated by a man. And he wasn't even real! "Look, don't get all uppity on me. I'm still feeling a little confused."

"How you feel is of no concern to me. I want answers, and I want them now." He loomed over her, his face sharp in the bright sunlight, the shadows of his cheeks, nose, and jaw in sharp contrast. Man, was he gorgeous when he was angry. Kind of a Daniel Day-Lewis and young Mel Gibson sort of guy.

"You said your house. Where is that, exactly?"

His eyes narrowed as he stared down at her, as though assessing her guilt or innocence. Nonsense. She wasn't guilty of anything except creating this wildly impossible scenario in her mind, probably while she slept. She'd even conjured up the riding crop, which he slapped against his thigh again. She watched, fascinated by the rhythmic smack of leather against fabric-covered muscle.

My God, was he going to use that on her?

Now would be a good time to wake up. She pinched herself, but all she got for her effort was a small pink welt and a dangerous look from the whip-wielding hunk standing over her that said, "Lady, you are crazy."

"I'm not crazy," she answered to his unspoken remark.

"I'll be the judge of that. Now, again, what were you doing in my house, in my daughter's nursery?"

"I was trying to comfort her. I can't stand to hear a baby cry."

"Who let you in?"

"No one."

"How did you—"

"No one was around. I just sort of . . . dropped in."

"Dropped in? What nonsense are you speaking? And why do you look like . . . that?" he asked, indicating her from head to foot with one sweep of that dangerous-looking whip.

"If I'd known I was going to be visiting, I would have dressed better," she said weakly, looking down at her jeans, green-and-brown striped stretch velour top, and oldest pair of tennis shoes. At least she still had her fanny pack. No one had taken away her personal possessions. The whole look wasn't exactly elegant, but then, all she'd been doing was cleaning the museum.

Besides, he wasn't real. She wasn't having this conversation.

She *prayed* she wasn't really having this conversation.

"Your clothes are obscene. Not even my field hands would wear such tight trousers. As for the rest . . . You must know that your clothing is not appropriate for a female."

"Not appropriate . . ." she repeated, looking at herself. The top was the height of fashion at Lerner's. Her moderately tight jeans were faded, soft, and comfortable. She wasn't dressed strangely. If anything, *his* clothing was odd, right out of one of those history books in the museum gift shop.

"Oh, no," she whispered, a horrible idea creeping into her mind.

"What is it now?"

"Please," she said, looking up at his hard face. "Tell me your name."

His eyes narrowed again, but he finally answered. "Jackson Durant."

She felt light-headed again. *God, don't let me faint right now. I'm onto something here—something I don't really want to know, but I can't avoid asking.* "Then this is Black Willow Grove?"

"Yes, of course."

"Oh, my God." She ignored him, ignored the dizziness that again threatened to send her into a faint, as she scrambled out of bed. Before she fell on her face, she walked to the window. If she could just see something familiar . . . But nothing looked the same. No roads, no traffic lights, no grove of live oak trees across the street from the museum. No telephone or electric lines strung overhead. Her Beretta wasn't parked outside. Just cleared land as far as the eye could see, fields of some crop sending shoots toward the sun.

There was also no flood, however. No sign of water seeping out of the banks of the Mississippi.

"What are you looking for?" His voice came from directly behind her. For someone who clomped around in those high riding boots, he could move awfully quietly when he wanted to.

Oh, no. He and his little daughter would die in 1849. She was talking to a dead man.

"Like I said," she whispered, "I'm a little confused."

"Why?"

"Why . . . ?"

"*Why* are you confused?" he asked angrily before spinning her around. She got one good look at his stern face before the dizziness overcame her. All the stress of traveling back in time, of realizing she was actually in the plantation house she'd seen only as a model, of being interrogated by a man written about in history books, hit her with a jolt. To her embarrassment, she sagged toward him.

He caught her with strong hands, hauling her upright, brushing her body against his solid, warm chest. Accidentally, she was sure. He seemed to hate her for some reason. Right now, she was too disoriented to ponder why.

"Sorry," she whispered. She couldn't seem to get her feet beneath her.

He said nothing, sweeping her into his arms when he realized she couldn't stand on her own. In three quick strides, she was back in the bed, deposited fairly gently by such an angry man. She closed her eyes against the swirling sensation. The last time she'd felt this way was after a ride on the Tilt-o-Whirl with her niece and nephew, Sandy and Justin. The memory usually made her smile.

"Are you injured?" he asked, his tone less harsh.

"I don't think so. My head is spinning," she answered weakly, bringing one hand up to shield her eyes from the bright sunlight. "Can you close those drapes a little? The sun seems to bother me."

He made some small sound, then stalked across the floor to the wide, tall windows overlooking his fields.

His plantation. My God, she really was back at Black Willow Grove, sometime before 1849, when it would be destroyed by the flood. How could this have happened? She'd been listening to the baby cry, then she'd pried off the plastic covering of the replica. She clearly remembered reaching for the pink doll, then feeling a real baby in her outstretched arms. But the whirling sensation had happened so fast, the feeling of the warm, live infant had been so fleeting.

She'd thought she'd imagined all this. But if that were true, she was still imagining. She was caught in a dream of her own design. Or she really had traveled back in time. Either way, she had to play this out. She had to be smart, crafty, and wise.

At the moment, she wanted only to be clear-headed and coherent.

She didn't feel up to thinking about anything. Instead of being twisted into the sky and landing in Oz, or falling down a rabbit hole and finding herself in Wonderland, she'd plunged into a dollhouse and through the barrier of time.

She pushed herself to her elbows, noticing that the man who called himself Jackson Durant had closed the drapes.

"I'm sorry I'm so much trouble," she said carefully. "I must have hit my head."

"When?"

She thought about her answer carefully, trying to remember details from the book she'd read, trying to imagine what the heroine of a novel would do in this situation. "When I . . . lost my clothes."

"And why did you lose your clothing?"

"I don't remember," she hedged, knowing she had to find out more about the time to come up with a good answer. She had a feeling Mr. Durant would cross-examine her with more skill than Perry Mason. To avoid any more questions, she fell back to the pillows in what she hoped was a dramatic fashion.

"I'm not feeling too well. Could I have a glass of water?"

She opened her right eye just a bit, watching him stride to the doorway.

"Birdie! Send someone up here right now," he called downstairs.

She watched him by peeping through a partially raised eyelid as he paced the floor, a large, black panther if she'd ever seen one. Wild and angry, confined in this beautifully decorated house. Why? Why did she feel that he was confined, and why was he so angry?

He stopped pacing and stared at her, as though he knew she was watching him. She pretended to be ill, lying against the fluffy pillows, relaxed on the outside but as tense as could be inside. She hoped he couldn't see that about her. She didn't want him prying into her soul until she had a reasonable story concocted.

She needed to stay here in the house until she figured out what was real, what had happened. If he kicked her out, where would she go, what would she do? And then she'd have no way back, even if she could find a portal into 1998. She wasn't sure how she'd survive on her own in the 1800s. One thing she remembered from history lessons in high school was that women didn't have much opportunity in this age. No voting, no land ownership, no rights. She didn't exactly have a nineteenth-century set of skills, either, to get a menial job.

Like cleaning a museum. Randi had a feeling that her cumbersome, heavy vacuum cleaner would beat the heck out of trying to suck the dirt out of rugs without a modern convenience.

"Yes, Mas'r Jackson."

"It's about time," Randi heard him mutter. And *Mas'r* Jackson? How politically incorrect was that?

Come to think of it, in this part of the country, the menial tasks on a plantation were performed by slaves.

Oh, darn. Another horrible thing to consider. Scratch the *Wizard of Oz* comparison. She'd landed smack in the middle of *Gone with the Wind*!

"Get her some fresh water right away, then fix her some tea and toast. She'll also need clothes. Get some of Mrs. Durant's things out of storage."

"Yes, Mas'r Jackson."

"And make sure Suzette is feeding Rose. I don't want her left alone again. The entire staff is going to have to tend to these chores more diligently until the governess arrives."

The governess? And where was Mrs. Durant? She couldn't ask those questions right now. Randi knew she had to convince him that she wasn't a hundred percent of her usual self.

"Yes, Mas'r Jackson."

Randi heard the sound of a servant's scurrying footsteps across the highly polished wooden floor. Through one partially opened eye, she observed the man she'd come to associate with a caged animal. He certainly had the sleek, hard body to make the image work.

"Does anyone ever say anything to you but 'Yes, Mas'r Jackson'?"

He whirled, making her think he was about to pounce. "What did you say?"

"Sorry. I was thinking out loud."

"I don't care what you think, I only require the truth. If you're feeling well enough to make sarcastic remarks, you're sufficiently recovered to answer my questions."

"But, I—"

The servant returned with a decorated porcelain pitcher filled with water, and a matching glass. Randi eyed the pieces with envy, thinking about how much they'd fetch at one of the local antique stores. Maybe she could load herself up with a few choice items before stepping back through the portal into her own time.

That would go a long way toward putting her into the black.

Now you're getting punchy, a little voice reminded her. She'd better concentrate on existing in the present, because time had run out. "Master" Jackson wanted answers, and he wanted them now.

She waited until the young black girl poured her water and handed it to her. Randi smiled, but the girl didn't meet her eyes. How were these people treated? Was Jackson Durant one of those horrible slave owners who beat his "property"? She shuddered at the thought of who had received lashes from that riding crop in his hand.

"Drink your water," he commanded.

She jumped, then automatically replied, "Yes, sir," before draining the glass.

"I'm glad to see that you've developed a better attitude."

Better attitude, my foot, she felt like saying. But she didn't, holding her tongue as she stared at the riding crop he bounced idly against his thigh. Didn't he get calluses from all that abuse? She would never, of course, ask him.

"I'm feeling a little bit better," she replied meekly.

"Good. Now, how did you get into my house? Why are you here?"

"I think I'm supposed to be here," she replied carefully. "My memory is a little fuzzy."

"Fuzzy?"

"Confused. I'm having trouble recalling all the details. Sometimes I just have . . . impressions." *Or improvisations*, she should say.

"Have you always had this problem, Miss Galloway," he asked, folding his arms across a wide chest, "or is this a recent phenomenon."

"Oh, a very recent phenomenon," she answered

quickly. "By the way, how long have I been here? I have no idea how long I slept."

"Perhaps an hour. I came into the house for luncheon, apparently right after you sneaked upstairs and entered my daughter's room."

"I didn't sneak upstairs," Randi defended herself.

"Then I ask you again, how did you get into the house?"

"Really, Mr. Durant, I'm not sure. I don't remember much. I heard a baby crying and followed the sound." That much was certainly true. Randi shrugged. "All of a sudden, I was holding her in my hands, and then you walked in."

Somewhere she'd heard that if you wanted to tell a good lie, make sure there was a lot of truth sprinkled in. Well, that story was full of the truth. She seriously doubted that Jackson Durant would believe her, however. He didn't look convinced, his black eyebrows drawn together and his forehead wrinkled.

"I can't stand to hear a baby cry," she admitted when he remained silent.

"I can't either," he said softly, his gaze drifting out the door and toward the stairs as though he, too, listened for the sound of his daughter's cries.

But the wistful look didn't last more than a few seconds. He reverted back to his severe expression. "So, I go back to my earlier question. Who are you?"

"My name is Randi Mae Galloway. That's R-A-N-D-I."

"You have a man's name," he remarked with another frown. "Why is that?"

She shrugged. "My father was expecting a boy."

"That's a cruel thing to do—to name a child something so inappropriate. And look at how you're dressed. Obviously that name has influenced your actions."

"Now, wait a minute!" she said, sitting upright, her blood boiling at his high-handed manner. He had no right to insult her clothing or the name her parents had lovingly chosen. She'd been named after both her Uncle Randy and her Aunt Mae, and it was none of his business.

On the other hand, she reminded herself, she had to be nice to this man who others called "master" and who held her fate in his hands as surely as he wielded that vicious whip.

"I'm sorry," she said, sagging back against the pillows. "I'm a little sensitive about my name."

"Where did you get those abominable clothes? I've never seen such fabrics or such a cut of cloth," he said, flicking his whip toward her in such a natural, casual gesture that she recoiled.

Her fear must have showed, because he said in disgust, "I'm not going to beat you. Not yet, anyway. Just answer my questions and we'll be done with this discussion."

Discussion? Was it just her, or did he seem to be doing all the talking? That's hardly what she'd come to know as a *discussion*. But again, she held her tongue, thinking about how very much in control he was over his plantation and all the lives around here. He was right: He could whip her and no one would stop him.

Instincts said he wouldn't commit such a barbaric act, but common sense reminded her that he could. She didn't want to take a chance.

"I found these," she said carefully, adjusting herself on the bed so she wasn't plastered against the headboard. She slid her feet to the floor. "My clothes were damaged, and I had to wear *something*."

"How were your clothes damaged?"

"During the accident aboard the . . . paddlewheeler." That was what those big, fancy boats were called, she hoped.

Her lie was interrupted by the arrival of a tray of tea and toast, brought by the same servant who'd brought her water. The shy young woman placed the tray on the bedside table, then moved back as though she awaited further instructions. Randi reached for the delicate china and poured tea into the small cup before looking for the sugar. She knew that artificial sweetener hadn't been invented yet.

"The accident, Miss Galloway."

"Yes, my suitcase fell overboard, and when I tried to grab it, I fell in, too."

"Your what?"

"Suitcase." Was that the wrong word? She couldn't think of another word that meant the same thing! "You know, the box that I was carrying my clothes around in," she answered, sketching out the dimensions with her hands. "Where's the sugar, please?"

She'd directed the question to Mr. Durant, but the young servant stepped forward, opened a box, and cut off a piece of brownish stuff. As it dissolved into the hot tea, Randi figured out that even white granulated sugar hadn't been invented yet, either.

"Your trunk," he suggested with an arched eyebrow, bringing her back to their discussion of her story.

"Yes! My trunk. I'm afraid I jumped into the muddy water after it, and ruined my clothes." Of course, she'd never jump in the Mississippi, but he didn't know that. She wasn't about to admit she was terrified of the water.

"That was a foolish thing to do, but I don't understand why your clothes would be ruined. Wet and dirty, perhaps, but not ruined."

"Shredded," she embellished. "Caught on something underneath the water and ripped to shreds."

"Rocks, no doubt." He seemed to be taking her story seriously, which was good. She wasn't sure what she'd do if he denied all possibility of her claims. "Were you injured then?"

"Yes, I hit my head when I was pulled back into the boat."

"So," he said, folding his arms again. "You remember all of this, but not how you walked into my house?"

Ah, so he had been trying to set a trap. "No, I don't actually remember everything that happened that horrible day," she said, adding a dramatic flutter of her hand for emphasis. "I relied on what others told me, since I hit my head."

"And this was how long ago, Miss Galloway?"

"Just a few days."

"No one could find you anything else to wear except these inappropriate trousers and ill-fitting shirt?" His riding crop again flicked toward her chest.

She scooted back on the soft mattress, which threatened to swallow her into its depths. "No, I suppose not."

"I find that hard to believe."

She shrugged, since she didn't have an answer.

"Where were you headed when this accident occurred?"

She glanced around the room, then answered with the partial truth. "Here."

"Black Willow Grove was your destination?"

"Yes."

"Miss Galloway, I was not expecting you. I have no idea why you were journeying to my plantation."

She crossed her fingers in the depths of the feather mattress and said a silent prayer that her next lie would work. "Well, that's very simple. *I'm* your daughter's new governess."

Chapter Three

"Don't be ridiculous. The only person who was supposed to be on a packet was Miss Agnes Delacey. And you, Miss Galloway, are a far cry away from that proper young lady."

"No, not really. You see, she's actually a very good friend of mine."

He gave her a look that said that she and the saintly Miss Delacey weren't in the same league. Heck, he probably doubted they were the same species.

His continued interrogation and blatant skepticism were interrupted by two servants who brought in an armload of dresses, undergarments, and shoes. One of the women carried what Randi assumed was a sewing basket. Good Lord, she really was in *Gone with the Wind!*

Jackson Durant's eyes narrowed while he watched the women enter. "We'll continue this conversation later," he said, before starting for the door.

"Wait," Randi called out before he disappeared into the depths of the house.

"What is it, Miss Galloway?" he asked impatiently, riding crop clenched against his thigh.

"I don't want to be a bother. Won't Mrs. Jackson miss these dresses?"

"Mrs. Jackson," he said deliberately, as though the very name angered him, "is dead. She won't miss these frocks."

With a turn of his heel, he strode from the room, leaving Randi alone with two servants.

"Please, put those down on the bed," Randi said softly.

So, his wife was dead, leaving him with a baby to raise and a plantation to run. No wonder he was so curt. Some might even say he was rude. She hadn't known him long enough to form a firm opinion, but first impressions told her he was an extremely results-oriented man who didn't have time for foolishness. Not a warm, friendly type. Not exactly a people person.

She sighed, then pushed herself off the bed. With outstretched arms, she twirled in front of the two attentive women. "Make me into an acceptable lady, please," she asked. With wide-eyed disbelief, they continued to stare at her hair, her clothes, and her shoes.

"Okay, I know we've got our work cut out for us, but you'd be surprised. Really, I clean up pretty well."

Jackson galloped away from the house, his mood as dark as the gelding he rode to the far cotton fields. What a ridiculous female! Dressed like a disreputable boy, with unusual-colored blond hair shorter than his own, she should have been nearly indistinguishable from any young male. Unfortunately, she didn't look—or feel—like a boy. Curves in all the right places, firm and sweet-scented, she'd sent him reeling when she'd swooned in his arms.

How was he supposed to stay angry with her when she was constantly feeling ill? For someone who looked healthy, she certainly didn't have a strong constitution. He only hoped Randi Mae Galloway had no illnesses that might be passed along to Rose. She'd held his precious child in her arms, and who knew what else she'd done—or would have done—without his presence in the nursery?

The gelding snorted, pulling against the reins. Jackson held him in check, not wanting a mad dash that could destroy the fragile young plants beneath the horse's powerful hooves. He wanted order in all things, but unlike his control over this animal, his life never seemed to achieve such a blessed state. That ridiculous young woman's appearance in his house was just another example of how little control he seemed to possess at times.

Randi. What an absurd name—as strange as her clothing and shoes. The woman was a walking contradiction. Dressing like a male, sounding and acting like the most fragile of women, she possessed both a smart mouth and a vivid imagination. He didn't believe for a minute that she'd lost her trunk and the clothes she wore in some accident aboard a packet. Why she wanted to be at Black Willow Grove remained a mystery, but one he would solve. However, there was no reason to let her know he was suspicious of her story or her activities. Common wisdom said that if he gave her enough rope, she'd hang herself.

Jackson slowed the gelding to a trot, then to a walk, as he neared his newest cotton field. His overseer strode between the last two furrows, near where a shallow levee separated the land from the Mississippi. Between the green plants, the field hands pulled weeds from the rich soil, tossing them aside to be trampled underfoot.

Only the best, most sturdy vegetation for the plantations along this exclusive section of river. Nothing as lowly as a weed would be allowed to live in the select confines of the elite.

Jackson narrowed his eyes, his hands tightening on the reins. He was one of the wealthy planters now. He'd sold his smaller plantation downriver for the opportunity to join these men. He was now one of those who'd pushed the river back from the fertile land, who commanded thousands of field hands, and produced millions of dollars from almighty cotton.

He'd paid the price in blood and sweat. He was one of them.

His overseer began to walk toward him, but Jackson waved the man away, content to sit in the shade of a cottonwood tree and watch the hands work the land.

This section of land had been part of the marriage settlement between him and his neighbor, Thomas Crowder. Pansy Anne Crowder, the polished, accomplished daughter of one of the region's wealthiest planters, had been a prize in herself. Jackson still had trouble believing he'd been the man who'd won the hand of the fragile beauty. Their marriage had been so brief that at times he thought his vague memories of polite conversation and even more polite couplings were nothing more than a dream. They'd married, honeymooned in New Orleans, settled into Black Willow, and then Rose had been born.

Within a week of the birth, Thomas Crowder's fragile, delicate flower had died of childbed fever, never recovering from the rigors of bearing their daughter. Her father blamed Jackson, of course, for planting his seed in such fertile but precarious soil.

Jackson had not blamed himself; one of the reasons he'd married Pansy was for the purpose of producing children, not because he'd loved her to distraction. He left love to society's poets. Jackson was too busy building an empire. And empires were much easier to build with land from a wealthy and generous father-in-law.

Thomas no longer had his daughter, but he did have a grandchild. If he wanted to see Rose in the future, Jackson had reminded him, he should uphold his end of the marriage bargain and sign over the land he'd promised.

Personally, Jackson thought his daughter would be better off without the influence of her bourbon-swilling, meddling grandfather, but in fairness to Rose, he would allow her to grow up knowing the man. Jackson thought that concession was very open-minded of him.

With a nudge of his boot heels, he urged the gelding toward the overseer. "Brewster," Jackson said with a nod, "how goes the work today?"

"The soil is wet, but the weeds not too plentiful," the man said, wiping his head with a cloth.

"We've had no rain this week, but I see the river is up."

Brewster settled his hat on balding head. "Might be a good idea to build up this levee a bit, just in case the snowmelt upriver pushes the Old Man over his banks."

"See to it, then. Weeding will do us little good if the cotton is under water."

Brewster wiped his head again. "It'll be done."

Jackson nodded, then turned the gelding back toward the house. He wondered what he'd find when he walked in this time. If there was a God in heaven, Miss Randi Mae Galloway would appear more like a proper young lady and less like a lowly field hand.

Then perhaps he could deal with her better, more objectively. And he would find out why she'd claimed to be a friend of Miss Agnes Delacey . . . and Rose's new governess.

*   *   *

After tea and toast, corsets and lacing, Randi felt much more like a genteel Southern lady. Unfortunately, she'd learned that eating and lacing didn't go together very well, and that using the primitive facilities in yards of petticoats and skirts was not the easiest task a woman had ever performed.

As a matter of fact, she'd gotten so tired from her ordeal of fitting and dressing that she needed a nap. In her time, she'd slept about one hour since midnight. Right now she should be sound asleep, about three hours away from the buzz of the alarm clock that roused her each morning at seven o'clock.

She glanced at the stack of her comfortable clothing, neatly folded on the room's only chair, and wondered if she should hide these twentieth-century garments. Probably. Jackson Durant would no doubt order them destroyed since he found her so repulsive. And her fanny pack! Fortunately, he'd ignored that item when asking questions earlier. She couldn't let him get his hands on her money, driver's license, or keys. She wouldn't be able to explain those so easily.

"Loosen up this dress, will you, Melody?" she asked one of the two servants who'd played lady's maid and seamstress for the last hour.

"Yes, ma'am," the girl said, tackling the endless row of hooks and eyes that ran from neck to hips on the least fancy of the three dresses they'd brought in for her to try on.

"How is Mr. Durant to work for?" Randi asked in a conversational tone as Melody continued her task.

"The master is just fine, ma'am," she replied in a respectful, almost automatic tone of voice.

"No, I mean really. Is he short-tempered, mean, unreasonable?"

"No, ma'am."

"Would you tell me if he were?"

The girl was silent for a long time, but Randi felt her

fingers working on the fastenings near her waist. Soon they were all undone, and Melody tackled the laces on the corset they'd convinced her was necessary for all ladies.

"The master is fine," she finally said.

"He seems a little angry to me. I wonder if he's always been that way."

"I wouldn't know, ma'am. I've just been here the last year, after Miss Pansy married the master."

Pansy? His dearly departed wife's name was Pansy? Well, Randi supposed that was an appropriate name for a Southern belle. And with their daughter's name of Rose, Jackson Durant had a whole flower motif going. To him, accustomed to such feminine names, the name Randi must seem totally wrong.

But Pansy? Oh, well. Randi shrugged out of the dress, leaving on the camisole and pantaloons they'd insisted she wear instead of her underwire bra and serviceable cotton bikini underwear with the Mickey Mouse logo.

"I'm going to take a nap now," she announced. "Thanks for all your help, and I'm really grateful that we didn't have to alter much on the dresses. At the moment, I'm just too tired to appreciate them. Could one of you wake me for dinner? I've got a feeling I'm going to be famished."

The two servants looked at each other, then Melody spoke up. "Yes, ma'am. I'll wake you in time to get ready for dinner."

"Thanks." Randi sank into the bed, feeling smothered by its depths once again. She rolled to her side, then stared out the window. In just a few seconds, she heard the door close as the two women left. Good. She needed to be alone, to think about what had happened and maybe figure out why. Not that she was really good with big pictures or high-concept ideas. She was more of a detail person.

The only "detail" she could figure out right now was

that her life was in the hands of an angry, skeptical man.

Outside the wide window, she could see for miles. Green carpeted the land. She suspected that in a few months, there would be white bolls of cotton on each of those plants, and she'd see men and women with long sacks, harvesting the cotton for endless, back-breaking hours.

Jackson Durant would no doubt be out there, tapping his whip on his thigh, scowling at the workers. She just hoped he didn't decide to abuse anyone in her presence. Randi wasn't about to let that happen, and explaining her actions might be even harder than convincing Jackson she was really his daughter's new governess.

Speak of the devil . . .

She pushed herself to one elbow, watching him thunder back home on a black horse that seemed to suit his persona exactly.

If he thought he was going to barge in on her and start another interrogation, he had another thing coming. She was too tired for more of his questions and comments.

With another sigh, Randi rolled over in bed, facing the door. If Jackson Durant did enter her room, she wanted to know about it.

When she awoke, the room was dark except for a small lit candle sitting on a chest near a doorway. Randi felt disoriented for several long moments as she forced herself to breathe evenly, to let her eyes focus on her surroundings. For the second time in the last twenty-four hours, she realized that she'd traveled back in time, that she was actually in Black Willow Grove's plantation house.

Her fingers brushed against the fine cotton chemise and pantaloons she'd been given earlier. How in the world was she going to dress by herself? Even the servant had struggled with the row of hooks down the back of the dress Randi had worn earlier.

She'd find a way, though, she vowed as she struggled into the heavy skirts, pulling up the bodice and slipping her arms into the tight sleeves. Clothing from the 1800s was so uncomfortable; how had the women ever accomplished any chores wearing such dresses?

But then, women who dressed like this didn't do chores. They definitely didn't dust furniture, clean toilets, or vacuum carpets. With a sigh, Randi fastened as many of the hooks as she could, then slipped on the narrow leather shoes that had been provided. The late Mrs. Durant had longer, narrower feet, making these shoes a poor fit. Randi remembered thinking that all the boots and shoes the museum displayed were equally narrow and usually smaller than her own size seven and a half. With a sigh, she thought of the comfortable tennis shoes she'd hidden in the very top of the cherry armoire, behind decorative carved scrolls. Too bad she couldn't wear her Keds instead.

As she walked to the door, she vowed that she'd find someone to help her finish dressing, then seek out Mr. Durant. He'd left in a huff earlier today, claiming she couldn't be a friend of the new governess, Agnes Delacey. Randi knew it was up to her to convince him that not only had Agnes sent her as a replacement, but that she'd be the best darn governess in the entire state of Tennessee.

She pulled the door open a crack, looked both ways down the hall, and started to slip outside. Her foot connected with something lying across the doorway.

"I'm so sorry! she exclaimed, bending down to help the servant to a sitting position. "I didn't know you were there. Did I hurt you?"

"No, ma'am," the young woman replied in a shy voice.

"Why were you lying there?"

"So's I can help you dress," she explained, struggling to her feet.

"You have to lie on the floor?"

"Yes, ma'am. That's the way we do these things."

"But that's so uncomfortable!" Randi shook her head. "Never mind. I shouldn't say a word. Where you sleep is your business."

"No, ma'am. The mas'r had me sleep here. Lebeau tol' me so hisself."

"Lebeau?"

"He's in charge in the house, ma'am."

"That will be all, Melody."

"Yes, Mr. Lebeau." The girl lowered her eyes, standing at the doorway as though she was a part of the furnishings. Randi's heart went out to her. How could everyone be treated so . . . indifferently? This whole system sucked. No wonder they'd had a big war over the issue of slavery.

Even though Lebeau was also black, he didn't treat the servants any nicer than "the master." God, she hated that word!

"I need her to help me dress," Randi said, standing a little straighter and jutting out her chin, "then I want to see Mr. Durant."

"Mister Jackson is downstairs. I'll see if he's available."

"Don't bother," Randi said. "I'd rather surprise him."

The tall black man raised his chin, looking down at her as though she'd just suggested grabbing a few beers with the queen. He was a good-looking man, in a well-groomed and businesslike fashion.

"Melody, help Miss Galloway with her needs. I'll escort you downstairs when you are ready," he said, before retreating down the hallway.

As soon as he was out of earshot, Randi pulled the girl inside the room, then kicked off the tight slippers. "Okay, just who is he and what's he like?"

"You want to know about Mr. Lebeau, ma'am?" Melody asked, confusion obvious on her expressive face.

"Of course. Haven't you ever heard that you should know your enemies? I'm not sure why, but I think Lebeau is not real happy with me." Or maybe he just didn't know how to treat her—another servant or a guest? She didn't know the answer to that question either.

"Yes, ma'am."

"Are you just being polite or do you actually agree with me?"

"Ma'am?" Melody asked in a bewildered tone.

"Never mind," Randi said, presenting her back. "Just help me get fixed up for my next interrogation by Mr. Durant." She ran her fingers through her short, streaked blond strands. There was nothing she could do about her hair, but maybe he'd overlook that one twentieth-century style if the rest of her looked more "respectable."

Melody lit several candles, then went to work on dressing Randi properly. While the servant adjusted the skirt over the layers of petticoats, Randi wiggled her feet inside the too-narrow shoes, wondering if there was a shoemaker around who could stretch them out. She wondered how long she'd have to tolerate these uncomfortable clothes and the angry man who thought her unfit. Before she could dwell too long on the depressing topic of being lost in the past, she was combed, corseted, laced, tied, and buttoned.

Melody stepped back, her hands folded demurely. Randi's heart went out to her in ways the girl would never understand. How could she explain to a slave in the 1800s that she couldn't tolerate these conditions, and that she didn't believe any of them should be expected to tolerate them either? No one should be considered inferior because of their race or the circumstances of their birth.

Randi felt like hugging the girl. Instead, she smiled and said, "Thank you, again. I wouldn't be able to do this without your skills."

Melody looked up for only a second, but Randi could tell she was surprised by the kindness. Didn't anyone ever praise the people on this plantation? Was everyone as harsh and unhappy as Jackson Durant and his henchman, Lebeau?

She had a good mind to march downstairs and tell him exactly what she thought of his lifestyle. But that wouldn't gain her what she needed, and she doubted her opinion would sway him even a tiny bit. With a sigh, she headed for the door.

As she expected, the tall black man stood at the end of the hallway. "Come with me, Miss Galloway," he said. His tone of voice wasn't at all shy, pleading, or coaxing. He obviously thought of this house as his domain, and seemed to sense that she was as out of place in this lifestyle as she was in these clothes.

"Lead on," she murmured, struggling with the long skirt and too-tight shoes. With luck, she wouldn't fall flat on her face. With control, she wouldn't tell Jackson Durant exactly what she thought of him and his wealthy, parasitic life.

But Randi Mae Galloway, outspoken, unconventional middle child, had never been very good at keeping her opinions to herself.

She made her way down the steps carefully, holding her skirts up slightly with one hand, grasping the banister in a white-knuckled grip with the other. Before long, she was following Lebeau down a short hallway that led to an open door.

"Please, don't announce me or anything," she asked him. "I'd rather not interrupt him if he's busy, and if he's not . . . Well, I'd just rather let him see me on his own."

Lebeau tilted his head back, peering from spectacles

perched halfway down his wide nose. "As you wish," he finally said before turning away with a very slight bow, leaving Randi alone in the hallway.

"Okay, it's now or never," she mumbled to herself. Consciously relaxing her tense body, she released her grip on her skirts.

She tiptoed to the doorway and looked inside. She was prepared to face Jackson Durant on his turf, to play the sweet-tempered young lady to the best of her ability. What she wasn't prepared for was the sight of the man who'd been nothing but angry and macho toward her, now holding his happy, gurgling baby daughter in his arms. Surrounded by all the masculine decorations, he looked as endearing as a Hallmark card commercial, as poignant as a Kodak ad.

Her hand drifted automatically to her flat stomach and she swallowed the lump in her throat. She would not cry in front of him . . . and now was not the time to mourn the emptiness of her own arms.

Before he noticed her, she forced herself to stand straight, then pasted a smile on her face. By God, she'd get through this time-travel business even if it meant giving an Oscar-caliber performance that Dorothy, Alice, and Scarlett would be proud of.

Jackson knew he flouted convention, but he couldn't stop this one departure from common wisdom. Each evening after Suzette fed Rose, he spent time with his daughter outside the nursery. Sometimes, they sat on the veranda and listened to the sounds of frogs and crickets. She'd watch the lanterns and doomed moths with glee, pushing with her dimpled legs until at times Jackson thought she might walk right off of his lap.

Other times he'd carry her to the stable, where Rose would reach chubby fingers toward the horses and squeal in delight. In a few years, he'd teach her to ride. A good seat was necessary for a man, but admirable in a woman. Before she danced her first waltz, she'd be able to clear a three-foot fence with ease. Rose would ride to the hounds or pursue any other equestrian event she cared to try.

Tonight, rain threatened, sending thunder and occasional flashes of lightning through the northwest sky. Jackson settled on pacing his study with Rose cooing over the colored spines of his books and decorative items on his shelves. She reached for everything she saw, and he knew from experience that whatever she snagged would be immediately placed in her mouth.

"This is a crystal decanter, young lady," he informed his infant daughter. "Crystal could cut your mouth, so I won't let you hold it. Isn't it pretty, though? When you're older, you can have all the beautiful crystal you want. When you marry, I'll send to France for the finest service money can buy. You'll be the envy of all your friends."

Rose cooed and smiled, wiggling toward the glasses and decanters on the cherry sideboard that matched the massive desk and wall of shelves. This room was Jackson's favorite, a retreat where a man could run his empire in comfort. Every time he sat down in the tufted leather chair and reached for a gold-embossed sheet of paper, he reminded himself that he deserved every penny he pulled from the unforgiving clay soil.

Rose squealed, reaching toward a vase that he'd been told was from an ancient Chinese dynasty. He didn't care; he was more interested in forming his own dynasty at Black Willow Grove. But for that to happen, he needed a wife and a son. He loved Rose with all his heart, but one day she would marry and move to her husband's land, leaving this plantation without a male heir who could run it properly.

Before long, Jackson knew he'd have to make the social rounds, looking for a new wife. He had several months, however. No one expected him to marry for at least a year after Pansy's death. And Thomas Crowder would not take to Jackson's new wife replacing the deified Pansy as mistress of Black Willow Grove.

This time, Jackson vowed, he'd find a woman with a more sturdy disposition. He already had his land; he didn't need to marry within his immediate social circle. Perhaps he'd travel to New Orleans. Or he could go north, to St. Louis. He'd bring up the subject very subtly in conversation among the planters, just to see if a northern wife would be acceptable.

Speaking of acceptable—or unacceptable—he wondered how Miss Galloway had fared with the female apparel. He only hoped the outer trappings made her behavior less suspect. The answers he wanted still burned in his gut. His reaction to her could only be called disturbing. He'd never seen a woman defy convention so thoroughly.

"You'll never act or dress that way," he told his daughter with a touch of his forefinger to her pink button nose. "You're going to learn what to do and say so you'll never feel awkward, so no one will ever question your right to walk into one of these rooms."

Rose babbled, a serious expression on her face, as though imitating him. The idea caused a curious lump in Jackson's throat.

With a powerful lunge, Rose squealed and turned away from the sideboard. Following her line of vision, Jackson felt the air leave his lungs. Standing just inside the doorway of his study was a woman like none he'd ever seen before. Short, straight, pale hair framed an intriguing face with pink-tinged cheeks and rosy lips. Her round breasts filled out the bodice of the green gown quite nicely, emphasizing her small waist. He'd seen more of her in detail, of course, when she'd been wearing the tight trousers and strange bodice. She hadn't looked all that appealing then, but now . . .

His heart slammed against his ribs, reminding him

58

for just how long he'd been without a woman. Damn it, of all the inappropriate women who might stir his lust, why this one?

She smiled shyly, then twirled slowly in a circle. "I told the servants I cleaned up real well. What do *you* think?"

Chapter Four

Randi blinked away the moisture in her eyes, keeping a smile on her face while Mr. Durant gave her a thorough once-over. A little too thorough, her woman's instinct told her. She felt like the only female at the Rebel's Yell Bar & Grill on dollar beer night.

"Do I look more presentable, Mr. Durant?" she asked sweetly.

His wandering gaze snapped back to her face. "You appear . . . much improved, Miss Galloway."

"Well, thank you very much," she said, hoping he didn't pick up on the fact she was being somewhat sarcastic.

He frowned a moment later. "Your hair is too short."

Her hand automatically went to the pixieish strands, which she'd tucked behind her ears and smoothed as much as possible into a conservative style. She'd refused Melody's offer of a hot curling iron to put ringlets around her face. How ridiculous would that look? "Short hair is easier to take care of," she offered.

"No doubt you're correct, but still, the style is not appropriate for a young lady. Not unless you've been ill."

"Ill?"

"If your hair was cut to aid in your recovery."

Personally, Randi thought that was the most ridiculous custom she'd ever heard. Since he obviously thought she should know about this silly habit, she'd better not say anything else or she'd get in trouble.

"Oh, yes." She shrugged. "There's not much I can do about the length of my hair. It's not like changing from jeans into dresses."

"Jeans?"

"That's what the pants I was wearing are called."

"I've never seen anything like them before, and I don't care to view them again."

"A lot of people like them," she said, her feelings slightly hurt that he didn't like the way she looked at all. There was no pleasing this man, even if she tried to look presentable.

"They're too . . . fitting."

"Fitting? You mean tight?"

"Yes, I suppose you could use that term." He practically squirmed, like he was recalling the sight of a creepy-crawly bug.

"So you're not really opposed to jeans, just to how they look on me because they're too tight?" she said carefully, trying not to let him goad her into saying or doing something unladylike.

"I would be opposed to such tightly fitting garments on anyone, Miss Galloway. Besides, I believe you claimed those aren't your clothes. Why would you care if I approve of them, on you or anyone else? My point is that they are inappropriate."

She raised her chin, controlling her temper with a promise to return to her own time as soon as possible, and never wear another dress again as long as she lived. "Of course. I respect your opinion."

He seemed surprised by her comment—or her ability to control herself. "Very good. Since there's nothing we can do about your hair, I'm pleased that the dresses fit so well."

Actually, she wanted to say, *they're as uncomfortable as hell*, but she didn't. She kept that silly little smile glued to her face. "Thank you for loaning me the clothes."

"They're a gift, Miss Galloway, not a loan. I assume with your trunk resting at the bottom of the Mississippi, you'll be needing them."

"Yes, of course."

"You did mention your trunk fell overboard, didn't you?"

"Yes. You know how hectic things can be with boarding and . . . unboarding."

He looked amused for just a second, but quickly hid his expression by turning and walking across the room.

Rose apparently didn't like his actions, because she began to fret and wiggle.

"She's a lovely baby," Randi said.

Rose let out an ear-piercing shriek, contradicting Randi's compliment.

When Mr. Durant turned back toward her, he was frowning. "I don't know why she starts to cry like that. She's fine one moment, then begins to cry."

"Are you sure she's not colicky?"

"She doesn't cry after feeding. The servants have said they've treated other babies with that disorder, but Rose is not suffering from a problem with her digestion."

"Maybe she just wants attention. She could be trying to get you to do what she wants you to do."

"Miss Galloway," he said with exaggerated patience,

. "she's only eight months old. I hardly think she's capable of deliberation."

"I wouldn't be so sure."

"Although I admire my daughter's attributes, I try not to give her more than is reasonable."

"Well, then maybe her nature is just more changeable. My nephew Justin was the same way when he was a baby—laughing one minute, fussy the next. We finally decided that he was just temperamental."

"Rose has a sweet temperament," he said defensively, frowning more as he grappled with the wiggling, crying baby in his arms.

"Of course," Randi said, hiding a smile. Anyone could see that Jackson Durant adored his daughter. How it must have hurt to lose his wife so soon after Rose's birth, at a time when most families are just beginning to bond. Randi had seen the phenomenon with her sister and brother-in-law after the birth of their son Justin.

"Would you like for me to take her?" Randi offered.

Jackson Durant looked as though she'd asked him to strip naked and quack like a duck. Randi barely suppressed a giggle at the image.

"No, she's fine," he claimed, even as Little Miss Rose puckered up for a really good fuss.

Randi took a chance and walked toward father and daughter. "Look, Mr. Durant, I realize you don't know me from Adam, but I'd make a great governess for your daughter. I know all about children. I have three nieces and nephews, and believe me, I've handled just about anything they can come up with. Why, with a sweet girl like Rose, I wouldn't have any trouble at all."

He looked skeptical, but Randi could tell he was wavering. Rose continued to alternately whimper, then shriek, adding to the atmosphere of desperation. He finally loosened his hold on his daughter. "You can see what you can do," he reluctantly offered.

Randi smiled at the baby, then held out her arms in

a universal offer to "come to me." Rose sniffled, then quieted, then returned the smile with a tentative one of her own. Urging the baby with facial gestures and soothing noises, Randi continued to hold out her arms.

Within seconds, Rose leaned in her father's grasp toward Randi, holding out her own chubby arms. Randi settled her hands around the baby's middle, then pulled her away from her reluctant father.

She settled the baby on her hip as if she'd held her a hundred times before, then turned her smile on the frowning man who obviously didn't want his daughter in the arms of a near-stranger. "See, I told you I was good with babies. Do I have the job?"

"A decision of that magnitude is not so easy, Miss Galloway."

"Of course it is. Either you trust me or you don't," she said with much more confidence than she felt. To hide her nervousness, Randi turned her attention back to Rose, who was reaching for her hair. "Rose trusts me, don't you, sweetie?"

Rose gurgled and grabbed, making Randi smile despite the lingering pain her memories caused. She loved babies; she'd always loved being around them, smelling that unmistakable baby smell, watching them discover the world. She wanted a child, *her* child, but that wish hadn't been granted. Someday . . . after she'd achieved her other dreams.

Randi Mae was going to be the Galloways' first career woman, as soon as she returned to her own time. And to do that, she had to stay at Black Willow Grove and very close to young Miss Rose.

"I don't know you."

"Then get to know me, Mr. Durant. I'm really very friendly."

"That," he said succinctly, "is exactly what I'm afraid of."

"What do you mean?"

"Has no one brought to your attention the fact that you're an extremely unreserved young lady?"

Her smile faded as she realized he'd misinterpreted her actions and her remarks. Instead of viewing her as friendly, he'd seen her as too forward, too aggressive. In short, she was acting like a twentieth-century woman.

Randi bowed her head, affecting her most submissive pose. "You're right, Mr. Durant. I've been told this before. I'm sorry."

She peeked at him through the fringe of her bangs. He seemed surprised, his head slightly turned, his eyes narrowed and assessing. "You've had no success changing your behavior?"

"Not very much, but I'm working on it," she answered honestly. In truth, she'd never seen any reason to curb her natural exuberance. Now that she was living in the nineteenth century, she certainly saw the need to act differently.

Come to think of it, she hadn't yet determined how far she'd traveled back in time.

"I won't have someone influencing my daughter who possesses less than the highest moral and personal standards."

"Of course. I understand. However, I am really very good with babies. I can tell you from experience that Rose is too young to be influenced by social rules. Right now, she's more interested in colors and sounds than she is in using the right fork or judging the length of someone's hair. In short, Mr. Durant, I think that I could enhance her care without harming her at all."

Randi waited for his reaction, praying that he didn't immediately reject her offer. If he'd just give her a chance . . . If she could find her way back home, then she wouldn't influence this baby at all. She'd be out of the past, and things could go on as they should.

Which meant, she realized with a start, that sometime in the near future Rose and her father would die in the rising muddy water of the Mississippi. Despite the hand she placed over her mouth, Randi couldn't suppress a moan at the image of them trapped in this house, the river covering their heads, pulling them under to a watery grave.

"What's wrong, Miss Galloway?"

"The river . . ." she tried to explain, but realized she couldn't. There was no way he'd accept the fact that a flood would come. She had to improvise, and fast. He looked at her as though she was acting strangely again, which, she supposed, she was.

She took a deep breath, trying not to alarm baby or father. "What I meant was that my head still hurts from falling into the river."

"When you lost your clothes."

"That's right. I hit my head, too."

"Yes, I seem to remember you mentioning that."

"I have a headache sometimes."

"And you can't remember things correctly."

"Exactly," she said, glad that he'd been paying attention earlier when they talked. "As a matter of fact, one of the things I'm having trouble recalling is the date. Could you please tell me?" She shifted Rose to the other hip, not taking her eyes off the baby's father.

"The date?"

"Yes. The month, date, and year, please," she asked politely.

He took two steps toward her, then folded his arms across his chest. The sleeves of his shirt pulled taut against his shoulders, emphasizing his lean but muscular build. And he was tall, looming over her short frame in a way that made her feel extremely vulnerable. Again, she reminded herself that she had to be very careful around this man . . . around all these people in the past.

The only one she could possibly let down her guard

around was this sweet baby. Her arms tightened around Rose as Randi blinked back the tears that constantly threatened when she thought of the tragedy yet to come.

"Today is April 5, 1849."

His words slowly registered. Less than a month. By the end of April, the plantation would be flooded. Jackson Durant and his daughter would be swept away, drowned in the horrible, muddy water that rarely gave up its victims.

She felt weak, her stomach churning. Normally, she was as healthy as a horse, but since she'd heard the baby's cries inside the replica, and especially since she'd been hurled back in time, she hadn't felt very well. The knowledge that everyone she met was going to be either homeless or dead didn't help.

"I'm sorry, Mr. Durant, but my head is really hurting. Perhaps I'd better lie down now," Randi said quietly, not meeting his gaze. Instead, she buried her face next to Rose, breathing in the distinctive baby fragrance, feeling the soft, warm skin that was so darn alive.

How could she let this baby die? Was that why she'd gone back into the past—to save a life? She wished she had some answers, but knew that she might never find out the reason she'd fallen into the dollhouse. Or the way to back to her own time.

The tug of the baby jolted Randi into awareness. "I'll take Rose from you," her father said.

"I could put her to bed," Randi said, reluctant to let go of the infant. Rose felt so good, so right, in her arms.

"No, I'll have Suzette perform her usual duties. You obviously need your rest, Miss Galloway. I'm sure falling into the river and losing your personal belongings is quite unsettling. We can talk some more tomorrow, when you're feeling better."

"Yes, tomorrow . . ." Randi said, distracted by the sight of the very virile man and his sleepy baby daughter, wishing her head wasn't swirling with images and feelings she'd rather not face. As Mr. Durant settled Rose more comfortably on his shoulder, Randi's hand drifted to her stomach, feeling the emptiness more strongly than ever.

"Do you need Lebeau to show you to your room?"

"No, I'll find it."

"Did you have a meal this evening?"

It seemed he thought her hand on her stomach meant she was hungry. If only he knew about her loss . . . but then, he wouldn't allow her around his daughter. Having short hair and wearing jeans was sin enough to be condemned. She didn't dare admit she'd slept with a man who wasn't her husband.

"Melody brought me a plate to my room earlier."

"I can have something sent from the kitchen, if you'd like."

"No, that's okay. I'm not really hungry." Besides, she could just imagine him waking the cook to fix something complicated and time-consuming for her. She couldn't do that to the servants, who no doubt worked hard without having extra duties. If she were at home, she'd pop a Lean Cuisine dinner into the microwave, but she knew prepackaged food wasn't an option in this time.

"Very well." Mr. Durant walked toward the doorway, but stopped before leaving. "Please don't linger, Miss Galloway."

"Of course not." Apparently he didn't want her wandering around his house unattended. She couldn't really blame him; after all, he didn't know her very well, and she wasn't sure he totally believed her story about losing her clothes. The lie was already told, though, and she couldn't take it back. Besides, she didn't have a better story.

She raised her skirt slightly, following him to the

door. Once in the hallway, he motioned her to precede him up the stairs.

"I'll have someone nearby in case you require any assistance during the night."

"I'm sure I'll be fine," she lied, knowing she'd felt this emotionally whipped only once before in her life. She wouldn't think about that other time, however. She had enough on her mind for now.

Randi walked slowly up the stairs, depressed and confused about her reason for traveling to the past, her options while she was here, and how she'd return. The longer she stayed, the more she'd care about the little girl in her daddy's arms.

If she didn't watch herself, she might even start caring about Jackson Durant. She'd be better off staying half-afraid of him, half-angry at him. He certainly gave her plenty of ammunition.

"I insist," he said, breaking into her thoughts, bringing her back to their conversation. And reminding her of how bossy he was.

Randi stopped on the landing where the stairway split into two sections and continued upward. Turning toward the "master," she asked, "Do you mean that someone will sleep outside my door?"

"That's common, Miss Galloway, or have you forgotten?"

"No, I haven't forgotten. I just don't appreciate the custom."

"Nevertheless, you're a guest in my home. I would feel remiss as a host if I didn't make one of the servants available to you."

"Someone like Melody."

"Yes," he said, his tone suspicious.

"I don't want her sleeping on the floor. I'd feel terrible knowing that she didn't have a bed."

"Miss Galloway, the conditions of my servants are hardly your concern. I assure you that she'll be quite comfortable. It's an honor for her to stay in the house."

"Rather than in the slave quarters," she finished for him, knowing she was again stepping over the bounds, but unable to stop herself from expressing her disapproval of the lifestyle of this time.

"Exactly. Now, if you'll continue to your room, I'm sure everyone will be able to get settled for the night."

"Can she sleep inside my room?" Randi asked, not budging from her place in the middle of the landing.

He stepped closer. "Why is this important to you?"

"I . . . I'm not sure. All I know is it feels wrong to make another human being lie on the floor like a dog just because I might need a drink of water or have a bad dream."

"Do you have bad dreams often, Miss Galloway?" he asked, stepping closer.

"No," she said, ignoring memories of the occasional night tremors that had no form or substance, waking her from a sound sleep, drenching her in sweat and making her shiver in dread.

"If you don't wish to start now, I suggest you get to your room. My patience is wearing thin."

"I'll go," she said, tipping her chin up to look into his eyes, "but if you send Melody to me, I'm having her sleep inside my room."

His eyes flared with some emotion Randi couldn't determine, then his lips settled into a thin line. "Do what you must, but remember I'll judge your character by your actions. If you wish to be employed at Black Willow Grove, you'd best keep that in mind."

"I will. But I must also remind you that strength of character is one of the traits you'd want for your daughter."

"What I want for my daughter, Miss Galloway, is my concern. Now get to your room before I have *you* sleeping on the floor."

She opened her mouth to argue, but quickly realized

further comments would do no good. "Very well, Mr. Durant. I just wanted to express my opinion."

"I'm well aware of your unseemly preference for expressing yourself, Miss Galloway. Now get to your room. I'll expect you downstairs for breakfast. We have other things to discuss."

She turned and ran up the remaining stairs, glad she didn't trip over the long skirts or catch a step with the ill-fitting shoes. With a last glance at the man behind her, she slipped inside and shut the door.

As soon as she was alone, with a single candle lighting the darkness, she slumped against the door. Exhausted, disheartened, and unsure of her future, she wanted to be safely back home. She didn't have an easy life; her family had few material possessions and even fewer plans to change their lives. But they had love. They had each other.

In a month, Jackson Durant and his daughter wouldn't even have that . . . except they'd be forever together in death.

She absolutely couldn't begin to care. Losing another baby would be like having her heart ripped out and stomped all over again.

From his second-floor veranda, Jackson watched the half-moon rise through low clouds hurrying southeast, as though they were glad to have given up their moisture and were now free to play. More rain up north meant a rise in the river level, which no one needed. He was worried, even though his neighbors didn't think much of his concerns. When he'd built the levee to its current level around the bend of the river for his new cotton field, Thomas Crowder had laughed, calling Jackson a fussy maiden aunt.

He'd endure some ribbing from his peers if his actions meant he'd saved his crop. He wasn't about to underestimate the Mississippi, which was both the giver and taker of life.

Years ago, stories told by many men, from experienced boat captains to stevedores, had impressed him. One old man had been on board the early steamboat *New Orleans* during the earthquake at New Madrid in 1811, which had changed the course of the river and destroyed the town. Another claimed that once the Mississippi had been so wide with floodwater, he'd been unable to see the far bank. Jackson didn't know if all the stories were true, but he'd seen enough of the river to believe most of the tales were at least possible.

Chances were the water level would recede once the snowmelt from up north had passed by, but Jackson had been a cautious man too long to ignore any possibility.

Thankfully, Brewster was also observant and cautious. The overseer had lived alongside the river for thirty years, had built up new levees and shored up old ones, had watched cotton fields flood and seen livestock swept away. Not this year. Black Willow Grove would be safe behind thick, strong walls of earth. His precautions probably weren't necessary, but just in case, Jackson wanted to be prepared.

He wanted to be prepared when it came to Miss Randi Galloway, too, but he had no idea how to anticipate her questions or her answers. She was as unfathomable as the river and nearly as unpredictable. Her only consistency seemed to be the story of traveling to Black Willow Grove for the purpose of taking Miss Delacey's place as Rose's governess. He didn't for a moment believe that Miss Galloway had jumped or fallen into the river after her errant trunk, then ripped up her clothes, hitting her head in the process, leaving her memory full of holes.

He wondered how long she'd worked on that story. He wondered *why* she'd felt it necessary.

A CRY AT MIDNIGHT

She frustrated him even as he felt amazement at her ability to spin such tales. While he'd told his own share of lies, he'd constructed his own much more carefully. He had never spoken the first words that came into his head. One thing he was certain of was that the real story of her odd clothing and manners would be even more interesting than the concocted version she clung to.

At times, he'd wanted to smile at her tale. Fortunately, he'd stopped himself in time. He didn't want his guest to believe that he found her amusing, not when he was determined to find the truth.

Persistence was a trait he'd always possessed. Patience was a virtue he'd developed over the years. And he could still tell the difference between someone who held four aces and someone who tried to bluff with a single pair.

Chapter Five

Randi nearly missed breakfast the next morning, but fortunately, Melody woke her in time to get dressed in the various necessary undergarments and fastened the hooks and eyes of a bell-skirted, low-waisted lavender dress. The bodice fit tightly, right up to her neck. The upper sleeves were also snug, but flared out at the elbows—a truly ridiculous feature. How could anyone tolerate all that material bunching up around her forearms when she could barely move her shoulders?

Casting a covetous glance to where she'd hidden her tennis shoes, she forced her feet into the too-tight leather slippers. Then, still fuming over the fashions of the 1800s, Randi carefully descended the stairs, following the smell of savory meat and yeasty bread. Her stomach growled in response, making her aware that she hadn't eaten a meal in a long time.

She wanted to linger over the rooms of beautiful, ornate furniture and heavy, lush fabrics, but she figured she should get to breakfast while it was still being served. The "master" might be a little peeved if she ignored his directive to meet this morning. Perhaps later she'd have time to look around the house.

She found the dining room, the long table set with one place at the end, another setting halfway down the side. Jackson Durant presided, looking up at her over the edge of his newspaper.

"I'm glad you decided to join me, Miss Galloway. I was afraid you'd decided to take breakfast in your room."

Based on his comment last night, she assumed sleeping in, then snacking on a half-dozen Hostess minidonuts wasn't an option, but she wasn't about to argue with him this early in the day. "I hope I didn't keep you waiting."

"Not at all. I've already eaten. However, I'll have coffee while we talk."

She cast a covetous glance at the sideboard's steaming contents.

"My intention is not to starve you," he said with amusement in his voice as he nodded toward the chafing dishes.

Deciding not to wait for him to change his mind, she took a plate from the sideboard and reached for a silver serving-dish cover.

Before she could lift the lid, he rang a bell. Immediately a servant—little more than a boy—entered, went toward her, and served.

"I can get this," Randi said quietly, hoping not to alert "the master" to what was bound to be unorthodox behavior.

"Since Miss Galloway is intent on serving herself, please fetch her coffee."

"Coffee would be great." Anything to help get her through another interrogation by the man who held her fate in his hands—even if he didn't realize it.

As soon as she took her seat, their conversation began. "Tell me about your relationship with Miss Agnes Delacey."

Randi popped a bite of sausage into her mouth before answering, taking her time chewing the unfamiliar taste. Not unpleasant, just different than the Jimmy Dean patties her mother cooked. She watched Mr. Durant out of the corner of her eye, but he seemed patient.

"This is very good," she said, stalling for time.

"Yes, our cook is the best. Now, about you and Miss Delacey."

"We met at school," Randi improvised. "She was from a very good family, of course, whereas I . . . well, we didn't have as much."

"Your circumstances were reduced?"

"Yes, that's a good way of putting it." Again, she tried to stay as close to the truth as possible to spin this tale. Maybe she wouldn't blunder too much.

"And why didn't Miss Delacey make this trip?"

"She fell and broke her leg," Randi said impulsively. "She knew she wouldn't be able to get around, up and down those stairs, taking care of a baby, so she asked me to take her place."

"Did she send a letter along with you, explaining her reasoning?"

"Yes, but it was in my trunk," Randi said, thinking that was a perfectly reasonable explanation. "She was so anxious for Rose to be raised with a woman's influence that dear Agnes insisted I come. Fortunately, I was available to leave at a moment's notice."

"You didn't have to quit your employment with another family?"

"No, I didn't. They didn't require my services anymore."

"Really? But I suppose your letters of recommendation were also in the trunk."

"That's right," she said brightly, glad that he was going along.

"Perhaps we can write to your former employer and get the letter replaced."

"No, we can't." She absolutely couldn't allow him to check into her background. She'd never survive such scrutiny.

"Why not?"

"They're gone. They're in . . . Europe. England, France, Spain. All those European countries."

"How very nice for them," he commented in a way that sounded almost sarcastic. Of course he wasn't being sarcastic. She didn't imagine he had much of a sense of humor, and doubted he'd expend any of his limited supply on someone as trivial as her.

"I'm sorry," she said, when that was far from the truth. "Perhaps you'll allow my actions to speak for me, instead of judging me by what's on a piece of paper."

"Miss Galloway, I believe that's exactly what I'm doing," he replied, shaking open his newspaper once more.

He'd sounded even more sarcastic that time, although she couldn't imagine why—or even how he'd be so suspicious. After all, he'd barely questioned her story yesterday. Despite his belief or distrust of her, she had to forge ahead. There was no other option but to stay at Black Willow Grove until she found out what was going on.

She used the opportunity to eat more of her breakfast. Eggs with a creamy sauce, two kinds of sausages, and some kind of corn dish that she didn't recognize. She was hungry enough that she wasn't too concerned about the type of food, only the quantity.

After several more bites, the silence stretched to uncomfortable lengths. The only sound in the room was the clink of her fork and the rustle of his newspaper. She wondered what type of news was reported in an

1849 paper. Probably nothing really interesting, like Brad Pitt's newest rumored romance or two-headed alien babies.

"What are you reading about?" she finally asked, curiosity getting the better of her intended reserve.

"Nothing that would interest you," he replied non-committally.

Male chauvinist, she wanted to scream. "Why don't you let me be the judge of that?"

He folded the paper and placed it beside his coffee cup, gesturing for it to be filled.

As soon as the young black servant filled both their cups, Mr. Durant spoke. "United States reaction to the political revolutions of last year. It seems the great thinkers of our time are split on whether change should be embraced or feared."

"Democrats and Republicans in Congress at it again," she said, remembering the way her father always bad-mouthed politics.

"Democrats and Republicans? Do you mean those who believe in democratic and republican forms of government?"

Oops. She'd done it again. Didn't the political parties go back that far? Did they have different names? She barely paid any attention to politics except to vote. "Yes, that's what I meant," she said carefully, looking down at her plate.

"The *Communist Manifesto* has generated some sympathy among the more liberal members of our society."

"The liberal press." Now there was a term she'd heard a lot.

"A quaint way of phrasing, but yes, the articles and books that have gone to press are more in favor of exploring change than they are of keeping the status quo."

"What do *you* think?" Randi asked, finishing off her last bite of egg and looking at him through the fringe of her bangs.

He seemed taken aback at her question, but quickly recovered. The term "a cat always lands on its feet" came to mind, except in Jackson Durant's case, if he was a cat, he was a pretty big, dangerous one.

"I believe political change is highly overrated. Most of the time, only the politicians change. The lives of people are disturbed, often violently so, but return to normal within a matter of months or years."

"My dad says the same thing, except his way of saying it is, 'damn politicians are all alike,' " Randi said, giving her best John Galloway imitation.

At the foot of the table, Jackson Durant actually smiled. It had been just for a moment, but he'd definitely found her amusing. Randi smiled in return, her heart feeling much lighter.

"You shouldn't curse," he chastised, although she didn't hear any bite to his words.

"I wasn't really cursing," she defended herself. "I was quoting."

"You're arguing semantics."

She shrugged. "You'll have to take that up with my dad."

His smile slowly faded. "And where would I find him?"

Her mind raced. She couldn't say, "Just north of Memphis," because that's where they were now. She named the first big city that she knew had been around since the mid-1800s. "New Orleans."

"Really?"

Randi folded her napkin carefully and placed it beside an odd-looking spoon she hadn't used. "This was a really good breakfast. If you don't have anything else to discuss right now, I'd like to go upstairs and see Rose."

"I haven't determined if I'll allow you to be her governess," he reminded her.

"I know, but since I'm already here, I could at least

visit her, couldn't I? I promise not to do anything . . . inappropriate. I won't curse or giggle or anything terrible like that."

"My terms for raising my daughter are not to be questioned, Miss Galloway. She has a special place in this society, one I intend for her to enjoy. I won't have her future jeopardized."

"I'll be a vision of propriety. And if any society patrols come around, I promise I'll hide."

Another smile threatened. "I'll allow your visit on those terms."

"Thanks," Randi said, starting to get up from the heavy chair.

He rose quickly from his place at the head of the table. She paused, having seen this kind of gallantry in movies, and waited for him to come around to the side.

Without a word, he pulled the chair out for her. She smiled and acted as genteel as possible, as though a man seated her and helped her up from the table all the time.

"I'll see you later, Miss Galloway. Please stay out of trouble."

"I will," she said, hoping she could keep that promise.

Jackson waited until his intriguing houseguest went upstairs, then called for Lebeau to meet him in the study. While he waited for his butler to arrive, Jackson stood at one of the wide, tall windows that overlooked the front lawn of Black Willow Grove. The rain that had threatened for several days hadn't fallen, leaving the ground firm and covered with newly green grass. Flowering trees along the side of the house bore witness to spring, while life abounded in the many birds that searched the ground for insects.

No one else could imagine that disaster could threaten during such sunny, perfect days. But there was something about the river this year that had him worried. As soon as he had finished his correspondence, he would ride upriver to check low-lying areas for any flooding.

If the Mississippi was rising, he'd have to warn his neighbors, although he doubted they'd put much stock in his intuition. They'd been planting cotton in this river bottom for up to twenty years and felt they knew more than a new resident. The fact he'd been around the Mississippi all his life would matter little to them; they knew the *land*.

"Mas'r Jackson, you wanted to see me?" Lebeau said in a loud voice that echoed down the hall, in case anyone was listening.

Jackson turned and faced the man who'd been with him for twelve years. Tall, austere, and private, Lebeau gave most people the impression of an educated, loyal slave—but that wasn't entirely true. Loyal to a fault, but hardly a slave, Lebeau had bought his freedom twenty years ago. He'd taken his name from the town in Louisiana where he'd lived when he left the plantation, since until his manumission he'd simply been called "Samson."

Jackson knew the man's biggest regret in life was that he hadn't been able to purchase the freedom of his wife and child, who had later been sold through an auctioneer and taken to Alabama. Although he'd searched for them for years, and Jackson had helped, they'd never located his family. If Lebeau was aloof, he had good reason.

Jackson walked to his desk, then motioned for Lebeau to take a chair. "I'd like for you to do an investigation on our houseguest."

"Miss Galloway?"

"Yes. She's not who, or perhaps what, she claims to be. Her story of losing her trunk off a packet, tearing her clothing, and even why she traveled to Black Willow Grove holds water like a sieve. She claims to be a friend of the governess I hired, but I don't believe that's the case. I think Miss Galloway has never met Agnes Delacey. I hardly believe they went to school together. Miss Galloway doesn't appear to have any finishing school qualities."

"Did she mention which packet brought her here?"

"No, she didn't, and I didn't press for an answer. Although at first I was furious to find her in my daughter's room, I now believe she has no ill motive for wanting the job of governess."

"She is a most straightforward and stubborn young woman."

"Exactly. I wonder where she developed such a personality."

"How deeply do you want me to investigate her background?"

"Not too much at the moment. For now, see if you can locate a packet that docked nearby and had an incident such as the one she described." Briefly, Jackson relayed Miss Galloway's story, up to and including his assumptions about her short hair.

"So ask around the docks, check with the stevedores, the pilots, or the captains. Whatever you can find. If someone as unusual as our Miss Galloway disembarked, she would be remembered."

"Amen to that," Lebeau said, rising from the chair.

"Oh, and Lebeau," Jackson began as the butler started to leave.

"Yes?"

"Ask the servants who have had contact with her if she's said or done anything unusual. Anything that would tell us more about her."

"I'll see what I can find."

"Thank you. This is really important to me," Jackson admitted. "Hell, anything involving Rose is important."

"I understand." Lebeau walked out of the room, as tall and imposing as he'd been years ago, when they'd met in Baton Rouge. How they'd changed since that night when the only thing standing between Jackson and two riverboat-savvy thugs was an angry black man who spoke like a gentleman and carried a length of chain that weighed half as much as a grown man.

No one knew all his secrets, Jackson knew, but Lebeau came as close as anyone. And what he didn't know for a fact, he'd probably guessed by now, but Jackson had no fears trusting his past to the quiet, dignified man with demons of his own.

Randi spent much of the morning on a quilt in the nursery, playing with Rose. The baby was a delight, full of energy, full of life. Whenever she began to think along those lines, Randi stopped herself. If she dwelled on what was to come, she wouldn't be able to go forward. She'd curl up on her bed on the second floor, pull the drapes, and be miserable.

But she felt that this child needed her. God knew, she needed this child. "Did you call me back to the past?" she asked the gurgling baby. "Was that really you I heard crying in the dollhouse?"

Rose couldn't answer, of course, but she did focus her bright baby blue eyes on Randi's face, grinning as though she knew some wonderful secret.

"I wish you'd share it with me, sweetie, because I'm awfully worried about you and your daddy."

By the time Suzette, Rose's wet nurse, came to take the baby for her feeding and nap, Randi felt as though she was being separated from a child she'd known much longer than two days.

With the baby down for a nap, Randi wandered downstairs. She noticed a few servants going about their tasks, but they paid little attention to her. She saw nothing of the tall black man, Mr. Durant's butler. No telling what he did during the day. Perhaps he turned into a bat and hung from some dark rafter. He had that kind of personality.

In one of the front rooms, she ran her hand along the polished, dark furniture. Ornate carved wood adorned each piece, and brocade fabrics covered the seats and some of the backs of chairs and the settee. She'd seen similar pieces in the museum, or, she realized with a jolt, these could be the actual pieces of furniture. Unlike the items that existed in 1998, these were all so new, the wood shiny, the upholstery vivid, the seats plump with evenly distributed padding.

The walls were painted a soft green in this formal room, with tall silk draperies that must have cost a fortune. Not exactly off-the-rack at Sears, she thought as she ran her fingers along the heavy gold-and-dark-green cord and tassel.

At the end of the room stood an elegant fireplace, complete with carved mantle and marble inlaid stones around the opening. As was the rest of the room, the fireplace was spotless; not even a pile of ashes indicated that anyone used the room or lived in this house.

Darn, it was cleaner than the museum!

Shaking her head at the cold, formal elegance of Jackson Durant's home, she wandered farther down the central hallway. This is where she'd found him this morning at breakfast, but she wasn't looking for him again. As a matter of fact, she really didn't want to see him for a good long while. He'd only start asking more questions, and she hadn't thought of any new answers.

What she'd really like was some lunch. The hallway ended with a glass-paned door. She looked outside and discovered some beautiful gardens to the left. Low hedges circled a stone statue of some half-nude woman. A double row of white blooming trees formed kind of a lane that looked inviting, especially since a bench faced the alley formed by the trees.

To the right were several buildings, one of them with

a smoking chimney. She opened the back door, followed her nose down a short covered walkway, and found herself in a large, bustling, rustic kitchen.

"Miz Galloway," Melody said, leaping up from her own plate of food. A short, overweight woman named Birdie, whom Randi had met yesterday, sat beside the maid, but she didn't jump up. Instead, she looked with assessing eyes. Randi felt as though she was being judged, and could only wonder if she measured up to Birdie's unknown standard. Melody had told Randi that Birdie ran the household staff, whereas Lebeau ran the house.

"Don't get up," Randi said. "I thought I might be able to get a plate for lunch. Nothing fancy, please."

Birdie turned and addressed the cook, who was stirring a large, black pot. "Fix Miz Galloway some of that ham and cornbread, and put some greens on there." The older woman turned to Randi. "You like greens, girl?"

"Yes, ma'am, I do," she said with a smile, grasping her hands behind her back. She felt as though she'd passed Birdie's test.

"Melody, you go set the table in the dinin' room for Miz Galloway."

"No, really, that's not necessary. I'd rather go outside, if that's okay. Maybe I could eat in the garden." Randi didn't want to intrude on the servants' lunch, and she knew her presence would be disruptive. They probably had little time of their own. "Master Jackson's" chores would keep them busy, she was sure.

"Whatever you want," Birdie said, looking her over once more.

"The weather is very nice."

"If'n it don't rain," Birdie said with a huff.

Rain. That meant possible flooding. Randi didn't want to think about that at the moment, either.

She thanked the servants for the plate of food, then

walked to the bench beneath the flowering trees. She had to place the food down first, because she hadn't yet gotten the hang of all the petticoats beneath the full skirt. At least these dresses didn't have those metal hoops and baskets she'd seen in a book on drawing costumes. She didn't think she could handle sitting in one of those contraptions.

Within a minute, however, she was settled back on the bench, munching on tender ham and crumbly cornbread. The greens were wild, a bit stronger than the turnip greens her mother favored. Overall, this food was very similar to what she was used to in her own time—more familiar than the breakfast dishes. She realized she was eating food the servants prepared for themselves, rather than the fancy dishes a wealthy, elite man like Mr. Durant would prefer. She found the situation ironic; she was much closer in social class and taste to his servants—his slaves—and yet she'd told him she was a governess suitable to raise his daughter in the privileged manner he wanted.

Randi laughed. There couldn't be a less qualified person in all of Tennessee to teach Rose how to become a proper Southern belle.

She was just starting on her second piece of cornbread when her meal was interrupted by a deep male voice.

"Continuing in your unorthodox ways, Miss Galloway?"

She chewed quickly, but the dry cornbread seemed to stick in her throat. She coughed, gently at first, but then in earnest.

Her eyes began to water, obviously alarming her cat-footed host. He placed one large hand high on her chest, and used the other to whap her on the back.

She shook her head, trying to tell him that his ministrations weren't necessary. Apparently he wasn't paying attention. Either that or he'd decided to ignore her feelings.

"Stop struggling, Miss Galloway. You must relax your throat."

Her face felt flushed. Her eyes watered. But slowly, she quit coughing until only an occasional small hacking sound escaped.

"Sorry," she said. Her voice sounded hoarse and raw.

"I should apologize," he said, surprising her with his admission. "I shouldn't have startled you like that."

"No, you shouldn't," she agreed, "but this is your house. I was just enjoying the nice day."

"Until I interrupted your meal."

She shrugged. "I didn't say that."

"Nonetheless, I'm sorry I caused you to choke on Cook's cornbread."

He continued to loom over her, one arm resting on the back of the bench, but the other . . . Well, she was extremely aware of his large, warm hand. "Er, Mr. Durant? You can move your hand now. I'm not choking anymore."

He seemed startled, then looked down. Sure enough, his fingers were still splayed across her upper chest. Of course, she was demurely covered by the high-necked lavender gown, but she was pretty sure that touching her this way wasn't considered appropriate.

Jerking his hand away, she nearly laughed at his expression. He seemed horrified and embarrassed, all at the same time.

"It's okay," she said with a reassuring smile. "No harm done."

"I apologize for my behavior."

"Hey, I was choking. You rushed to my rescue." She shrugged. "No big deal."

"No big deal?" he asked, clearly confused.

"It's an expression where I come from, meaning that you don't need to worry."

"I see. You don't consider impropriety to be a 'big deal'?"

"Of course I do, but you didn't mean to be improper. You just forgot."

He looked unconvinced. "Do you always find excuses for inappropriate behavior?"

She looked up at him. "What do you mean by that?"

"I mean," he said, leaning a bit closer, his expression intensifying until he barely resembled the man from their previous encounters, "what if my action was intentional?"

Her heart sped up, her breath caught in her throat. He was so close she could see his dark, dark eyes and inhale his unique scent. He'd been out riding, she could tell, because the smell of horses and sunshine came with him to this shady garden spot. He seemed to be sensing her also, because his nostrils flared ever so slightly, and his eyes narrowed.

"Was it intentional?" she whispered, her gaze locked with his.

"What do you think?"

Think? How could she when he was so close? But she forced herself to look away, take a calming deep breath, and focus.

As much as his dark good looks and off-limit status excited the woman in her, something told her this seduction scene wasn't genuine. He wouldn't have seemed so surprised and embarrassed if he'd meant to come on to her. He wouldn't have pulled away, then changed his mind. No, he was up to something, and the realization caused a sudden jolt of disappointment.

"I think," she said slowly, clearly, "that this is another one of your tests. You don't have any interest in me as a woman. You're just trying to figure out if I'll make a suitable governess."

"That's what you think?" His eyes narrowed. "But what if you're wrong?"

The hand that had braced her chest now rested gently against her neck, just below her ear. She figured he could feel her pulse beating strongly and could sense her rapid breathing. She hoped he didn't read too much into her reaction, because she wasn't some bed-hopping tramp that fell for a great body and sexy eyes.

"Your heart is beating fast," he said softly.

"I'm a little nervous."

"Why is that, Miss Galloway?"

"Because I don't like to be toyed with. I don't want to play your games."

"You still believe I'm testing you?"

"Absolutely."

"Then let me see if I can convince you otherwise," he whispered before his lips descended to hers.

Chapter Six

Even as his lips touched hers, Jackson knew he was insane. There was no other explanation. He'd told himself that he couldn't be attracted to such an unusual young woman; he certainly didn't trust her. Yet he couldn't stop himself from kissing her.

Her lips were soft and warm, parted in surprise. He took advantage of that slight fissure to coax her into a deeper kiss, to ease his tongue into her mouth. He swallowed her gasp of surprise, then lost himself in the familiar tastes of ham and cornbread, and in the unfamiliar sweetness of her growing passion.

His head swirling with desire, he pressed closer as he settled onto the bench beside her. At the first touch of her hand on his shoulder, he urged her back against his arm. She sighed and grasped at his shirt, her fingers raking his skin in a response that excited him beyond reason. He reluctantly left the heaven of her lips to place nibbling kisses on her jaw, below her ear, and the edge of her high-necked dress. How he wanted to unfasten the damnable cloth that kept him from tasting more of this unique woman. How he wanted her. . . .

When he traced a path back up to her lips, however, she turned her face. Undeterred, he continued to kiss her cheek, her jaw.

"Mr. Durant," she whispered, "stop."

He drew back, just enough to see if she was really denying him, or if she was merely being coy. Passion burned brightly in her green eyes, but also defiance. He reminded himself that she was no shy, retiring woman. She'd also said she didn't want to play games. Would she try to play one of her own?

He tested her, trying to kiss her again, but she pushed against his chest.

"I meant it, Mr. Durant. I'm not going to be your toy."

"I never thought you were."

"Are you saying this whole seduction scene was spontaneous, that you really wanted to kiss me?"

He pulled back, unaccustomed to having his word questioned—especially by someone with secrets of her own. "If you can't tell the difference, I won't bore you with a declaration."

Jackson pushed himself up from the bench, anxious to be away from his infuriating houseguest as soon as possible. However, when her eyes traveled the length of his body and paused on his obvious arousal, he stopped. Her eyes widened; she knew what his body's response meant.

"As you can see, Miss Galloway, I obviously wanted *something* from you."

Her gaze snapped to his face, her eyes narrowed in disgust. Without waiting for her coming tirade, he strode away from the once-peaceful garden and toward the house.

He was insane. Taunting her, taunting himself. He didn't *want* to want her. He should be repulsed by her behavior, her short hair, her lies. But for some reason he had yet to understand, he was pulled toward her with a force he'd never felt before.

His boot heels clicked across the stone walkway, then he opened the door with enough force to rattle the windowpanes. Cautioning himself to be quiet for Rose's sake, he didn't slam the door. Instead, he inwardly raged as he took the stairs two at a time, heading for his solitary bedroom and a change of clothes. He would get out of the house, visit his neighbors, and take out some of his frustration through sound, logical arguments.

If that failed, he'd put his fist through a wall.

"Too long without a woman," he mumbled as he jerked off his rumpled shirt. That was the only explanation for his irrational, overly emotional behavior. He should have a mistress, someone compliant and sweet, with flowing dark hair and adoring eyes. Not some hot-tempered, short-haired young woman with a huge imagination and little experience to perpetuate her fraud.

Unfortunately for him, he'd never believed in taking one of his slaves for a mistress. Nearly every other planter he'd met had indulged in the practice, but Jackson had seen the fear and loathing on the faces of some of the women. He couldn't lose himself in a body that shrank away from his touch, with a woman who could barely tolerate his physical needs.

No, he needed someone willing and sweet. Hell, he needed a new wife. In just four months, he'd be free to marry. As soon as Lebeau solved the mystery of Miss Galloway, Jackson vowed he'd start a search for a suitable young woman. Someone who didn't kiss like an angel and rake him with eyes that burned like the devil.

Randi waited until the totally infuriating "master" slammed into the house. She didn't want to risk running into him anywhere near a bedroom. He'd probably assume that she wanted a little more of his interrogation. The jerk. At first, he'd kissed her like he meant it, then he'd decided to see how far he could push her. She knew the minute his kisses had turned from genuine to a controlled seduction.

She recognized the move from Cleve's lovemaking repertoire. Too late, she'd realized that he could change from charmingly genuine to genuinely slimy in a blink of his disarmingly innocent blue eyes. Whenever he'd acted that way, she knew he wanted something. A little loan until he got a new job. An introduction to a family friend who needed to buy something Cleve was selling, or give him a job when he wasn't.

Randi's family might be poor, but they were honest. She hadn't recognized Cleve's get-rich-quick schemes and unethical behavior until they were well into their relationship. Until it was too late . . .

She'd been such a fool. But, she thought, rising from the bench and picking up her plate, she'd already beat herself up enough over her big mistake. Live and learn, that's what her mother always said.

Randi looked down the alley formed by the blooming trees and sighed. "Mom, I wish you were here. I need you. I need my family."

There was no answer, of course. A gust of wind shook the limbs, making a few white blooms fall to the ground like snowflakes.

Would she ever see her family again? Sit down for Sunday dinner at the Early American breakfast table they'd owned for as long as she could remember? Play with her nieces and nephew, see the new ones born? Or get to realize her own dreams, with her family seated proudly in the audience?

She blamed the moisture in her eyes on the gusty wind, but she knew that wasn't true. With a heavy heart, she returned the plate to the kitchen, hoping none of the servants had witnessed the embarrassing exchange between herself and their master in the garden, or commented on her watery eyes. What would they think of her if they knew she'd kissed him back like a love-starved idiot? Would they assume she was some weak-willed bimbo, or sympathize with her over his planned seduction?

My God, did he do this often? Randi remembered stories and movies about the omnipotent slave master who took any female on his plantation to bed, whether she was willing or not. Would Jackson Durant do that? She shuddered at the thought. Surely he couldn't . . . not when he'd pulled away from her when she'd insisted.

But then, she wasn't a slave. Heck, she wasn't even technically a servant. He'd never said she could be Rose's governess. He hadn't kicked her off the plantation either, but he might now, since he knew she wasn't about to fall into bed.

She walked as quietly as possible up the stairs, praying she didn't run into him because she wasn't up to another confrontation. Her mind still swirled from all the unanswered questions that couldn't be resolved . . . not yet, anyway. She'd have to find out soon. Within a month, the plantation would be underwater, their lives threatened.

Randi climbed up to the third floor nursery, but found Rose still sleeping. Suzette was on a pallet, also napping. She looked too young to be a mother herself. In sleep, especially, she looked like she should be taking driver's education, planning on a dress for the Junior/Senior Prom, or begging her parents for a ticket to some popular rap artist's concert.

The uncertainty of life in the 1800s, of her status here at Black Willow Grove, and of her ability to return to her own time pushed Randi downstairs to the solitude of the bedroom she now called her own. But for how long? A sob escaped her as she stumbled down the steps, tripping over her long skirts. She picked them up high and ran into the room, shutting the door, turning the key to lock out the world.

She couldn't lock out her thoughts, however. With tears streaming down her cheeks, she sank to the feather mattress, skirts billowing around her. She fumbled to the table beside the bed, but couldn't find the box of tissues that should be there.

Only in the twentieth century, she realized. That was the last straw. She gave into the frustration and fear, and cried until her chest ached and her throat felt raw. Ignoring the knocks on her door, she curled into a ball, hugged one of the soft, full pillows, and fell into a fitful sleep.

Jackson's temper cooled before he left the house to visit his neighbors. After he'd gained control of his body and calmed his mind, he realized how his houseguest might have mistaken his intentions. After all, he'd given no indication earlier that he'd wanted to kiss her, or found her attractive. He'd gotten the impression that she was slightly afraid of him—after she'd pushed him beyond his limit.

He'd reluctantly decided that he should apologize for his actions. He shouldn't have treated her as though she was a woman of easy virtue, even if her clothing and every other indication screamed that she was no shy, innocent miss.

So he stood outside her room, ready to offer a formal apology for his inappropriate actions. From inside he heard the sound of muffled sobs. Damn it, the girl was crying. He hated women's tears. Pansy had cried quietly, with no great emotional display. Jackson assumed she'd merely wanted attention, or a new bauble.

This woman cried like a child. Unrestrained. Messy, no doubt. He knocked several times to no avail. He tried the knob, but found the door locked. With a firm set of his lips, his jaw clenched, he descended the stairs.

Let her cry. He'd tried to offer his apology. Tears hadn't been necessary to force him to take action.

His black gelding's reins were held by a stableboy just outside the front door. With a quick vault into the saddle, Jackson put his heels to the horse, galloping away from Black Willow Grove and the sound of crying that echoed in his mind.

Five hours later, still angry and frustrated, he cantered back to the stable. He'd wasted the afternoon on small talk and gentlemen's pursuits. His neighbors hadn't wanted to listen to his theories on the river. They'd wanted to know which of his horses he'd race at their annual event in May. Thomas Crowder had insisted that Rose have a woman's influence, hinting that Jackson's household wasn't an entirely appropriate one in which to raise a daughter.

Jackson had promised him that a proper governess was on the way. He'd also hinted that he'd search for a suitable mother for his daughter after their crops were in and his period of mourning was over. That declaration had produced a chilling look and thin-lipped glare from Pansy's mourning father.

The rest of his neighbors had wanted to share a cigar, a glass of bourbon, and talk politics. Anxiety over Europe's "Year of Revolution" had spread to the upper class, mostly Protestant minority of European extraction, who ruled a land inhabited by everything from black slaves to wild savages to the destitute poor. Needless to say, the planters didn't feel entirely secure in their holdings, though they talked as though nothing could threaten their lives.

He let out a snort of disgust at these men who worried more about the turbulent political situations of far-distant countries than they did about a river that had flowed through the land for thousands of years, long before man had claimed the rich soil for his own. As far as Jackson was concerned, if events didn't affect the price of cotton, they might be interesting, but they came very low on his list of priorities.

Right now, top on his list was to find out what Miss Randi Galloway really was—governess or thief, innocent young lady or scheming woman of ill repute, he reminded himself as he entered the house to clean up before dinner. He hoped Lebeau had discovered some pertinent information during his trips to Randolph and Sugar Creek. He'd set aside time for his butler's report after dinner.

Of course, he also needed to spend his regular evening visit with Rose. He knew regularity was important in the life of a child, so his foul mood should not interrupt their interval together before bedtime.

The colors of sunset gilded the stairway in oranges and golds as he climbed to his bedroom. With any luck, his valet would have warm water waiting. Even if he were eating alone again tonight, he would dress for dinner, as was expected of gentlemen of his social standing. A small price to pay for all he'd gained in the last fifteen years.

Lost in his thoughts, he turned the corner of the landing and strode down the hallway—and ran into the object of his frustration.

"Mr. Durant!" she cried out, grasping his arm for support. She'd obviously been upstairs in the third floor nursery. A spot he identified as baby drool marred the bodice of her pale green daydress.

He gently held her upper arms, resisting the inappropriate urge to pull her close. "I'm sorry, Miss Galloway," he said, striving for a formal tone even as his heart began to pound and his body tightened from the feel of her warm, womanly body so very close. The fact that she was attired demurely in a high-necked dress that showed very little flesh made no difference. "I wasn't paying attention."

"Apparently I wasn't either," she said breathlessly, her gaze locked with his. "I didn't hear you coming."

He searched her face in the fading light of the hall, looking for signs of her earlier tears. He saw none. As a matter of fact, she looked remarkable composed. Her lips appeared rosy, her lashes unusually dark. Did she use cosmetics? If so, that was more evidence that she was no innocent miss.

"I wanted to talk to you," she said, interrupting his examination.

With a sigh of resignation, he released her arms. She took a step back.

He wished he'd met with Lebeau first. Jackson didn't want to face any recriminations or questions without knowing more about her outrageous story. And yet he felt he owed some explanation for his earlier behavior. He'd rather wait until he felt in control of both his erratic heart rate and his position as master of Black Willow Grove. Alone in this half-darkened hallway wasn't the best place to mention their kiss in the garden. Still, as a gentleman, he owed her.

"I want to apologize for my behavior earlier. I should never have pressed my . . . needs upon you as I did."

"Your needs," she said, her brow furrowing.

"Certainly you know what I mean."

"Yes, I think I do. You mentioned needs rather than anything more complimentary to me. But that's okay. I understand."

"You understand what?"

"That you don't feel anything special for me. Any port in a storm. Isn't that right?"

"That's not what I said," he said, feeling his frustration level rise.

"That's what I heard you say."

"I don't wish to discuss my motives any further, Miss Galloway. I hope you accept my apology."

She seemed to consider his request, her head slightly

tilted and her brow somewhat furrowed. "I accept. I shouldn't have kissed you back. I'm not sure what came over me."

"We'll put that behind us, then."

"Okay. But I still wanted to talk to you."

"I was preparing for dinner."

"Oh." She wrinkled her nose, confirming his suspicions that his afternoon with the other planters had left a mark on his person. "You smell like a bar."

"A bar?"

"I mean," she said quickly, "that you smell like cigar smoke and liquor."

"I've been visiting. That's what men of my position do, Miss Galloway, along with running their plantations." He wondered why she didn't know about the customs of the wealthy. Had she never been employed in an upper-class family? She apparently hadn't been raised in one, since she was searching for employment with no references. If her family had fallen upon hard times, they would have at least known others who would have offered a position as governess or companion.

"Well, I've been thinking. That's what I do."

Her saucy retort deserved a smile, but he quickly tamped down the urge. "And what have you been thinking about?"

"My status here at Black Willow Grove. I need to know whether you're going to let me stay on as Rose's governess. I can't just keep living here without some sort of job."

"Are you accustomed to working, Miss Galloway?"

"Yes, I am. And I work hard. I'm good with babies and children. I've already told you that."

"I'll consider your request. At the moment, I need to change for the evening." He started to walk away, then realized he was being rude for not considering how she would take his abrupt dismissal.

He looked at her over his shoulder. "Would you care to join me for dinner?"

"Yes," she said, her smile lighting up the dim hallway.

"Then I will see you downstairs in fifteen minutes."

Thankfully, she let him escape to his bedroom. His reactions to Randi Galloway were becoming stronger and more disturbing.

"Please, Lebeau," he whispered as he closed his door, "have the information I need before the night is through."

Randi hurried down the stairs, holding up the skirt of the uncomfortable dress. She needed to find Melody and ask the maid what she should wear to eat dinner with the master. Randi had heard that the wealthy "dressed for dinner," but what exactly did that mean? And was the custom the same in the previous century?

She found the servants in the kitchen, again interrupting their meal. "I'm sorry," she explained to the young black woman, "but Mr. Durant asked me to join him for dinner, and I'm not sure if I should wear this dress. He said fifteen minutes."

"That dress has a spot on it, Miz Galloway."

"Please, call me Randi," she reminded the maid.

"Yes, Miz Randi," Melody replied automatically. "I can get that spot out for you, but Miz Durant always wore a fancy dress for dinner. That's a day dress."

"Oh," Randi said, holding out the skirts and looking at the fine detailing of lace and cording. "I don't think I have time to change. Besides, I'm not Mrs. Durant—not even close."

"You fit her dresses just fine. I'll look through the trunk."

"You don't have time for that, girl," Birdie said from her perch on the other side of the table. "Melody, you get that spot out. The master'll understand Miz Randi didn't have time to change. Lord knows, you don't keep a man waiting for a meal."

Randi smiled. "That's true. They can be real bears when they're hungry."

"The master's strong on keepin' to schedule," Birdie continued, gesturing with a spoon. "He expects everyone to be on time."

"I see." So, he was as stern and authoritarian with them as he'd been with her. Maybe even more since they couldn't just up and leave.

As if she could. Then how would she get back to where she belonged?

Within a few minutes, Melody had unhooked the back, placed a folded rag beneath the fabric of the bodice, and removed the spot. With more patting and a little heat from a small iron instrument resting on the hot stove, the dress looked fine.

Randi smoothed the skirts of the green dress. Between the demands of the "master" and his teething daughter, she was going through clothes pretty fast. "Okay, I'm as ready as I'm going to get." She looked around the kitchen, where the cook and serving staff—including the slightly built boy she'd noticed at breakfast—prepared to carry the meal into the main house.

"I hope you have a good dinner, Miz Randi," Melody said shyly.

"Thank you," she replied warmly, giving the helpful girl a squeeze on her shoulder. Apparently not all of the people in the past were suspicious of her. At least a few seemed to like her. She wondered if Jackson Durant would ever feel that way. Probably not. And she didn't have any reason to *want* him to be attracted to her, even though her feelings had been hurt just minutes ago when he'd referred to his "needs" rather than any real desire he might have experienced.

She preceded the servers into the house, arriving in the dining room first. Should she be seated or standing?

She wished she knew more about the customs of the time. She should have paid more attention to history in high school. If she'd known how much the events and philosophies of each period influenced the architecture, she would have studied those boring dates, revolutions, and explorations more diligently.

This opportunity to study history firsthand was an entirely different experience. She had to admit that after getting over her initial shock, she could look at what was going on around her with a little more interest. When she got back to her own time, she was going to have some vivid memories of this bygone era.

She watched a server carry in what looked like condiments for the table. Two others brought in silver chafing dishes. They worked quietly in the background, leaving her alone.

She folded her arms across her chest and wandered around the well-decorated room, taking in the expensive-looking flocked wallpaper, the elaborately carved and gilded mirror over the fireplace, and the wide, detailed crown moldings at the ceiling. Not even the museum curators could have produced a more beautiful setting for the heavy cherry and mahogany furniture. There was seating for twelve around the table, a long, marble-topped sideboard, and a huge china cabinet. As a matter of fact, everything in the room was on a grander scale than she could have ever imagined.

She should sketch this room, she thought suddenly. Besides helping her remember the details for when she returned to 1999, the activity would give her something to do while Rose napped, or after she went to bed at night. That is, if Jackson Durant gave her the job.

"Pardon me for being late," he said from the doorway.

She jumped at the sound of his deep, disturbing voice, but tried to hide her reaction by turning toward him and smiling. "I've only been here a minute."

"I see dinner is ready," he said, striding toward the long table. "Would you like to be seated?"

Randi picked up her skirts, hoping she didn't trip as she walked to the chair he stood behind. As she allowed him to seat her at the table, she felt very much a part of this time, like a pampered princess.

But, she reminded herself, she was no princess . . . and she was only playing dress-up in a make-believe land. Sooner or later, she'd go back to her own time, where she was much closer in social class to the people serving the food than to the master of the house, who took a seat at the head of a table that cost more than her dad made in six months.

"Tell me, Miss Galloway," Jackson Durant said from his thronelike chair, interrupting her thoughts, "since you want to become Rose's governess, what is your philosophy of child-rearing?"

Chapter Seven

"My philosophy?"

"Yes. What are your views on the care and raising of children?"

She seemed surprised by the question, but he wasn't about to let her off the hook. Especially since he'd learned from his valet that Lebeau hadn't yet returned from his fact-finding mission . . . and she was pressing for an answer to her request to become Rose's governess.

"I think babies need lots of attention and stimulation."

"What type of stimulation?"

"Light, color, sound. They need to hear people talking, and not just baby talk. They need to be spoken to just like older children. That helps them talk when they get a little older."

Her explanation was interrupted by the arrival of their plates, loaded with medallions of beef, onions baked in a puff pastry, and a colorful relish. Jackson appreciated the efforts of his cook. While other planters had sent away for French chefs, he'd seen that expense as unnecessary. Instead, he'd sent his cook to New Orleans for training with one of the best restaurateurs in the city. His efforts had been rewarded in much-improved meals.

A rich red wine was poured, then he motioned the servants away. He watched Miss Galloway look askance at her forks, finally choosing one. She blushed when she realized he'd been observing her. Taking pity on her, he turned his attention to his own meal. After two delicious bites, he directed their conversation back to the topic.

"Very well. I suppose our views on infants are similar."

"Good. I'm glad you're more . . . open-minded."

"What do you mean by that?"

She looked up from her plate. "You know . . . progressive. I know that a lot of people in your position might not spend much time with their children. They let them be raised by servants, don't they? I noticed that first night that you aren't like that."

"I believe that children should know their parents. After all, the child will inherit your estate, so he should know your values."

"That's an interesting way of looking at it," she said, a furrow in her brow. She frowned at her meal. He supposed her viewpoint was directed at him and not the tender fare.

"So you have had dealings with the planter class," he stated.

"Some," she said faintly. He decided not to pursue that remark, lest she start accusing him of inviting her to dinner so he could interrogate her again. She had unusual views on what was appropriate for him, in his position, and what was equitable for her. She continued to interest him because of her unique ability to turn around the most conventional and usual situations into points of contention.

Sometimes, she even made sense—a disconcerting notion.

"Are you enjoying the meal?" he asked, deciding that was neutral ground.

"Yes, it's very good. I could use some salt, though."

"The salt cellar is just to your left, Miss Galloway."

She looked around, obviously not seeing the object. Jackson motioned to one of the servants, who lifted the porcelain lid and provided a sprinkling of salt to her plate.

"Thank you," she said with a smile to the cook's son.

She was extraordinarily polite and sensitive to the servants. He wanted to know why. Had she been in such a situation, and was therefore empathetic to the staff? Another mystery he intended to solve, once Lebeau returned.

They ate in silence for several minutes, finishing the first course with the polite clink of silver on china, the occasional sip of wine.

The plates were cleared and a compote of dried fruit in brandy sauce was served.

"I think you're trying to get me drunk," Miss Galloway observed after taking a bite of the rich dessert.

"I beg your pardon?"

"All this wine, and this sauce. What's in it, brandy?"

"That's correct. Do you like it?"

"Yes, but I may be tripping up the stairs in this long skirt."

He frowned, not knowing what she meant by that remark. He'd seen his wife's dresses on the itinerant young woman, and they didn't seem too long at all. In fact, he was surprised by the fit. Pansy had seemed much more ethereal, her fine blond hair pulled back from a delicate face in a becoming, modest style that wouldn't suit Miss Galloway at all. She filled out the bodice more than his wife, also, but seemed oblivious to the swell of her rounded breasts beneath the concealing clothing.

He was not unaware of her charms, however. Jackson shifted in his chair and averted his eyes from the silhouette of his houseguest. He couldn't wait four months to start looking for a new bride; he realized he had to find some outlet for his passionate nature. A suitable mistress, perhaps. Even a good courtesan would see him through a short courtship with a proper second wife. Since Miss Galloway's arrival, his celibate status had been proven his Achilles' heel.

Despite her remarks about "getting her drunk," he noticed she finished every bite of her dessert. She'd used the incorrect spoon, but he wasn't about to point that out. Hopefully, she'd be long gone before Rose had need of such instruction on the proper usage of flatware.

Or you could just get Lebeau to instruct Miss Galloway, a little voice whispered in his ear. The idea shocked Jackson; he wondered where, in his convoluted mind, that thought had come from. He didn't actually want her around. Certainly, he didn't think of her as an appropriate governess for his precious daughter.

Did he?

Disgusted, he whipped his napkin off his lap and threw it beside his plate. "If you're finished," he said in a measured tone, hiding his wayward thinking, "would you care to join me in the study?"

"Well, okay," she said tentatively. "Is something wrong?"

Apparently he hadn't concealed his aggravation as well as he'd thought. "Nothing for you to be concerned about, Miss Galloway."

He motioned to one of the servants. "Have Suzette bring my daughter down now."

The young woman nodded and hurried away.

Jackson rose from his chair, then walked to behind Miss Galloway's seat. He looked down at her short, short hair, noticing again how the various colors blended together to form a light shade of blond. He'd never seen hair that looked like this.

"Mr. Durant?"

"Yes, Miss Galloway," he said, pulling out her chair so she could rise from the table. As she'd predicted, she did seem unsteady. Perhaps she wasn't accustomed to the potent wine he preferred.

He took a risk to his libido by guiding her from the dining room with a hand beneath her elbow. She seemed surprised at first, then smiled at him in a shy way he found captivating.

He would get a mistress as soon as possible, he vowed as they walked to the study.

"Is it necessary to call me 'Miss Galloway'?" she asked, her brow wrinkling as she took a seat on the settee beneath the window.

"What would you have me call you?" he asked, walking to the brandy decanter. He had need of a bit more reinforcement than the glass of wine he'd consumed at dinner.

"Could you call me Randi, at least when we're alone? I understand how you'd want to keep up appearances for others. The staff, neighbors, and so forth."

"That's very understanding of you," he said, amused at her request, turning to face her across the room.

"And I want to call you Jackson, not Mr. Durant," she added.

He froze, the snifter suspended in midair. "That's very forward of you."

"How can you say that after . . . And besides, it's only fair. Why would *you* call *me* by my first name when I have to be more formal?"

"Why, indeed? Are you totally unfamiliar with my position as your benefactor?"

"No, but we do things a little differently where I come from."

"And where would that be, Miss Galloway?"

"Randi, remember? Why is that so important to you?"

"The question is, why is it so important that you keep me from knowing where you family lives, where you went to school, or who was your last employer?"

"I . . . I suppose I want you to trust me for who I am, not where I come from."

Her words echoed in his head, reminding him of things he'd said before. His own thoughts, long buried under layers of wealth and respectability. His needs, forever denied by an unforgiving society. Yes, he understood her request—far more than he would ever admit to her or anyone else.

"I'll call you Randi when we're alone," he acquiesced. "And as of today, you are truly my employee."

"I am? As Rose's governess?"

At his nod, her face glowed with delight. Impulsively, she sprang up from the settee, flew across the room, then threw her arms around his neck. Giving him a quick hug, she exclaimed, "Thank you! You won't regret this."

Very carefully, he stepped back from his exuberant new staff member. "I hope you're right, Miss . . . Randi," he said, striving to control his reaction to both her display of affection and the feel of her breasts against his chest. She was only expressing her gratitude, he told himself, not soliciting a passionate response.

At that moment, Suzette walked into the room with Rose, who gave a squeal and reached for the two of them.

Jackson's face turned hot with a blush as rare—and as inappropriate—as Randi Galloway's actions.

*　　*　　*

Once Randi began her duties, she felt much more settled into her life in 1849. Having a job took her mind off some of her troubles, giving her focus. Although she still hadn't solved any of her other problems—like finding out why she was here and figuring out how to convince Jackson to move out of the house before the flood came—she felt more confident that she could accomplish her task.

Already she could tell that he wouldn't put his daughter in danger. He loved that baby just like the best twentieth-century father. His love for Rose was the first thing Randi had admired about Jackson, but the more she was around him, the more she decided he wasn't the cruel slave master, the insensitive chauvinist, or the social status–seeking elitist that she'd once assumed he would be.

Not to mention the fact that he was drop-dead gorgeous, and more appealing now that she'd gotten to know him better.

Whatever was going on in her brain—and with her hormones—she could now look back on their kiss in the garden and remember the first few moments of wonder and passion before her suspicion had kicked in. She'd accepted his apology, and she now believed he wasn't trying to get more information from her by kissing her senseless. He'd been caught up in the moment, too, and if he'd changed in some subtle way, he'd simply tried to get control of his passion.

Jackson Durant was definitely a man who liked to be in control.

Something was bothering him today, she could tell. He'd been restless at breakfast, and when she'd asked if anything was wrong, he'd said that it was nothing serious. Lebeau had gone off on some business, he'd said, and he was awaiting his return. Jackson had looked at her closely when he'd revealed why he'd been such a bear. Randi didn't know why, but she was thankful he'd at least told her a little of his reasons for feeling tense and temperamental.

She wasn't afraid of him—at least, not usually. She didn't think that he was going to whip her, shake her, or do anything else that was possible behavior for a man who could become quite angry. His anger seemed to be directed at situations rather than individuals.

Rose's cooing brought her back to the present. She'd taken the baby to the garden, spreading an oiled cloth—given to her by Suzette to protect them from moisture—and a thick quilt on the ground beside some low shrubs. The baby pushed herself up and crawled around awkwardly on the colorful quilt, chasing rays of filtered sunlight and errant, floating petals from the flowering trees behind them.

"No, you can't eat that," Randi told the baby, who'd grabbed a handful of blossoms and was in the process of moving them toward her mouth. "Are you hungry? I think you need some more solid food," she told the baby, who protested the confiscation of her "snack" with a high-pitched squeal.

She wished she could phone her mother for advice, or call her sister Tanya or her sister-in-law Darla to ask when their children had started on cereal. How much solid food should Rose eat, and what would be comparable to modern baby food? Could anything hurt her gums when she was teething? She had lots of questions that hadn't come up before because Randi hadn't been totally responsible for her nieces and nephews. She was a great baby-sitter, but having full care of Rose was more like being a mother than an aunt.

The thought of herself as a mother caused a sharp pang of longing. For however long she had with Rose, she'd enjoy the baby's sweetness and revel in the sense of wonder the infant expressed about her world.

With a tentative smile, Randi seated Rose on her well-padded bottom and handed her a thick, dense biscuit that Suzette said all babies needed when they were teething. Sure enough, Rose stuck the hard object in her mouth and started working it with her gums. Soon, the gooey mess ran from the corners of her mouth onto her clean white embroidered dress.

Randi dabbed away the mess with a wet cloth she'd learned to keep close by. Without constant cleanups, Randi had discovered, she'd be swapping out dress after dress on the baby. Considering the fact that all of Rose's clothes were hand-washed and ironed, the extra work for the servants seemed unnecessary.

One thing Randi had changed was to simplify her young charge's wardrobe. A baby didn't need long skirts and voluminous bed sacques, as Suzette had called the nightgowns babies wore much of the day. Randi had asked for several of the garments to be cut off so Rose could crawl around without getting tangled in her clothing.

"Plenty of time for that later," she'd told the gleeful baby, "when you have to wear uncomfortable dresses like mine."

Rose was a wonderful, intelligent, active baby. Randi knew she shouldn't be so attached to the infant, but she couldn't help herself. How could anyone not love Rose? Leaving her behind in the past was going to be unbearable, but Randi tried not to think of that. First, she had to find a way to get home. She'd gotten here by following the sound of a baby's cries into a replica of Black Willow Grove. Unfortunately for her, there were no replicas of twentieth-century Tennessee for her to use as a time-travel device. She didn't have a clue how to create one, either, or to explain her needs to Jackson.

She couldn't say, "Build a tiny little three-bedroom ranch-style house with an asphalt shingle roof, beige wood siding, and brown trim." Not only would they think she was crazy, but the materials they'd need didn't exist. Black Willow Grove had been so detailed and accurate. She couldn't imagine any replica she'd build—or supervise building—would possess such marvelous elements.

The only way she could show them what her home looked like was through sketches. Could she reproduce a good copy of her reality and not forget many of the features? She wasn't sure if she could draw accurate detail to scale. But she could practice. Besides, she loved to draw, getting lost in whatever she was creating.

Maybe if she tried to re-create her parents' house or even the museum as it existed now, she'd preserve the memories of her world. She had a horrible feeling that if she stayed too long, the images would fade in her mind. She wouldn't be able to remember . . . and then she'd be stuck here forever, waiting for a flood to claim their lives. Or she would lose the chance to escape through Black Willow Grove since the house would be destroyed.

Perhaps Rose and Jackson didn't really perish in the flood. Maybe they fled too, except no one knew. Maybe the historians assumed they died.

Within a few minutes, Rose's chewing motions slowed and her eyes became heavy. Randi eased her to the quilt with a minimum amount of protest from the infant. She sang softly, humming whenever she forgot the words to Elton John's "Candle in the Wind." She kept getting the words to the Marilyn Monroe version mixed up with the newer lyrics written for Princess Diana's funeral, but both songs moved her. She especially remembered that he called Diana "England's Rose," so the song seemed very appropriate. The princess's death was tragic, but this baby deserved a chance to grow up, to love and have children of her own.

By the time the baby was asleep, Randi had tears in her eyes.

If she couldn't convince Jackson of their fate, she wondered if she could leave them to be victims of the flood. With a sniffle, she wiped the moisture away from beneath her eyes, patted Rose gently on her back, and continued to sing softly.

"I seem to find you in the garden often," Jackson's deep, soft voice said from behind her.

She pivoted, sniffling again as she looked up past his tall black boots, thigh-molding breeches, and his trademark riding crop resting in one hand against his leg. Thoughts of tragedy flew from her head as his very alive, very masculine presence overwhelmed her senses. A cutaway coat emphasized his broad shoulders, and the somber, dark colors accented his blue-black hair and tanned complexion. The man looked too good to be true, so composed and handsome that she had to remind herself to breathe—especially when she remembered how they'd been "discovered" by Suzette in the study last night.

Randi was sure that the impromptu hug she'd given him must have seemed like more of a romantic embrace, because Suzette had smiled shyly at her when they'd put Rose to bed. Jackson, of course, had been too much of a gentleman to mention the incident. He'd been even more embarrassed than she about the impropriety of post-dinner hugs. Of course, if he hadn't given her the wine and the brandy sauce, she probably wouldn't have acted so impulsively!

He'd been even more courteous that evening, but she couldn't forget his attractive blush. If she'd believed in princes and fairy tales, here was tangible proof that Cinderella's dreams could come true. Of course, this wasn't a ball, and Randi wasn't wearing glass slippers.

She did owe him some justification for her sniffles since she couldn't yet tell him the real reason she'd been moved to sadness. "Rose is just so perfect, so special, that she brings tears to my eyes."

He looked at her with a wistful smile that seemed to say, "I don't believe you for a minute." But he didn't give voice to his doubts about her explanation. "What was that song you were singing to her? I don't recall it," Jackson said, kneeling on the quilt and smoothing his daughter's fine blond hair with one large hand.

" 'Candle in the Wind,' " Randi replied. "And I doubt you would have heard it around here."

"Another custom specific to your homeland?"

She nodded, wishing she could tell him the truth, but knowing she couldn't. He'd never believe her story.

"It's nice. Different, but nice." He shifted his focus from his sleeping daughter to Randi. "Rather like you."

She felt herself blush. "Thank you. I was afraid you didn't like the fact I was different."

"I'm growing accustomed to your eccentricities."

Randi smiled. "That's what you call it? I'm glad you've figured me out."

"I haven't figured you out at all. I'm just growing more familiar with the way you say and do certain things, your unique views on life and equality, and the way you feel very passionately about certain issues."

Like you, she wanted to say. *I feel very passionate about you*. She couldn't admit that to him, though. To encourage this insane attraction would be the height of stupidity. They were from two opposite worlds— wealth and relative poverty—and two distinct times. She couldn't forget their differences for a minute.

Randi looked away from his intensely personal expression. "Rose just went to sleep. I think she wore herself out crawling around, exploring the world here in your garden." She patted the baby gently on the back and smiled at the peaceful way Rose slept. "I've had to really watch her because she keeps trying to eat all the flower petals that fall from the trees."

"I'm not sure if the flowers are edible, but I suppose the air is good for her."

"Yes," Randi said, hoping that was true. Rose didn't seem to have any allergies or other bad reactions to being in the fresh air and sunshine. Of course, Randi didn't allow her in the sun for long. No one in the 1840s knew about SPF 35, that was for sure.

"Are you coming or going?" Randi asked, looking over his finely tailored garments that fit him like a glove.

"Going. I've been summoned to my former father-in-law's plantation to meet with some of the planters. I believe the subject is the crisis in hiring skilled workers," he said with a sigh of resignation.

"I suppose you don't believe this is very important."

"What I don't believe," he said with a bit of steel in his voice, "is that we can compete with the lure of gold fields."

"Gold fields?" Where had she heard that before?

"Surely you've heard of the gold strikes in California," he said rather incredulously.

"Oh, yes, the gold strikes," she said, suddenly remembering her high school history class. "Sutter's Mill."

"That's right. That was the start. Now every man who wants to become rich has packed up a cart or a wagon and headed west."

"That must be really hard. I mean, there are no trains, no roads, no easy way to get there."

He tilted his head and stared at her thoughtfully. "You say that like there should be all of those things. What do you mean?"

Oops. She'd goofed again, letting her knowledge of the future seep through into the conversation. "I didn't mean anything like that. I must mean that compared to civilization, they'll have a hard time living in such a distant place." She didn't know if California was a state, a territory, or another country at the moment, so she played it safe.

"I'm sure it's quite rough out there, but men are willing to risk everything for a chance to make money quickly and easily."

Randi shrugged. "You can't really blame them. Not everyone is born wealthy. I'm sure it's easy for you and the other planters to forget that people need to hope for a better future."

He looked at her as though she'd just said something incredibly stupid. Well, she wasn't apologizing for her little lecture. The rich might think they could control all the wealth forever, but they were wrong. Lots of people earned their way into the upper class . . . some of them even without winning the lottery!

"All I'm saying is that they're pursuing the American dream by going to California to search for gold."

He continued to look at her with a blank expression.

"You know, the American dream?" Maybe that phrase wasn't in use yet either. Oh, well. She could bluff this one. "People started coming to American for opportunity, right? Religious, political, and personal. That's the American dream."

"A telling phrase. I hadn't heard it before."

"Well, that's okay," she said. "I'm sure you'll hear it again." *If you live that long. If you listen to me about the flood.* She didn't say that, of course.

He pushed himself up from the quilt. "I must leave."

"There's something I wanted to ask," Randi said, struggling to rise so she didn't have to talk too loud. She didn't want to wake Rose.

Jackson reached down and took her hand, pulling her up with ease. She wondered how nineteenth-century guys looked without their shirts. Did they ripple and bulge like models and actors of her day, or were they a bit more ordinary looking, like most of the guys she'd known in the real world?

She had no business wondering about Jackson Durant's abs or pecs. "Thanks," she murmured, tearing her gaze away with effort.

"What did you need?"

Again, the word *you* sprang to mind, but she tamped

down the thought. "I was wondering if I could have some paper and a pencil. My hobby is sketching."

"Of course," he said, still holding her hand.

She gently tugged her fingers from his grasp. He seemed surprised, as if he'd forgotten they were still touching. Darn it, this attraction thing was building on both sides. Apparently she was going to have to be the one to keep their relationship in check. Strictly business—especially saving the lives of him and his daughter.

"Where would I find paper and pencils?" she asked. Her voice sounded a tiny bit breathless—not a good thing when she'd just vowed to keep their relationship professional.

"In the study. My desk is locked, but the paper you'll need is in the bottom of the credenza. If you have any trouble finding what you need, ask Birdie . . . or Lebeau, if he's back from his trip."

"Okay," she said. "Thank you."

"You're welcome." He continued to look down at her, his eyes heavy lidded.

If she stayed where she was, he was going to kiss her. She knew it as well as she knew her name. With a quick intake of breath, Randi stepped back.

Her movement seemed to break the spell. He blinked, then frowned. "Good day, Miss Galloway."

"Randi," she reminded him, wondering why she'd insisted they become more informal.

"Randi," he repeated, saying her name with such softness and depth that her knees felt a bit weak.

She sank to the quilt, using Rose as an excuse to put more distance between her and the most unsuitable man she'd ever been attracted to. This guy was even a worse catch than Cleve, because with all his faults, at least her former lover had been born in the same century as she.

"Good-bye. Have a good time," she said cheerfully.

118

Jackson frowned. "I sincerely doubt that is possible, given the men I'm visiting."

Randi chuckled. "Okay. Then I'll just say drive carefully."

"I'm riding." He walked toward the path behind the house.

"Of course you are," Randi called, smiling. "Have a nice day."

He stopped, then turned back to look at her. "Miss Randi, are you teasing me with more of your odd phrases?"

"Yes, sir." She loved looking at him, whether he was perplexed or serious, smiling or frowning. At the moment, he looked surprised, and perhaps a bit teasing himself.

He didn't answer, just turned back to the path and walked away, swinging the once-threatening riding crop against his thigh.

Chapter Eight

Lebeau returned to Black Willow Grove late that afternoon, just before the rain started to fall. Heavy gray clouds rolled in from the west with rumbling thunder and occasional flashes of lightning. Jackson had the lamps lit early, then retired behind the closed doors of the study to confer with his butler.

As he poured them both a cognac, Jackson realized his palms were damp—a condition he couldn't blame on the wet weather. He wanted to confirm his suspicions that Randi was lying about how she'd arrived at his plantation and why, but was he was ready to hear the truth? From Lebeau's somber expression, Jackson deduced the news wasn't good. He hoped that she wasn't a common criminal or woman of ill-repute. He'd hate to dismiss her from his home, but he would in an instant to keep Rose from being exposed to such elements.

"Tell me what you learned about my houseguest," Jackson said as he handed Lebeau the brandy snifter.

"Thank you," the butler said, taking a sip and savoring the mellow flavor with closed eyes and a blissful expression. He opened his eyes and gazed at Jackson. "This is one of the few vices you've corrupted me with."

"Not for lack of trying," Jackson answered, remembering his earlier, wilder years along the river, when he and Lebeau had more in common than anyone else knew. They'd been outcasts of sorts, searching for their futures among men who rarely talked of their pasts. Now they were both respectable, although in different ways.

Lebeau leaned back against the settee. "You were right. No one had seen or heard of Miss Galloway."

"No lost trunk?" Jackson sipped the imported brandy and tried to keep his mind from racing.

"Nothing about a young woman with short, blond hair and unusual clothing."

"How about on the road to the house. Did anyone see her there? Any servants . . . field workers?"

Lebeau shook his head slowly. "Not a soul."

"How did she get here?"

"Have you asked her?"

"She won't talk. She gives some vague answer that could mean anything from she walked unobserved in the front door and up the stairs to she magically flew into the house." Jackson shook his head. "I don't know what to think about her."

"Why don't you ask her to leave?

"Because I don't think she has anywhere else to go, and because . . . because she truly believes she's here to watch over Rose."

"You've let her take care of your daughter?" Lebeau asked incredulously.

Jackson held up his hand. "I know it sounds like I've lost my mind, but you should see her. She's very good with Rose. She cares for her."

Lebeau shook his head. "I never thought you'd trust

that baby to a woman who wasn't the best."

Picking up an intricate needlework bookmark that his wife had made for him as a wedding gift, Jackson stared at the tiny stitches and delicate flower pattern. He kept the piece displayed out of habit, even though she would never walk into the study again to see that her gift was appreciated.

The best. He wasn't sure how to measure what was best in a woman any longer. Pansy Crowder had possessed all that was admirable in a woman: beauty, manners, breeding, modesty, and obedience. He'd assumed that he would be happy if his wife was such a paragon of womanhood. Looking back on their ten-month marriage, he couldn't say he'd been happy. Proud of possessing such a beautiful, cultured wife, but nothing more.

He'd rarely laughed with her. At the most, she'd smiled as though her face might crack. And in the bedroom . . . Well, Pansy had been as obedient and modest as humanly possible. He'd been almost relieved when he'd discovered she was with child. Out of deference to her delicate condition, he'd refrained from the "joys" of the marriage bed. He wasn't sure which of them was more grateful to forego that most intimate aspect of married life.

"That young woman has you tied in knots," Lebeau observed.

Jackson placed the bookmark on the desk, then looked at his friend. "Actually, I wasn't thinking of her at all. I was remembering my wife."

"I'm sorry. I didn't mean—"

"Don't apologize. The truth is, I'm not sure anymore what's best in a woman. I can't imagine Pansy mothering a child. Randi has a way with Rose that is . . . refreshing. She's happier now, crying less."

More and more, Jackson found himself remembering his own mother. She'd smiled easily, and was ready with a hug or a scold as needed. Although she hadn't possessed great beauty or fine bloodlines, she'd been a loving, warm mother. She'd also worked hard making a home for their family when she could have given up hope. He'd forgotten the importance of a mother's hugs and caring concern until he'd seen Randi with his own daughter.

"Then you've hired Miss Galloway to be Rose's governess?"

"I told her she had the job. Of course, that was pending any negative report that you brought back."

"I'm sorry I don't have any news about her. Maybe she came from the other direction by wagon or coach."

Jackson shook his head. "I don't think so. She jumped on the river story too fast, as though that was the first thing on her mind. She could have just as easily told a story about a spooked team and overturned wagon as the reason for her lost clothing and faulty memory."

"I see your point. What do you want me to do now?"

"Keep asking, but don't go out of your way. Maybe we'll come across someone on a packet returning to the landings."

"There might not be as many packets as normal. We have trouble coming, I'm afraid."

"The river?"

Lebeau nodded. "I talked to a navigator who'd been working upriver, and he said the snowmelt has pushed the Missouri over its banks earlier this month. The runoff is heading south, and with the heavy rains north and west of here, we're bound for trouble before long."

"Damn," Jackson muttered. "I suspected as much, but I'd hoped I was wrong. How bad did he say the water levels were up north?"

"Bad. The worst he's seen since being on the river before the paddle wheelers."

Jackson cursed beneath his breath, then walked to the window and looked out into the blackness. Beyond the veranda, rain pounded the delicate grass of his lawn, and in the fields, he knew the young cotton plants were equally vulnerable to the downpours. He reminded himself that rains came every spring, and yet each year he managed to produce a crop. He would find a way this year, too.

"Damn it, I've got to convince them to build the levees higher all along the river, not just at my turn. If the water leaves the banks upstream, my measures won't matter. We'll be flooded with no way to divert the water away from our houses or crops."

Lebeau looked at him long and hard, in that wise and patient way Jackson had come to know.

"What?"

"After all these years, you still think you can control this river?"

"Not the whole river. I'm not that stupid or naive, but I will do whatever is necessary to keep it away from my land."

"The river might not be so obliging."

"The river can go to hell. I haven't worked this hard to build up Black Willow Grove so the Mississippi can claim my land."

"The river claims what it wants," Lebeau said, rising from the settee.

"Then I hope to God it wants someone else's land, because mine is going to be protected if I have to set every man on this plantation to work building a levee like no one has ever seen before, from Sugar Creek around the bend and north to the Hatchie."

Lebeau shook his head. "I'll do my part, but—"

"You run the house. Let me worry about the river and the other planters."

"I'll go do that," Lebeau said. "I imagine things have gotten out of sorts around here since I've been gone."

"Not so much that I've noticed, but then, I'm not as observant as you about everyday matters."

"Nothing to do with Miss Galloway, I'm sure."

Jackson frowned. "I get enough sarcasm from her."

Lebeau opened the door to the hallway, then said in a louder voice, "I'm sorry, Mas'r Jackson. I'll try to do better next time."

Jackson shook his head at Lebeau's charade—at their charade, he should say, since both were participants. They didn't have much choice, however. The slaves would resent his status, even as they aspired to his position. Explaining the relationship between master and freeman was too daunting to consider. Jackson's carefully maintained secrets could even be revealed.

Not to mention the other planter's distrust of freed slaves. They didn't want freemen stirring up unrest among the field hands upon which the whole economy depended.

Jackson closed the door, then picked up Lebeau's glass. Removing a handkerchief from his pocket, he carefully cleaned all traces of brandy from the snifter. Not even Birdie needed to know that the master had shared a brandy with his butler.

"You are a little terror tonight, you know that?" Randi and Rose lay face-to-face on a quilt on the nursery floor. Rose squealed in delight and reached for the simple stuffed toy from Suzette.

Apparently Rose's daddy wasn't going to come up to get her tonight. Suzette said he was behind closed doors in his study with Lebeau, who had come back from his mysterious trip. No telling what they were discussing. She hoped the topic was rising water rather than fallen nannies. That's exactly what she felt like— someone caring for another woman's child and lusting after the husband. Sad, but true. She couldn't seem to help herself, she thought with a sigh.

Rose yanked the toy up and down with her pudgy arm before throwing it across the room.

"Good shot, sweetie! You're a regular Joe Montana, you know that?" Randi said with a laugh.

Rose shrieked again, reaching toward the toy.

Randi was about to crawl across the room after the strange stuffed animal when it was handed to her by a large, masculine hand.

"I think she wants this back," Jackson said, his voice showing some amusement.

Randi scrambled to sit up after handing the toy to Rose, who promptly stuck it in her mouth. "We were just playing."

"I can see that," he replied, folding his arms across his chest and staring down at her. "Where did you get that toy?"

"I asked Suzette for something. Rose didn't have anything to play with."

"She's only eight months old."

"I know, but she gets bored very easily. She needs lots of mental stimulation, remember? Is there something wrong with the toy?" Randi couldn't see anything objectionable, but then again, she couldn't tell what kind of animal the darned thing was supposed to be.

He nodded toward the cloth toy. "It's the kind the slave children play with."

Randi felt herself heat up, kind of like a percolator. It started in her gut and worked up to her neck and cheeks, bubbling up into an all-out sense of outrage. How dare he think a sweet little . . . whatever—cow or horse or pig—was unsuitable for his precious daughter? Especially when she was having such a great time playing with it.

"You're a snob, you know that?" she said, pushing herself to her feet. She jabbed a finger at his chest. "If you don't think this toy is good enough for Rose, then why don't you just tell her that? Go ahead, destroy her happiness by jerking it right out of her hands. Maybe then your uppity sense of propriety will be satisfied."

"I never said the toy wasn't good enough for her. I just wondered where you got it."

"Oh," she said, feeling the hot bubbles of outrage pop into warm mist around her head.

"What makes you automatically assume the worst about me, Randi Galloway? Is there something in your past that causes this resentment toward anyone who is successful?"

"I don't have anything against success," she said, tilting up her chin as she looked into his dark eyes, "but I don't like people who think they're better than others."

"And you assume I think I'm better than someone else?"

She knew she was looking at him like he was crazy, but she couldn't help herself. "You're a planter. You *own* other people. Don't you think that's a big clue as to how you think?"

"I hadn't really thought of it like that," he said, looking at her in an assessing way she couldn't read. "Our economy is based on the production of cotton, which has little to do with thinking you're better than someone else."

She raised her arms to make a point, then let them fall to her sides. "Never mind. You're not ready to hear this. You're too much a part of this whole crazy era to understand what I'm talking about."

She started to sink to the quilt to cuddle up with Rose—the least-complicated person Randi had met since her journey to the past. Jackson apparently had other ideas, because he surprised her by grasping her upper arm.

"Stop that!"

"I'm just trying to keep your attention. You have a habit of getting frustrated and stopping a conversation."

"I don't think arguing further would do any good. Now please, let me go."

He released her arm, but continued to stare at her. "Why are you so ready to dislike me?"

"Does it matter?"

He drew in a deep breath, then stepped back. "It shouldn't."

She shivered, hugging her arms. She didn't want to admit anything to him, yet she felt compelled to answer her own question. "I don't like what you represent, but I can't say that I dislike *you*."

"Then I believe we're evenly matched, because while I don't like knowing you're lying about how you arrived, I can't dislike you, either."

"How do you know I'm lying? Not that I'm admitting I am, of course," she added quickly.

"Give over, Randi," he said gently. "No one saw you arrive on a packet—especially in a way you described. An occasion such as losing your trunk overboard, then jumping in after it, would have been remembered."

"No one remembered me?" she said in a small voice, looking down at Rose.

"No one."

"Well, I suppose they just weren't there," she said bravely.

"You just won't give up, will you?"

She turned her attention back to Jackson. "When the time is right," she said softly, "I'll tell you whatever you want to know."

He watched her intently as though he was judging the truth in her statement. Silence stretched between them until she felt as tight as a guitar string. Finally, Rose let out a squeal.

Randi looked down, grateful for the interruption. Rose had crawled to her dad and was trying to get his attention by pulling on his pant leg. Randi couldn't keep herself from watching his reaction.

His expression changed from thoughtful intensity to

unconditional indulgence. With a smile, he bent down and picked up his daughter.

Delighted with this turn of events, Rose squealed again and reached for the collar of Jackson's coat. He snuggled her closer, a look of love on his face. Randi turned away from the sight, unable to watch father and daughter any longer. Her heart hurt too much to see them happy, growing together as a family when their time might well be limited to less than a month.

She felt responsible for their lives because she was the only one who knew what was going to happen. But could the future be changed? She had no idea. Perhaps when she arrived back in her own time, Black Willow Grove might still be standing. In that case, a replica would hardly be necessary. Did that mean she couldn't go back if the future was changed?

She wished she had someone to ask about this and so many other questions. But for once, she was on her own. Without family or friends, the lives of two people in her hands, she hoped she made the right decisions about what to say, and when.

"I hope you know when the time is right," Jackson said, breaking into her thoughts.

She froze, her hands clenched into fists. My God, had he read her mind? "What? What are you talking about?"

He looked at her as though she'd talked in tongues. "You said you'd tell me where you are from when the time is right."

"Oh, yes." She breathed a sigh of relief. "I will. I promise."

"I hope that's a promise you will keep."

"I don't think I have any choice."

His expression told her he was confused by her change of demeanor and her words. Well, she couldn't help the way her thoughts kept straying to their fate.

"Very well." He handed Rose over to her. "The hour is late and my daughter needs her sleep. I have a long day tomorrow also. I'll say good night to you both."

Randi snuggled the baby close, grateful for the warmth and life she represented. "Good night."

After Jackson left, Randi stayed with the baby even after Suzette arrived to feed her before bed. She didn't want to leave, didn't want to let this little girl out of her sight. But she knew she must, just as she must make the tough choices and try to follow her head instead of her heart. If she listened only to the longings in her soul, she'd never get home, and two people might perish in the muddy depths of a river that had claimed more lives than she would ever know.

Randi recognized the importance of eavesdropping, but she hadn't planned on hearing quite so much when she'd ventured downstairs the next evening. She'd seen the men ride up on fancy horses and in beautiful carriages several hours ago from her second-floor window. For all she knew, this could be the nineteenth-century equivalent of boys' night out. But apparently this get-together was more important than a bunch of guys shooting the breeze, playing cards, and sharing some brews.

Sitting with her knees drawn up to her chest in the landing of the stairwell, she felt like a little girl listening to adult talk long past her bedtime. She wore the lavender gown, but she'd abandoned both the uncomfortable petticoats and the poorly fitted shoes. Her bare toes curled on the highly polished wood. The sensation was delightfully wicked, making her a bit nervous as she tried to stay totally in the shadows. If Jackson found her here, he'd blow a gasket. She didn't dare inch forward though, as much as she wanted to grasp the railing and lean against the solid wood so she could get just a tiny bit closer to what was going on downstairs.

Unfortunately, she couldn't see into the room from her vantage point. She could hear and smell, though.

The men meeting in the parlor were generally loud and opinionated. They smoked enough cigars to keep a servant busy lighting the smelly, disgustingly soggy rolls of tobacco. She could only speculate on the amount of brandy or bourbon they were consuming this evening. Already two servants had entered and left through the open double doors, carrying laden trays in and empty ones out. How long did this overindulgence last? She thought that the hour must be close to eleven, although she hadn't heard the grandfather clock in the hallway chime yet. Given the fact that the day started dreadfully early in this time—even before the sun came up—she found their late-night meetings a bit strange.

This whole planter society was definitely a man's world, she thought with distaste. Of course, things might have been different if Jackson's wife were alive. Other women might have visited Black Willow Grove, but probably not tonight, when the topic of conversation centered around the masculine subject of saving the homestead from Old Man River.

Randi could almost hear the male chauvinists in the room below saying to their "little women," "Now, honey, don't you worry yourself about a thing," then patting them on the hand in a condescending manner. Of course, that would be after the woman had given birth, plowed a field, and cooked a meal. Thank heavens *she* wasn't the wife of any of these male chauvinists. Molding herself into a man's image of an ideal woman, being demure and accommodating, was something she'd never do. Besides, she couldn't accept this lifestyle. The heck with Jackson's rationale that the society was based on the economy of cotton production. His explanation sounded more like an excuse for these men to keep on overindulging in self-gratification.

She snorted in disgust at the image of those cigar smoking, liquor-swilling jerks, then clamped her hand over her mouth. She had to remember to keep her opinions to herself, especially when eavesdropping in the middle of the night.

"You haven't lived in these parts for long, Jackson," one of the men said in a placating tone. "You don't know how the river behaves around here."

"I know this river as well as anyone," she heard Jackson answer, "and I know that the bend in the river is a weak point we can't ignore."

"The water rises every spring, Jackson. You know that. Just because some of those fur-trappin' cold-bloods upriver panic over a little floodin' doesn't mean that we have to start buildin' levees."

"Not just a little flood, Will," Jackson answered. "The worst some have seen in years. And it's coming this way."

"Well, of course it is, son," a particularly patronizing neighbor said, "but that river has a long way to go before it gets to Tennessee, and all that water might just dry up or soak in before we get a chance to see any of it."

"You really believe that, Thomas? Are you willing to risk your granddaughter's heritage on hopes that water-saturated land can hold even more rain and floods?"

Silence. Randi found herself holding her breath, waiting for someone in the room to agree with Jackson. They had to take whatever steps were possible to save themselves . . . to save Jackson and Rose and Black Willow Grove. Randi had agonized because she hadn't found an opportunity to convince him of the importance of protecting against the flood, but apparently her warnings weren't necessary. He already knew they might be flooded.

So why was she here? If not to warn of a coming flood and tragedy, why had she come back in time? She couldn't do anything to divert water. She wasn't an engineer, or even a draftsman—yet. Since they were forewarned, they should be able to save themselves.

The volume of the men's voices lowered. She heard the clink of crystal, probably as glasses were refilled. A moment later, she pulled back into the shadows as a servant walked out of the room with a decanter-laden silver tray.

These planters couldn't pour their drinks out of plain old bottles, she supposed with an unusual amount of loathing. Only the best for them. Did any of them know they were living on borrowed time? If the flood didn't get them this year, then the Civil War would, sooner or later. When had it started? The 1860s, she thought, but then, history had never been her best subject.

Why these men bothered her so much, she wasn't sure. She'd had some doubts about Jackson's morals and practices, but after last night had decided he wasn't such a bad sort. Okay, he was spoiled by wealth and position, and didn't understand much about women who weren't obedient servants or polite wives.

Despite those drawbacks, he seemed different from the other men. Maybe he was just smarter than most, she thought, shifting once more on the hard floor.

Jackson *was* different, and not just in looks—although she couldn't ignore how he filled out the shoulders of his coats and the backside of his pants. She was especially fond of those thigh-hugging breeches and tall black boots. The riding crop still caused her to cringe a little, even after she'd decided he wasn't going to hit her—or anyone else, most likely—with it.

With a sigh, she propped her chin on her hand and stared at the doorway, wishing they'd decide something soon. She was pretty tired of sitting here, but if she went back upstairs, she was equally sure something exciting would happen that she'd miss.

Just as she'd shifted on her weary butt for about the twentieth time, the voices of the men rose again, except they all seemed to be talking at once. Seconds later, the first two walked through the doorway. Randi scooted back farther into the shadows.

Lebeau appeared with a servant, who began handing out tall black hats and other items, including a few more riding crops.

"We'll try your plan," one of the men said in a bored tone of voice, "but I don't expect much to come of these rising waters."

"Don't forget the warning system," Jackson said, entering the foyer from the parlor.

Randi's heart sped up at the sight of his lean body and straight posture. Compared to the rest of the men, he was a god among peasants. He looked particularly appealing tonight in a fitted, short double-breasted jacket and thigh-hugging trousers. Unfortunately, the tails of his jacket hid his well-sculpted rear.

"I know, I know," the bored man said. "We'll set the bells up along the levee, and use riders if there's a break."

"I know you think this is a waste of time, Franklin, but believe me, if we do have a crisis, you'll be glad we took these measures."

"I'm sure you're right," the man said, settling his top hat firmly on his head, "but this is a damned inconvenient time to start taking workers away from the fields."

"Jackson's convinced we won't have any fields," a jovial man said, slapping him on the back with a thick, stubby-fingered hand, "if we don't protect ourselves from a flood."

"A regular Noah," a third man said with a smile that didn't reach his eyes.

Jackson turned to the man, who was getting his hat from Lebeau. "God hasn't spoken to me, Thomas, but if He does, I'll be sure to ask Him when and where we can expect a levee breech."

A smattering of chuckles followed, then the men moved toward the door. Randi counted a total of five, excluding Jackson. She wondered if these represented all the families or plantations in the area. She hoped so. If they were all prepared, all united in their goal to keep floodwaters out, maybe history would be changed.

They didn't sound too convinced, though, come to think of it. And she hadn't done anything to influence anyone—especially Jackson. As she sat on the landing and contemplated what she'd heard, she became more and more convinced that the other planters weren't going to carry through their end of the deal. Maybe their lack of diligence had led to the flood that would take Jackson's life.

And Rose's life, too. With a wistful, breathy sigh, Randi looked up into the darkness. She couldn't let that baby die. Not in the muddy waters of the Mississippi. Not before she'd had a chance to live.

The slamming of the door downstairs jolted her back to reality. She had to get back to her room before someone realized she was here. Someone like Jackson Durant.

"I'm going upstairs to check on Rose," she heard him say to Lebeau. "I won't be back down, so go ahead and lock up the house."

"Yes, Mas'r Jackson," the butler said in his dull but dignified tone. He motioned for the servant who'd been helping with hats to go into the parlor, probably to clean up the mess. There must be a bucket-load of cigar butts in there, judging by the amount of smoke that had poured out of the open doorway.

Randi tried scooting back up the stairs so she didn't attract attention, but the hem of her dress caught on a splinter of wood.

"Do you think they'll listen?" she heard Lebeau ask in an entirely different tone of voice, low and conspiratorial. How odd. She paused, no longer thinking about the worrisome hem.

"No, I'm sorry to say. But maybe I've planted the idea

of a possible flood in their heads. Perhaps they'll pay more attention when the water starts to rise."

"They'll pay attention when the field hands are wading between the furrows, trying not to get bit by snakes to care for their cotton."

Snakes? She hadn't thought of snakes, but conceded that their presence was likely. The idea of slithering snakes lurking in the muddy water caused another shiver to pass through her, almost diverting her attention away from the conversation below.

"And when their carpets begin to float away," Jackson added.

Randi frowned, trying to figure out what was different. Tone of voice, she supposed. Jackson talked to Lebeau in a way that was downright friendly. She hadn't expected that in a master-servant relationship.

She even heard Lebeau chuckle.

That caused her to lean forward, pulling against the still-captured hem. The fabric gave way with a slight ripping sound.

She hadn't thought the noise too loud, but as she inched back in the shadows, she knew her presence had been discovered. Her only options were to make a mad dash for her room—as if Jackson wouldn't know which person had been eavesdropping on the stairs—or try to bluff her way through this.

His heels clicked against the marble entry files, then came to stop on the first step on the stairway.

"Miss Galloway, I presume?" he said in a resigned, yet amazed, tone.

"Good evening, Mr. Durant," she said in her most refined voice. She cautiously tucked the hem of her skirt over her bare toes.

"What in the name of all that's holy are you doing, sitting here on the landing?" She could tell that resignation had won out. He didn't sound amused. Thank heaven he hadn't noticed her bare feet.

"Getting rhubarb pie," she improvised in a small voice, smoothing the gown's skirt closer around her, hoping he didn't notice she wasn't wearing any petticoats.

"We don't keep rhubarb pie on the stair landing," he said in grave voice. "Besides, wouldn't you have used the back stairs if you'd wanted to go to the kitchen? And we don't sit around in the shadows like a second-rate spy." He started up the steps.

"I wasn't spying," she said in defense of her original position. "I was merely going downstairs when I heard voices."

"So you decided to spy." He stopped two steps down from the landing, looming over her without threatening too much.

She shrugged. "Are you trying to hide something?"

"Of course not, but that's hardly the point. I will not tolerate this kind of behavior from a governess. You most certainly cannot teach my daughter decorum when you behave in such an outrageous fashion."

"I'm sorry," she said, thankful he didn't have his whip with him tonight. He was working into a real snit, and she didn't want to see or hear that tap-tap-tap of leather against fabric-covered muscle.

"Get yourself up to bed now, and this won't happen again."

She struggled to rise, but her legs had been bent awkwardly for too long. The minute she tried to put weight on them, she stumbled.

He reached for her arms, pulling her upright so fast she heard another, louder rip. "Oh, no."

She looked down. The hem of the gown was partially torn off, lying across her bare foot like a tattered flag that said, "Look at me."

He did. And he groaned. "Miss Galloway, you continue to amaze me." His grip on her arm didn't slacken; if anything, his fingers seemed to tighten.

She shrugged, ignoring the warmth in her cheeks that told her she was blushing. "The shoes don't fit."

"That is no excuse for walking around like a field hand."

Something inside her seemed to snap. Whereas she'd been embarrassed just a moment ago by her bare feet, she now focused only on the practical nature of her outfit. And standing in front of her, looking like an actor out of some big-budget historical epic with an unlimited wardrobe, was the man who kept putting her down.

She twisted from his grasp. "Why should I tromp around in some really narrow shoes, all laced up in a dress with more petticoats than a fifties' poodle skirt? I'm tired of being miserable in my clothes, do you hear? I want my comfortable shoes back. I want some clothes that don't require help to get dressed. Most of all, I want everyone to quit staring at me like I've lost my mind!"

"Miss Galloway, you obviously *have* lost your mind. I'll see about putting you on a packet tomorrow, although I don't suppose you'll tell me where you're from or if you have anywhere to go. That, however, is your problem."

He brushed past her, reeking of cigars and brandy, his jaw set as he stared straight ahead.

"Wait!"

He paused, but then continued to walk.

She rushed after him, holding up her skirts. "You can't kick me out of your house! I've got to stay here."

"No. I won't have you influencing Rose with your behavior."

Randi caught him as he was halfway down the hallway to the attic stairs. "Please, I've got to stay!" She grabbed his rock-solid arm and pulled him to a stop.

"What you're doing isn't helping your case," he said, looking down at her hand, partially around his upper arm.

"Maybe I'm not being very smart about this. I know I've got a temper, but please, you must listen."

"Why should I listen to any more of your lies? You haven't told me the truth about where you're from or why you're here." He shrugged off her hand as if she were of no consequence.

"I've thought about it a lot, but I can't figure out why I'm here," she wailed. "Please, you've got to trust me. I know what's going to happen in the future."

He stopped. In the dim light of the upper hallway, his jaw twitched. "What did you say?"

Chapter Nine

"Premonition," she said, easing the word out as though she'd never said it before. "I can tell what's going to happen. I know there's going to be a flood."

A vision of haggard old crones, throwing chicken bones to foresee the future, warred with his interest in her absurd claims. He'd known seers in his past—far into a childhood that was so distant the memories seemed to belong to another man. Voodoo and black magic–induced claims, performed by African slaves from the Caribbean, were common where he'd grown up. Most of the "seers" deceived just for the profit of a few coins, but some of them had given eerie predictions of things to come.

He remembered one old woman who'd lived not far from his family. She'd come to their door one day, seeking him out, saying she had something important to tell him. The memory of her greasy, stale scent rushed back, along with the fretful, damp wind that had swirled threadbare skirts against her legs like ancient drapes at a broken window. She was so poor and ragged that she'd caused a shiver to run through him.

"Beware the flames," she'd said with wild, fevered eyes and a raspy voice. She'd taken his shirt in her bony fist and pulled him so close that he'd smelled her bad teeth. "Fire will destroy, but if you're honest and true, you'll escape to a new life."

He'd pulled away from her, disgusted by her ratty state, unwilling to believe her absurd claims. He'd sent her on her way without a coin—not that she'd asked for one.

Less than a year later, his parents and younger brother had died when smoke filled their house as they slept. Neighbors had rushed to put out the flames, but they'd been too late to save his family.

Jackson had left home months before to seek his fortune. He hadn't died as the old woman had predicted, but not because he was honest or true. Quite the opposite, in fact. There'd been little honesty in his life since leaving his family behind.

Except for Rose. In his daughter, he saw the future. Not literally, not like Randi Galloway proposed. But in her life, his would live on. He hoped he'd have other children; a son to inherit Black Willow Grove was essential. Children were his future, not some vague or dire predictions by disturbed women who thought they foresaw events yet to come.

"You're only claiming you have the sight because you heard us talking. Your desperate grasp at saving your position is pathetic."

"I listened because I already knew about the flood," she claimed, once again grabbing his arm. "Please, you've got to believe me. I didn't mention this earlier because I thought we had time to . . . because I wanted you to learn to trust me. But now there's little time left, and you must listen to me."

Her voice had grown more pleading as she continued, but Jackson hardened his heart against her anxiety. "There's nothing you have to say that I want to hear."

"Even if I tell you that Black Willow Grove will be destroyed, that a hundred and fifty years from now, nothing will remain of this magnificent house?"

"You don't know that."

"I do. I've seen the future. There'll be a museum built on this very spot, and they'll re-create the furniture and locate many of your treasures. There's nothing you can do to save the house, but you can save yourself and Rose."

"What are you talking about?" He jerked his arm away from her grasp, alarmed by her desperate claims. His heart beat fast and hard as he realized she was more delusional than he'd imagined.

"You and Rose . . . both lost in the flood, along with the house."

"Your imagination is running wild. Floods don't tear down houses like this," he said, sweeping his arm wide. "Black Willow Grove is built to last a hundred years or more. Water may rise to fill the lower floor, but when the flood recedes, the house will still stand."

"I don't know why, but the house won't withstand the flood. I can't explain what happens in detail, only the final result."

He grasped her upper arms, giving her a small shake to stop her raving. "None of this is true! You're imagining this outcome to justify your existence. For some unknown reason, you've decided you want to be here with my daughter. I have no idea where you came by your knowledge of her, or how you came to be on my plantation, but this madness must stop."

Tears filled her eyes as she sagged against him. "I'm not mad," she whispered.

He couldn't push her away without being deliberately cruel, and despite what others may think of him, he rarely acted out of anger. He'd been furious with this young woman when he'd found her holding Rose that first day, but now he felt sadness for such a loss of a spirited, if unconventional, soul to the horror of madness. "I'm in a better position to judge that than you are," he said more gently.

"No. You don't understand."

"I don't understand because you've made no sense."

He felt her shake her head against his chest.

"Come," he said, tugging on her arm. "You need rest."

"I can't leave here," she said in a small voice that cut through to his tattered soul.

"We'll talk tomorrow."

He led her away from the attic stairs, down the hall toward the bedroom she'd been using. From the corner of his eye, Jackson saw Lebeau in the shadows beside the stairs leading to the first floor.

With a shake of his head and a frown, Jackson let his butler know his services weren't needed. Lebeau turned and silently descended the steps.

Jackson led her into the candlelit room and toward the bed, making sure she had what she needed for the night. A single taper burned on the chest on the far wall. One of the servants had laid out a night rail and cap. A pitcher of water and a fresh towel rested on the washstand.

"Shall I send Melody in to help you?" he asked, remembering Randi's complaints about her dresses.

She looked around the room as though seeing it for the first time. "Is she around here?"

"I imagine she's gone back to her quarters at this late hour."

"Oh." She sank wearily to the bed. "I don't feel very well, but I don't want to wake her up." She reached around with her right hand, bending at an awkward angle as her fingers skimmed along her spine. "Can you . . . would you unfasten these hooks? I can't reach them."

"That's not a good idea," he said, taking a step back.

"Because it's unconventional?" she asked with just a hint of her former spark.

"An unmarried woman should never be alone with me in a room, much less ask me to unfasten her clothing."

"I didn't invite you in, but since you're already here, I'm just being practical." She raised her chin, as if she dared him to question her logic. In the golden candlelight, her green eyes glistened with unshed tears and uncommon defiance.

"Did it ever occur to you that there's a reason society has rules?"

"Believe it or not, I'm familiar with rules. I just don't happen to believe they're useful except as guidelines."

"That is a ridiculous statement."

"What do you expect from a crazy woman?"

He turned and walked toward the door. "I'll have Lebeau fetch Melody for you."

"Don't bother," Randi said, pushing herself up from the bed. "I mean it. I don't want her sleep disturbed just because you're too afraid of me to unfasten a little row of hooks and eyes."

"I am not afraid of you," he said, clutching his hands into fists to keep himself from waving his arms like a lunatic. If he stayed around her much longer, he'd be as crazy as she was.

"Go on," she said. "Go hide in your study with all your cronies, and believe what you want. I'm not crazy, and I know what I know." She turned away from him, walking to the window where faint moonlight illuminated the pale lavender of her dress.

He paused in the doorway, watching the straight line of her back, her unusually squared-off shoulders. She stood more like a man than a woman, he realized. Not that she wasn't feminine. Her curves would entice any man to explore more than a row of fastenings down the back of her high-necked bodice. He'd already tasted her lips, and knowing how she kissed did nothing to quench his curiosity about unleashing her full passion.

With an inward sigh of resignation, he shut the door—from the inside of the bedroom.

Her shoulders slumped as she leaned against the window frame. He thought he heard her curse, and she definitely wiped a hand beneath her eye as she continued to stand and stare into the night.

He walked toward her, not trying to hide the slight tap of his half-boots on the wooden floors.

She jumped, holding a hand to her throat in a feminine gesture as old as time. "I thought you'd left," she squeaked breathlessly.

"I decided to put you out of your misery of uncomfortable clothing. However, I don't want anyone to know about this. Do you promise you won't tell?"

She coughed discreetly. "I promise."

"Very well. Come here."

The words hung heavily in the air as she continued to stand beside the window. Moonlight cast a silvery glow over the swells of her breasts and shadows beneath the enticing curves. The waistline of the dress dipped past her narrow waist. She seemed to feel his gaze settle there, because she placed one hand over her flat stomach as she held a breath.

He seemed a bit breathless himself as he stared at this strange woman.

When she walked out of the stream of moonlight and into the golden candle glow, he felt the increased warmth as she turned from cool silver to glowing bronze. He clenched his fists again, this time to keep his hands from trembling.

Her gaze didn't waver as she stopped before him, looking very much like an offering to the gods. He wanted to pull her to his chest, settle his mouth over hers, kiss her until they both melted from the heat. He knew this desire was wrong. He tried to tell himself she wasn't the kind of woman he needed or wanted, but his body wasn't listening.

He prayed she continued to look into his eyes, because the cutaway coat hid nothing of his arousal.

"I trust you to be a gentleman," she whispered.

He sucked in a deep breath, then swallowed the denial he wanted to shout. If she only knew . . .

"Turn around," he murmured hoarsely.

She presented her back. Her short hair bared a graceful neck, tilted forward slightly. He wondered how it would feel to kiss her there, just above the high collar of the lavender dress. Would her shorn hair be soft or coarse? Would the strands irritate or delight? Just a little lower, and he would find out.

"Are you having trouble seeing?" she asked suddenly.

Her question snapped him back to reality. "No," he said in a strangely hoarse voice that didn't sound like him. "Just a moment."

Starting with the top fastener, he concentrated on dispensing with them as quickly as possible, on not thinking about how warm she felt beneath his knuckles, or how soft her skin brushed against his fingers as he worked each hook loose.

By the time he reached the waist, his hands trembled with the effort to keep himself from caressing instead of merely undressing her. How he wanted to peel away the fabric and feel her supple warmth beneath his hands. He couldn't resist sweeping his fingers along her spine, from waist to neck. Belatedly, he realized she wore no corset. The knowledge caused a wave of dizzying desire to speed through his body like a bolt of lightning. His hands settled firmly on her shoulders, ready to spin her around and kiss her senseless.

"Jackson?"

146

His name, sounding so trusting and sweet on her lips, made him pull his hands away as though she'd grown as hot as a burning coal.

"This is the reason," he ground out through clenched teeth, "that society has rules. Don't tempt me again to break them."

Randi sank to the bed as soon as Jackson firmly shut the door. She'd planned to check on Rose, but wouldn't be doing that now. She'd also planned not to get caught on the stairs, lose her temper, or blurt out the truth about what was going to happen in the future.

She buried her head in her hands, still unable to believe what she'd told Jackson. God, how could she have been so stupid? Now he wanted her to leave Black Willow Grove. At the least, he wouldn't let her around his precious daughter. Rose meant too much to him to let a crazy woman take care of her.

Then, to top off her totally stupid night, she'd practically challenged him to defy all his conventions and unhook her dress. She'd wanted him to admit that his rules—society's rules—were too confining. Instead, she'd given him a reason to be even more careful. Despite what he thought of her, he still wanted to make love. Between guys she'd dated and her brother Russell's friends, she'd been around enough men to see the symptoms.

She sat up, running her hands through her short hair. She had it just as bad as Jackson. She'd wanted his hands to linger on those hooks and eyes. She'd wanted him to turn her, hold her close, tell her he believed her and wanted her. But that wasn't going to happen. She mustn't forget that despite the passion that sizzled every time the two of them were alone, he wasn't going to trust or believe her unless she proved to him that what she'd predicted would really come true.

Unfortunately, she didn't remember enough of the

historical account of Black Willow Grove to impress him with details. And there hadn't been specific information about dates or names leading up to the tragedy in the book. She knew more about the people since she'd gone back to the past than she ever would from reading a book written nearly 150 years after they'd died or fled.

Now that she saw them as living, breathing people, her sadness was much more intense. She'd nearly collapsed from the pain earlier, suffering their loss so acutely when she'd told him the truth. Even if he didn't believe her, she'd tried to save the lives of his family and staff.

Maybe blurting out a half-truth wasn't such a bad thing. Maybe warning Jackson was redemption in itself . . . but maybe it wasn't. How would she know before it was too late for other action? How could she save them, or save herself?

Disgusted by all the questions that raced through her head with no answers, Randi stood up, then shrugged out of the confining dress. Beneath the uncomfortable garment, she'd worn only a soft, thin chemise. She knew that Melody had been scandalized by her decision, but she simply couldn't stand a corset she didn't need. Apparently she was a little more petite than Mrs. Durant, so the dress fit.

The moonlight beckoned, so Randi walked to the window and leaned against the frame. High clouds drifted across the night sky, but were they full of moisture? She'd grown weary of staying inside while the rains pounded the earth, but without an umbrella to shelter her, or a reason to be outside, she'd confined herself to the indoors. Rose had been equally unhappy with the weather, fussing and refusing to nurse to the point that Suzette had become frustrated.

Of course, she'd never show that to "the master." As far as Randi could tell, no one told anything unpleasant to Jackson, and no one dared to show any emotion. No matter what Suzette or Melody or Birdie felt, they kept their opinions to themselves. Only rarely did Randi get a glimpse into the other women's feelings. To them, she was an outsider—and white. They thought that unlike them, she was free to go. They didn't realize that she was tied to this place by bonds stronger than legal ownership.

If she didn't find her way back home, she may very well become a casualty of the flood that would sweep over this land in a matter of weeks. She couldn't face the rising water, the knowledge that there would be no dry land beneath her feet, that she couldn't simply wade out of the river to a safe place. She shuddered when she remembered what had happened when she was a child, the horrible feeling of being sucked beneath the muddy water. She couldn't breathe, couldn't see, even though she was only a foot or so beneath the surface.

By the time she'd been pulled out of the river, she'd been half-dead from fear. The Mississippi's taste had lingered for weeks, maybe months. When the river was high and fast, the air thick and humid, she still tasted the muddy water.

Tomorrow, she'd tell Jackson Durant a story he'd believe about her premonition. She'd beg his forgiveness for eavesdropping on his meeting, and swear she'd never misbehave again. She'd wear the uncomfortable clothes without complaint, care for Rose with the highest sense of propriety, and never criticize him or his rules again.

Tonight, she needed to think of a good reason for her knowledge of the future. Something a conservative, nineteenth-century man would believe. She wished she had a clue what that might be. At the moment, her mind continued to churn with a thousand images, none of them focused enough for a logical, realistic plan of action.

A breeze drifted in the open window, fluttering the drapes that she'd snuggled next to. She looked up into the night sky once more, seeing darker, thicker clouds. The air felt heavy, humid. She shivered, hugging her arms, swallowing her sudden sense of panic.

The Mississippi tasted exactly the same, in her time or this one.

The next morning, Jackson wasn't looking forward to seeing Randi. He flicked out his napkin and settled the cloth in his lap. After a restless night of snatched sleep between disturbing dreams of a woman's tears and rising water, he'd come to breakfast early. Perhaps she wouldn't come downstairs; she obviously wasn't accustomed to rising at dawn and getting to work.

As he accepted a plate from Cook's son Thomas, Jackson wondered again what type of position Randi had held or family she'd grown up in where she didn't have to rise early. She didn't look or act like a pampered daughter, yet she was unfamiliar with the most basic functions of a working household.

She was as much a mystery today as she'd been nearly a week ago when he'd found her standing in his daughter's nursery. After last night, she shouldn't be his problem any longer. She should be on a packet headed south, back to a city where she supposedly had at least one friend named Miss Agnes Delacey.

Jackson stabbed a bite of sausage. Randi Galloway didn't know Miss Delacey. He'd bet his next year's crop on it.

As if his thoughts had conjured her up, Randi walked through the doorway of the dining room, looking even worse than he did after a nearly sleepless night.

"Good morning," she said, not meeting his eyes.

He settled back in his chair, folding his arms across his chest. "I've had better. Are you here for breakfast?"

"No," she said, casting a glance at the buffet server.

"I came down to apologize for my words and actions last night."

"Please have a seat," he said, frowning at her subdued attitude. He didn't fancy having her stand halfway down the long table, head bent as she studied the carpet.

"I'd rather not." She paused, taking a deep breath. "This won't take long."

"As you wish," he said, picking up his coffee cup. "What did you want to say?"

"I'm sorry," she started, blurting out the words as though she couldn't wait to say them, or perhaps because she was afraid to wait lest she lose her nerve. "I've had dreams of the flood. I suppose I just added you and Rose to my dreams. They scared me to death, and when I heard the other planters and you talking about the possibility of a flood, I overreacted. I'm sorry."

He studied her. She was lying again, just as when she'd told stories about how she'd learned about the governess position, how she'd arrived here. "Why are you telling me this?"

"Because I don't want to leave," she pleaded, finally looking him in the eye. "The truth is, I have nowhere else to go. I'm afraid that if I leave here, something awful will happen."

"To you?"

She nodded. "And to you, too . . . and Rose. Despite my behavior, I really do care about her. She's a wonderful child. I've grown very close to her these past few days, and I can't stand the thought of my dreams coming true."

For once, he felt she was telling the truth. About not having anywhere to go, about caring for Rose. Jackson sighed in resignation. "Are you willing to live by my rules?"

"Yes! I'll do whatever you say. I'll behave, I promise. I know I haven't been the best—"

He held up his hand. "Enough. Tomorrow we'll attend church services, where you'll have a chance to pray to God for the deceptions you've perpetrated. After that, I hope you'll conduct yourself in a more circumspect manner."

"I will!" He had the alarming premonition that she was going to run the length of the table and fling her arms around his neck. He wasn't sure how he'd respond if she did such an outrageous thing.

Ridiculous. Of course, he'd push her away. Gently, so as not to harm her. But firmly, so she understood that this physical attraction they shared would not be encouraged.

"Then I suggest you assist Suzette with her duties for today. I'll consider your position here, although I'm not sure I'll trust you with the care of my daughter until you are more forthcoming about your past."

Her shoulders, which she carried so proudly, sagged, and the sparkle went out of her eyes. "I understand. I'll do as you wish."

He had the immediate and disturbing vision of her lying in his bed, her small, curvy body naked beneath soft sheets and moonlight. He pushed the image aside. She would not be doing *that*, despite his wayward thoughts. He apparently needed to attend church services as much as she.

"Be prepared to leave at this time tomorrow morning," he said brusquely. "If there's nothing further, I'd like to continue with my breakfast before it grows even colder."

"I'm sorry," she said again, looking like a whipped puppy as she turned around. Before she reached the doorway, she looked back over her shoulder. "Thank you," she said in a flat, dull tone that was so unlike her usual tone of voice.

He broke eye contact, turning his attention back to

his sausage and eggs. "You're welcome. I will see you tomorrow morning, Miss Galloway."

He knew the use of her proper name would serve as a slap in the face to her, since she valued the informality of Christian names so much. He hardened himself against the thought and refused to look at her. In just seconds, he heard her footsteps as she walked away.

Jackson Durant, master of Black Willow Grove, had behaved as was appropriate and proper, but as he sat alone at his long table, he wished he could become the younger, more carefree man he'd once been. That man would have teased and laughed with Randi Galloway. He might have even pulled her into his lap and fed her from his plate.

But that person was long buried in the past. He'd made a decision, and by God, he would see his dreams come true in a society where behavior and breeding were as important as money.

He hadn't just bought his way into this society; he'd become exactly what was expected of him. He could ask nothing less of those in his household.

Chapter Ten

The next day, Randi awakened with the first light of
dawn, knowing she had to be especially careful with
her appearance and demeanor, today and every day until she managed to get home. After yesterday's humble
apology in the dining room, she realized just how difficult her charade was going to be. Not only would she
need to be aware of every word coming out of her
mouth, but she had to watch her body language as well.
She also couldn't show anyone that she lusted after the
master of Black Willow Grove—or that he returned her
feelings of desire. No, she was going to be a paragon of
womanly virtue from now on if she had to bite her
tongue and clamp a hand over her mouth.

She used the cool water in the washstand to clean up
as much as possible, wishing for all the world she had
access to a nice, hot shower. All week long, she'd had
one bath, and only because she'd asked for a tub to be
prepared. The tub had turned out to be something

called a hip bath, a totally unfulfilling bathing experience.

Without a shaver for her legs, deodorant, lotion, and shampoo, she supposed *how* she bathed wasn't as important as just getting clean. Baking soda and harsh soap could only do so much, and using a straight razor was downright painful.

Today was especially important because she'd be seeing some of Jackson's friends and neighbors, and she didn't want to embarrass him. She'd done enough to make him suspicious of her; she couldn't afford another mistake.

She was used to going to church with her parents, but over the past ten years the dress code had become much more casual. Women wore slacks and blouses, men were free to come in shirtsleeves and no ties. She knew in Jackson's church she'd be expected to wear her "Sunday best." In 1849, that would be the pale green dress, she guessed, although judging the function and quality of these clothes was difficult since she didn't know what other ladies wore.

Melody slipped inside the door, her arms full of what looked like yards and yards of plaid fabric.

"I brought you a dress Miss Pansy never wore. Suzette and I finished up the hem and bows for you."

"That's so sweet," Randi said, folding her damp towel on the washbasin, then walking up to the maid. "What does it look like?"

Melody shook out the dress. So much plaid! She'd look as big as a house in this, Randi thought, but she didn't dare share her sentiments with the girls who had worked so hard to get a new garment ready for her to wear to church.

"Now, you're sure this is appropriate for church?"

"Yes, Miss Randi," Melody answered, her hand caressing the slick, polished-looking fabric. "Miss Pansy was havin' the dress made for herself for church and visitin' when she found out she was carryin' a baby. The waist was too tight, so she never had it finished up."

"Okay, I trust your opinion," Randi said dubiously. "Let's see if it fits."

Melody helped Randi don the new dress and voluminous petticoats. This particular garment even had a small bustle made out of horsehair, Melody informed her. When Randi turned and looked into the cheval mirror in the corner, her eyes widened. Yards and yards of brown and green plaid jumped back at her, flounced from the low, pointed waist, and decorated with small tailored bows down the front of the skirt.

"My goodness," she said.

"Yes, ma'am. Isn't it the prettiest dress you've ever seen?" Melody said with a sigh.

"I've never seen anything like it," Randi answered honestly. "You're sure I should be wearing this to church?"

"Yes, Miss Randi. I know it's awf'ly fine, but it's not too fancy for church."

With a last glance in the mirror, she started toward the door. "I guess I'm ready."

"No, ma'am! We need to do your hair, and you'll need a bonnet for church."

"I will?" A bonnet sounded even uglier than the dress.

"If you'll come to the kitchen, we have the curlin' irons hot."

Curling irons? Randi obediently followed Melody down the back stairs to the hallway, then out the door to the detached kitchen.

Within a few minutes, the short hair around her face had been curled into ringlets, and a muddy green-colored taffeta bonnet had been settled on her head. She was sure she looked ridiculous, but Melody, Birdie, and Cook all said she was dressed appropriately.

Suzette came into the kitchen with Rose perched on

one hip. They all settled at the table as Suzette nursed the baby. Randi ate some toasted bread and blackberry jam. She learned that the slaves had their own church, which Jackson "allowed" them to attend. They seemed thankful for his progressive attitude, but Randi found the whole idea of controlling their religion or access to church horrible. No matter how long she stayed in the past, she'd never get used to this culture. She couldn't wait to get home, where although everything wasn't perfect, at least the Constitution guaranteed equality.

But, Randi thought, taking Rose from Suzette after the baby finished nursing, she'd sure miss this baby. She'd even miss the strong feelings of desire that passed between her and Jackson Durant, no matter how misplaced those passions were.

Before long, Birdie announced that it was time to leave for church. Suzette hurried upstairs with Rose to change the baby into nicer clothing and a fresh diaper.

Randi's heart began to beat faster as she crossed the covered walkway to the main house. Jackson wasn't around, so she settled on a formal bench in the entryway to wait for him. The longer she sat, the more fidgety she became, but she was determined to behave properly.

A few minutes later, Jackson strolled downstairs, Suzette holding Rose several steps behind.

Randi watched him with greedy eyes that took in every detail, from his dark brown coat and tailored vest to the high-pointed collar and intricate printed neck cloth of his white shirt. His trousers were tan, tapered at the bottom over a pair of dark brown leather boots.

At least they'd match, she thought to herself with a smile.

He adjusted the cuffs of his shirt beneath his coat sleeves, then looked down at her. "Are you ready?"

"Yes," she answered, hoping her voice sounded properly demure instead of breathless and throaty.

"I haven't seen that dress before," he said as she stood up.

"No, it's . . . new."

His eyes skimmed over her, then he nodded. "Very well. The carriage should be brought around by now." He motioned to Suzette, who handed Rose to Randi.

"You'll take care of my daughter during the services," he announced. "She's just been fed, so she shouldn't be any trouble."

As if he could predict these things, Randi thought. But she held her tongue. "Okay, I'm ready," she said, perching the baby on her hip, venturing a slight smile in Jackson's direction.

He frowned. "Not that way. You look like a washerwoman. Hold her properly."

Randi's smile faded. "Yes, sir." She cradled the baby in her arms. Not only was this dress uncomfortable, just like all the rest, but now she had to hold Rose in an artificial and arm-killing fashion.

This is the price you have to pay, she told herself. *Just don't say a word.*

Jackson shifted on the hard oak seat as the sermon drew to its climax. He hoped Randi was able to hear the minister clearly from the servants' benches in the rear of the church, but he didn't dare check on her. He'd turned to look at her once and found her eyes burning with anger. Rose wasn't giving her any trouble, of that he was certain; he hadn't heard her fretting or cries.

The only other reason Randi might be in a temper was because he'd directed her to sit in the rear. Since she was caring for an infant, she was expected to be able to remove the child quickly if she started to disrupt the service. Surely Randi hadn't expected him to invite her to the Crowder family pew, where he sat with Thomas and Pansy's younger sister Violet. To have a servant sit with the family was highly unusual, unless a governess for older children sat with them to see that they behaved during the sermon.

Even if he'd wanted to ask Randi to sit with him so Rose would be in the family pew, he wouldn't have done so. To go against convention meant explaining his reasons to Thomas, and then tolerating the inquisitive gazes of the other planters. Such a minor point wasn't worthy of openly flouting the rules of society.

The minister built his sermon to a crescendo. The very rafters of the church seemed to tremble in reaction to his impassioned plea from the Gospel of St. Paul. Immediately following, the choir launched into their final hymn, their voices blending together quite well on this surprisingly pleasant Sunday. The weather had remained clear. The rain that had threatened last night hadn't yet arrived, so their ten-mile trip to the church in Randolph had been uneventful.

Jackson stood with the rest of the congregation for the benediction. Although he hadn't been raised in this faith, he'd taken to the services rather well, he thought. This was the church where Rose had been baptized, and where she would no doubt marry when she came of age. Perhaps he would even see a grandchild baptized here, among the other planters' families.

"An excellent sermon," Violet whispered as Jackson gathered his gloves and hat.

"Yes, the reverend was in fine form today." In truth, Jackson thought the man had gone on too long in his admonishments to the faithful, but what did he know about religion? Surely the minister had a better grasp of the needs of the congregation.

"Will you be joining us for dinner?" Violet asked, her girlish voice somewhat deeper and more refined, he noticed. She was growing up fast, her fine blond hair curled in ringlets around her pretty face. Just two years ago she'd been far less mature, but now she was growing into a stylish and appealing young lady.

The observation made him feel older than his thirty years.

"I fear I won't have that pleasure today," he replied with a smile as he offered his arm. "I must escort my daughter home, then oversee some important improvements to the property."

"You're off building more levees, aren't you?" Violet asked in a way that sounded coquettish. Surely she wasn't setting her cap for him. The idea that Pansy's little sister would think he'd be interested made him feel decidedly uncomfortable. Still, he couldn't openly address the issue without feeling foolish. What if he was wrong?

"The flood is something we've discussed, and we're all taking precautions, so you won't need to worry."

"I'm not at all worried," she replied with a shake of her ringlets. "I don't think there's going to be any old flood this year. Just some dreary rain and more mud," she added with distaste.

"We need the rain for our crops."

"Well, it's a mess on our hems and slippers!"

Jackson smiled at Violet's attempts at flirting as they neared the back of the church. Out of the corner of his eye he saw Randi holding Rose. They'd best be off soon. Rose looked as though she was beginning to fret.

He conversed briefly with Thomas, offering help to shore up the levees to the north. As he handed Violet over to her father, he bowed to them both and made his excuses. Within seconds, he walked to where Randi waited.

"Are you ready to leave?"

"I'm more than ready," she said in a cool tone of voice that told him she was indeed peeved about something.

"The carriage should be outside." He urged her forward with a hand to her elbow, but she pushed ahead, walking through the crowd with her shoulders back and her head high. She showed particular interest in the Crowder family. No doubt Randi was curious about Rose's relatives. Probably some of the other women at the back of the church had told her their identity.

She didn't seem inclined to talk, so he remained silent as his driver guided the team along the rutted road.

"Did you enjoy the sermon?" he finally asked when she failed to comment on their journey or his daughter's growing displeasure at being held so long.

"I'm sure it was fine."

"Could you hear it clearly? I assume Reverend Bond's voice carries especially well."

"All the way to the back of the church," Randi answered.

Jackson mulled over her choice of words, finally deciding that she was indeed unhappy at their seating arrangements.

"Surely you realized that only family members sit in the pews," he said cautiously.

"I do now," she said, not meeting his eyes.

"That's a social custom that is the same everywhere."

"Not where I come from," she said sharply.

"Ah, yes, that mysterious land of Randi Galloway. Are you ready to tell me exactly where that kingdom is located?"

She remained silent, her lips pressed together until they looked bloodless.

"I didn't think so." He crossed his arms and fell silent, his own mouth tight with displeasure. There was no talking to the woman, so why did he try? Her concept of what was proper defied every principle he'd subscribed to for years.

Rose began to fuss just as they crossed Hurricane Creek. He leaned over the side, checking the water level. The placid, normal depth mollified his apprehension about rising water. Perhaps they would be safe after all.

"The creek looks normal," he told Randi, hoping to

ease her fears about an impending flood. She was busy with Rose, however, and didn't answer or look at him.

They continued in silence toward the house. He felt Randi's seething resentment as she bounced Rose on her lap. What did she expect from him? She'd apologized for her earlier behavior and promised to be a vision of propriety. He should have also required her to take a vow of amicability. The woman acted as no other, and he didn't understand why he didn't send her on her way with a few dollars and his wife's old dresses.

She should be grateful to have a roof over her head and food to eat. Instead, she seemed to believe the world should march to the cadence of her bizarre values. How could she profess to have high moral principles when she refused to answer simple questions and lied about other equally important issues?

Damn it, she'd needed this visit to church to think about her station in life and the importance of truth. True, the minister's sermon on humility and chastity hadn't dealt directly with Randi's major problems, but just being in the building should have prompted some feelings of redemption in her.

Instead, she was in an even worse temper now than earlier.

He apparently didn't understand women—at least not women who made their way in life somehow other than on their backs. He got along famously with them, their relationships simple and straightforward. He needed a trip downriver to an exclusive bordello where he could lose himself in the soft, scented depths of a woman who knew how to please a man. No expectations other than coin, no demands for anything other than decent treatment. Hell, he enjoyed giving more than they expected, pleasing them if at all possible. He'd never been a selfish lover, even with a whore.

But until he knew for certain that the water coming downriver wasn't going to flood his land, he wouldn't leave. He'd keep his desire in check until the crisis passed, then he'd head for New Orleans and a well-deserved week of carnal pleasure. He'd forget all about Randi Galloway, rising water, crying babies, and difficult in-laws.

Randi carried Rose upstairs to Suzette, who was napping on the narrow bed in the room beside the nursery. Without a word, she handed the fussing baby to her wet nurse and tromped back downstairs to her bedroom.

She couldn't remember being this angry and frustrated in her entire life, she thought as she jerked off the ugly bonnet and threw it on the bed. Even when she'd told Cleve that he was going to be a father, and he'd stared at her with a growing look of horrified comprehension, she'd been more hurt than frustrated. She'd wanted to hurt him—she couldn't deny that basic urge to shake some sense into his scheming, self-centered head—but she'd simply walked away when she'd realized he didn't care.

He hadn't wanted to be a father. Jackson Durant, on the other hand, enjoyed being a dad. He was good with Rose, although Randi knew he was too restrained. He only showed her affection when they were in private, she'd noticed. Before long, Rose would notice his behavior, too, and she'd want to know why her daddy didn't love her.

If Randi were ever going to speak to him again, she'd bring the problem to his attention. However, he'd no doubt question how she knew what Rose would think. Another premonition? He'd scoff at her explanation. He'd also tell her his behavior was none of her business.

Whose business was it? Probably that eye-batting Southern belle who'd draped herself all over him at church this morning. Did the man have no shame? That little blond bimbette was way too young for him, even though she'd apparently decided to sink her hooks in.

Randi sank to the low-seated upholstered chair, pushing her petticoats down when they threatened to jump up and smother her. She hated these clothes, she hated this time, and she especially despised Jackson Durant. The big jerk.

When Melody came into the room a few minutes later, Randi lifted her head from her propped up elbows and blinked back tears that threatened to spill out of her burning eyes.

"I want to go home," she said, as though the young maid could help her achieve her goal.

"Where is your home, Miss Randi?" Melody asked, laying out one of the plain gowns on the bed.

"Far, far away," Randi whispered, resting her chin in her palm. "I don't know how to get there."

"How did you get here?"

Randi frowned, thinking back to what seemed like ages, but in actuality, had been only a week. The replica had been the key, but she'd also heard a baby crying. The little plastic doll in the nursery hadn't been Rose until Randi had touched her. Then somehow she'd fallen into the past through the dollhouse.

Could she fall back into her own time? She couldn't build a dollhouse, but maybe her sketches would take her back.

She'd been practicing the last two days so she could create a reasonable version of the room at the museum that she'd left. She wasn't sure if she could go back somewhere else. Besides, showing up out of the blue in her mother's kitchen, or popping into her bedroom at some odd hour, would be unsettling to her family. She didn't know if they'd believe her right away, because the story was totally preposterous. She wouldn't believe time traveling could occur if it hadn't happened to her.

"Miss Randi?"

She looked up, suddenly remembering she wasn't alone. "I'm sorry. What did you say?"

"I asked if you wanted me to unfasten that dress for you?"

"Yes," Randi said, pushing herself up from the low chair. "I sure do. I've got things to do."

"Are you havin' a meal with Mas'r Jackson?"

"No! Absolutely not."

Melody looked at her with a confused expression on her face, but didn't say anything. Within minutes, Randi wore one of the plain dresses, although she yearned to pull on her faded, soft jeans and comfortable shirt.

She hurried Melody out the door, then pulled out a clean sheet of paper and a pencil. She placed the completed practice sketches of the rooms of Black Willow Grove on the bottom of the stack.

Alone, she lay flat on the floor and reached underneath the bed. Tucked between two bed slats, her fanny pack snuggled next to her jeans and velour top. She eased the straps from beneath the boards, then held her prize close. Already she felt more comfortable.

After locking the door, she settled cross-legged on the bed and unzipped the fanny pack. She brought each item to her nose, inhaling the familiar, twentieth-century fragrance of plastic and chemicals in the mascara, the waxy, perfumed smell of lipstick, and the odor of worn leather from her wallet. Her keys jangled on the souvenir Graceland key ring, the brassy scent rubbing off on her fingers.

She breathed deeply, homesickness swamping her. She wanted to be at her mom and dad's house, sitting down to rump roast cooked with potatoes, onions, and carrots. Her mom fixed green beans when she could find good tender ones. And the inevitable Jell-O salad, which no one really liked that much, but her mom made anyway because it wouldn't be Sunday without congealed fruit salad.

And those melt-in-your-mouth, brown-and-serve rolls. Her family went through at least two packages of them. The bread wasn't gourmet. Heck, they weren't even as good as the cook's yeasty loaves, which she'd come to enjoy so much this week. But those little rolls were such a tradition that no other type of bread could substitute.

Her stomach growled, but she ignored her hunger. She had more important things to do than eat. She should have at least an hour or so before Rose wakened from her nap. Besides, didn't she get a day off? Or did she have a job? Jackson hadn't really resolved that issue, except to say that she could help Suzette care for Rose.

Someday, Randi thought with a grimace, she was going to have to start talking to him again. When she did, she'd ask about her job.

She no longer believed there was a reason she'd gone back into the past. She'd gotten pulled into some natural phenomenon, maybe, like a wormhole she'd seen in a space movie once. She wasn't supposed to be here, Jackson wasn't going to believe her, and she needed to go home.

With renewed determination, she started sketching.

Chapter Eleven

Jackson longed to strip down to his shirtsleeves and join the hands working on the levee. He wanted to experience the burn of tired muscles and feel honest sweat roll down his face and neck. With a sigh, he folded his hands over the pommel of the saddle and resisted the urge to dismount and throw caution aside with his fancy coat.

This dangerous thinking was Randi Galloway's fault. His jaw clenched when he recounted all the ways she'd criticized his decisions, his judgment, his very life. What possible reason could she have for believing she was right and everyone else was wrong? Who had raised her in such an unorthodox manner to produce this free thinking?

She wasn't going to tell him. He'd pushed her, angered her, and yet she'd resisted every opportunity to admit how she'd arrived in his home. He should ship her off. He should be done with her disruptive influence before her ideas spread to his staff or even his daughter.

Randi Galloway wouldn't be happy until he espoused the views in *Letters on the Equality of the Sexes*, marched into church with a copy of *The Bible Against Slavery* under his arm, and quoted Thoreau.

The black gelding shifted beneath him, pulling at the reins. Jackson sat up straighter in the saddle, suddenly as restless as his mount. With a nudge of his boot heel, the horse leaped forward. Jackson reined him to a controlled canter, passing by Brewster with a salute from his whip.

Out of sight of his field hands, he urged the gelding up the levee to where the earth lay flat and even, putting heels to the horse until wind whipped past and tore at the fabric of Jackson's fine clothes. Too soon, he had to slow his mount, guiding him back to the woman who had destroyed his peace of mind as surely as the threat of flood.

He had half a mind to confront her again. He could confine her until she relented. If he wanted, he could withhold food and water, lock her away, refuse her requests to see Rose or anyone else. If she complained to the authorities, Jackson could explain away his actions. No one would listen to an odd young woman with no past who pretended to know the future.

But as he thought of the possibilities, he knew he would do none of those things. Force would bring out the stubbornness in her, and besides, he couldn't live with the knowledge that he'd abused a woman. His actions in the past had occasionally been illegal, sometimes even immoral in a strict biblical sense, but he'd never hurt a woman through conscious action. He wasn't about to start now, when he was a respectable member of planter society.

He knew in his heart that if he took any action against Randi Galloway, he'd be reacting to the unwanted physical response she evoked in him. The fact that she was a liar didn't affect how much he wanted her. Hell, he didn't know if she was an innocent young woman or an experienced courtesan. The worst part of his dilemma was that he didn't particularly care; he just wanted her naked and needy in his bed. The image caused an uncomfortable reaction that he was helpless to satisfy at this time.

When the threat of flood was past, I'm going to New Orleans . . . maybe for two weeks. I might not get out of bed the entire time.

The sight that greeted him as he reined the gelding to a trot did nothing to improve his black mood. Descending from the family's imported, blue lacquered carriage was Violet Crowder. Thomas stood beside the groom who was handing his daughter down, restlessness giving his plump features a decidedly nasty aura.

Unfortunately, his former father-in-law spotted Jackson before he could slip around the gardens toward the stable. He took a deep breath and prepared for an afternoon of mindless chatter with two people he did not have the time or inclination to entertain.

"Thomas Crowder, may I present Rose's new governess, Miss Galloway?" Jackson performed the introduction with the goodwill of a wolverine with a toothache.

Randi smiled slightly, then, not sure what else was expected, performed a little curtsy like she'd seen in an old movie. Not one of those all-the-way-to-the-floor bobs, but just a slight dip.

Thomas Crowder looked her over as if she were a slightly green-tinged slice of beef in the meat case, frowning at her short hair and who knew what else. "Jackson said he was sending away for a governess."

"Yes, well, I'm here," she said, not certain what she should say to this man who was Rose's grandfather.

"Miss Violet Crowder, may I present Miss Galloway?" Jackson addressed the blond bimbette with a big heaping of Southern hospitality. Randi found his attitude disgustingly male.

"Well, aren't you just the most unusual governess?" the young woman said, a sickly sweet smile on her face.

Randi clamped her lips together and forced herself to smile in the same sickening manner right back at the bimbette. "Violet is Rose's aunt," Jackson announced.

Randi blinked, comprehension dawning as she realized the connection between these people and Jackson. He was courting his wife's sister? How disgusting. She'd known Violet was too young for him, but she hadn't realized that she was practically a relative. Didn't they have laws against that in the old days?

Fortunately, Rose was behaving like the little sweetie she was, although she was somewhat clingy. She would need a nap soon, and she wasn't going to tolerate a lot of passing back and forth between these critical relatives. She grasped the fabric of Randi's bodice and held on for dear life.

"Why don't you take a seat over here, Miss Galloway," Jackson said, indicating a chair near the empty fireplace.

She walked between the Crowders on one side and Jackson on the other, feeling somewhat like she'd endured a mini-gauntlet. She felt the gaze from three pairs of eyes following her movements. Now would not be a good time to trip over these long skirts.

Violet chose a chair near Jackson, who stood with his arm on the mantle, watching Rose. Thomas settled his stout frame on the ornately carved, brocade-covered settee.

Silence stretched uncomfortably until Rose let out a squeal and reached her arms up to her daddy.

Grateful for the distraction, Randi looked up at Jackson, expecting him to pick up his daughter. But he didn't. He turned and addressed Thomas Crowder instead.

"As you can see, Rose is fine," Jackson said.

"Time will tell," Crowder said.

Randi felt like socking the old grouch in his paunchy stomach.

"I thought having a governess was one thing that would ease your mind about my daughter's upbringing," Jackson replied, emphasizing the fact that Rose was *his* daughter, *his* responsibility.

Even if he wouldn't pick her up.

"Of course she needs a governess, Papa," Violet chimed in. "Even if our dearly departed Pansy were still here with us, a governess is entirely necessary."

Randi wanted to chime in, "Really?" but held her tongue. Didn't any of these women raise or nurse their own children?

"Yes, but a suitable governess is the key to raising a well-behaved child. Are you sure about this young woman's credentials?" Thomas Crowder added gruffly.

Jackson looked down at Randi, his narrowed eyes unreadable. "She suits Rose just fine. I'm satisfied with the care she's providing . . . for now."

His message was clear: Don't screw up again. She was trying, she really was. But having them talk about her as though she wasn't here, as though she weren't important, made her so angry she had a hard time staying put in the chair.

"Papa is planning a ball for the first week in May," Violet announced. "We haven't had any guests or parties for a long time."

"I was under the impression you were in mourning," Jackson said, turning his attention back to the bimbette.

"Oh, of course, but Pansy has been gone for ever so long."

"Only eight months," Jackson answered.

"But almost a year," Violet said brightly. "Why, you'll

be out of formal mourning before long, and I'm just sure you'll be looking for suitable wife."

"And a mother for Rose," Jackson added.

"Of course," Violet said, casting a quick, dismissive glance at the baby. What a horrid mother she'd make, Randi thought. Violet was so self-centered that she couldn't see beyond her next party, her next conquest. If Jackson married her, Rose wouldn't have a mother. An older sister, maybe, but definitely not a mother.

The image of Jackson and Violet locked together in a passionate embrace flashed into Randi's mind, giving her a queasy feeling in her stomach and the beginning of a pounding headache.

As if the baby could sense her mood, Rose began to fret, reaching for her father again. Once more, Jackson ignored her. Randi noticed his jaw was clenched, his lips pressed together in displeasure. She wasn't sure whether his expression showed he was irritated at the situation or at his daughter.

She wasn't confused about her own feelings, however. She was furious that he'd shunned his child, for whatever reason. He never acted this way when they were alone with Rose. Apparently he had different standards around his guests. Maybe he was more superficial and calculating than she'd thought.

Spurred on by anger, she said, "I'm sure Rose would just love a new mother, especially one who can plan parties and looks beautiful in her dresses."

Violet smiled in agreement, but Thomas Crowder's face took on a distinctively angry shade of red. Jackson's eyes shot fire across the few feet separating them.

"What a ridiculous statement," Crowder said. "Jackson, are you going to tolerate that kind of sass in your own home?"

"Miss Galloway has a disturbing tendency to speak her own mind. She's also gifted with an unusual sense of humor. I'm sure she meant no insult." He paused, looking down at her without any amusement. "Did you, Miss Galloway?"

"No," she answered, breaking eye contact and taking a deep breath. Her arms tightened around Rose, the one person who seemed to appreciate her for who and what she was.

However, Rose must have been aware of the stressful situation because she started to whimper and wiggle. She'd been good for some time now; she wanted to get down and crawl around. She'd especially like to stick some of the fabric roses on Violet's dress in her mouth, Randi knew from experience.

"Would you like me to take her to the nursery now?" she asked, wanting to leave this tension-filled room. She didn't understand what was going on, but whatever family drama was being played out, it wasn't her business. If Jackson wanted to play rob-the-cradle with Violet and ignore his own daughter's needs, then she couldn't stop him.

Not that he'd listen to her. Not that she had any influence over him. And not that she *wanted* to dictate his lifestyle or his love life.

All she wanted to do was go home. Her sketching was progressing nicely, the details of the museum room were coming back to her. She felt closer to her own time now that she'd started to draw.

"I think that would be a good idea," Jackson answered.

"I do, too," she mumbled, holding Rose close when she reached out one more time toward her daddy. The baby's pleading gesture tore at Randi's heart until she barely had time to mutter, "Nice to meet you," before fleeing the room. By the time she reached the landing of the stairway, tears burned her eyes.

"I'm sorry, sweetie," she whispered to the baby. "Your daddy is being a horse's patootie, but that's not your fault."

She hurried to the nursery, but not before Rose was in an all-out snit. Randi handed her over to Suzette for feeding, then retreated to her own room. She needed the comfort of her sketching, but most of all, she needed to concentrate on her goal—leaving this century and these people behind.

Maybe fifteen or twenty minutes later, the fancy Crowder carriage pulled up to the house. The Crowders stepped inside, then Randi noticed one small gloved hand wave from an open window. What a silly bimbette! Seconds later, the carriage departed.

Through her closed bedroom door, Randi winced when she heard the front door slam. Damn! Jackson must be angry about something. She hoped she wasn't the reason his temper was in an uproar. She didn't want any more scoldings or threats from him.

She didn't want to think about him going to parties, meeting other young women, marrying one of them so he'd have the obligatory wife for himself and mother for Rose—and doing so even if the woman wasn't a really good and caring person.

Within a few minutes, she heard the door slam again. She unwound her legs from where they'd been as she was sitting on the bed sketching, then walked to the window just in time to see him gallop off on a reddish-colored horse.

Jackson was really in a snit. She had a sneaking suspicion she was a big part of whatever was bothering him . . . and that she'd find out about it, sooner or later.

He felt so guilty about ignoring his daughter earlier that he spent extra time with Rose that night. He curbed his bad temper, provoked to the breaking point by both Thomas Crowder and Randi Galloway. What was he going to do about her? She continued to defy convention, and today she'd openly insulted his dead wife's family.

Rose seemed unusually sedate tonight. She didn't spend as much time reaching for things on his shelf or desk, but rather played with his collar, cravat, and buttons. She seemed fascinated by his face, running her chubby hands over his lips and nose, exploring to her heart's content.

He let her. By God, indulging her playfulness was the least he could do after ignoring her pleas for attention when the Crowders had visited. He'd wanted to reach out, but propriety had kept him in check. Rose couldn't understand right now, but she would someday. She'd learn that society's expectations had to guide their lives, far more than fleeting emotions.

"It's the price we pay," he told Rose, leaning back so he could look into her wide blue eyes. "You'll see that someday."

He knew without a doubt that Randi didn't understand why he'd refused to hold his daughter. How could she not understand something so basic? Where had she lived or worked where a father responded to his child regardless of the guests present or the social situation in which he found himself?

Of course, children were rarely in the company of adult visitors, so perhaps the scenario hadn't come up before.

He nestled Rose close and strode across the room, angry that he was finding excuses for Randi's behavior. He was angry that he couldn't put her out of his mind—or out of his house.

After standing at the window for several long minutes, watching the fleeting clouds move across the moon, he realized that Rose no longer wiggled or explored. He patted her back, rearing his head back to look at her. Sound asleep, she looked so innocent and pure—so perfect—just as Randi had said that day in the garden.

Randi. Damn it, what did he have to do to get her out

of his mind? She was everywhere. In the house, the garden. In his study, in Rose's nursery, and even the church. He couldn't travel in his carriage without remembering her anger at being relegated to the back pews at church. He couldn't stroll the grounds or walk the hallways without seeing her, sitting on the landing or on a quilt, having lunch or playing with Rose. Smiling, crying, fuming. How could a woman tie him in such knots after fewer than two weeks?

With a sharply indrawn breath, he turned away from the window. Rose needed to get to her bed, and he needed . . . No, he wouldn't finish that thought. He *needed* a well-practiced whore to satisfy his needs.

He *wanted* a crop-haired termagant with rounded curves and enough passion to make his blood boil.

He took the stairs quickly but carefully, aware of his precious burden. Perhaps he would be able to give Rose over to Suzette quietly, then retire to his study. The brandy he'd purchased through his contacts in New Orleans beckoned. He might curse the morning sun tomorrow, but tonight, he planned to deplete his stock of fine liquor.

Randi waited until the house was quiet and the clock chimed eleven, then ventured downstairs. She'd used up the pencil lead and had no way to sharpen her only sketching instrument. There had to be a dozen more in Jackson's study. Now was the perfect time to replenish her supply, or to find a pencil sharpener—although she doubted anything like that existed in 1849. Her sketch was coming along too well to be stopped by a technical problem.

She'd half-expected to be summoned downstairs for a confrontation with Jackson earlier, but none had arrived. She felt a sense of reprieve, but knew her luck was only temporary. Sooner or later—probably tomorrow—he'd ask her about her sarcastic comment regarding a new mother for Rose who looked good in dresses and planned parties like a pro.

But darn it, they'd made her angry by talking about women as though that's all they were good for. Okay, maybe Violet wasn't good for anything, but most women were. Violet didn't even respect the memory of her own sister, setting her sights on the husband just months after he'd become a widower. So much for sisterly love, Randi thought, tiptoeing across the thick carpet runner.

No candles or lanterns were lit in the hallway, although she saw a faint glow coming from inside Jackson's study. She'd heard him come upstairs earlier, she thought, so this must be the equivalent of a night-light. Certainly the room wasn't bright enough for him to be working so late.

She paused at the doorway, her hand cool against the smooth, fluted woodwork. A lamp burned very low on the desk, but there were no papers lying there, no sign that anyone was up at this hour.

She'd just slip in, get another pencil, and get back upstairs before someone caught her sneaking—

"Miss Galloway . . . of course," a deep, disembodied voice said from the depths of the study.

She froze, her hand covering the scream that threatened. Her heart beat so fast she thought her chest might burst. Suddenly there wasn't enough air in the room.

"What are you doing here?" she whispered.

"I should be asking you the same thing."

"I meant in the dark. Lurking around the study." She squinted into the shadows, finally locating him beside the window, half-concealed by heavy velvet drapes.

"It's raining," he said softly, his words slightly slurred.

"I hadn't noticed. I just came down to get another pencil."

"Stay."

"No, I really can't," she said, inching backward toward the door.

"I insist."

Chapter Twelve

"Why?" she asked cautiously, still hoping to inch toward the door. If she could just make it out of the study, maybe her heart wouldn't pound so hard, or her breath catch in her throat.

"Maybe I want the company," he said, turning toward her. His face seemed shadowed and almost menacing in the near-darkness. "Does that seem so odd?"

"Well . . . yes," she answered. He didn't seem like the kind of man who wanted company, except the companionship of men similar to him in status and interests. She had a hard time imagining Jackson Durant snuggling up on the couch beside her and asking about her day—or expecting her to do the same.

He let out a disbelieving snort, then walked toward her. Randi resisted the urge to cower against the furniture, but she couldn't stop the tingling of her nerves in reaction to his nearness. As he stepped closer to the candle, his features seemed to soften and glow. Only an optical illusion, she told herself, but that didn't stop her from thinking that he was the most handsome, most interesting man she'd ever known.

"I'm a man, just like any other," he said, as though he could read her thoughts. "Why do you find it so absurd that I'd like company from time to time?"

"Maybe because you seem so self-sufficient . . . and so confident. I can't imagine what we'd have to talk about."

"Can't you?" he asked, stopping too close. She breathed in his scent, plus the smell of some liquor she couldn't identify. "We've talked in the past."

"About Rose, about me." Actually, she'd always thought of those talks as interrogations, but she wasn't going to mention her observation at the moment. Jackson was in a strange mood tonight, one she wasn't sure she should encourage—although the idea carried a certain feminine appeal she couldn't deny.

"Then I suppose we've exhausted our topics." He eased closer, taking her hand in his and examining her fingers as though they were the most fascinating subjects in the world.

"We could talk about you," she offered, gently trying to pull her hand out of his grasp.

"I'm not very interesting," he said, smiling slightly as he focused on her face instead of her hand. He held her fingers firmly but gently, not letting her escape so easily.

"I don't know about that. I imagine you've done lots of interesting things in your life."

"More than I care to remember," he said in a husky, distracted voice. "More than you would care to know."

His admission sounded dangerous . . . and exciting. "Why don't you let me be the judge of that?"

"Why don't I kiss you instead?" he asked, pulling her hand to his shoulder, capturing her waist with his other arm.

"That's not a good—"

Her words were cut off by his lips, descending without caution or restraint, taking her breath and every coherent thought in her head. The scent and taste of liquor was intoxicating, but not as much as his kiss. He kissed her as though their lips had met millions of times before, and yet with a gentleness that surprised her. He eased his tongue inside, testing her response.

And oh, how she responded. Her arms snaked around his neck, her breasts brushed, then fit tightly, against his chest. He pulled her close, his arousal pressed against her stomach. She forgot to breathe.

She broke away from the kiss when her head began to spin, but he wasn't ready to let her go. With determination and skill, he stepped them back. Her thighs brushed the desk. As soon as she was pinned between his muscular legs and the solid wood, he kissed her again.

She knew she shouldn't return his passion. She should break away, save her sanity and her chances of leaving here with her heart intact. But her body wouldn't listen, rising on tiptoes to kiss him back, opening her lips and inviting him into her body, her soul. She'd wanted to know what desire felt like with Jackson, and she'd gotten her wish. How could she ignore the feelings she'd wanted so badly?

His mouth slanted across hers, kissing her deeply, his breath quick and hot against hers. Then he broke away to caress her cheeks, her neck, the skin below her ear, with his lips. She moved against him, earning a groan of approval from deep inside his hot, rigid body.

"I want you," he whispered against her throat, where her nightgown gaped open. She hadn't buttoned the confining garment all the way to the top, as she probably should have. Now she was glad, because the narrow vee gave Jackson better access.

"I want you too," she admitted. "But with no questions, no problems, no complaints. Do you understand?" she whispered against his silky, long hair.

"I never understand what you say." He kissed his way up the other side of her neck as he worked more buttons free. "You're a mystery to me, Randi Galloway. I don't know who or what you are. All I know is that you make me crazy with longing."

Alarm bells began to ring, faintly at first, but then louder as the implication of his words sank in, as his clever fingers slipped inside the opening of her nightgown. He wasn't going to follow the terms she'd given. He wanted answers to his questions, a resolution to the mystery. He didn't even like her—he disapproved of everything that was important to her—and yet he wanted to make love with her.

Or maybe he just wanted sex.

"Jackson, wait."

"I've waited for over a week. Why torture ourselves any longer?" His hand caressed the top of her breast, then slipped lower.

"Because I meant what I said. Because you're not thinking clearly. You've been drinking."

"I think too much," he whispered against her parted lips. "And sometimes you don't think enough. But not this time. Right now, neither one of us needs to think at all."

"But—"

He kissed her deeply, passionately, as his hand cupped her breast and his fingers sought her hardened nipple. They both moaned; she couldn't tell where one sound began and the other one ended.

She tried to push against his upper arms, but he was solid and strong—and aroused. Very aroused. She ignored the demands of her body that urged her to press tighter, to push up her gown and wrap her legs around his hips until he eased the empty ache inside. Making love—having sex—wouldn't solve their problems, although she knew without a doubt the feelings would be so wonderful, so fulfilling.

But giving herself body and soul to Jackson Durant, who didn't share her values or even her century, would present new obstacles.

She broke from his demanding kiss. "Will you stop asking me questions? Tonight, tomorrow? About who I am, where I'm from?"

"Don't ask me to do that!"

"I have to. And what about other . . . complications? What if I got pregnant?"

"Don't back away from what we feel."

"I have to! One of us has to think, and you're obviously not in any condition to reason."

He buried his head between her neck and shoulder. "I'm not drunk."

He felt warm and solid, although she knew the sensation would be fleeting when they pulled apart, as she knew they would. "Maybe you're not drunk, but you've been drinking. Believe me, I'm not flattered to think you want me only because the alcohol is speaking," she scoffed. Frowning against his hair, she sobered when she added, "Jackson, I *can't* get pregnant. Do you understand? I will not allow myself to get involved with you—to get hurt by you."

"I won't hurt you."

"You can't help but hurt me," she whispered, stroking his black hair. "You'll never believe who or what I am. I know that now. And I can't start caring about you more than I do now. Not when you . . ."

"When I what?" he asked, pulling back to look at her.

"Never mind."

"Are you talking about your dreams? They're only dreams," he said, stroking her cheek, then down her neck. "You'll be safe here at Black Willow Grove."

"No, I won't. None of us will. And even if I believed

you, if I thought the disaster wouldn't come true, there's something else you should know."

"What?"

She took a deep breath. "When I was younger, my brother Russell and I built a raft to float on the Mississippi. We used driftwood, lashed it together, and had a grand adventure planned."

"What happened?"

She laughed, the sound hollow and sad in the silence of Jackson's library. "We weren't very good shipbuilders, I'm afraid. The water was high, the current fast. Our raft lasted long enough for us to be swept into the deeper water, then it started to break apart. I tried to hold on to the driftwood, but the river twirled it around, pulling it under. I screamed. I swallowed water. Horrible, muddy water." Randi shuddered, closing her eyes against the memories. "Russell was a good swimmer. He pulled me to the shore, half-drowned. I thought I was dying, but he saved me."

She looked into Jackson's black eyes, the candlelight causing flickering golden images that distracted her from the horror of the near drowning. "I've never gone into the river since. I can't stay here. I won't be able to stand it, even if the water only gets to the bottom floor of the house. I'd look out the windows and see nothing but the muddy flood, and I'd know . . ."

"Know what?" he asked softly.

"Know what will happen," she whispered, looking away.

"You don't believe that I'll protect you?"

She placed a hand on his cheek, the late-night stubble real and very male against her palm. "I believe you'll try. I also believe that this house will not survive."

"Dreams," he said. "Nightmares. That's all they are."

She shook her head. "I wish they were."

"You told me—"

"I told you what you wanted to hear. I told you what

184

I needed to say in order to stay. But Jackson, I *know*. Something terrible is going to happen here. I thought I could come and save you . . . save Rose. But not if you won't listen."

"I've listened," he said, pushing away from her.

Her arms slipped from his shoulders, hanging empty and cold in the darkened study. "You don't believe me."

"Of course not." He ran a hand through his hair, then turned away. "But I believe that you're convinced you know the future. I see no harm in you thinking a tragedy will happen. When the flood passes us by, you'll see that I'm right."

She remained silent, his nineteenth-century rationale easy to accept only because he wasn't calling her a lunatic. Still, she couldn't drop the subject. "What if the flood doesn't pass by?"

He turned back to stare at her, his eyes intense and burning. "I'll see that it does."

She took a step toward him, touching his cheek with her palm. "I know you'll try. You love Rose. You love Black Willow Grove. If anyone can save this place and the people who live here, it's you."

She stepped back until she reached the doorway. Placing one trembling hand on the frame, she said, "But I can't stay. I must go home . . . before—" She stopped, unable to continue because the image of leaving him and Rose was too overwhelming.

Before he could respond, she hurried from the study, her arms wrapped around herself as she fled to the relative safety of her room.

Her heart breaking for what could never be, she turned the lock on her door, then pushed aside her paper and stubby pencil.

There would be no more sketching tonight.

Jackson came downstairs late the next morning after a night of fretful sleep and nightmarish dreams of his own, and settled in his study behind a closed door. He blamed his foul mood on the brandy, which had left him with a cottony mouth and pounding headache. What a waste of the imported spirits he'd spent a good sum to acquire.

But the real waste was the passion that he *hadn't* shared with Randi. They would have been so good together. He'd known it, deep inside his soul, from the first time they'd touched.

He didn't know who she was, but now knew why she believed she was here. To save him and his daughter. He'd been alarmed about her predictions of a flood destroying Black Willow Grove at first. Those feelings had changed to concern for her mental abilities, then, last night, anger that she didn't trust him to keep them safe.

This morning, frustration warred with that anger. He wanted to believe she'd escaped from an institution, that her premonitions of disaster were caused by nearly drowning on that raft she and her brother had so carelessly built. But when he looked into her eyes, he didn't see madness. He saw sincerity and openness.

Randi Galloway seemed even more open and honest in her feelings than his mother, who had always told the truth, even when her family wanted to hear a comforting lie. As a child, he'd wanted assurance that times would get better, and they'd have plenty of food to eat and warm blankets when the damp cold wind blew through the boards of their shack.

She'd never promised him those things. All she'd said was they would have each other, and somehow they would get by. She'd told him to say his prayers before she tucked him in beside his younger brother each night on their narrow cot.

She'd asked him not to leave when he was only fourteen years old, tall but thin as a rail. Full of anger and dreams, he'd said he'd be back with a pot of gold that would take them all out of poverty.

He hadn't come back in time, though. The pot of gold hadn't materialized as quickly as he'd hoped, and he'd found that he'd lied to the one woman he'd loved. His family had died in a fire, in their sleep, alone and wondering what had happened to their oldest son.

The son with all the dreams, who had lied when he said he'd be back to take them all away.

He rested his head between his hands on the desk where he'd almost made love to Randi last night. A brandy-induced headache pounded in his temples, but the pain wasn't as severe as that in his heart. He missed his family, especially the strong woman who had made their shack a home. He wished he could go home, just one more time, and find the closeness he'd known in the poverty they'd shared.

He'd found no strong women, no real closeness among the planter families. He'd forgotten the importance of strength . . . and maybe even love. When he'd looked for a wife, he'd wanted land and family. Connections to the wealthy, the elite. Acceptance into their society. Pansy had been exactly what he was looking for, and everything he now realized he didn't want.

A knock interrupted his musings. Jackson lifted his head, running his hands through his hair. "Come in."

Lebeau opened the door, slipping inside silently. "Miss Violet is here to see you."

A vision of her blond loveliness did nothing to dispel the unease he felt about his dead wife's sister. Violet was looking for a sign that he welcomed her interest. She'd never understood that he was being polite only in a familial manner. A gentle snub would set her straight.

"Tell Miss Crowder that I'm unavailable." He sighed. "I'm not feeling my best, but don't tell her that."

Lebeau raised one eyebrow, gave Jackson an assessing look, then left the library.

Jackson went to the window that overlooked the

187

lawn. He heard faint voices, then the front door closing. In a moment, the Crowders' carriage wheeled down the drive, the horses at a fast trot.

Smiling, Jackson returned to the desk. He was just taking his seat when another knock sounded.

"Yes. What is it?" He wasn't in the mood for any more interruptions.

A feminine hand pushed open the door, then the object of his most recent frustration poked her head inside the study.

Her expression betrayed her feelings clearly: embarrassment, caution, and the same frustration he felt. "Sorry to bother you."

"No bother. I assumed Lebeau wanted something else."

"I need a new pencil, or a way to sharpen the one I have."

"Of course. Come in."

As she slipped inside, he noticed that she wearing the lavender dress this morning. She looked prim and proper, the opposite of the disheveled, passionate woman he'd kissed and caressed last night. He tore his eyes away, focusing on the grain of wood, the sparkle of brass. Memories of their minutes together burned a path through his gut, producing an arousal he hid by remaining seated. He pretended to look for a pencil when in fact he knew exactly where he kept the writing instruments.

"Here you go," he said, trying to sound normal, even cheerful, as he handed Randi a handful of the requested items. Only then did he look at her again.

She'd plastered a strained smile on her face. "Thank you."

"You're welcome."

She backed away, the color in her cheeks high. "I'd better get back to Rose. She's with Suzette."

"Of course." He nodded. "Until later then."

"Yes . . . later."

She closed the door behind her. Jackson slumped in his chair, feeling much older than his thirty years. At the same time, he felt as awkward as a lad. What could he say to her after drinking too much brandy, trying to seduce her when she was in his employ? He'd never coerced a woman into his bed; he didn't believe he'd tried to press his advantage unfairly with Randi. But perhaps he had. He wasn't thinking too clearly—last night or this morning.

Soon, he'd return to his senses.

With a sigh, he walked across the room to the credenza and pulled out a surveyor's map of the area. He needed work to keep his mind busy and off Miss Randi Galloway's charms. He'd made a mistake last night, allowing himself the luxury of wallowing in his desire for his daughter's governess. He should never have kissed her the first time; he shouldn't have done the same— and more—last night.

At least she wasn't angry with him. For that, he was grateful. They could return to their previous uneasy relationship. In time, they'd forget that in a moment of brandy-induced passion, he'd kissed a woman he'd grown to admire for her strength of will, and she'd kissed him back with an honesty he'd all but forgotten.

Chapter Thirteen

Randi felt lucky that Jackson hadn't made a very unpleasant scene over their encounter last night. She'd been half-afraid that he'd accuse her of being a loose woman, or scheming in some way, or come up with another reason to distrust her. He hadn't. Apparently he wasn't as narrow-minded as she'd once thought—although he wouldn't exactly qualify as a sensitive, 1990s male.

Of course, not many men she knew would fit that description. Sometimes she thought those guys were dreamed up by magazine editors and talk-show hosts.

With a sigh, she picked up Rose from the quilt they'd spread on the floor earlier. Rain kept them indoors, making Randi nervous about the water level. Time was running out, and despite the widespread belief that the river wasn't going to rise very far or very fast, she knew differently.

"Your daddy is too cocky for his own good," she told the baby, holding Rose high over her head and twisting her gently from side to side. Rose squealed in delight, drooling down onto the bodice of the lavender dress.

"Oh, you stinker," Randi said, smiling at the baby's apple cheeks and pink-bow mouth as she settled the infant on her hip. "You just love to get me dirty, don't you? Do you know how much trouble it is to change out of these dresses? And I can't just throw them in the washing machine, either, like I can my jeans and sweats. Somebody has to wash these with their very own hands."

Randi tickled Rose's tummy until she giggled and wiggled. Only when she looked up did she notice Suzette standing in the doorway, a look of confusion on her face.

"Oh," Randi said, "how long have you been there?"

"I heard what you said," Suzette answered cautiously. "I don't know what those words mean, but it sounds to me like you're talkin' 'bout things I never heard of."

Randi took a deep breath. "You're right. You haven't heard of washing machines or jeans or sweat suits. They exist only where I come from."

"Where's that, Miss Randi?" Suzette asked tentatively, easing into the room with an armload of folded diapers.

"Far away from here," Randi answered, looking out the window at the pounding rain as she bounced Rose on her hip. "I wish I could go back home, too. I'm afraid . . ."

"What's you afraid of?"

"The river," Randi said softly. "The rising water."

"Birdie said the water ain't gonna come as high as the house, but we're gonna have wet fields and poor crops. She knows 'bout things like that."

Randi shook her head. "I think the river will get as high as this house, Suzette. I know we're all in danger if the planters don't build high levees and watch carefully every day."

"Mas'r Jackson will take care of us," Suzette responded automatically.

Randi smiled as reassuringly as possible. After learning that Suzette had been raped by her former owner, Randi found the girl's faith in any man incredible. "I know he'll try. At least he's aware of the problem. He seems to be more concerned than the rest of the men around here."

"Birdie says he'll take care of us."

"Do you like that? What if you had to take care of yourself?"

"All alone?" Suzette asked with alarm in her voice, her dark eyes wide.

"No, I mean what if you didn't have a 'master' to tell you what to do and when? What if you could go out and get a job where you were paid a wage for working? Would you like that?"

"I don't know, Miss Randi. Maybe . . . But Birdie says we're better off here at Black Willow Grove 'cause we have a good master."

Randi sighed. The concept of slavery was so ingrained that many of the people who worked the fields and in the house didn't have any idea how they'd get by without someone providing food, clothing, shelter, and direction to their lives. How sad. How were they going to survive after the Civil War?

"Suzette," Randi said, walking over to where the slim young woman straightened Rose's diapers, "some day in the future, maybe fifteen years from now, you might not have a master any longer. You might be free to get a job you'd like and make your own decisions."

"Are you an abolitionist?" Suzette asked with narrowed eyes.

"Well, I hadn't really thought about it, but I suppose

I am. I don't believe it's right for one person to own another one."

Suzette scoffed. "You'd best not tell anyone 'round here 'bout how you're thinkin'," she advised. "The planters'll run you out of the county for certain."

Randi smiled. "I'm sure you're right. I'll keep my opinions to myself. Or just between you and me, okay?"

Suzette nodded. "I'd best feed Miss Rose her dinner."

"I think I'll go change. She drooled on me again, and now I can tell she's also wet." Randi handed the happy baby over to the nurse, then grimaced as she held out the damp section of her dress. "I sure wish you had Pampers."

"What's that, Miss Randi?"

She laughed. "Never mind. I'll see you later."

Randi walked down the narrow stairs to the second floor, musing over her conversation with Suzette. Slavery wasn't something she'd ever thought about in 1999. The concept seemed far removed from modern life, except when some group made it an issue—usually when they were arguing politics. She hadn't paid much attention one way or the other, but now she had to worry about the fate of people other than Rose and Jackson.

What had happened to the rest of the people who'd lived at Black Willow Grove? Had they escaped with their lives, only to be sold somewhere else? Had Suzette stayed with Birdie, or had Melody learned to be more outgoing and competent as a lady's maid, as she wanted to become? Where would Lebeau go, with his dignified manner, superior attitude, and strange relationship with Jackson?

She sighed as she entered her bedroom. *Her* room. How odd that in only two weeks, she'd come to think of this as hers. She'd be gone from here before the month of April began, if she was lucky. And if she worked hard to find a way home.

Crossing to the window, she looked out at the gray,

late-afternoon gloom. She could barely see the row of trees that made the pleasant shaded alley of the garden. The light rain had started yesterday and hadn't let up one bit. Rubbing her arms against the chill, she was just about to turn away from the window when she heard a shout and saw a rider galloping toward the house.

Randi pivoted toward the glass, her fingers gripping the windowsill. What was wrong? Surely no one would run their horse into the ground unless his mission was important—even urgent. She watched until the rider disappeared under the porch, then she turned and hurried toward the stairs.

"Mas'r Jackson!"

Jackson pushed himself away from his desk, the urgency he heard in the unknown man's voice pulling him toward the entry.

Lebeau was already there, restraining the wet, dripping man from venturing farther than the marble near the front door.

"What's wrong?" Jackson waved Lebeau off, approaching the restless messenger.

"A packet tried to get away from a snag of branches and ran into Mas'r Franklin's levee. The people onboard got shook up real bad, some of 'em hurt pretty serious. Mas'r Franklin says he needs you and any hands you can spare to help."

Jackson turned to Lebeau. "Get Brewster to pick twenty strong men loaded in two wagons. I'll need a horse." Jackson hurried toward the stairs, then called back over his shoulder. "Have Birdie get together some linens and whatever food we have prepared and can spare. They'll need meals."

"Yes, Mas'r Jackson," Lebeau said, his own tone more urgent as he started off the other way to carry out his orders.

"Get yourself some coffee and cornbread in the kitchen," Jackson called back to the messenger. "I'll ride with you if you're returning to Eastland."

"I am. Thank ya, Mas'r Jackson."

He hurried up the stairs, deep in thought over what else he'd need, when he saw a lavender flounce on the landing.

Jackson looked up into the wide eyes of the woman who haunted far too many of his waking moments.

"Eavesdropping again, Miss Galloway?" he asked, brushing past her on his way to his bedroom.

"No, I just . . . Well, yes, I was," she said, her footsteps hurrying along the hallway behind him.

"I'm sorry. I can't talk right now."

"I know. The emergency at Franklin's plantation."

"Right. I'm not sure when I'll return. I hope I'll be back by late tonight. Please make sure Rose is well attended while I'm gone."

"That's what I wanted to talk to you about," she said, following him into the one room he didn't want to visualize her entering—or more. Even the atmosphere seemed intimate, the near-darkness pervading the interior of the house where lamps had yet to be lit.

"I'm sorry. I don't know what you're talking about." He yanked at his cravat. "And as I'm in a hurry, I must ask you to leave."

"I can help with the people who are injured."

"Now you're also a physician?" he scoffed as he worked the buttons at his cuffs.

"No, but I've had a course in first aid."

"First aid?" He looked up. She looked concerned, but also disheveled, her bodice spotted and her skirt hopelessly wrinkled. "What are you talking about?" he asked impatiently. More strange words and unknown terms from the land of Randi. . . .

"It means giving aid to those who have been injured, until a doctor can treat them. I know how to treat

195

wounds, give CPR—that's cardiopulmonary resuscita-
tion—and set bones."

"Useful knowledge, I'm sure." He started on the buttons of his shirtfront. She was probably making up this
story, too, although he couldn't understand why. He
was certain that young women were not trained in
medical procedures, even in the strange world Randi
Galloway called home.

"I want to come and help," she said from directly behind him.

"You need to stay here and watch after Rose." He
didn't dare turn and face her, not when he had to
change quickly and leave his house for Eastland.

"Why?" Her voice reflected disbelief. "Suzette's here."

"Randi, please. I'm in a hurry. Surely you can understand this type of situation is no place for a young
woman."

"Why?"

He finally turned around out of exasperation. "Because there will be blood and perhaps death. There
could be fire aboard the packet from the boilers or from
stoves that tipped during the crash. It is no place for
someone without a reason to be there."

"Even if I could help someone? Why can't you believe
that I know what I'm doing?"

"Because young women aren't trained in the skills
you claim to possess. I believe you may be imagining
you know more than you do about medical procedures."

"You don't believe me," she said, hurt evident in her
tone and her expressive face. She looked at him as
though she were disappointed, not in the situation, but
in *him*.

He ignored the emotions her accusation caused,
turning away from her in the near darkness of his bedroom. "I must change clothes now. Please excuse me."

"No! Listen, I know what I'm talking about. If there

are injured people, I can help. Haven't you ever heard of nurses? My God, what kind of backwoods twilight zone have I landed in?"

Jackson ignored her presence, as much as he could, and yanked off his shirt. "I'm warning you—"

"Right," she scoffed. "I'm not afraid of you."

He faced her, a clean but old shirt balled in his fist. "Even after last night?" he said, knowing he shouldn't bring up the incident, but unable to stop himself from goading her into fleeing.

"Especially after last night. Don't you realize how reassuring it is to know that a man will stop when you say no?"

Jackson closed his eyes, his body as tense as the air between them. "Randi, please. I can't discuss the issue with you right now."

"Then you shouldn't have brought it up!" she said with more spirit than he'd heard from her all day. Her unique tone of voice, her sass—as his mother would call it—should have irritated him, but he found himself hiding a smile instead.

And speaking of things coming up, he didn't dare draw attention to his trousers. Despite the urgent emergency, he was responding to her with far more enthusiasm than he'd believed possible.

"I'm coming with you," she said. "I'll ride in the wagon, if you want. But damn it, Jackson, I can help. Why would you deny these people whatever comfort I can offer?"

Why, indeed? Again, she was beginning to make far too much sense. He had to question his sanity. "Very well. Can you ride?"

"Well, not very much. My uncle trains horses, but they're too valuable for me to ride."

Of course she couldn't. Any other young woman would have said yes. "Then you can ride with me."

"Yes! I'll run and tell Suzette."

"Don't bother. Tell Lebeau. He'll make sure she knows."

"Okay." She paused only a moment, then leaned toward him. Before he knew her intentions, she'd placed a quick kiss on his cheek. "Thanks, Jackson. You made the right decision."

After she picked up her skirts and ran from the room, he smiled into the darkness, touching the spot where her soft lips had connected with his rough cheek. She wasn't the insane person; he was.

Randi had ridden horses a few times. Nice, calm, riding stable–type horses mostly, but once an older farm horse at one of her friend's grandparents' farm. Only once before had she been on the back of a spirited animal like the one Jackson mounted in front of his house, and Uncle Aaron promised she'd never have to ride one again.

She started to shake her head when Jackson extended his hand, but knew that he'd run off without her. She really needed to go to Eastland and help the people. How could she stand by when others were suffering? But that wild-eyed horse gave her a serious case of the screaming willies.

"How do I get up there?" she asked against the wind and rain. The bottom of her full skirts were nearly soaked through already, although her upper body was covered in an oiled slicker that one of the servants had handed her. Apparently, women didn't go out in the rain much. Pansy hadn't owned a raincoat.

"Lebeau, hand her up," Jackson directed.

Effortlessly, the butler placed his hands around her waist and deposited her into Jackson's strong arms. She barely had time to squeal before she was seated across his lap, her bottom nestled across the front of the saddle. His arms closed around her, holding the reins of the nervous animal. At least, the horse seemed nervous to her. She wished it would just stand still and behave.

"Hold on around my back," Jackson said, his voice husky and intimate against her ear.

Her heart raced as she snuggled next to Jackson. Just last night she'd experienced the explosive nature of their passion. How could she stand being this close to him for however long the trip took? She just hoped he couldn't tell how much he affected her, especially in such a serious, nonintimate situation.

Calm down girl, she told herself. *You're traveling to an emergency, not being swept away by Prince Charming.*

As the horse started to move, she realized the dangerous nature of her position. That front part of the saddle, gently sloped like she'd seen on Tennessee Walkers instead of the Western kind with saddle horns, pressed between her legs in a very vulnerable spot. With each stride, she became more and more aware of how long she'd gone without any passion in her life, and how much she'd like to experience these feelings in Jackson's arms, with his body firmly against hers.

"Quit wiggling," he said fiercely against her ear.

"I'm uncomfortable," she finally managed to say. "Maybe I should ride behind you."

"Could you just be still! I don't want to take a tumble off this horse. And I'd like to remind you that coming along was your idea."

He was right, of course, although she wished he hadn't used the word *coming* to describe her situation.

"Just one second," she pleaded. With an effort, she managed to angle herself away from the relentless saddle and higher across Jackson's thighs. "Does that hurt?" she asked when he groaned.

"Not exactly," he said hoarsely.

He put his heels to the horse, pressing her back farther against his muscular chest and stomach—and into the arousal that rubbed against her thigh.

"Oh," she said, her cheeks heating up as they continued on toward the wreck of the paddlewheeler.

She decided that horseback riding was the most delicious form of torture she'd ever experienced. She'd never look at being swept away by a dashing cavalier in those grand old movies the same way.

By the time Jackson galloped onto the scene at Eastland, some order had already been restored to the disaster. However, Randi immediately saw several crises illuminated by flaming torches, carried or stuck into the mud. First, high water trickled through a small break in the levee where the paddlewheeler was wedged. Second, the precarious angle of the boat made getting people and their belongings off the boat very dangerous.

Although there were waist-high railings around each deck, no one could stand upright. Women wailed and men shouted orders as possessions were carried with great difficulty by black field hands and white travelers alike.

The gangplank tilted at an odd angle. Men tried to stand upright with their heavy loads as they held onto a railing. Randi thought back to her original story of her trunk falling into the river and her jumping in after it. The scenario now seemed very probable—but she suddenly realized that falling off an upright boat would be virtually impossible.

If another paddlewheeler had crashed into a dock or levee, Jackson would have known about it. That meant he'd known all along that she was lying . . .

She didn't have time to follow through with that thought. With all the chaos, she needed to find where they'd taken the injured passengers.

"Who's in charge?" she asked Jackson.

"Franklin should be, but I don't see him. Let me ask around."

He rode up to a man who obviously recognized him. Dismounting from the chestnut horse that had carried them here so quickly, Jackson reached up and lifted her from the back of the nervous animal. Only once before did she remember being so grateful to be on dry land.

Of course, the sogginess below her feet wasn't really *dry*.

"Where's Franklin?" Jackson shouted to the man.

"At the house. They've taken the passengers there."

"The injured ones, too?" Randi asked.

The man looked at her with raised eyebrows, but answered, "Yes." His eyes raked over her, probably wondering who she was and why she was here.

"Can you ride by yourself to the house?" Jackson asked.

"Are you kidding? On that beast?"

He shook his head.

"Where is the house?" Randi asked, shading her eyes from the torches as she looked into the darkness.

"Not far," Jackson said, pointing away from the chaos. "Can you see?"

"Yes." Sure enough, the faint lights from the windows were visible through the gloomy twilight. "I can walk."

"I'll take her," the man said.

Jackson looked between them, then shook his head. "Thanks, but I believe I'll deliver Miss Galloway myself."

Within seconds, he'd mounted the horse. The man they'd talked to handed her up, his hands sweeping down her leg once she was settled on Jackson's lap. A shiver passed through her. The man thought she was a woman of no consequence, someone he could approach with no repercussions. Well, he'd better not try anything with her, because she'd kick him where it hurt the most.

Before she could reacted to the lecher, Jackson wheeled the horse away from the scene of the wreck and into the darkness. She held tight, settling her head

Victoria Chancellor

against his strong shoulder, feeling his heartbeat against her hand as it crossed his chest.

"That was Franklin's overseer," Jackson informed her. "Stay away from him."

"No problem." For once, she and Jackson agreed.

The ground was much wetter here than on Jackson's land. The horse struggled through sucking mud, slipping several times. Randi held tight, her left arm around Jackson's back, her right looped around his neck. He seemed to welcome her presence, encouraging her snuggling by holding her tight. Far too soon, the ride was over.

He reined in the horse beside the front porch. She felt his arms tighten as if he was preparing to lift her down. Her gaze raised to his, then caught and held. Lamplight from inside the house gilded his tanned skin with a golden glimmer and his dark eyes with a shimmering, mysterious look. He took in a deep breath, then leaned over her so quickly her breath caught. He kissed her deeply, fiercely, until she responded by meeting his tongue with thrusts of her own. As quickly as he'd placed his lips over hers, the kiss ended.

The distant sounds of footsteps and conversation filtered into her consciousness as Jackson lifted her from across his thighs and onto the porch. He looked as unsteady as she felt. Leaning against a white column, she couldn't turn away from his intense look.

He broke eye contact, looking toward the doorway. "Franklin!" he called out.

Within a few seconds, a middle-aged man in a rumpled coat and mud-spattered pants joined them.

"This is Miss Galloway, my daughter's governess. She has some knowledge of the healing arts."

"We could use some help. The doctor is setting broken bones."

"I'll do whatever I can," Randi offered the flustered planter.

"But with the greatest care," Jackson added. When she looked up at him, she saw possession and desire written on his face. For me, she thought, amazed that she'd evoked such strong emotion in a man who prided himself on control.

"You will be cautious, Miss Galloway," he added. "I'll be back for you later."

With those meaningful words hanging in the rain-drenched air, Jackson pivoted his horse and galloped across the muddy lawn, back toward the wreck. She shivered, knowing that if he decided to take her somewhere dark and private when all this was over, she'd gladly go. No thoughts of her future or past, no worries about when she could leave or how.

As she followed Mr. Franklin into the house, she felt as though she were losing herself in the past. Frightened by the idea, she knew she had to keep her head on straight, even when her mind was spinning from Jackson's kisses.

Chapter Fourteen

The hard physical labor felt good. Jackson had discarded his coat, working alongside stevedores and weary travelers, planters and field hands. They hurried to get the heavily laden vessel unloaded. Items in the lower deck had shifted to the submerged side when the packet hit the levee, keeping the boat wedged even further into the mud of the Mississippi.

They needed to get the boat out, whatever the effort cost. When—if—the water rose higher, the boat would be pulled loose by the current and run into the levee again. Next time, the entire earthen wall could collapse from the impact.

Another problem was that the wreck left many travelers without a place to stay, clean clothing, and hot food. Each planter could take a certain number of guests into his home, and no one should be terribly inconvenienced, but who knew when another packet could carry these stranded people to their destinations? And if the river continued to rise, as he suspected it would, then transportation could be a long, long time coming.

Working up to his knees in muddy water, he twisted a barrel free and passed it to a burly field hand who worked on Franklin's plantation, who passed it to a stevedore who usually worked the docks at Randolph's. Jackson's lower legs had gone numb an hour ago, at least. His arms and shoulders ached with the repetitive effort, but he hadn't felt this good in years. The only better outcome of this night would be to go home with Randi Galloway and make sweet love to her until they were both exhausted.

He'd stopped last night when she'd asked him to. He'd stop again, but he didn't think that's what she wanted. Holding her in his arms on the ride to Eastland, kissing her before he rode away from Franklin's house, he'd understood her desire was as great as his.

Yet he had to tell Randi they were unsuitable for any relationship more permanent. Surely she realized that, but for the sake of honesty, he needed to say the words. He would find a suitable woman among the planter class, and he would marry her for the sake of having an heir and a mother for Rose.

Having a liaison with his daughter's governess had a certain unpleasantness that he refused to heed. If he'd discovered another man in his position had taken advantage of a young woman's position in his home, Jackson knew he'd condemn the man as a lecher. Even knowing he was applying a double standard, he couldn't stop himself from thinking about Randi—and about losing himself in her warmth.

"Watch out!"

The deck beneath him shifted, along with the cargo, and Jackson slipped down into the dark water. Something crashed into his shoulder, sending sharp pains down his arm. A barrel rolled into his chest, knocking the air from his lungs and slamming him against the wall. He struggled from the water, gulping, panicked, shaking the water from his eyes.

Across the deck, he heard another man moan—the field hand, probably, who had been midway across the cargo deck when the warning was shouted. The torch they'd used for light had apparently fallen into the water, but he saw the bobbing glow of someone coming down the stairs, carrying a lantern or another torch.

"Over here," he called out.

Within minutes, three men helped him pull the other man from beneath barrels that had rolled and shifted, nearly burying him in a watery grave. The field hand's arm appeared to be broken, with a long gash that looked painful. Jackson's own bruises seemed insignificant as he helped the man to the fresh air and help.

Surprisingly, the rain had stopped. Fleeting clouds rushed across the half-moon, and a cool wind made him shiver in his wet clothes. The man he supported began to shake.

"Bring a wagon around," he called out to one of his drivers.

Within minutes, Jackson had the injured man loaded into the wagon with a blanket around his shoulders and bleeding arm.

"You'd better go too, Mas'r Jackson," the driver said, pointing to his side.

"That's his blood," Jackson said, turning toward the torch light and peering at his wet, clinging, stained shirt.

"Naw, Mas'r Jackson. I think you got a cut of your own."

He ran his fingers along the tear in the linen and found a slash across several ribs. He hadn't even noticed until now.

"I suppose I should have it bandaged." Besides, he'd get to see Randi again, find out how she was faring at the house.

He hoped she possessed some nursing skills, because he was in the mood for some coddling. Now that he'd noticed the slash on his side, the damn cut hurt like hell. Besides, he was wet and cold. He hoped Franklin had some clothes that would fit him because he hadn't thought to bring extras.

The wagon made slow time through the mire separating the partially breached levee from the plantation house. Jackson tried to concentrate on the logistics of water flow and levee repair, but he was shivering too hard to think. His shoulder ached and the cut bled slowly. His blood was the only warmth he could detect on his body.

By the time the driver pulled up at the front steps, exhaustion had claimed the rest of his energy. He helped the more severely injured man out, even though he shook uncontrollably himself. With the driver on the other side of the field hand, they pushed through the front door into light and warmth.

Jackson's eyes focused on the woman rushing to meet him, concern shining from her wide eyes. Her expression felt so warm, so intoxicating, that he almost reached out his arms to grab her. Instead, he held on to the injured man and continued walking into the house, hoping he didn't do or say anything in a weak moment that would embarrass him . . . or show others his inappropriate feelings toward his daughter's governess.

Randi rushed toward the three men: two black, one white, all three wet and dripping on the Franklins' marble foyer. When she got close enough to smell the muddy Mississippi River water, she also saw the blood on Jackson. The knowledge that he was injured and bleeding made her stumble, but she caught herself before she acted like a complete fool and embarrassed Jackson.

He was so sensitive about how others perceived him. Someday, she was going to have to find out *why*.

"What happened?" She looked first at the man they were supporting, one on each side. Jackson should be lying down, not holding up a guy so big that he looked like a professional football player.

"My arm's broke," the big man ground out.

"Hold still," she told him as she peeled the shirt away. The bone appeared to have snapped and broken the skin. Setting it would be awfully painful. She turned to look at Jackson's side.

"The boat shifted when we were unloading the cargo hold. He's hurt worse than I am," Jackson said.

"I'll be the judge of that. Where are you hurt?"

"Just a little cut on my ribs. Nothing important."

Of course he'd say that. "It's full of dirty river water. We need to get it clean, at least."

"As long as you treat him first."

"What's your name?" Randi asked the man with the broken arm.

"George, ma'am," he said through gritted teeth.

"Let's get you settled back in the kitchen, George. That's where the doctor has been taking care of the people who are more seriously injured. Not that there were that many, thank heavens."

"You're not going to take off my arm, are you?" he asked in fear and pain.

"Of course not!" Randi was shocked that anyone would jump to that sort of conclusion for a broken arm, even a compound fracture.

"I'll have to take a look first," the doctor said, joining them from where he'd been resting in the parlor.

"Please, don't let him take my arm," George pleaded to Jackson.

"I won't."

They went to the detached kitchen where patients could be laid flat for medical procedures. Thankfully, the stove provided heat against the damp chill outside. Folded towels rested on a nearby shelf. Not exactly a high-tech E.R., but this was all they had to work with.

George passed out from the pain of getting him up on the oak table.

"That's okay," she told Jackson, standing close beside him and pressing a clean cloth to his wound. "The doctor can set his arm while he's out cold."

"I'm not letting him take off the arm."

"Of course not! It's broken, not mangled."

Jackson looked at her as though she was crazy. "Broken arms are removed fairly often when they push through the skin like this."

"Really? Not in the land of Randi Mae Galloway."

Jackson tried a slight smile at their ongoing jest, but failed miserably. She'd never seen him so tired.

"Can you get us a chair?" she asked the other man who'd helped Jackson get George into the house.

"Sure, Miz Randi."

He even knew her name. How was that? She'd never seen him before. From the way he was dressed, she supposed he worked outside. Of course, it was hard to tell when even Jackson looked like a dockworker.

"For you, Miz Randi," the man said, setting a chair before her.

"Thanks, but it's not for me. For Jackson."

She urged him to sit, then began pulling the wet, tattered shirt from his body.

"What are you doing?"

"Getting you out of these wet clothes," she answered, tugging the sleeve down his arm.

"Miss Galloway!" His shocked tone of voice surprised her as much as the other occupants of the room, who all stared at her.

"What?"

"You shouldn't be doing that. You're an unmarried

209

woman," Jackson whispered in a fierce, condemning tone.

"Oh, don't be silly. You don't have anything I haven't seen before. I have an older brother, you know."

"Yes, I believe you mentioned that. However, I'm not your brother, and—"

"Hold still."

"Ouch!"

"You've got a nasty bruise," she said, pulling the shirt away from the wound and surrounding area. "Are you sure somebody didn't just beat the—heck out of you? You look like you just went a few rounds with Evander Holyfield."

"Who?" Jackson looked away from the doctor and turned his confused gaze toward her.

"He's a boxer." Vaguely, she remembered that the sport had another name, long ago, but she couldn't recall the name.

Jackson looked at her blankly. "I assure you, only barrels inflicted this damage, although some boxes were stored below."

"You may have broken some ribs. Does it hurt to breathe?"

"Not especially."

George moaned, returning their attention to him.

"I'll need assistance holding his arm straight," the doctor said.

Jackson started to rise, but she pushed him down in the chair. "Not you. We need to see how badly you're hurt before you start exerting yourself again. If you're feeling okay, then get yourself the rest of the way out of that wet shirt and find something dry to put around you."

She motioned for the other black man to come over. "We'll help you, Dr. Shelton."

"Aren't you going to disinfect the wound?" she asked when they leaned over the table.

"I don't think that's necessary. These people have much tougher skin, and they—"

"Dr. Shelton, that's ridiculous! He's just as prone to infection as anyone. Now where is that whiskey you used earlier? I saw you use some on that young man with the scrape on the side of his neck."

The doctor glared at her, but retrieved the bottle from the table beside the stove.

"A waste of good spirits," the doctor complained as he poured whiskey over the raw skin.

Randi insisted he wash his hands before touching the wound, then, with a minimum amount of grumbling and their help, he managed to pull the bone back into place. Thankfully, George stayed passed out through the entire ordeal. Randi didn't want to think how painful the procedure must be.

He started to bind the wound, but Randi interrupted him. "Shouldn't that wound be stitched?"

"He's a field hand, Miss Galloway," the doctor replied in a long suffering voice. "His scar doesn't have to look pretty."

"No, but skin is the best way to keep out germs. If the cut doesn't heal properly, it might get infected."

"What are you talking about?" Dr. Shelton asked incredulously.

"She knows many things from her homeland," Jackson interjected.

"I know that infections aren't caused by evil spirits or bad air," Randi said. "Look, if you don't want to sew him up, then I will." *As long as he stays passed out*. Otherwise, she'd have to stick a needle through his skin while he watched her and flinched, and she just didn't think she could do that.

The doctor shook his head, but headed for his medical kit. "I've never had such a fussy assistant before. There's a reason women aren't involved in the medical profession."

Randi laughed. "Just wait! You should only live so long."

She realized what she said, but couldn't take it back. Oh, well. No one would pick up on the fact she'd referred to the future, not just another place.

When she hazarded a glance at Jackson, she noticed he was watching her closely. Too closely.

The doctor began to sew the skin together, large stitches that wouldn't serve this poor injured man well at all. "Look, Dr. Shelton, I know you're tired. Why don't I finish that up? Women are good at sewing, right?"

No one seemed to notice her sarcasm, and the doctor gave her only a withering stare before handing over the needle. She'd never done this before, but her efforts must be better than that old quack's. Taking her bottom lip between her teeth, she tried not to wince too much when she poked the metal through George's ragged skin.

She'd watched a doctor in the emergency room do this to Russell one time when he'd fallen from the loft in a friend's old barn onto some sheet metal. Of course, he'd also gotten a shot to numb the area, an antibiotic, plus a tetanus booster. This poor worker wouldn't have any of those, so who knew what kind of infections he could get or pain he would suffer?

Just to be sure, she poured a little more whiskey on the wound, the needle, and thread. If she didn't think it would put her to sleep, she'd take a good swig herself.

"You have good hands," Jackson said, looking over her shoulder. Once again, he'd moved silently.

"Don't startle me when I'm doing this," she said. "I'm not exactly a pro."

"A what?"

"A professional. You know, like someone who went to school to know how to do this right."

"Your stitches are better than the good doctor's, and

he went to Harvard." Jackson grabbed the bottle of whiskey and took a long drink, grimacing when he swallowed.

"Really? Well, I didn't go there. Maybe the University of Tennessee . . . someday."

Jackson shook his head. "You're talking in riddles again."

"Sorry." She glanced down at his bare, bruised chest. "Shouldn't you find some clothes to wear? You look cold."

She didn't want to think about his olive-toned skin, lean muscles, or cold-pebbled male nipples. Cheeks warm, she turned back to her task of sewing up the worker's damaged arm, careful not to disturb the set bone. At least he wasn't bleeding any longer. She had no idea how to stop massive bleeding. First aid was the only course she'd taken, and only because she thought she should have those skills around her nieces and nephew.

As soon as she was finished sewing up the gash, she called Dr. Shelton back. He glanced briefly at the neat stitches, then set the bone in splints and bandages. Luckily, as they were finishing, George came to, moaning when he tried to move his arm.

"You need to keep the bandages clean and changed daily," Randi told him when she saw the doctor had little interest in treating George like a regular patient. "Don't take the splint off, though. That bone has to mend. If the wound gets red or feverish, you'll need medical treatment."

"Thank you," he said, looking around the room as though wondering who had actually patched him up.

"Thank Miss Galloway," Jackson said. "She did a neat job sewing up that gash in your arm."

Randi smiled at the man's thanks, then promised to come and see him if she could. Before long, he returned to his family. Finally, the doctor was ready to look at Jackson's injuries.

Sitting on the wide oak table, he looked very uncomfortable, Randi thought. Jackson didn't like to be the center of attention. He took another drink of whiskey, obviously trying to kill the pain.

The doctor had him breathe deeply, testing his ribs. After making sure nothing was broken, he cleaned the wound and bound it tightly with clean cotton cloth strips.

Randi stood back and watched, ready to intervene if the doctor performed an unsanitary or, in her opinion, unwise procedure. She wasn't taking any chances with Jackson's health—while she was here. Eventually she'd go back to her time, leaving him to his fate in this horrible, dirty, harsh world.

The idea made her swallow a moan, then blink back tears. When Jackson looked up and saw her, she yawned.

"Sorry," she said. "It's late."

"Yes, it is. I thought I should work on the boat some more, but I imagine they've finished unloading by now. We were almost done when the accident happened."

The doctor turned away from the table, loading unused bandages and vials into his bag.

"You definitely need to go home," Randi told Jackson. "You're covered in bruises, that cut has barely quit bleeding, and your ribs are going to be as sore as all get out tomorrow."

"You're predicting the future again," Jackson asked with a weary smile.

"Yes, and I'm as sure of that as I am the other," she said briskly, hating the way she couldn't stop eating him up with her eyes. Darn, but Jackson looked sexy even when he was dirty and injured. There was no fairness in life. Why did she have to be attracted to a man who looked that good? If he resembled a toad more than a prince, she might be able to resist her urge to run her hands over his tight, smooth skin. Soothe his lean ribs. Kiss his bruises until they healed.

"I'm going back to the parlor," the doctor said, yawning in earnest. "It's been a long night."

"That it has, Doctor. Thank you for patching me up."

"Anytime, Mr. Durant."

Jackson sent the driver from Black Willow Grove to find some clothes, leaving Randi alone with the object of her lustful thoughts. Not a good idea.

He wasted no time, pulling her forward between his legs as he stayed on the table. His trousers were still damp, but all she felt was the warmth of his body surrounding her. He smelled of muddy river water and whiskey, but she didn't mind. She wanted to brace her hands on his chest and show him how relieved she was that he wasn't seriously hurt. He could have been smashed, his arm or leg broken, or lots of injuries worse than some bruises and a gash on his side.

"Jackson, don't. Anyone could walk in."

"Then pretend you're treating me," he suggested, settling his hand on her waist. "Use some of your skills to make me feel better."

She had lots of ideas on how to make him feel better, but few of them involved medical skills. "Is that what you really want? I thought you were more concerned about appearances than that. Are you willing to risk getting caught kissing your daughter's governess?"

Chapter Fifteen

Jackson let the smile die on his face, weariness replacing the temporary boost from the two shots of whiskey. He let his hands drop from her waist, careful not to brush against any other part of her body as he rested his palms against his thighs. "You're right. That was the whiskey talking."

"And the pain and the exhaustion," Randi added, stepping back from between his legs.

He smiled slightly at her concerned expression, already missing her warmth and nearness. "Perhaps. I won't deny that I'm a bit sore, and I could use a good night's sleep. The problem is, so could the rest of these people."

"Then why don't we gather some of them up and take them to Black Willow Grove? That's what other planters are doing."

"Yes, bringing travelers into our homes is the usual procedure."

"Usual? You have these accidents often enough to

have a procedure?" she asked with wide eyes.

"Not too often. Sometimes a boiler explodes. Sometimes a snag on the river catches the paddle wheel or rudder."

"Sounds dangerous."

He tilted his head to the side and assessed her carefully. "You should know. Didn't you arrive on a packet? Haven't you heard stories of river travel, especially since you're from New Orleans?"

She broke eye contact, busying herself with folding the soiled clothes she and the doctor had used earlier. "Oh, I've been rather sheltered. My parents didn't talk much about disasters."

"But you know the perils of traveling on the river? You heard of the fire and explosion aboard the *Ben Sherrod*, didn't you?"

"Oh, sure. The *Ben Sherrod*. Of course."

"That was several years ago."

"Really? Well, it seems like just yesterday."

"1837, I believe."

"I was very young then."

"I suppose so. You never did tell me how old you are."

"Does it matter?"

"I don't believe so, unless you try to make up some ridiculous number. Thirteen perhaps, or maybe fifty."

That brought forth a smile. "No, I won't deceive you. I'm twenty-five."

"That old," he said, and smiled back as he eased himself off the table. He ached all over. Tomorrow he'd have bruises on top of bruises where he'd been slammed against the wall of the cargo hold.

"I thought you might think I'm too young to know much about children, but that's not true. I have three nieces and nephews I've cared for since they came home from the hospital."

"Hospital? Why were they in the hospital?"

"When they were . . . Oh, I meant, since when they

were born. They went to the hospital later, when they were sick."

"Confusing the two events seems odd. Is there something else you want to tell me?"

"No. Look, why don't I see what's keeping your driver? He should have some clothes for you by now. You can't sit around in those wet things all night."

She placed the soiled clothes on the end of the table and made a hasty retreat for the door, but not before he snagged her arm.

"Someday, you're going to tell me the truth."

She looked at him with what appeared to be sadness in her eyes. "You won't believe me."

"More premonitions?"

"No, but I've come to know you pretty well. At least I think I do. I know you don't believe me about the flood."

"How can I believe something based on your dreams?"

"What if they're more than dreams?"

"Are you telling me you can *prove* the flood will come and sweep Black Willow Grove away?"

"No, I can't prove that." She broke eye contact, looking down at his hand on her arm.

He let her go, too weary to argue, too confused by her words to consider what she might mean. Leaning back on his arms, he closed his eyes. In a moment, he heard the kitchen door close. Alone, he let the long day's events wash over him. He wanted to go home, back to Black Willow Grove, where he could keep his daughter safe. Where no flood would threaten them.

He would show Miss Randi Galloway that Jackson Durant could take care of his own.

Randi helped get the weary travelers settled, but not before dawn. A middle-aged couple, two young lawyers from St. Louis, and a very attractive widow who'd been cruising the Mississippi came to stay at Black Willow Grove. The lawyers were drunk, the couple grumbled about the disaster, and the widow had hungry eyes for Jackson.

Floozy, Randi thought, closing her bedroom door. The widow had better stay in her own room. If she caught the woman tiptoeing down the hall toward the master suite, she might just find herself tripping over a loose rug . . . or something. Melody had understood what Randi meant with nothing more than a raised eyebrow, and the young maid had gotten very good at slipping around the upstairs. She knew more gossip than anyone, but unfortunately for Randi, all Melody's knowledge seemed to focus on the servants. The "master" never did anything wrong, Melody claimed.

Well, he could just keep his nose clean for a little longer! Fooling around with the shapely widow wasn't something he'd want to confess to his upstanding fellow planters. Or maybe he would. Maybe the double standard was alive and well, and he was free to have affairs with women all he wanted—as long as he didn't sleep with any of the morally righteous daughters or wives of his social class.

Randi pulled off her stockings and shoes, thankful she'd worn her own footwear under the long skirts. She couldn't have made it through the night in those narrow, pinching slippers. She sank to the fluffy mattress and propped one foot over her knee, rubbing her heels.

She was bone-tired, but wondered if she could sleep after everything that had happened in the last twelve or fourteen hours. She wanted to drift into a state of unconsciousness and stay there as long as possible. Somehow, she didn't think she'd get her wish. Her mind kept replaying the night's events, from her frustration at not having modern medical basics to Jackson's accident.

She'd been so frightened for him when he'd arrived at the house with blood over the front and side of his once-white shirt. No telling what kind of bacteria or other creepy-crawlies he'd come in contact with in the river water. With no antibiotics or disinfectants to help him out, he could catch any number of ailments. Now she understood why so many people had died in the past of relatively simple injuries.

She wanted to go home. Pushing her sketches, paper, and pencils aside, she sank into the welcoming depths of the mattress. Perhaps she could go to sleep, despite all her doubts and fears. She'd keep one ear awake, though, she vowed as she drifted off. That lusty widow wasn't getting her hooks in Jackson—at least not as long as Randi Galloway was living under his roof.

By the end of dinner the next evening, Randi felt she might have been mistaken. She hadn't traveled back in time; she'd died and gone to her own personal hell. Jackson had asked her to join the houseguests, which was very considerate of him given her sometimes unofficial status in his home. He'd told the Crowders that she was Rose's governess, but she always felt as though Jackson might change his mind at any moment. Since governesses were servants, too—sitting in the back of the church and taking orders from the "master"—she certainly wasn't entitled to eat with family or guests.

Jackson was being nice, she thought as he smiled politely at the widow, which meant he wanted answers again. That's why he was including her. Testing her was more like it. Despite her best efforts to blend in, he always seemed to find a problem with her story, a discrepancy in her wording that gave her away. But he'd never guess in a million years that she was from the future.

And she didn't have a million years. If she remembered correctly, they all had under two weeks to get away from Black Willow Grove before the flood covered all this land.

The older lady discreetly cleared her throat, then patted her lips with her napkin and placed it beside her plate. This seemed to be a clue, because everyone finished what they were doing.

With a clink of his china cup against the saucer, Jackson finished his coffee and rose from his seat at the head of the table.

"If the ladies would like to retire to the parlor, I believe the gentlemen and I will have brandy and a cigar in the study."

The older lady nodded at her husband, who then pulled out her chair. Since both young lawyers had rushed to assist the widow, Jackson came around the table toward Randi.

"I'm surprised you aren't on the other side of the table," Randi whispered as she turned her head toward Jackson.

She felt his amused chuckle as a caress of hot air against the nape of her neck, sending shivers through her whole body.

"I think she's in good hands."

I'd like to be in your hands. She sucked in a deep breath and pushed the image aside. "That sounds pretty kinky, but I guess they're all consenting adults."

"What kind of word is kinky?"

"Never mind. I was just being catty—er, petty," Randi covered for herself. Darn, she was doing it again, and this time she couldn't blame the wine or the brandy sauce. She'd been careful with her food and drink since she'd discovered the large amount of liquor that could be reasonably consumed during a meal in this century.

"Don't worry about Mrs. Sanderson," Jackson said, looking across the table at the smiling widow.

"I'm not worried about her at all. I think she's looking for a new husband." Randi stood beside her chair and straightened her skirts.

"Quite possibly. She's young and attractive. I'm sure

she'll have no trouble finding suitors." Jackson placed his hand beneath her elbow and guided her away from the table.

"A rich planter would be nice, I suppose," Randi muttered as they passed the sideboard.

"What did you say?"

"Nothing. Never mind."

His hand tightened on her elbow before they reached the doorway. "Mind your manners, Randi Galloway. These people are guests in my home."

"I'm well aware of that." They had more of an affirmed status than she did. "Does that mean I need to join them in the parlor?"

"Do you want to?"

She paused, her mouth half-open to answer yes, she wanted to keep an eye on the attractive widow. But another part of her didn't want to be subjected to any scrutiny. No telling what kind of mistake she'd make if those women asked her questions.

"No, I believe I should go upstairs and check on Rose. She's teething and very fussy."

"Very well. I'll make your excuses."

"Thank you."

She gave him a little smile, then walked as quickly as possible down the hall toward the front stairs so she got another glance at the group as she turned to go up the steps.

Jackson was talking to them, looking tall and handsome in his deep blue cutaway coat and straight-legged trousers. His blue-black hair gleamed in the hall lantern light, and his tanned skin appeared smooth and healthy. No one knew how bruised and battered he'd been last night. None of his injuries was visible on the outside.

She had a feeling Jackson's polished exterior hid other secrets.

Picking up her skirts, she hurried upstairs before she

told Jackson that she'd changed her mind. Every minute seemed especially precious, and she didn't want to spend any of them hiding in her room.

On the other hand, she'd never get home if she didn't work on her sketch. After she checked on Rose and relieved Suzette for a supper break, she'd do just that—work on her sketch until it was so real she could reach out and touch her own world.

Jackson closed the door of his study, then filled each of four glasses with two fingers of cognac. At this rate, his supply would be long gone before he got to New Orleans again. And if the water continued to rise, they might be months away from traveling on the river. He needed to get back to Franklin's plantation and check on—

"Do you play?"

Jackson turned toward one of the lawyers, Douglas Templeton. "I'm sorry. What did you ask?" He handed the young man a glass.

"Poker. We'd like to have a game, if that's agreeable to you."

Jackson felt his heart falter and stop, then start again at an incredible pace. "Poker," he heard himself say, although his voice sounded far away. Without thinking, he handed a glass to the older, less-sociable man.

"Yes," Templeton said jovially. "I assume you play."

"Not much anymore." He looked down at his hands and was surprised that he appeared steady. He wasn't shaking at all.

"Well, then," Templeton's friend said with a grin, taking the last glass of brandy, "we'll try not to take too much of your money."

Jackson drew in a deep breath, then turned away from the men and composed himself. Poker. He'd avoided playing games of chance with his neighbors for the past three years, ever since he'd settled here. He'd always had a good excuse: busy with planting; emergencies in the fields; others to visit. No one questioned his aversion to gambling.

Now he felt trapped. He couldn't refuse such a simple, ordinary request without seeming churlish. Alienating his guests was not the mark of a gracious host, and he certainly didn't want word getting out that he was rude and boorish.

After another deep breath, he took a long swallow of his cognac. He would get through this evening, one way or another.

"Where do you keep your cards?" the other young lawyer, Richard Darley, asked from behind him.

Jackson turned and assumed what he hoped was a pleasant expression. "I'll get them."

Minutes later, they were seated at the game table he rarely used when entertaining—and never for gaming. Mr. Blessing, the older man, sat to his right, with Templeton directly across the table and Darley to the left. Two of them had chosen cigars from the humidor, and smoke curled toward the ceiling from the fragrant tobacco.

"Fine brandy," Blessing said, his jowly face already florid.

"Thank you."

Jackson's palms felt damp even before he opened the new pack of cards and offered them to Darley for shuffling. He nodded for the man to continue. Within seconds, they'd each taken a card to determine the deal. He won, of course. Curse his luck.

"Five card stud," he said in a dull voice, then looked up from the deal. "Jacks are wild."

Two hours later, only twenty dollars lighter in the pocket, Jackson said good night to the last of his houseguests. Everyone was tired from last night's events, so thankfully, even the men hadn't lingered too long after dinner. Mr. Blessing hadn't tried to hide his fatigue, yawning throughout the poker game.

Thank God that was over. He hadn't lost enough to encourage his guests to play again, thinking him an easy mark. Nor had he won enough for them to want to get their money back. He'd simply played his cards as dispassionately, as precisely, as possible.

"Gaming?" Lebeau said as he entered the study to tidy up.

"Under protest. My guests would have been disappointed if I'd been a churlish host."

"I don't suppose they'd believe playing cards was against your religion."

"That might be stretching the truth too far," Jackson said, a hollow laugh accenting his slight jest. If they only knew. . . . He snapped himself out of his reverie. "I hate to admit it, but I'm too tired to think about my guests or what games they want to play. I'm going to bed."

"I'll finish up here."

"Thank you."

Jackson made his way slowly upstairs, his weary mind unable to focus as images from the past and thoughts of the future flitted through his head. He wanted to sleep for a day, at least, curled up in a dark place where no disasters intruded, no secrets threatened his peace.

However, that wasn't going to happen. He had to be up at dawn tomorrow to confer with Brewster on adding even more men to the levee-building crew. Franklin also needed a visit to see if the packet had been dislodged from his embankment, or if he needed any more help with the wreck. If this infernal rain ever stopped, or if the threat of flood passed, then they needed to thin the cotton plants and begin the season-long check for pests and disease.

The door to his bedroom was open, a low-burning

lamp giving off a golden glow. He rubbed his bruised and torn side as he tossed his discarded coat on a chair. The bandage probably needed to be changed, but he had a difficult time seeing the cut himself. Tomorrow would be soon enough to check his injuries. Perhaps he'd ask Randi to do the chore for him. She had a soothing touch, even if she did cause his blood to roar and his heart to race.

Thankfully, his valet had left water and towels on the washstand. Jackson stripped off his cravat and unbuttoned his shirt. If he hadn't smelled of cigar smoke and spirits, he would have dropped to the bed and been asleep before his head hit the pillow.

He balled the soiled shirt and threw it in the direction of his coat, wincing as the cut on his side pulled taut. After quickly washing, he began to unbutton his trousers before remembering Randi's comment earlier. Rose was teething, fretting and fussing as she did at times. Was someone with her? If his child was alone and in pain, someone would pay.

He took only enough time to pull on a clean shirt before heading upstairs. He couldn't sleep without knowing his daughter was comfortable and safe, especially since he hadn't been able to visit with her after dinner as was his usual habit.

The third floor was nearly dark, with only the slight glow of a candle coming from the bedroom next to the nursery. He walked softly across the floor, careful of the plank that squeaked and of any toys that Randi might have left lying about. She had an annoying tendency to sprawl on the floor and act like a child herself. He sometimes believed she enjoyed playing as much as Rose. He'd never known anyone who placed such importance on being happy.

Stopping beside the crib, he reached out and gently touched his daughter's fisted hand. She lay on her back because Randi had said lying on her stomach was dangerous. Something about crib death that she'd known of from her home. Another mysterious phrase from the mouth of Randi Galloway.

"Sleep well, little one," he whispered to his baby as he placed a kiss on her forehead. Her skin felt pleasantly warm and very smooth. How could anything as sweet as this child have come from someone as coarse and tainted as himself?

"Jackson?"

His head snapped up at the whisper. Standing in the doorway was his daughter's governess, dressed in a flowing white nightgown. As he stood there, she ran both hands through her short blond hair, lifting the gown away from her body. His eyes strained in the darkness to make out details of her body, revealed by the candle's faint glow.

She looked like a wanton angel.

His blood pounding in his veins, his fatigue forgotten, he crossed the room and took her in his arms.

Chapter Sixteen

He kissed her like a man starving for affection, for love, and God help her, she couldn't hold back. As she parted her lips and welcomed his fierce invasion, she knew that Jackson was the man who could fill that empty spot inside. And she was the woman he needed to chase away the loneliness she sensed in his soul. With no other woman would he find the kind of love she could offer him.

For however long they had . . . until she could return to her own time, she thought as his hands molded down her back and pressed her tighter against his solid, real body.

A sob escaped her as she clung tightly to his shoulders.

"I'm sorry," he whispered, pulling back. "I didn't mean to hurt you. I . . . You make me crazed."

Her arms held him fast. "Oh, Jackson, you didn't hurt me."

"Then what?"

She released her hold around his neck, then took his hand and pulled him into the small bedroom next to Rose's nursery. She'd left a single candle burning earlier, and now she was grateful for the meager light. "I don't want to wake her. She was so fussy earlier."

"That's why I came up here, to check on Rose. Then I saw you and I couldn't stop myself." He tried to leave, but she held fast. "I apologize."

"Why? For being honest about how you feel?"

"I had no right. I've taken advantage of you enough, yet I never seem to remember that fact when we're alone together."

"Doesn't that tell you something?"

"What do you mean?"

"That we're both fighting something inevitable. I've never felt this way either."

He touched her chin. "Perhaps because you've never been in this situation before."

He didn't know how true his words were. She'd never traveled back in time, met a man from another culture, fallen in love with his helpless baby and, yes, him, too. But that's not what Jackson meant.

She placed her hand on his cheek and smiled into his troubled eyes. "Jackson, I haven't lived in a nunnery all my life. I know this will shock you, but I do know what lust feels like."

He went very still, his whole body tense. "What do you mean?"

She took a deep breath. "I thought I was in love once."

"You were engaged?"

She didn't want to lie to him. She and Cleve hadn't been formally engaged in the sense that he'd given her a ring. They'd talked of marriage, but always as a vague event, sometime in the future. But that was enough, though, wasn't it? "Yes," she whispered.

"You gave yourself to him?"

She heard the censure in his voice, despite his efforts to keep his tone low and neutral. Still, his criticism hurt. More than anything, she wanted to explain. He would never understand the morals and standards at the end of the twentieth century, though. They were 150 years apart in time—and at least that much in ethics.

"Don't tell me you never went to bed with a woman besides your wife," she asked instead of answering him directly.

"That's different."

"Because you're a man."

"Yes! And because I never seduced an innocent young woman into giving me something intended for her husband," he said, his whisper fierce, his body poised for flight.

She bit her bottom lip and swallowed a sob. Right or wrong morally, he was going to understand the comparison. And Cleve hadn't seduced her. Their attraction had been mutual—hadn't it?

"I can't explain what happened. You won't understand."

"As usual," he added, his voice a frustrated sneer.

"If I told you the truth, would you believe me, no matter how far-fetched, no matter how improbable my explanation seemed?"

"I can't guarantee that I'll believe something I haven't heard yet!"

"Jackson, I *know* you won't believe me," she said, gripping his unbuttoned shirt in both hands. "If I thought there was any way I could explain where I'm really from and tell you how I got here. I would in a heartbeat." She dropped her arms to her side. "Don't you understand how much it hurts me to keep all this to myself? I wish I could tell you. I wish you'd tell me that you'd understand."

He looked at her as though he'd never seen her before. "You expect too much," he said finally.

As she stood in that small bedroom where she'd chosen to sleep that night, Jackson walked away. She knew she'd given him too much to think about: Admitting she wasn't the innocent young miss he'd assumed she was, telling him that she couldn't explain where she was from, asking him to believe her no matter what.

She was expecting him to behave as though he loved her. She hugged her arms around herself and shivered in the cool night air. Just because she'd fallen in love with him didn't mean he returned the feeling. As a matter of fact, he'd be foolish to fall in love with someone as inappropriate, as out of place, as she was.

A whimper came from the nursery. She hurried toward the sound, thankful for a distraction from her young charge. Anything to take her mind off her compounding problems.

Randi settled herself and Rose on a quilt in a rare ray of sunshine that slanted through the third-floor window. The rain had stopped sometime during the night, but the ground was a muddy mess. They wouldn't be going outside yet. Rose continued to teethe, fussing and fretting while she gummed the hard biscuits Suzette provided.

"I know you're grouchy," Randi said to the restless infant, "but you're going to have to get through this on your own. I don't have any medicine to give you. I wish I did, sweetie."

Rose pushed up on her hands and rocked back and forth. She'd be crawling any day now, as soon as she got her knees and elbows coordinated. Randi smiled when she imagined Rose's delight at learning to crawl, then walk. They'd have to baby-proof the room, and put a gate across the stairs.

Her smile faded as she remembered she wouldn't be here to see Rose take her first step. She wouldn't be anywhere near Black Willow Grove. Either her plans would work and she'd return to her time, or she'd run— as far as possible from the flood waters of the Mississippi.

She was not going to drown in this plantation house—but Rose and Jackson would, if they didn't heed the warnings—hers and the ones given by a rising river and the plentiful rains.

Nature was teasing them today, giving them a glimpse of blue skies and fluffy white clouds, tempting new green leaves to unfurl and faces to lift to heaven. But the fair weather wouldn't last. Or, if the flood came from upstream, the sun would be shining on mile after mile of flooded fields, with no human face left to witness the destruction.

Randi sighed as she picked up her sketch paper and pencil. She should be more pleased with her efforts. The room she'd drawn looked complete, as much as she could remember. Pretty good work, if she did say so herself. If this didn't get her back home, she couldn't imagine what would.

She patted the baby absently on the back. Had she forgotten any details in the drawing? Anything that would make her sketch so inaccurate that she couldn't get back home? Her eyes scanned the depths of the room she'd drawn, trying to recall any chair or folded quilt, small table or leather-clad trunk that she'd left out.

"Did you draw that, Miz Randi?" Suzette asked in an amazed voice from behind her.

"Yes, I did. It's a room I remember from . . . from my home."

"It's real pretty." Suzette leaned closer to study the sketch. "You must be rich," she whispered in awe.

Randi looked up into Suzette's young, open face. "Why do you say that?" No one had ever confused her for someone with wealth.

"Because your folks have so many things they've got to put them all in one room," Suzette said, as serious as could be.

Randi chuckled. "This isn't where my parents live," she tried to explain. "This is a place I visited. It's a museum. Do you have those here?"

"I don't think so. What is it?"

Randi thought for a moment, absently patting Rose's back. "A museum is a place where things are collected. Some of them are valuable, some are just special. They put these things in big rooms and everyone can come and look."

Suzette peered at the sketch once more. "These beds and chairs and tables are special?"

"Where I come from they are. They're rare. They're very old."

"You like old things?" Suzette asked incredulously. "Why would you like old if you can have new?"

Randi smiled, holding up the drawing and looking again at the detail. She'd seen the items dozens of times, but she'd never thought of them as special. Just things to dust and straighten. Not things that someone had once used daily and treasured. "Maybe because someone else once loved them."

Suzette shook her head, but didn't make any more comments. Just as well, Randi thought, because she had no more answers.

Rose began to fret. Since it was her lunchtime, Suzette took her off to the rocking chair for feeding. The gentle sound of wood on wood, the occasional scuffing noise of Suzette's thin leather slipper, provided a peaceful setting that Randi craved.

She stretched out on the quilt, basking in the sunlight, her thoughts turned inward. She felt sad, disturbed by what she'd said to Suzette and about the facts she knew of the past.

What if she couldn't go back? What if she had to run

away instead? Where would she go? She had no money and very few real skills or knowledge of these times.

She took out fresh sheet of paper and idly began to doodle, something that had often helped her think when she was younger. Often, she'd talk with friends on the phone, then look down a half-hour later and find an elaborate, palatial home. Or sometimes a cartoonish figure of the person they'd been talking about.

Today she let her mind roam free, wandering through her options. If she stayed here, she might be able to get a job as a governess. She'd travel north, away from the reality of slavery and plantation life. She hadn't seen anything terrible at Black Willow Grove, but just knowing that people were kept against their will, forced to work long hours with no hope for a future, made her shudder. Besides, a war was coming that had been fought mostly down south, if she recalled correctly. She didn't want to be caught in the middle of two armies.

She propped her chin in her hand and tried to imagine not seeing her family again. The thought was too awful to consider. They'd always been close; she couldn't imagine not walking into her mother's kitchen, or watching television with her dad. And her brother's new family . . . she'd just gotten to know Darla well. They'd planned a ladies' night out in Memphis for Tanya's twenty-first birthday next month. They'd sat at Darla's table and laughed over whether they should splurge for a male stripper. After all, Tanya, the baby of the family, should have a twenty-first birthday she'd always remember.

Randi frowned as she realized she might not be there for her sister's birthday, just as she wouldn't see Rose's first steps or find out if Jackson survived the flood. If she ran away, she'd never know.

If she stayed, she might die, too. At the least, she'd be surrounded by water. Acres and acres of muddy brown river. She couldn't stand the image; she'd never survive the reality of smelling, watching, and eventually having to wade or swim through the flood.

She leaned her head down and closed her eyes. When she opened them, she saw not the Mississippi, but the sheet of paper. She'd sketched Jackson, a look of longing and loneliness on his face.

Randi closed her eyes again. She couldn't have Jackson. Even if she stayed to save them from the flood, he was not hers to love. He belonged to another culture, another time, and no matter how much she wanted him, they were as different as night and day.

As if nature wanted to emphasize her point, the shaft of sunlight disappeared. The nursery seemed instantly less vibrant, less alive. Even the gently rocking sound that had been so comforting fell silent. Rose was asleep in Suzette's arms, and Randi lay on the quilt with the sketch of the man who was breaking her heart without knowing, without ever believing, how or why.

Randi escaped the house full of people the next day by convincing Lebeau that she needed to go to Franklin's plantation to check on George's broken arm. The butler hadn't wanted her to leave Black Willow Grove; he frowned and said he'd have to check with Master Jackson. She'd stood her ground, though, and they'd left the plantation without Jackson showing himself.

She supposed he didn't want to see her, loose woman that she was. Well, she couldn't help how he felt, and she wouldn't apologize for what she'd done. By the time she and Cleve had progressed to a physical relationship, she'd thought she was in love. Cleve had been so much fun, so clever. Only later did she realize that most of what he'd said and done had been an act.

Whatever his faults, they weren't her concern any longer. At one time she'd thought they'd have a very special bond between them forever, but circumstances had changed. She didn't hate Cleve; she'd simply accepted his faults and moved on with her life.

Moving on from Jackson, Rose, and all the other people she'd met in the past would be entirely different. She wouldn't be able to forget them, no matter how long she lived. And she'd always imagine what might have been, if they'd lived under different circumstances. In the same century, for example. If they shared the same values, or wanted the same things in life.

How in the world could she be so attracted to a man she had absolutely nothing in common with?

"Whoa," Lebeau called to the team, pulling the buggy to a halt in front of the plantation house.

He stepped down into the mud that now made up the driveway of Franklin's home, which was closer to the river. Randi smelled the muddy water, felt it seep into her body. For a moment, as she looked across a narrow field toward the newly mended levee, she panicked. Sucking in lungsful of oxygen, she grabbed on to the buggy seat and told herself that she was in no immediate danger. No raging torrent on the other side of the earthen dam threatened to take her under. She felt with all her heart and soul that today was not her day to die. Still, she couldn't help shuddering as she relived the feeling of helplessness she'd experienced as a child.

"Miss Randi?"

She blinked, looking away from the line of trees swaying gently in the breeze. "Sorry. I was just . . . thinking."

He frowned. "Are you feeling poorly?"

"No, nothing like that. Let's see if Mr. Franklin is home."

Lebeau helped her down. Fortunately, where he'd "parked" the buggy was close enough to the house that only her soles got damp walking the few steps to the porch. She'd given up on trying to force her feet into the uncomfortable shoes and had gone back to her Keds.

She wondered if she'd be the one to ask about George. Probably. Lebeau and the rest of the servants she'd met seemed reluctant to speak to the plantation owners. She'd never get used to that color-coded deference, even if she did have to stay here.

"Is Mr. Franklin at home?" she asked the black woman who answered the door.

"Yes, ma'am. Please, come in."

Lebeau followed her into the house, keeping his distance, holding his hat in hand. She wouldn't have thought it of him after their first meeting, but she welcomed his silent presence. She didn't feel quite so alone, knowing he was there, knowing he was one more link to Jackson and Black Willow Grove.

Within a few minutes, she'd met with the blustering planter, who'd seemed genuinely confused about why she wanted to check the bandages on the man she'd helped the doctor treat two days ago. But he granted permission for her to see to the wound, as long as she didn't keep the others from their chores.

She promised she'd be good, then headed back to the buggy. Lebeau drove her around back to the slave quarters, where Franklin had told her the man was working with the "grannies." She wondered what in the world a strong guy like him was doing for the older women.

She found out minutes later when they pulled up to a whitewashed building that was a littler larger than the other cabins, which she assumed were the houses where the slaves lived. Two elderly women sat on the front steps watching over a dozen children, who raced around the muddy yard, grinning and yelling like children everywhere. They looked dirty but happy. The scene reminded her of schoolyard scenarios in her own time, except for the homemade, rough-spun garments the kids wore.

But she couldn't forget that these were slave children, destined to spend the next ten or fifteen years under a doomed system. They'd be adults before they were free, and then what would happen to them?

"Miss Randi?"

Lebeau again startled her out of her morbid thoughts. "Sorry. Do you see George?" She shaded her eyes against the noontime sun.

"Stay here with the buggy. I'll go ask about him."

She did as he suggested, watching the children play until the "grannies" called them in for lunch. With a sigh, Randi thought of her nieces and nephew, missing them so much. Without the laughter of the children, the atmosphere of the slave quarters seemed eerily quiet. They were all out working, in the fields or the house, and their cabins stood as a row of silent reminders on the Southern way of life.

She'd never thought of herself as part of the plantation culture because her relatives had come to Tennessee after the war, working for other farmers, probably in a similar capacity as these slaves. Her grandfather had leased land and grown cotton; her father had gotten off the farm to become a welder, then a supervisor at a small plant that produced iron and steel frames. None of her relatives had been wealthy people, but none of them had been owned by someone else, either. She wanted to believe she had a lot in common with the workers, but knew that one difference made comparisons impossible.

Lebeau came around the side of the building with George, his arm still bandaged and splinted. She just hoped they'd successfully disinfected the cut the other night. What she wouldn't give for some hydrogen peroxide, sterile gauze, and antibiotic ointment.

After Lebeau helped her down from the buggy seat, she turned to George and smiled. "How are you feeling?"

"I . . . I'm fine, Miss Randi."

"Mr. Franklin seemed confused to see me, and I suppose you are too. I just wanted to come by and check your wound."

"My wife treated it and changed the bandage," he said proudly. "She's a good healer." A little more shyly, he added, "My wife said those were fine stitches you set into my tough old hide. I thank you very much for that."

"You're very welcome. And if your wife is familiar with folk medicine, she probably knows more than that quack who was here the other night," Randi said, not trying too hard to hide her disappointment over both the doctor's skills and his attitude. What these people needed was a good E.R.!

She thought the saw the worker smile, but she wasn't sure. "Okay, then," she said. "Do you mind if I take a look?"

"No, Miz Randi, but you don't have to do that," he said, almost apologetically.

"I'd feel bad if your wound got infected and I didn't try to help."

He shrugged, obviously uncomfortable with her attention. Lebeau stood back, watching silently as she unwound the cotton fabric from the area of the splints where the wound was located. Being careful with the break, she removed the softer cotton pad from the lacerated cut—and gasped.

"What in the world is that on your arm?"

The man looked down. "Tobacco. My wife soaks the leaf in rum. She says it helps to heal a cut."

Tobacco? What an odd remedy. She peeled back the dampened piece, surprised to see the flesh appear smooth and healing nicely. "Whatever your wife is using appears to be working, but I wouldn't keep it on too long. I'd say your arm was going to be safe from infection, as long as it stays clean. Just don't get it wet with any water from the river that hasn't been boiled."

He nodded. Randi re-bound the injury, checked to make sure the splint was tight, and told him to be careful.

"Mas'r Franklin has me paintin' the meetin' house," he explained. "The work's not hard."

"I'll be back in a few days so I can check the stitches again. They should stay in for a week. If I don't get back, have your wife remove them with scissors she's held over a flame."

The man thanked her, and she and Lebeau set off for Black Willow Grove.

No matter where she went—back to her own time or north, away from the flood and this way of life—at least she knew she'd helped one person's life. Now if she could only get Jackson to listen to her. If only she could save him and Rose from a terrible, tragic fate.

Chapter Seventeen

A messenger arrived late in the day from Randolph, advising Jackson that a packet had arrived from up-river. It had had a difficult time docking due to high water and strong currents, but according to the messenger, the boat had room for passengers who wanted to continue downriver to New Orleans.

Jackson received the message with barely concealed joy. He'd found the older couple to be tolerable house-guests, requiring little entertainment or companionship, thankful for meals and cordial company. The two young lawyers tested his patience with their need for gaming, however, and pulled everyone else into their conversations of trials and judges, families and friends.

And then there was the Widow Sanderson, a healthy young woman who wanted a new liaison in the worst possible way. She hadn't gone so far as to show up unannounced in his bedroom, but he'd found her about the house at all hours of the day, seeking to engage him in conversations that could quickly change to far more.

When he looked at her coifed hair and calculating smiles, he kept comparing her to the usually unkempt and unconventional Randi Galloway.

She and the widow had at least one thing in common, however: Both had given themselves to another man. The thought caused Jackson to tighten his grip on the pen he held and clench his jaw in frustration. At least the widow had married the man she'd lain with, probably *after* the nuptials. Randi hadn't waited for sacred vows, but had jumped—with her usual lack of planning or foresight—into an intimate relationship with an unsuitable man.

Would she ever change? Had she learned from her ill-fated love affair? Probably not. She was willing to leap into a relationship with him as long as he didn't ask questions of her home, or her knowledge of floods, healing arts, and infant care. Her skills and attitude were too unusual to accept without question. She asked too much.

As he sat in his study, trying to get some work done on the plantation's account books while he waited for his guests to take their leave, he wondered if Randi wanted to go with them. She'd said she needed to get away from Black Willow Grove and the coming flood. Would this newly docked packet be the way out for her, too?

He threw the pen down in frustration. He owed it to her to mention the boat's arrival and its offer to take on passengers. After last night's disturbing encounter on the third floor, he wasn't looking forward to seeing her. No matter how much he told himself she was a foolish, weak, loose woman, he still wanted her—just as he had before she'd shocked him with her revelations.

Pushing away from the desk, he stalked across the room and into the hallway. Darley and Templeton were near the front door, grinning and giving him a wave down the corridor. He offered a weak smile and a dismissive wave in return before making a quick decision to use the back stairs. He wasn't in any mood to chat with the two lawyers, especially since they might insist on getting in one last game of craps or try their newly developed "skill" at monte.

Turning into the stairwell beside the butler's closet, he took the narrow, dark stairs two at a time. If he was going to see Randi again, he'd prefer that he get the encounter over with quickly. If she decided to leave, then so be it. She'd be out of his life for good. Somehow, he knew that once she left Black Willow Grove, she wouldn't come back.

"Miss Galloway," he called out at the top of the stairs, making sure she could hear his footsteps so she wouldn't accuse him of sneaking up on her. He'd found her past accusations amusing, since he'd rarely tried to keep silent. She was so often lost in her own thoughts that a gaggle of noisy geese could have waddled through the room without her raising an eyebrow.

He strolled into Rose's nursery, not surprised to see Randi struggling to rise from the quilt on the floor, fighting her skirts and petticoats. His daughter was sitting up, grinning and shaking what appeared to be a dried gourd in her hand as though it were made of the finest silver. He started to say something, but stopped himself. What did it matter if Randi chose common items, as long as Rose's toys were safe and made her happy?

"What is it?" Randi asked, her eyes wide and uncertain.

"Nothing to be excited about," he said quickly. She was no doubt thinking of disasters like the breach of Franklin's levee. "A packet has landed in Randolph. The guests are leaving."

"I'm sure they'll be happy to get to their destination."

"Yes, but that's not what I wanted to talk about." He

stood a little straighter to counteract the tension in his body. "You've mentioned several times that you couldn't stay. You now have the option of leaving on the packet, going back to New Orleans or wherever you're from."

"Leaving?" Her expression of surprise, even shock, seemed even more dramatic due to her paled complexion.

"Yes! You've told me over and over that you're frightened of the water, that you believe we'll be flooded, even that we would all die. Here's your chance to get out now, before the disaster you predicted."

A dozen expressions flickered across her face. Thoughtful contemplation, followed by confusion, doubt, panic. She shuddered, her arms stiff at her sides. He resisted the urge to cross the floor, take her into his arms and tell her everything would be fine. If he offered comfort and security instead of giving her the option she needed, he wouldn't be fair.

"I can't leave on the packet."

"Why?"

She turned away, looking down at Rose. "It's going south, to New Orleans, right?"

"That's correct."

"If it floods here, it will flood there. Besides, I'm going north, not south."

"Why?"

"There are too many customs down here that I can't accept."

"I thought you said you were from the South."

"Yes, but . . . I can't explain, okay? Just trust me when I say that I can't tolerate slavery or these differences in class. It's ridiculous, you know? Why can't people just accept each other for who they are inside, not how much money they have or the color of their skin?"

Why indeed? He'd asked himself the same question hundreds of times in the past. Far into the past, he amended. As a child and a young man, he'd hated the system that labeled him inferior because of his background and lack of money. When he grew older, he'd accepted the system and learned to live with society's restraints. He'd become part of the system, which was all that Randi saw in him.

He dared not reveal his other side. "You cannot change society because you think it unfair."

"No, I don't think I can. That's why I have to leave."

"To go north."

"Or back to my own . . . home."

Why had she hesitated on such a simple word? He wanted to ask, to demand the truth once and for all. Perhaps if he knew the whole story, he wouldn't feel this fascination with her. He'd be able to go on with his life, concentrating on the important task of protecting his family and land from floods, then focusing on his private life by finding a suitable wife.

When Rose reached up her arms to Randi, the sight made him smile despite his dark mood. His daughter was a little angel, especially when she wasn't fussing and fretting. Randi had blamed teething for his daughter's foul humor, but he suspected the baby was now happier due to the attention she received from her new governess.

If Randi left, Rose would lose the connection to a woman who showed her such care and affection.

"I'm pleased you aren't leaving today. Rose would miss you."

Randi turned wide, uncertain eyes toward him. "Yes, she probably will."

"Then you still plan on leaving sometime?"

"I must. I can't stay in this place forever. I miss my family, my customs. I'm trying to be honest with you about the fact that I must leave sometime soon."

"One of the few things," he couldn't help adding.

"I've told the truth about many things, but you don't believe me."

"Tell me everything and perhaps I will."

"No, you wouldn't. You'd think I was crazy."

"I don't see madness in your eyes," he admitted.

"And I don't see open-minded acceptance in yours."

He took a deep breath and raised his chin. "Then we're at our usual impasse. My guests are leaving and I must give my farewells."

"Don't let the widow linger too long. She may decide to stay."

Was that jealousy he heard in her voice? Not hardly. Randi must know that she couldn't be compared to the Widow Sanderson. He'd never given that lady the impression that he was interested in her affections, whereas with Randi, he'd been quite clear how much he wanted her in his bed.

But only in his bed. She would never be a suitable wife for a planter in this society, especially since she was opposed to all the customs upon which planter society placed so much importance.

"I'm certain the widow will be leaving promptly," he said as he turned and walked out of the nursery. He stopped at the door. "Unlike you, she has a destination in mind, and she knows her circumstances."

"You're right, Jackson," Randi said, snuggling up to Rose. "I've always had a problem with that. But my parents always told me that I could do whatever I wanted, if I wanted it enough. I believed them."

He didn't have anything else to say, so he let her have the last word. With as much frustration as he'd felt coming up to the third floor, he went back down—to say good-bye to his guests, and to try to get his life back in order.

Randi hugged a sleepy Rose and watched as the houseguests left Black Willow Grove in Jackson's carriage for the awaiting paddle wheeler in Randolph. She could have gone. Jackson was ready to let her go.

And why not, since she'd told him about her ill-fated love affair with another man, rebuffed his advances, and refused to tell him the truth about where she was from? Jackson was a man who placed a lot of value in having the very best, and to him, she simply wasn't good enough. She'd been looked down on before, by schoolmates and coworkers who placed more value on the right clothes, shoes, and accessories than they did on personal values and friendship. But former social slights hadn't hurt like this. She'd never felt as though a part of her heart had been stomped on.

The odd thing was that Jackson found her both morally *and* socially inferior. He hadn't mentioned anything about a permanent relationship—not that she could ever agree to one—but he'd obviously wanted to fool around. She supposed he'd never considered the fact that he was applying a huge double standard.

"I should have expected as much," she said to a cuddly Rose, who'd nestled against her chest, so trusting, so sweet. God, how could she leave this baby? Maybe she could take her back to 1999, away from the flood and certain death. Was there anything wrong with that—other than the fact that Jackson would be devastated . . .

But would he be any more devastated knowing that he'd caused his daughter's death by remaining stubborn to the end? Randi didn't know. Maybe he would rather he and his daughter perish together than be separated by 150 years.

Randi rocked back and forth, watching the carriage disappear in the distance. She hummed "Candle in the Wind" to Rose, since the baby liked the melody so much.

"You're goin' ta spoil that baby rotten," Suzette gently chided from the doorway.

Randi turned toward her, still swaying back and forth. "I know, but I love to hold her. She's such a sweet little thing. So trusting." And she didn't judge, didn't ask questions. Randi wasn't sure that she couldn't have loved her own child more than she loved Rose—not that she'd had the chance to find out.

Her biggest regret in life had been that she'd never gotten to hold her child. She'd been unconscious from hitting her head. By the time she woke up, there was no baby. Her arms had felt as empty as her womb.

Reluctantly, she settled Rose onto the crib mattress. She hugged herself to keep the warmth and cherish the unique baby smell. "I'll miss you," she whispered.

She couldn't take Rose away with her. As much as she loved Jackson's child, she would be changing history to try something that bold. Besides, Jackson would be devastated. He'd never understand why Randi had left. He probably wouldn't believe her if she left a note. He'd assume she'd gone north, and probably would spend his life looking for his child.

At least he wouldn't be here when the flood came, a little voice reminded her. Maybe that was the only way to get him away from Black Willow Grove. Or maybe she could just make him *think* she'd stolen his child.

Excited by this new idea, she tiptoed from the room, leaving Suzette to watch over Rose as she slept. Her sketch was complete, but she could put that aside for now. What she needed was a plan to get away from the plantation without anyone knowing where she'd gone.

Randi went back to Franklin's plantation the next day to check on George's arm. She sure hoped he continued to improve, because the thought of him getting a life-threatening infection that could cause an amputation made her green around the gills, as her mom liked to say. What did plantation owners do with field hands who only had one good arm?

"Lebeau," she asked as they traveled the muddy rutted road to Eastland, "what would happen to George if he lost his arm?"

"What do you mean?"

"Would Mr. Franklin sell him, do you think? Or would George be given different duties?"

"Depends on what jobs need to be done. There's always plenty of work, but a one-armed man can't do too much. Master Franklin might just sell him."

"Like to a neighbor?"

"Not usually. Causes too many problems."

"You mean like the person who bought him might think he got a bad deal?"

"No, that's not it."

"What, then?"

Lebeau sighed and flicked the backs of the horses with the reins. "If George is always thinking 'bout his wife and children over at Eastland, he might not keep his mind on his work."

"You don't think the new owner would buy the whole family?"

Lebeau shrugged. "Why should he?"

Randi couldn't believe Lebeau was asking her why someone should be civil or caring, especially since he was also a slave. Shouldn't he understand?

"I'll bet Jackson would buy the whole family," she said. "He'd understand why a man would want to be with his family."

"Yes, he would," Lebeau said in a low, thoughtful tone. His expression seemed closed. He sat in silence, looking only at the team, and Randi decided to be quiet for awhile. Maybe she shouldn't ask these questions, but she didn't have any other way to find out.

She stayed silent as long as she could, but before they arrived at Eastland, she had something she had to find out. "I asked Suzette what she'd do if she were free. She didn't have any idea."

"You asked that girl about being free?" Lebeau asked incredulously.

"Well, yes, I did. Is that wrong?"

"Why in the world would you ask her something like that?" he asked suspiciously, his dark eyes narrowed as he finally looked at her.

"Because I wanted to know! This way of life won't last forever, you know. Someday, you'll all be free."

"Are you some kind of abolitionist?"

"Suzette asked me that, too. Are you against abolitionists?"

"The whole South is against abolition."

"Yes, but you, personally? Surely you can't be against gaining your freedom." He didn't say anything, so she continued. "What would you do if you were free?"

He seemed to be thinking hard. The silence was broken only by the mud-cushioned footsteps of the horses and an occasional creak of the buggy.

"I expect that I'd go on being Jackson Durant's butler."

"Really? But why, if you could go anywhere, do anything you wanted?"

"Because . . ." He shook his head. "I shouldn't tell you this, but I'm going to so I can try to make you understand. I'd go on being his butler because I already am a free man. That doesn't mean a darn thing when you're black and in the South, though."

"You're not a slave? But you call him 'master' just like everyone else."

"No one knows, and I'm hoping you won't tell them. It's nobody's business but mine and Jackson's."

"One night, I overheard the two of you talking. I thought it was odd, but I couldn't imagine why. Now it makes sense."

"I call him 'mas'r' around the other slaves because it's expected."

"I can understand that, I suppose, since you're a role model."

Lebeau snorted. "I'm not trying to be any role model. I'm trying to make my life easier. I don't need them thinking I'm some uppity black man because I'm free and they're not."

"You don't care about your people?"

"Those people aren't mine, Miss Randi," Lebeau said, his eyes cold and assessing. "Those people belong to Jackson Durant. The two of us understand that. I sure hope you don't plan on upsetting things around Black Willow Grove."

Chapter Eighteen

"Jackson, I'd like to learn how to ride a horse," Randi announced the next morning just after breakfast.

She'd waited until he'd finished his meal, then approached him in the hallway. She hoped he'd be in a better mood now that he had his house back from all the guests and since the rain had held off another day.

"Why do you need to know how to ride?"

"Because everyone should know, don't you think?"

"Every lady," he said, brushing past her on his way toward the front door.

She closed her eyes for a second, feeling his insult deep beneath her skin. He was never going to let her forget that she'd gone to bed with someone who wasn't her husband. She supposed she should have lied to him, but that wasn't her style. She'd learned early in life that she couldn't keep up with lies, so she'd usually stuck to the truth. Just look at how poorly she'd lied when she'd first arrived here! Jackson had known all along she wasn't the governess he was expecting, she didn't know Miss Agnes Delacey, and she hadn't lost her trunk overboard from a paddlewheeler.

Still, he'd allowed her to stay and care for Rose. She hoped he'd tell her why before she left, but doubted he'd ever admit his feelings.

Catching up to him by running across the marble floor, she grabbed his arm before he went out the door. "Please, Jackson. I know you're frustrated with me, but I'd really love to learn how to ride. Couldn't we just call it payment for taking care of Rose?"

"Payment?"

"Yes," she said, getting irritated with him despite her vow to behave herself until she accomplished her goal— getting him and Rose away from Black Willow Grove. "People are usually paid for their services, aren't they? I'm not one of your slaves, although I know you're used to that particular system of keeping good help."

His face flushed with anger and he shook off her arm. "You go too far."

"Why, because I point out the obvious? Or because I had the nerve to touch you?"

Quicker than she could think, his hands closed around her upper arms and pulled her close. "I never denied you the right to touch me. In fact, I distinctly remember encouraging you to use whatever skills you possess to—"

She twisted out of his grasp, then slapped him as hard as she could across his cheek. Immediately horrified at what she'd done, she took a step back, then spun on her heel, picked up her skirts, and ran toward the rear of the house.

Flinging open the back door, she cut across the covered walkway, then ran as fast as she could toward the alleyway of flowering trees. White petals rained down on her as she pounded across the damp earth, her skirts pulled high, her lungs burning. She'd just reached the end of the corridor when she heard pounding of another kind.

She looked back in time to see a flash of red. Then a strong arm closed around her, lifting her against the heaving side of a horse that seemed on the verge of being out of control.

"Let me down!"

"Be still or I will. I doubt you'd survive being trampled, even though the ground is soft."

Randi immediately stilled. She'd seen the horror of broken bones in 1849; she had no desire to be a patient of that quack, Dr. Shelton.

"Relax. I'm pulling you up onto this horse because I'm certain you'll try to run again if I let you go."

"No, I—"

"Relax!"

With a command like that, how could she resist? Trying her best not to stiffen up, or pull against him, she let Jackson haul her onto the saddle of the nervous animal.

"I don't think your horse likes me here."

"If I can tolerate you, so can he."

Again, she felt his insult deep inside her soul. Biting her lip so she wouldn't say anything else, she sat silently across the saddle as they galloped away from the house.

How unlike the ride to Franklin's plantation that evening last week! This ride felt angry and stiff. She had no urge to melt into Jackson's warm body, nor did she sense any desire in him to hold her close. On the way to Eastland, he'd asked her to hold him around his neck, encouraged her to snuggle close. Now, he seemed to want to be as far from her as possible without shoving her off the saddle.

If he didn't want to be around her, why not just let her go? Why not let her run away, foolishly, without any food or money? Why not stop the horse, deposit her near the road, and tell her good riddance?

Jackson's actions didn't make any sense to her—not that she was in any emotional condition to consider his reasons rationally. The only thought that popped into her head was that he was carrying her off because he didn't want to murder his daughter's governess inside the house. She'd probably seen too many television shows, she rationalized.

They rode in silence for what seemed like a long time, but Randi knew it couldn't have been more than ten or fifteen minutes. The air was heavy with the smell of muddy water as Jackson urged the chestnut up the steep levee by the Mississippi. Randi's heart seemed to skip a beat as the horse faltered, then got his footing and surged to the top.

She gripped Jackson's coat lapel as he pulled the animal to a stop. The horse's sides heaved with exertion, and Randi felt the same when the reality of where they were hit her. Stretched before them was Old Man River, out of his banks and raging strong over willows and up the trunks of huge cottonwoods. Snags of driftwood spun and dove beneath the current, then reappeared farther downstream.

It was so similar to the time she and Russell had taken their driftwood raft out onto the river, only this was worse. Much worse.

"How long has it been this way?" she whispered.

"Not long. The packet was able to leave early yesterday, but I had word the current was running faster." He looked out over the wide expanse of river, then added, "I'm surprised."

She was, too, not to mention alarmed. "Doesn't this make people nervous? Surely they'll take extra precautions against the flood."

"I hope so."

When the horse shifted beneath them, Jackson started, as though he'd forgotten that they were still sitting together on the mount.

"Sit still," he told her before dismounting.

Within a few seconds, Randi was standing on the solid, damp ground. Through the soles of her feet, she could almost feel the power of the water as it rushed past, much too close for comfort.

"How sturdy is this levee?" she asked nervously, stepping back.

"Reinforced and packed solid," he said, walking the horse a few yards farther down the earthworks. "The best I can build."

I suppose I should be reassured by that comment, she told herself as she followed a respectful distance behind the chestnut.

Jackson didn't walk far. Apparently he'd found a dryer spot, because he loosened the girth, removed the saddle, and spread the blanket on the ground. Since there were no branches around, he tied the horse's reins to a ring on the saddle.

She hoped the animal didn't get spooked and leave them here. She wasn't ready to spend any more time than necessary beside the raging flood, especially when she kept seeing driftwood and dead animals floating and dipping past like log rides at Opryland.

"Sit," he said, motioning to the blanket.

There was barely room for two, but somehow they both managed to settle fairly comfortably on the ground. Jackson sat with his elbows propped on his spread knees, his black boots resting flat on the clay soil. Randi tucked her long skirts around her ankles and tried to keep her knees together by looping her arms beneath her legs.

"I apologize for the seating arrangements. I wasn't expecting this when I left the house."

"Then why not just go back? Why have you brought me out here, except to torture me with the sight of the river?"

"I didn't realize you'd consider it torture."

"Really? Maybe I wasn't clear about how terrified I am of the water."

"The water isn't that close to us here. This levee is plenty high to handle any flood that they've had in recorded history."

Randi remembered a few years back, when they'd called the Midwest's rising water a "five-hundred-year flood." She supposed Jackson wouldn't believe her if she reminded him that "recorded history" wasn't very long. "So why am I here?"

"I'm not sure," he said, looking down at the dirt. "I shouldn't have insulted you in the entryway."

"Are you apologizing?"

"Yes, damn it!"

"Well, I'm sorry I slapped you. That was . . . unexpected. I don't think I've ever slapped another person in my life."

"I'm glad to hear that. I don't surround myself with violent people, especially those in contact with my daughter."

"No, you don't want that. You don't have to worry, because I've never struck a child."

He nodded, then remained silent for several long seconds as he watched the water rush by. "Why won't you talk about yourself, Randi?"

"I already told you that you wouldn't believe me."

"And what if I don't?"

She drew in a deep breath. "You might send me away."

"You're leaving anyway. You've said so many times. What difference does it make if you leave in a few weeks or tomorrow?"

"I . . . I know I have to leave. I know what's going to happen."

"From your dreams?"

"Look, I can't tell you how, okay. Please don't keep asking."

He sighed. "All right, how about another question? You arrived here saying you'd come to care for Rose. Why did you say that?"

"Because I think that's true. She was a child without a mother and she needed me."

"Then she'll still need you after the flood passes."

Randi looked down at her lap, blinking back tears. All she could do was shake her head.

"Is there something special about my daughter? How did you know that she needed you?"

"I heard her crying . . . in my mind. I knew I had to find out why she was so sad."

"Certainly you've known other babies. You take care of her as though you've done this many times before."

"My nieces and nephew," she added quickly.

"If they mean so much to you, why aren't you home with them?"

"Because Rose needs me!" she said, the words rushing past her frozen throat. "She was lying there crying all alone, and I couldn't stand it! No baby should be like that, all alone, not knowing that someone loves her. Not feeling the warmth of hands holding her, not knowing a mother's love. No baby . . . no baby . . ."

She buried her head in her hands, her chest heaving as she cried for the baby she'd never held, for the life that a senseless accident had snuffed out so prematurely.

She barely felt his arms come around her, but then she was crying against his shirt, her hands clutching his lapels. He murmured words she couldn't understand, his hands stroking her back. When she shivered, he took off his coat and snuggled it around her shoulders.

"I'm sorry," she said, gulping in air. "I'm trying not to cry."

"Maybe it's best that you just go ahead. Let go of

whatever is bothering you. Sometimes the secrets we hold so dearly haunt us."

She knew his words held a more meaningful message than she could decipher right now. Her mind refused to think beyond the pain of losing her own child. Her secret . . . the one she didn't even talk about to her parents, because she didn't think they'd understand the emptiness she lived with every day.

"What baby haunts you, Randi?" Jackson asked softly.

"My baby," she answered, dabbing her eyes with her sleeves. "I lost my baby before she was old enough to live on her own."

"You had a miscarriage?"

"I had an accident. I slipped down the stairs on the ice last winter. One minute I was carrying in my groceries, the next I was lying at the bottom of the steps, bleeding. It happened so fast . . ."

She paused, sniffing back tears. Jackson held her, the rubbing of her back comforting as she relived the pain and shock.

"The doctors tried to help me, but I was bleeding inside. They said the placenta detached. She didn't have a chance of surviving at five months. They can work wonders with premature babies, but not that young."

"Of course not. Babies sometimes die."

"Not so much in my . . . home."

Thankfully, he didn't say anything about her near slip. "Losing the baby wasn't your fault. It was an accident."

"I know, but I keep thinking that I could have been more careful. I didn't know there was any ice on the steps. There hadn't been any snow or sleet. . . ."

"It was an accident," he said again gently.

"That's what my family kept telling me, over and over, until I believed them."

"And the father?"

"He didn't want to be a father. The pregnancy was an accident. I thought we'd been careful, but I still got pregnant."

"He didn't offer to marry you?"

"No, and I wouldn't have married him if he had. I didn't realize until too late that Cleve would have been a miserable husband and an even worse father. He was too tied up in himself, always scheming, always making big plans, telling me all these wonderful things." She shook her head, still not sure why she'd fallen for such a good-looking, insecure, untrustworthy man.

"I learned from him not to depend on anyone else for my happiness. I'd wanted our relationship to work out so much that I overlooked the fact that his stories never quite seemed true. I didn't ask him tough questions because I wanted to believe he was the kind of person he said he was.

"No, he would have made a terrible father. If my baby had lived, I would have let her see her dad, but when she was old enough to understand, I would have told her that she just couldn't believe at least half of anything he said."

Jackson eased his arm from around her shoulders. "Truth is important to you."

"Yes."

He sighed. "Sometimes people don't lie, but they don't tell the whole truth."

"If they know that the whole truth would make a difference, then they're lying."

"You're quick in your opinion. Are you so sure?"

"Yes."

"Then if I haven't told you the whole story of my life, does that mean I'm lying?"

"Only if there's something in your past that you're keeping from me on purpose, something you know would be important."

He squinted into the mid-morning haze, not answering her.

"What are you keeping from me, Jackson Durant?"

He still didn't answer, but turned to her, cradling her jaw in one hand. "I'm sorry about your baby." He kissed her sweetly on the forehead, then leaned back just a little and looked into her eyes. "And I was wrong to condemn you for thinking yourself in love."

This time he kissed her on the lips, gently at first, then stronger, more sure. She parted her mouth, kissing him back with a growing awareness that they'd shared some truth today. Maybe not the whole truth, but they'd come to a new level of understanding on this earthen levee. She hadn't expected to tell him about her baby. She hadn't expected him to comfort her, admit his mistake, and understand that society condemns far too easily.

He twisted over her, pushing her back onto the saddle blanket. When he broke their kiss to caress her neck, she breathed deeply. The smell of the muddy river was tempered by the slightly sweet smell of horse and the alluring scent of Jackson.

His fingers molded her breast through the cotton of her bodice and thin chemise. Her nipple was hard as a pebble and aching as she arched toward him. "I want you to touch me," she whispered into his ear. "I want to touch you."

Her words seemed to enflame him. He kissed her again, hard and urgent, and moved one leg over hers as he slipped his hand beneath her back.

"Damn all these hooks," he said, breaking the kiss as his hand skimmed down her spine.

She chuckled despite the situation—heavy arousal and urgent need. "I've said the same thing myself. I don't know how women stand these dresses."

"What? Never mind," he said, nuzzling her neck. "I'm

insane to make love to you on a levee in broad daylight. On a saddlecloth, in the dirt."

"Then I'm insane, too, because I would have let you," she said, hugging him close. "I still would, except maybe I'd ask if we could go somewhere more private."

"Are you sure?" he asked, pulling back to look into her eyes.

"Yes, I'm sure. I may be wrong again, but I don't think so. I've wanted you for a long time, too. I knew we shouldn't. I knew you didn't trust me, maybe even that you didn't like me."

"I didn't understand you."

She smiled lovingly at him. "You still don't."

He smiled back. His expression, along with his tousled hair and rumpled shirt, made him appear young and carefree. "I'm willing to listen."

"Then maybe I will tell you . . . sometime. I can't promise," she warned as she ran her hand through his raven-black hair.

He kissed her again, deeply but less urgently. Gently, but thoroughly. She knew he was still aroused; she felt the hardness against her thigh.

"What is going to happen now?" she whispered when the kiss ended.

"Arrange our clothes. Saddle the horse. Go back to the house."

"Will you teach me how to ride?"

"A horse?" he asked, grinning down at her.

She pushed against his shoulder. "Yes, a horse. I think I can manage the other."

"Really?" he answered, rolling off her and kneeling on the blanket. "I may test your skills . . . later."

"I hope you do," she said, pushing herself up on her elbows. "I've always been good at taking tests."

Chapter Nineteen

Jackson knew he couldn't run upstairs to his bedroom with his daughter's governess in the middle of the day, but he had big plans for later that night. He was certain his intentions showed clearly because Lebeau greeted him with a raised eyebrow as he eased Randi off the horse onto the front porch.

"Suzette was looking for Miss Randi," Lebeau told them.

"What's wrong?" she asked, brushing dirt off her skirts.

"Little Miss Rose is running a fever. She wanted your advice."

"I'll go up to her right away."

"I'll go with you," Jackson said, dismounting quickly and handing the reins to Lebeau. "Would you have him taken around to the stable?"

Lebeau nodded. "I don't think it's anything serious with Miss Rose."

"I'm sure it's not," Randi said over her shoulder as

263

she hurried to the house. "Probably just a normal temperature with her teething."

Jackson followed, watching the sway of her skirts as she walked quickly up the stairs. He resisted the urge to reach out and grab her hips through the muslin of her dress. Her body—what he'd felt of it before he realized they were about to make love in broad daylight on the top of a levee—had been firm, yet nicely rounded.

He thought back to the first time he'd seen her and how she'd been dressed. The odd shirt with stripes across the bodice had emphasized the swell of her breasts, and the soft, plush fabric had felt very inviting. The blue trousers had been molded to her legs, clearly showing the round curves of her bottom and the tempting vee where her legs joined.

He wondered if she still possessed the strange clothing—and perhaps if she would wear the items for him in private.

"Suzette?" Randi asked when she reached the top of the stairs.

They walked into the nursery to the sound of Rose's fretting. Jackson hadn't realized how uncommon the intermittent crying had been lately until he heard his daughter fussing again.

"Miz Randi, she's a little warm and flushed. I don't think she's serious-ill, but I thought you should look at her."

"Come here, precious," Randi said, taking the baby from Suzette. She bent her blond head close to Rose's head; her hair was nearly the same color as Randi's own. Jackson noticed that if anyone saw them together, they'd think Randi was Rose's mother.

The thought intrigued him. . . .

"Let's look at your gums," she said, walking with Rose toward the window. "Suzette, would you bring me a clean, wet cloth please?"

Randi carefully washed her hand, then inserted a finger in Rose's mouth despite her protests. "Jackson, come here and help, please. You're tall."

His surprise was short-lived as he walked to where they stood. She handed him the baby. "Try to hold her still so I can see her teeth. I think one of the upper ones is coming through, which is probably why she's fussy and a little feverish."

Between the two of them, they managed to accomplish the task, although at one point he thought he heard a muffled giggle coming from Suzette across the room. She wasn't accustomed to seeing him caring for his child, but he felt a sense of accomplishment in helping Randi check his daughter's mouth.

"Yes, there it is. I sure wish I had some ice or teething medication," Randi said.

"It's nearly May," he reminded her.

"I know that. I wish you had an ice maker."

"Why would anyone want to make ice?"

She looked at him as though he were crazy. "To preserve food, cool down drinks, treat baby gums. I could name a dozen more reasons."

He frowned, wondering how she'd come up with the idea of making something available only in nature. Randi Galloway had the most powerful imagination he'd ever encountered. As he stood near the window and gazed over his land, his thoughts weren't nearly as creative as hers. Whereas he'd once lived by his wits, he now thrived on the orderly planting, thinning, weeding, and picking of cotton.

There were few ways to improve production beyond taking good care of the plants. He'd increased his profits by using his workers more effectively, making sure they were healthy. In some cases, he'd given papers of manumission, freeing them to become wage earners who'd stayed on to share their skills with others. Most of the improvements he'd made to Black Willow Grove he'd learned at his first plantation in northern Louisiana.

However, in none of his experiences had he discovered a place where women wore trousers, sported short hair, dreamed of ways to make ice, or could treat serious injuries with the skill of a surgeon.

While he pondered Randi's unique perspective, she took the baby from his arms. "You might as well go, Jackson. I'm going to stay with Rose and see if I can help her. She likes me to rub her gums when they hurt, and that's about all I can do to help."

"Very well," he said, resisting the urge to kiss his daughter's downy hair . . . and Randi's soft, pink lips. "I'll see you later."

"I hope," she said, the wistful quality of her voice making him stop and smile.

Before he said or did anything revealing in front of Suzette, he turned and walked quickly down the stairs. He had to get his mind off his attraction to Randi and start thinking about what else he could do to ensure Black Willow Grove's safety.

One thing he could do was take extra precautions with the house, since Randi kept insisting that it would be destroyed in a flood. To his knowledge, large houses like his were never harmed extensively by rising water. For one thing, they were elevated slightly so at least two feet of standing water were necessary to get inside the house. If water did rise that high, some plaster and flooring would need repairs, but the structure itself would not be damaged. He'd heard of levee breaks near a frame house that caused a flimsy structure to be swept away, but that could hardly be compared to a house as large and well-built as his, more than a mile from the river.

Still, so she would be reassured, he'd build a second levee around the house. Workers would take dirt from the closer field, which he'd planned to plant corn in this coming month. The disruption would be small since the levee didn't need to be more than two to three feet tall.

His pace quickened as he descended the stairs. When Randi saw he was serious, she'd feel much more sure of their safety. Then she'd stop talking about leaving Black Willow Grove—and him.

From the third-floor nursery, Randi watched the men build a new levee around the house. She saw Jackson, too, striding among the workers, black dirt clinging to his boots and pants—the same pants that covered his legs earlier, when they'd lain together on that small blanket on a very different levee.

As she watched them work, she realized what Jackson was telling her: She was safe. He was building this new levee to show her a flood wouldn't threaten the house. She could stay dry inside this grand building, and didn't need to leave Rose—or him.

She wished she could believe, but history wouldn't have lied about the fate of Black Willow Grove. Other homes had survived; she'd visited them as a teenager with her high school classmates on field trips, and once her family had taken a vacation to Natchez.

Besides, the museum was built on this exact spot, according to the books. The land looked a little different. The trees that grew around this plantation house had disappeared years before the museum was built. The river was in about the right spot, though, and the slight hills looked the same, except without telephone lines, fences, or roads.

She'd grown to love this house. Every time she thought about the destruction to come, she became sad. Of course, it was difficult to think beyond the deaths of Rose and Jackson. She had to find a way to save them. Something awful was going to happen, but he'd never see it coming if he was so certain they were safe behind two levees.

Rose had dropped off into a restless sleep. Randi decided to go downstairs and look into her fanny pack one more time. Perhaps she'd overlooked something that could help Rose deal with this teething pain. Maybe an aspirin, which could be ground into powder and given to the baby in some mashed-up fruit. Under normal circumstances she'd never give adult aspirin to an infant, but she didn't have much choice if she wanted to relieve Rose's pain and fever.

She tiptoed from the room, then hurried down the stairs. After locking the door, she knelt beside the bed and pulled the fanny pack free of the bed slats.

The familiar imitation leather pouch felt good in her hands. She longed to go back to her comfortable jeans and pullover top, but didn't dare. She was lucky that she'd been accepted so warmly by Jackson's servants. Showing up in twentieth-century clothing would be frowned upon by everyone, from Jackson to Lebeau to Birdie, even though they'd accepted her tennis shoes without too many odd looks.

Dashing back upstairs, she sat in the rocker as spring sunshine slanted through the wavy panes of glass. She unzipped the fanny pack, then placed her wallet, car keys, and lipstick on her lap. She felt around the inside seams and found nothing but an empty, balled up foil candy wrapper and a fuzzball of indistinct origin.

"Darn it," she whispered. She would just love to have something useful from her own time. Medication, deodorant, disposable razors, toothpaste. Who needed a wallet and car keys when there weren't any places to show your ID and no car to drive? Heck, there weren't any roads to drive on even if her 1992 Beretta suddenly materialized like Cinderella's coach.

Randi flipped open her wallet, turning to the photos of her family. Russell and Darla with little Sandy, taken at one of the mall photo shops in Memphis last Christmas. They looked so happy and so real. She could almost reach out and touch them. The next photo was a single picture of Justin, taken at the house during his birthday party. His chubby pink cheeks were dotted with birthday cake, and his stubby fingers were streaked with icing. That first birthday party had been a fun day.

The final photo was a formal sitting of her parents, taken a few years ago for their twenty-fifth wedding anniversary. Her dad had tried to smile, but he always appeared more gruff than gracious when he wore a suit and tie. Her mother, on the other hand, looked radiant, thrilled to be in the photo as she sat beside the man she loved.

Randi sighed, missing them so much. How many times would she have turned to her mother for advice these past few weeks? She would have loved to have confided her attraction to Jackson to her sister Tanya, who enjoyed giving advice more than most people. Randi knew that even Darla, who had married into the family four years ago, would have commiserated with her over the church incident, the unfair way the people of this century treated servants, and the lack of good, hot showers.

With a sigh, she snapped her wallet closed and placed it back inside the fanny pack. She zipped up her belongings and tucked the pouch beside her on the chair. She'd hide it later, when she went downstairs again. At least she'd gotten to "see" her family again.

After she went back to her own time, Randi wanted to remember Jackson and Rose in the same way she remembered her relatives—with love and good memories. There was no way to photograph them, so the next best thing would be a sketch. She'd been practicing, filling her hours with rooms and architectural details, but she could try a portrait sketch. She was no great artist, but she might be able to portray them pretty well. At least she had the motivation to create their image—to remember them forever when they could no longer be a part of her life.

She retrieved her sketch pad from the top of the chest of drawers, then moved the rocker closer to Rose's crib. Using a light touch, she began to draw the peaceful face of the sleeping child.

Jackson came in through the back door after spending the day constructing the new levee, dirty and sweat-stained like his workers. Randi watched him from the shadows in the hallway. He looked exhausted but satisfied with himself. She smiled at the image, one that was more endearing because she suddenly felt she was seeing through the layers of sophistication and breeding to the real man.

"You've had a busy day," she said, stepping into the glow of light from a wall sconce.

"You surprised me."

"I'm sorry. I didn't mean to hide. I was just on my way to the kitchen to check on dinner." She took another step toward him.

"I'm filthy," he claimed, taking a small step back. "I need to bathe and change."

"I know, but that doesn't mean I have to stay away, does it?"

He looked surprised. "I wouldn't think that a lady would want to be around me until I was more presentable."

"So now I'm a lady?" she asked, then chuckled at the image of herself all dressed up and styled like Violet or some of the other women she'd seen at church. "Really, Jackson, I thought you knew me better than that." She stepped a bit closer. "I'm a woman, not a lady."

"I meant it as a compliment," he said intimately.

"I know, and I'm flattered. I just wanted to let you

know that I don't care how you're dressed or whether you have some honest sweat staining your shirt. Fancy clothes don't make the man."

"Then what does?" he asked, his tone soft and truly inquisitive.

"What's inside," she said, closing the gap and placing her hand over his heart. "You have real warmth inside here. And love. You love Rose, and you love Black Willow Grove."

"They're my whole life."

"I know. And if you didn't have that love inside you, you'd be empty in here."

"I feel very full inside right now. If I weren't so dirty, I'd take you in my arms and show you."

Randi smiled. "I'd let you, too." She let her hand drop from his chest and stepped back so she wouldn't be tempted to ignore his dirt and sweat, let her arms creep up around his neck, and plaster herself to his body. He was uncomfortable with the way he appeared, and she didn't want to make him even more aware of the hard work he'd done today. She imagined he didn't participate in physical labor that often.

On the other hand, he had a lean, muscular body that screamed "I work out." She sincerely doubted he had a weight bench and treadmill hiding in his bedroom.

"I'll let you go, then," she said. "When will you want dinner?"

"Give me half an hour. You will dine with me, won't you?"

"I'd love to." She'd like to dine *on* him, come to think of it. Her stomach clenched and she felt herself grow warm at the idea of feasting on a clean, damp, very warm Jackson Durant.

A wicked idea formed in her mind, one she couldn't ignore. "Jackson, since you're tired and you have to bathe and change anyway, why don't you have dinner in your room? That way you wouldn't have to get all dressed up, and you could relax for a change."

"That's a bit unusual."

"Yes, but I think you deserve to pamper yourself a little. After all, you've put up with houseguests for three days, you're under a lot of stress, and this is your house. If you want to do something different, then why not?"

He smiled at her. "Why do I suspect you have another motive for urging me to dine upstairs?"

"Me?" she answered innocently. "Why would you suspect *me* of anything?"

He laughed. "Because it seems to me that your mission in life is to get me either aggravated or—" His eyebrows rose and he leaned forward to whisper, "Miss Galloway, are you trying to seduce me?"

"Oh, absolutely," she whispered back, her hands clasped behind her back. "Is it working?"

"If I weren't filthy at the moment, I'd show you how well."

"You can show me later. Now go take a bath, put on something comfortable, and I'll have dinner brought up soon."

"Both Cook and Birdie will be scandalized."

"They'll get over it."

He laughed again, then headed up the back stairs. Randi watched his legs and backside, trying to imagine him naked. The thought was so inspiring that she sucked in a deep breath, turned, and hurried toward the kitchen.

"Jackson is going to have dinner in his room tonight," Randi told the two women who were busy fixing the meal. One stirred a small kettle, and the other was taking some delicious-smelling rolls out of the oven.

Birdie walked in from the other direction. "Is Mas'r Jackson feelin' poorly?"

"No, he's just tired, and he came in late. I saw him in the hallway and he said he'd eat his meal upstairs. I think that's a good idea. He won't have to get dressed up to sit in that big dining room."

"Um hmm," Birdie said, looking into the rough-hewn china cabinet and pulling out a big platter. "Sounds like takin' a meal upstairs was your idea, Miz Randi."

"Why, I'm surprised you're so suspicious of me, Birdie," Randi said, hardly keeping the amusement out of her voice. "Do you mind?"

"No. Mas'r Jackson did work mighty hard today, right alongside the field hands. I ain't never seen a white man work that hard."

"Maybe he feels strongly about saving his home from the flood."

"There ain't no flood yet."

"No, but I think there will be."

"You been tossin' the chicken bones or lookin' at the tea leaves?" Birdie asked suspiciously, with just a hint of skepticism.

Randi chuckled. "Neither one. Let's just say I have a feeling."

Birdie nodded. "Mas'r Jackson'll take care of this house," she predicted. "He's powerful fond of the place."

"I know. But sometimes I remind him that people are more important than things."

Birdie scoffed. "I ain't seen a planter yet that thought that way."

"Well, until today, you hadn't seen one working alongside his field hands," Randi reminded her. "Maybe today will be the start of a new way of things. Maybe . . ."

"Maybe what, Miz Randi?"

"Nothing," she said, then shook her head. "I was just thinking out loud." Randi shook herself out of her thoughts of the future and turned her attention back to the present. "I think I'll fix myself a tray too, and eat upstairs."

"Go right ahead," Birdie said. "I'll be bringing the mas'r his supper directly."

"He's going to take a bath first. You might want to wait a half-hour or so."

Birdie nodded just as Jackson's valet came into the kitchen.

"Mas'r Jackson needs a tub of hot water," he announced.

"I'll get out of your way in just a second," Randi said, easing toward the stove. She grabbed a plate, then let the cook dish up spoonfuls of the various dishes. She didn't know their names, but from the smell, they were having some kind of chicken in sauce, a white, diced-up vegetable that smelled a little like turnips, and greens. "Give me an extra roll, please," Randi asked, unsure whether she'd like the turnipy thing tonight, but knowing she'd love the bread. Her mother said she was still a little picky when it came to veggies, but who could eat something that smelled like stinky feet?

"Thanks." Randi slipped out of the kitchen, past Jackson's valet, and into the house. Skipping up the back stairs, she walked quickly to her room. She had to give Jackson some time to bathe and get dressed, but the urge to join him right now was nearly overwhelming. As she eased the door closed, she took a deep breath and looked around for something to occupy her time.

Her sketching. She set the dinner plate down on the chest of drawers, then walked quickly to the bed. The drawings of Rose lay in a half-circle on the quilt where Randi had left them earlier. They were good, if she did say so herself. She'd created the tiny one for her wallet, so she could place it next to her nieces and nephew.

She needed one of Jackson, too. Maybe he'd pose for her. That might be a good ice-breaker, in case they were a little uncomfortable. Especially at first. They were taking their relationship to a new level, and although she was really excited about the prospect of finally making love to Jackson, she was nervous. Whatever happened could change the outcome of the future. If Jackson learned to trust her, perhaps he would heed her warnings . . . finally. If that was enough to save the house, then he and Rose wouldn't die in 1849.

Randi didn't know how their survival could change the future. Would there still be a museum on the site? Would she have a job cleaning there, or would there be a replica of Black Willow Grove for her to reach inside? If the house survived and there was no museum, how would that affect her travel back to the past?

Maybe she'd never gone back. Or maybe she couldn't go home.

Shaking her head against the depressing concepts that she couldn't resolve, she picked up the miniature picture. Yes, this one deserved to be in her wallet. She lay the paper down on the bed, then got down on her knees and retrieved her fanny pack from beneath the bed. She had just enough time to place her latest treasure in a plastic sleeve right behind Justin, hide her belongings again, then get ready for her special night with Jackson.

Chapter Twenty

"That will be all for tonight, Micah," Jackson said as he stepped from behind the folding screen and tied his robe around his waist. "You can take the water out in the morning."

"Yes, Mas'r Jackson." Micah picked up the damp towel and soiled clothing, then silently let himself out the door.

He remembered some of Randi's first criticism—that people never said anything to him but "yes, Master Jackson," and "no, Master Jackson." He'd thought her remarks preposterous then, but now, he saw some truth in her observations. He could go for days with no conversation except for that of Lebeau's. If they hadn't been friends for years and been through so much together, he doubted even the freeman would really talk to him.

He hadn't realized how much he'd missed arguing with someone before Randi came into his life. For the past several years, he'd been so careful to blend in, so circumspect in his actions, that his life had become silent and dull.

Randi was never silent or dull. She sparkled with life and energy. She resonated with passion and opinion, stated firmly and surely with a curious blend of emotion and logic. He'd never known another woman like her, and knew that he'd never meet anyone who stirred his soul like the young governess with a mysterious past.

As if thinking of Randi had conjured her presence, she peeked around the door. "Is it safe to come inside?"

Jackson smiled. "That depends on your interpretation of 'safe,' " he answered, giving his belt a last tug. "However, you're very welcome to come into my lair."

"Geesh, you sound like the Big Bad Wolf," she answered, slipping through the partially open door with a plate of food in one hand and a sheaf of papers and pencils under her other arm. She wore the green gown he'd given her and the unusual shoes she'd arrived in.

He didn't know what she meant by that comment, but decided, as he walked toward the door, to take her remark as a compliment. "You have your hands full," he said, taking the plate of food from her and closing the door. With a discreet click, he turned the lock.

"I didn't know if you'd have enough food for me, so I brought a plate. But don't worry. I told Birdie and the cooks that I was eating in my room, too."

"Very clever of you."

"Thanks!" She appeared nervous, clutching papers close to her body, holding pencils in a white-knuckled grasp over her breast.

"Why don't you sit at the table?" he asked, gesturing toward where his dinner awaited. Micah had set the covered plate on a linen cloth with flatware, crystal stemware, and a small candelabra. Jackson had suggested wine, telling his valet that the spirits would help him sleep. No one had questioned him, of course. Jackson now wondered if the staff had any idea of what might go on here tonight.

If he told them, even to shock their sensibilities, they'd simply say, "Yes, Master Jackson," and go on with their tasks. Their extreme deference rankled, but he had no idea what to do about these sudden, errant thoughts.

He didn't want to think about his relationship with his servants tonight, anyway. He didn't want to think much at all. Action was his goal, and the sooner the better.

Not that he would rush Randi. He wanted her to be comfortable with the situation, yet excited about the evening to come. He simply wanted both the comfort and the excitement to commence as soon as possible. His body had remained in a perpetual state of readiness.

He followed Randi across the room, set her plate down opposite his, and pulled a chair out for her. She settled in, smoothing her skirts around her bottom and thighs with a caress he longed to imitate—only without the fabric separating his fingers from her flesh.

He took a deep breath, reminding himself not to hurry Randi. First, they needed to have dinner, perhaps drink some excellent wine. He knew how spirits relaxed her.

"Your dinner has gotten cold," he commented, leaning toward her setting. "Would you like to share mine?"

"No, I doubt I'll even taste it," she said, laughing a bit nervously.

"Perhaps some wine would stimulate your palate," he suggested, reaching for the bottle of Beaujolais.

"Normally, I'd accuse you of trying to get me drunk, but I think maybe tonight you don't want me passed out."

"No, never that. You should try to relax, though. If you don't want to be here, you can leave at any time."

She reached across the table and covered his other hand with hers. "Jackson, I know that. There's no place else I want to be. I'm just a little nervous. Despite what you may think of me, I don't just jump into bed with anyone."

He felt his cheeks grow warm with her candid remark. "I never said you did."

"I know, but you might be thinking it." She sighed, easing her hand away. "I thought I was madly in love with Cleve Sherwood. I was wrong, but I know how I feel about you."

"How?" he asked, handing her a glass of wine, hoping his hand didn't shake and reveal his equally nervous state.

She paused, taking the glass, looking away from his searching gaze. "I care for you very much," she said softly.

"I care for you also," he admitted. He didn't have a word to express how he felt about her. In all honesty, he'd never felt this way about another woman—not that he'd ever known a woman like Randi.

She sipped from her glass. "I don't know much about wine, but this is very good."

"I'm glad you like it. Try it with your coq au vin," he suggested.

"My what?"

"Your chicken," he said, smiling slightly behind his own wineglass. He hadn't known the name either when he was younger, but to mingle in this society, a knowledge of all things was necessary. Lebeau knew about wine, food, and manners. Jackson couldn't have had a better teacher. If the planters had any idea where their neighbor had gotten his fine manners and how he'd stocked his wine cellar, they would be shocked.

"Oh." She took a small forkful of food, then looked up. "This is good, Jackson." She chewed some more, swirling the taste around on her tongue. "Is there wine in this sauce?" she asked, her voice betraying her suspicion.

"Yes, a bit. But don't worry; the alcohol dissipates in the heat."

"That's your way of telling me that eating this meal is not going to get me drunk, right?"

"That's correct," he said, smiling at her playful expression.

She took a few more bites, followed by several sips of wine. He did the same, barely tasting the food as he watched Randi across the table. Lamplight gilded her hair gold and silver, while the candles on the table highlighted her rosy cheeks. His earlier exhaustion dissipated as surely as the spirits in the coq au vin.

In the silence of his bedroom, awareness seemed to grow. Of Randi, the woman. Of the privacy they shared. Of their mutual desire. He didn't know where the feeling came from—deep inside his soul or flowing between the two of them—but he welcomed the sharp-edged anticipation. He placed his fork on the plate, resting on his half-eaten dinner. His eyes focused on Randi, and hers on him, he drank his last sip of wine and blotted his lips with the linen cloth.

Without words, he pushed away from the table and took her hand in his. She rose, a nymph from the sea or a statue come to life, her eyes warm with a golden glow only partly induced by candlelight.

"Are you sure you want to be here, with me, alone?" he asked.

She nodded. "I'm sure. There's only one thing I ask."

"What's that?" He pulled her closer, until her breasts just lightly brushed against him.

"If possible, I don't want to risk getting pregnant. Can you . . . you know?"

"Withdraw?" he answered for her in a whisper.

"I suppose. I just . . . I can't go through that again."

"I understand." The image of Randi, round with his

child, caused a rush of excitement and yearning to race through his body. He didn't want to withdraw; he wanted to bury himself deep inside and never come out. "I'll do what I can to protect you," he promised.

He understood her reasons. She'd recently lost a baby; she didn't want to experience anything similar to that tragic event. Still, the image of his child growing inside of her haunted his mind even as his body prepared to claim Randi as his own.

For how long? his long-lost conscience asked. Shocked by the question, he stilled, staring deeply into her eyes. "For as long as we have together," he answered without thinking.

"What?"

"Us," he whispered before taking her lips in a claiming kiss.

Her hands crept around his neck as his own slid down her back, pressing her close, feeling every curve and indentation along the way. He wanted to strip away the layers of clothing that separated them. The urge to tear the fabric in two darted into his mind, but he dismissed the primitive instinct. That action would neither comfort nor excite Randi, but rather would frighten her into running from his room.

He worked his way up her back, then began unfastening her dress. She moved restlessly, then broke the kiss with a gasp.

"Darn hooks," she whispered, her breath hot against his neck. "If this wasn't one of my only dresses, I swear I'd tear it off myself."

He felt as though she'd punched him with a soft velvet pillow. In an instant, his hands grabbed the cotton fabric and tore the garment in half, all the way down her back.

"Wow," she said, then demanded another long, mindnumbing kiss. Her hands pushed his robe from his shoulders, then stilled when she encountered his white linen shirt. Her fingers balled the fabric in her fists as she leaned back and looked into his eyes.

"Do it," he murmured, and she did, ripping buttons loose as she bared his chest. The sound of carved bone hitting the wooden floor and scattering about the room seemed to enflame her even more. Her fingers caressed his chest as she moaned into his mouth.

He'd never felt this excited before. Randi's passion was honest, her responses natural in a way he'd never expected a woman to react. Not practiced, not reserved. Just true to her desire.

With an answering moan, he pulled the bodice down her arms, separating long enough to strip the dress from her body. The chemise she wore was thin, and he could see the dark, tight peaks of her breasts through the white embroidery. Instead of ripping that garment from her as well, he knelt down, pulled the torn dress the rest of the way down her hips and legs, and placed his mouth over her nipple.

She grabbed his head, holding him to her as she trembled and moved against him. He wanted to taste her flesh, kiss every golden inch of her, but the abrasion of the thin linen was such sweet torture that he dared not allow himself such a luxury yet. Instead, he slowly eased the chemise up her legs, caressing the backs of her knees and thighs as he pushed the garment higher.

"Where are your pantalets, Miss Galloway?" he asked softly as he neared her rounded bottom.

"Back in my room, Mr. Durant."

"What a naughty young woman you are."

"I know," she murmured, urging his head back to her breast. "You'll forgive me, won't you?"

He didn't answer as his lips closed over her nipple again. This time he took her deeply into his mouth, suckling hard until her knees buckled and she gasped.

In an instant, he steadied her with both hands on her buttocks, gripping her firmly as he stood. She trembled, holding tight to him as he raised her from the ground and rubbed her against the part of him that wanted desperately to be inside her.

"Please, Jackson," she whispered against his neck as he held her higher off the ground. Her legs parted, then snaked around his waist. His breath caught in his throat, then he growled his answer into the sensitive skin of her shoulder.

With her locked around him, he strode across the room, easing her onto the bed. To his surprise, she didn't release him, but kept her legs around him as he stood beside the bed. "I love these big, high beds, don't you?" she asked, her eyelids heavy with desire.

He pulled the shirt and robe from his arms with two swift jerks, then yanked at the buttons of his trousers. She wanted to help, but only slowed him down.

This was not the time to go slow.

"Now," he whispered, straining against his linen smallclothes.

"Now," she answered, her legs still locked around his hips.

His hands ripped open the thin material of her chemise. The tearing sound echoed in the silent room. Her legs locked tighter around him, but eased when he caressed down her glowing body to her inner thighs.

Her breasts were perfect, enough to fill his hand, with rosy nipples that begged for his touch. He obliged, tasting her, savoring the flavor of warm, fragrant, womanly flesh. Her stomach was flat. He couldn't tell that she'd ever carried a child. He leaned down and kissed the expanse of skin between her hipbones until she grabbed his hair and pulled his lips away from her soft flesh.

"Jackson," she murmured, her eyes damp and luminous.

He knew then that she loved him. The feelings he wanted to express came to his lips, but wouldn't push

283

past the barrier of his hopes and dreams. Instead, he lowered himself and kissed her tenderly, deeply, until she moved against him once more.

Only then did he pull the torn chemise from beneath her and toss it aside with his trousers. Only then did he stand before her naked and proud, and let her feast her eyes on him.

"I want you," she said after her eyes had caressed him intimately. He felt nearly bursting with emotion and desire, but vowed to make this night last, to love her completely.

He lifted her farther onto the mattress, then lowered his body on top of hers. With a soft sigh, she cradled him between her thighs and sought his lips once more. With seeking hands, she urged him tighter against her damp warmth. Finally, after an eternity of kisses, he eased inside, to the place where he so desperately wanted to be . . . to the comforting home that he'd searched all his life to find.

She moved with him, gasping his name, enthusiastic in her response. She knew what she wanted and urged him to give it to her. Yet all the time, she gave as much in return. More, because he wanted to please her with a passion as strong as his desire to fill her completely. When her movements quickened, he urged her on. When she gasped his name and stiffened, he took her lips hard and sure. When the spasms racked her body, he followed her to that mystical place where souls join and hearts beat as one.

At the very last second, he managed to pull himself from her quivering body. With a roar, he found his own release, joined in the heart forever, but not in the flesh. She sobbed and held him tight as he collapsed on her sweat-dampened body.

As his mind drifted to a place of sweet dreams and even sweeter reality, he moved enough to pull a cover over them. Then he slept, held tightly in her arms.

A CRY AT MIDNIGHT

*   *   *

Randi awoke to the sound of thunder, rumbling in a long, booming vibration that gently shook the house. She opened her eyes and looked out the bedroom window, closed against the night's chill. A faint flash of lightning, not too close, lit up the inky sky. More rain. With a sigh, she snuggled back against Jackson's warm chest.

Making love with him had been the best, the most incredible, experience of her life. She'd known they'd be explosive together, but she hadn't realized exactly how much. Jackson seemed to need her more than air or food. In fact, she felt as though he was feasting on her. Not in any negative way; he just relished every kiss and caress like a starving man would devour a feast.

She'd never been a feast before. In the darkness, she smiled. She rather liked being the appetizer, the main course, *and* the dessert.

Another rumble of thunder made her think of their situation outside these four walls. More rain might mean a higher water level, more chance of flooding. Would the main levee along the river hold? Would the smaller one around the house help, once it was finished? She hoped the answer to both questions was yes.

The restless urge to capture the magic of this night filled her with energy. She eased away from Jackson, careful not to wake him when he so desperately needed his sleep. She couldn't believe they'd made love not once, not twice, but three times during the past hours.

And he'd already been exhausted from working all day. Geesh, she wondered what they might have done if he'd been completely rested. Could her body take Jackson at 100 percent?

With a smile, she swung her legs out of bed, turning her warm pillow into his chest so he would still think she was there. She suppressed a groan at the soreness between her thighs and the sensitivity of her breasts as the sheet slid over her body. She was out of practice—as if any previous encounter could have prepared her for Jackson.

Since her dress and chemise were ruined and she hadn't worn any undergarments, she searched along the dark floor for his robe. She definitely remembered that at some point last night, he'd been wearing clothes. A fortunate flash of lightning helped locate the paisley-patterned garment lying in the tangle of his white shirt and black trousers.

She slipped the soft robe around her naked, slightly aching body, then inhaled Jackson's scent. The smell acted like an aphrodisiac—as if she needed one, she thought with a smile. Walking carefully across the floor meant avoiding her torn dress and the beautifully set table near the fireplace.

On each mantle throughout the house she'd seen matches, so she assumed Jackson's bedroom would be no different. Sure enough, with only a minimum amount of searching and aided by occasional flashes of lightning, she lit a new candle. The ones that had been burning earlier must have gone out.

The golden glow made the room seem cozy, more intimate. As her eyes adjusted to the new level of light, her gaze strayed to Jackson's large, high bed. His body lay relaxed, yet still impressive, beneath the white sheet. During the last hours, she'd tried to memorize each muscle, each bone, each plane of flesh. She'd tasted his skin. Her nails had dug into his back and buttocks.

Now she wanted to memorize him another way. She found her paper and pencils in a chair, then tiptoed to the bed. As she hugged her supplies close to her chest, she watched him sleep. He looked younger, more vulnerable, than she'd ever seen him.

Because of her . . .

Silently pulling up a chair, she positioned her candle

on the bedside table and balanced the sheets of paper on bent knees. Within seconds, she'd started a new drawing of Jackson, tousled and relaxed in sleep. Her pencil flew as she captured his essence on paper.

She didn't know how long she'd been sketching when a loud boom of thunder made her look up from the paper. The storm was moving closer. Rain pelted the windows.

"It's raining." Jackson's soft, sleepy voice startled her as much as the thunder.

"Did I wake you?" she whispered.

"No, I think the thunder did. What are you doing?"

"Sketching."

"In the middle of the night?"

"It's closer to morning, I think. This is one of the few times I've seen you completely relaxed and still for more than two minutes."

He reached across the bed and captured her left hand. "There's a reason I'm relaxed," he said, his voice deeply seductive. "Come back to bed, *chérie*, and I'll give you something better to do than draw my rough face."

"Rough face?" she asked, resisting his gentle tug. "Why would you say that?"

"Because I'm not blond and handsome like the young men around here."

"That's the silliest thing I've ever heard," she said, wondering if his earlier exhaustion and the over-exertion of making love three times had completely addled his brain. "You are without doubt the most handsome man I've ever met." She let her words sink in, then added, "And even if you weren't, I'd still love to look at you. Your face has character and strength, as well as great gentleness and passion."

He seemed surprised. "You see all that in my face?"

"Absolutely."

"You should light more candles, *chérie*," he said gruffly, obviously uncomfortable with her praise.

She put her paper and pencils down on the mattress, then scooted out of the chair onto the bed. "I think you're just fishing for compliments," she teased, pushing him back onto the pillow. "You know darn well you're the best-looking man in Tipton County. Maybe in all of Tennessee."

He actually blushed. Randi laughed, leaned down, and kissed him. "I just love getting in the last word."

"As you said, if I dispute your opinion, you'll simply say I'm hoping for more praise. Perhaps I'd best be quiet."

She eased closer, pushing her pillow out of the way so she could lie next to him. "That's the way I like my men, Jackson Durant. Handsome and silent."

He laughed, pulling her on top, holding her fast with his large, strong hands on her hips. "And this is the way I like my women, Randi Galloway. Beautiful and . . ." he paused while his fingers worked the knot of the belt loose, "naked." He spread the robe wide, his eyes taking in every inch of her body.

Her blush matched his earlier one, plus her nipples puckered and her thighs tightened around his hips. "Darn it, Jackson, I was already sore," she mumbled before she leaned down and kissed him deeply.

Chapter Twenty-one

Jackson looked at Lebeau's raised eyebrow and felt compelled to answer. "I overslept. Yesterday was quite draining."

"Yes, I imagine it was."

The knowing look his friend gave him made Jackson pause at the bottom of the stairs. "What do you mean by that?"

"Only that I was concerned when you hadn't arrived for breakfast, so I went upstairs to check on your health. From the sounds coming from inside your room, I at first thought Miss Galloway was murdering you in your sleep. However, I soon came to realize that my first assumption was wrong. Just the opposite, in fact."

Jackson felt his face heat up like a woodstove on a cold winter's day. "I assume no one else noticed."

"I believe Suzette commented on Miss Randi's absence in the nursery this morning, but I steered her away from that line of thinking. She believes that a temporary problem of digestion kept her away from Little Miss Rose."

"Good. I wouldn't want anyone else to suspect—or to know."

"Ashamed of yourself?" Lebeau asked, folding his arms across his chest.

"Of course not! I'm concerned for her reputation."

"Then you're not ready to declare her your mistress."

"No! She's not . . . Hell, I'm not sure what she is."

"I suspect you should give that some serious thought, my friend, because you can be assured that Miss Galloway will certainly be contemplating more formal arrangements."

"She has no intention—"

"Perhaps she didn't before. Trust me, an unattached woman—and a free-thinker at that—will not accept your vague assurances of a pleasant future for long."

"Since when did you become an expert on women?"

"I didn't say I was an expert on *all* women. I simply claim to know something of the way *her* mind works."

Jackson scoffed. "If you would so kindly tell me, I'd be eternally grateful."

Lebeau gave him a long, hard look. "Think back to your younger days, my friend," he said, his voice low and intense, "to when you had high ideals and even higher hopes for the future. To when each day was lived with an intensity of purpose long forgotten as we age. Forget the fact that she is a woman, or your lover. Only then will you understand her."

Jackson stared at Lebeau, wondering where the words, the passion, came from. Had Randi worked some magic on him, too? "What did she say to you to make you feel so strongly?"

"Not much . . . and yet everything I needed to hear." Lebeau shook his head again. "I should see to our supplies. The water is rising, and we may need another trip to Randolph before the road washes out."

"That bad?"

"Yes. The lumber I ordered was delivered just a short time ago, and the driver said his wagon had become stuck twice on the drive out."

"You're right. We need to stock up on everything." Jackson felt as though he was coming out of a trance—albeit a warm and wonderful one. For a scant few hours, he'd forgotten his responsibilities and problems. Now, in the wan light of a dreary, rainy morning, he needed to face reality. "Tell me if you need anything from me. Otherwise, I'm going to see about the small levee around the house."

"You might want to extend it around the cabins, as well. I'm sure the field hands won't fancy floating if the main levee breaks."

"You're right again. I'll have Brewster start on that as soon as we get a sufficient height around the main house."

Lebeau started down the hall toward the back door.

"Thanks for reminding me about the workers."

The black man turned, his face unreadable in the dim hall light. "No need to thank me. As Miss Randi reminded me not long ago, they're my people, too."

Jackson frowned as the butler walked toward the kitchen. He'd never heard Lebeau say anything that joined him to other freemen or to any slaves. As a matter of fact, he'd always seemed to avoid the subject. Randi had caused this change? Jackson wondered just exactly what she'd said to make Lebeau shift his thinking so radically.

He didn't have time to ponder this development, Jackson reminded himself as he strode to the front door. Constant monitoring would be necessary from that point on. One large snag, a runaway boat, or simply a surge of water could create an opening in the earthen dam. And a small opening could become a large crevasse in hours, even with men working around the clock.

He squinted against the rain slanting across the porch, dampening his trousers and shirt. Brewster had the men working, slipping as they used shovels and trowels to pack the mud into position on the new levee. Jackson felt the urge to join them, to do whatever was necessary to protect his house and the people he loved. Rose, whom he'd checked on this morning before going out, and Randi, who held a place in his heart he hadn't realized was empty before.

He should tell her how he felt, he realized, looking upward as though he could see through the many feet of wood to where she was now dressing. The problem was, he didn't know how to say the words. He hadn't known he was capable of romantic love until this morning, when he'd opened his eyes and looked into her softly glowing face.

She loved him. She would stay at Black Willow Grove now, and they would all be safe. Together, they'd make a home for Rose, the baby they both loved. Randi would want another child. In time, he'd find a way to defy convention and marry his daughter's governess.

If he were strong enough in both reputation and wealth, he would be able to do anything he wanted. No one would dare shun Rose if her father were the richest man in the county. No one would dare talk about his wife behind her back if they thought he could find out and be offended—not if his anger meant financial ruin.

So, he must save Black Willow Grove, replant the crops, and survive this rise in the Mississippi. The flood would pass them by, or, if it didn't, would do minimal damage to the plantation. He would be in a better position than his neighbors, and he would take full advantage of that position to increase his wealth.

The sooner he could claim Randi as his own, the happier he would be.

Happy. He hadn't thought of life in those terms much in the past fifteen years, but he did now. Despite the rising water and the rain that poured from the sky, he felt hope take root in his soul. Together, he and Randi would be able to accomplish all the things he wanted to make them happy.

Randi watched the new levee construction from the third-floor nursery, holding Rose on one hip. The rain hadn't let up all day, but despite the miserable conditions and mud, the men worked on. Jackson was right there in the midst, his once-white shirt plastered against his body, his mud-colored pants sticking to his legs.

She knew he had to be tired; they hadn't slept much last night. She'd fallen asleep after lunch, unable to keep her eyes open while rocking Rose. Of course, she'd been relaxed by a warm bath and comforted by dry, clean clothes. Wet and cold would go a long way toward keeping Jackson awake. She just hoped the combination didn't make him ill. He was working darn hard to keep them all safe.

Would this muddy mass hold back water? She didn't see how, but Jackson knew more about the construction than she did. Too bad sandbags hadn't been invented yet. She could see how they'd be much more effective than simply packing dirt around logs or boards that had been driven into the ground.

Maybe she should mention sandbags. They might be able to sew up something. But how? Without sewing machines, the process could take weeks. They didn't have that long. In fact, if the history books were correct, they had only days.

"What am I going to do about you and your daddy?" she asked the baby.

Rose squealed and reached for the glass, her chubby fingers tracing the path of rain down the panes. Randi leaned closer to the window, watching as Jackson walked over to speak to the only other white man out there. The overseer, she suspected. He didn't seem to be a bad sort of man—not like the stereotypical, evil, whip-wielding ogre in historical movies. That didn't make his role in the social system any less repugnant, though. She'd never get used to these class distinctions.

When Jackson turned and started for the house, Randi carried the baby out of the room and downstairs. If only for a minute, she wanted to see Jackson. They'd been separated all day after being virtually inseparable all last night and this morning. Now she understood why people went on honeymoons—so the demands of the real world didn't interfere with what was really important. Her heart beat faster as she descended the stairs as quickly as possible with her precious burden.

She knew Jackson would feel uncomfortable being confronted while wearing his wet, muddy clothes, but she didn't let that stop her. He'd just have to get used to letting her see him no matter what he was wearing— or wasn't wearing, she thought with a smile as she turned the corner at the last landing.

"Jackson," she said breathlessly as she spotted him coming in the back door. She walked down the last few steps and stopped, hugging Rose tight.

"Randi," he said, his voice intimate as he walked toward her.

She felt his gaze skim over her body like one of his firm, sure caresses. Her skin heated up as she remembered exactly how he'd made her feel last night—all woman and well loved.

"I know you're tired and wet. I just wanted to come down and see you," she said breathlessly, feeling very much like a teenager with her first case of puppy love. However, her feelings for Jackson weren't fleeting. She'd thought she was in love once; this time she was sure.

"I'm filthy," he said, spreading his arms to show her the mud.

"And cold, I'm sure. Would you like to have dinner in your room again tonight?" she asked, knowing she hadn't kept the twinkle out of her eye when Jackson gave her a sly smile.

"I'd like that very much."

Randi smiled back, stepping out of his way so he could go on up the stairs. "I'll just go tell the kitchen your plans."

"Why don't you have a plate sent up for yourself, too? That is, if you wouldn't be uncomfortable telling the staff."

"No, I . . . I don't think I'd mind," she said, surprised that Jackson would want to announce their relationship to the world. She'd thought *he* was the one who was uncomfortable with any sort of illicit affair, but maybe not.

"I'll see you soon, then. Bring Rose in if you'd like. I haven't been able to spend much time with her."

"Okay." Randi's smile faded as Jackson continued up the stairs. He was acting rather strange for a man from this time. Suddenly, he was open about their relationship and being the model dad. What had caused this sudden change? She meant to question him gently later.

She pushed open the back door and walked the short distance to the kitchen. Within a few minutes, she'd given them directions to bring dinner for two to Jackson's room. Even though she used the excuse that he wanted to spend time with Rose, they looked surprised.

Randi didn't say anything. She shrugged, smiled, and hoped they understood. However, she wasn't about to make any excuses for the way she felt about Jackson. She loved both father and daughter, and she wanted to spend as much time with them as she could.

For as long as I have, she reminded herself as she

crossed the covered walkway to the house. She hadn't seriously tried to return to her own time, so she didn't know if she could. She couldn't imagine going off and leaving Jackson and Rose, even if she was convinced they'd survive the flood. But she also couldn't tolerate living in this century, under these restrictions, and knowing that the entire way of life was going to change before Rose grew into a teenager. Jackson hadn't believed her when she told him about the flood; he sure wasn't going to believe that a civil war would tear this country apart and probably cause him to lose his beloved plantation.

With a sigh, she continued on to her room. There she placed Rose on the hooked rug and wiggled one of the soft cloth dolls that seemed to follow them room to room. Kneeling on the floor, Randi retrieved her fanny pack, then her wallet. She turned to the empty sleeves where Rose and Jackson's portraits belonged. The time had come to place the sketches next to the rest of her family, because no matter what happened, Randi would always think of them as hers.

She carefully creased, then tore the paper along the straight edge of the table. With a kiss to each small drawing, she placed them facing each other in the wallet. "What's going to happen to us?" she asked, knowing there were no answers. Not yet.

She took another look at her family, then folded and snapped the wallet. Using a bit of her lipstick and mascara, she freshened herself up for an intimate dinner with Jackson. When she turned back toward Rose, the infant was rubbing her eyes.

"Tired, sweetie?" she asked, reaching down to pick up the baby. Rose seemed to have grown in just the three short weeks Randi had been here. The little girl glowed with health, her pink cheeks and porcelain complexion a perfect match to her name. "Just like a little English rose."

Humming her favorite tune, Randi carried the baby upstairs to see if Suzette had come back from her quarters. Sure enough, the nurse was waiting for them.

"I heard you were eatin' with Mas'r Jackson tonight," she said as Randi walked through the door.

"Oh, yes, we are. He's pretty tired from working and wanted to spend some time with Rose. He misses her, you know."

"Um hmm," Suzette said, unbuttoning her bodice.

"Where I'm from, it's not uncommon to have a less formal dinner. My mother only set a fancy table three or four times a year."

"Um hmm," Suzette repeated, positioning the baby across her lap. "I'm sure goin' to his bedroom is all about seein' this baby."

"Well, mostly," Randi said, trying to sound convincing. "Does it bother you to know I'm going to his room?"

"No, it don't bother me. I just hope you know what you're doin'. Mas'r Jackson is a fine-lookin' man, but he's not gonna marry anyone but one of these fancy plantation women."

"Someone like Pansy Crowder."

"That's right. That's the kind of woman these men want. Pretty and just about as worthless as can be."

"She sure had a beautiful baby, though."

"She did that," Suzette said, stroking the baby's soft hair, "but then she went and died."

Randi shrugged, not knowing what else to say. As far as Suzette was concerned—and she probably reflected the opinion of everyone who worked in the house— Randi fell in the gray area between slave and eligible wife. She shouldn't be a casual plaything for a wealthy planter, but she wasn't worthy to be his wife either.

"I don't know what to say, Suzette. I love Jackson."

"I know you do, but I'm afraid that man will break your heart."

Randi nodded. "You may be right, but I couldn't live

with myself if I didn't spend this time with him. I also realize that because of what happened to you, you're sensitive to the issue of masters of the plantations and the women they . . . love. But it's not like that between Jackson and me."

Suzette nodded, then switched Rose over to her other breast. "This baby will be finished with her dinner soon. Will you be takin' her to Mas'r Jackson's room?"

"Yes, I will."

"She'll be sleepin' soon."

"So will Jackson, probably. He looked pretty tired."

Ten minutes later, Randi carried the sleepy baby down to the second floor. Jackson's valet was leaving, closing the door behind him. She waited until the man went down the servants' stairs, then continued on to the bedroom.

She eased inside, noticing the room was lit with more lamps than last night. Again, dinner was spread on the table near the fireplace. A sense of déjà vu drew her forward, but the load in her arms reminded her this was not yet a romantic rendezvous.

"She must be heavy," Jackson said, coming from behind the screen, belting his robe around his waist.

"She's getting heavier all the time. Especially this time of night. I think I've been carrying her around for hours." Randi handed the baby over, noticing that Rose immediately snuggled up under her daddy's chin.

"You probably have. Birdie says you spoil her."

Randi chuckled. "No more than I spoil my nieces and nephew."

"Do their parents complain?" he asked, rubbing his chin against Rose's downy blond hair.

"Heck, no! They'd be shocked if I didn't spoil them rotten."

"You come from an unusual family," he commented softly, but she heard no criticism. Perhaps they were making progress.

"Not really. Maybe different from your family. My parents aren't rich, or maybe even successful by your standards. But they are happy, and they raised good kids." She spread her arms wide and twirled about in the middle of the room. "Just look at me!"

Jackson laughed. Rose shifted in his arms. "She's sleepy."

"Suzette just fed her. Normally, I'd go ahead and put her down to sleep, but I knew you wanted to see her."

"You're spoiling me, too."

Randi grinned. "I'm doing my best."

Jackson smiled, then sobered. He looked at her with a hungry intensity that made her heart pound. "It's working."

She stared at his lean face, wanting him again. So soon, so much. "Why don't I take your daughter to her room?"

"I'll pour some wine."

Randi smiled, stepping close to take Rose from his arms. "I won't be long."

Jackson leaned down and kissed her lips, strong enough to cause butterflies to start fluttering, but not so demanding that her knees turned to jelly. "Hurry back," he whispered, careful not to wake his little girl. "There's something we need to discuss."

"Really?" Randi leaned back, trying to steal a hint from is face.

His expression betrayed nothing, however. "Just come back soon. I want to have time to talk and . . .

Chapter Twenty-two

Jackson settled across the table from Randi, the scene reminding him of last night in many ways, yet with such fundamental differences. For one thing, she no longer appeared as nervous. They both knew the extraordinary experiences to come, and he liked to think she was filled with as much anticipation as he.

"To another wonderful evening," he said, raising his wineglass to touch hers.

"And morning," she said, smiling in a seductive way that made his heart beat fast. They both took a sip.

"You will be merciful and allow me some rest, won't you?"

"Perhaps," she answered, "if you're very, very good."

He leaned forward, resting his forearms on the table. "You didn't have any complaints last night."

Her gaze skimmed his face, down his neck, and back again. "No complaints at all."

"Good, because there's something I'd like to ask you."

She shifted in her chair, setting her wineglass on the table. "What is it?"

He took a deep breath, feeling uncharacteristically unsure of himself. "Randi, I don't know exactly how to say what I need to say. I've followed my dreams for fifteen years now, building this plantation into something I'm very proud of. I also have a daughter who is a joy. Before you came to Black Willow Grove, I didn't know I was missing anything else in my life."

He reached across and took her hand in his. "In the weeks you've been here, I've learned about your unusual views on life, your differences, and even the things we have in common. You've filled a place in my heart that I didn't know was empty."

"Oh, Jackson. That's so beautiful," she whispered, her hand squeezing his, her eyes bright with tears.

"I know you're worried about the flood, but we've taken every precaution. I don't want your bad dreams of disaster to keep us apart."

"Jackson, I can't—"

"No, wait. You've always told me you had to leave, but that was before last night. I realized this morning that my life is not complete without you. I want you to stay."

Her brow furrowed and her eyes appeared troubled. "In what way? I've already gotten a lecture from Suzette and a bunch of raised eyebrows from everyone else."

"In time, I want to make you my wife."

His words fell heavy in the silence of the room. Randi stared at him, panic and sadness in her eyes. He'd thought she'd be surprised, of course, but not this. "What's wrong?"

"Jackson, I . . . I don't know what to say."

"You're refusing my suit?" he asked, a feeling of incredulous unreality settling over him.

"No, not really. I mean, I don't want to refuse." She

pushed back from the table, her skirts swirling around her as she paced across the floor. "There are things about me you don't know. Things I haven't told you."

"I'm aware you have a mysterious background, and I've stopped insisting you answer."

"I appreciate your understanding, but this is important," she said from near the window, where rain still ran in rivulets toward the saturated earth.

"What is important? My God, just tell me," he said, rising from his chair and tossing his napkin on the table. He walked toward her, ready to take her in his arms if that would help her over this hurdle she had yet to cross.

"No, I need to sit down," she said, more anxious than he'd ever seen her. He was becoming alarmed himself. What was so terrible that she experienced such reluctance to tell him?

"You're not already married, are you?" he asked, a growing nervous energy coursing through his body.

"No!" She sank into a nearby wing chair. "I wish it were that simple."

"Randi," he said, taking the chair across from hers and holding her icy hands in his, "just tell me what the problem is. Surely we can find a way to solve whatever is plaguing you."

She began to tremble. Alarmed, he pushed out of the chair, pulled the cover off the bed, and draped it around her shoulders. Kneeling in front of her, he took her cold hands once more.

"Keeping this secret is causing you more distress than anything you could tell me."

"I know," she said, her voice faint. "But I know you're not going to believe me, and I don't want to see the expression on your face once I tell you my secret."

Jackson had never felt such intense frustration. He wanted to force her to tell her hidden truth, but knew of no way. How could he convince her that he wouldn't react poorly to her secret when she'd given him no clue as to what she was hiding?

He ran a hand through his hair. "Please. I promise I will try to understand whatever you have to say."

She closed her eyes, her hands balling into fists inside his grasp. "I don't want you to hate me," she whispered. "I'm not crazy, Jackson. What I'm going to tell you is the truth."

"I'm listening."

She raised her eyes. "I'm not from New Orleans. I was raised in a small town just north of Memphis, not too far from here."

"Do I know your family?"

She dropped her eyes from his and scoffed. "No, you don't. You couldn't know anything of my family." She looked at him again. "Please, Jackson, sit down in the chair. Get comfortable, and then let me tell my story."

He obliged, letting go of her hands with reluctance. She seemed to need this space between them, settling back into the chair as though she might blend right into the fabric and padding.

"I already told you what happened last winter with my pregnancy. I left out that losing the baby made me think about where my life was going, what I wanted to do. I realized I'd put my dreams on hold. I'd forgotten what I'd wanted and settled for what I had."

"I don't understand."

"I know you don't," she said with compassion, then took another deep breath. "All my life, I'd wanted to be an artist or an architect. I drew cartoons when I was young, then animals and trees and anything else that interested me. I found out my big love was drawing buildings, inside and out. It's called perspective drawing. I seemed to have a talent for it. Before long, I was creating new designs. My art teacher in high school encouraged me to go to college."

"High school?"

"I don't know what you call it now. You go to high school for the last three years, usually. You know, like after grammar school?"

"You wanted to go to the university?"

"Yes, but no one in my family had ever gone."

"Randi, you are a young woman," he reminded her. "There are no universities for you to attend."

"Not now, but there will be."

"What do you mean?" he asked, sitting up straighter. He felt a tingling of concern that Randi was not facing reality.

"I mean that in the future, there will be universities for women all over the place. All of them, as a matter of fact. It's going to be illegal to discriminate because of a person's sex."

"You mean you hope that there will be such things," he said, the tingling increasing.

"No, I mean that in the future, that's the way it's going to be."

"How can you be so sure?"

"Because that's where I'm really from, Jackson. The future."

His mind fell empty for several seconds as he tried to make sense of what she'd said. Finally, he asked, "How can you be from the future?"

She shrugged. "I don't know how it happened. One minute I was in the museum, trying to finish up and go home, and the next I was standing in Rose's nursery, holding her in my hands."

"You mean that it seems like you were one place one minute, and somewhere else the next," he said carefully. "You simply don't remember traveling to Black Willow Grove or entering the house."

"No, that's not what I mean. I was in the museum, which is built right here where the house now stands, and I heard a baby crying. Actually, I'd heard the same sound for the past two nights. I couldn't stand it any longer. I thought someone was playing a sick trick on me, reminding me of the baby I'd lost. So I grabbed the plastic cover, ripped it off the replica of Black Willow Grove, and reached inside to see if the little baby doll was somehow connected to wires."

"What replica of Black Willow Grove? What are you talking about?"

"I already told you the house was destroyed in the flood. They found sketches made by your former slaves, and eventually they built something that looks like a dollhouse. They'd just placed it inside the museum when I started hearing the cries of a baby. They were Rose's cries, Jackson. Somehow, I heard her nearly a hundred and fifty years into the future."

"A hundred and fifty years! Surely you don't expect me to believe you come from this place that many years distant?"

"I said you wouldn't believe me," she said sadly.

"How can I believe something that's—"

"Crazy?" She finished the sentence for him.

"Randi, you must admit that your story is preposterous."

"I know that, Jackson. Why do you think I waited so long to tell you? I can certainly understand why you're reluctant to believe me, even though my feelings are hurt that you won't try. You should know that I'd never intentionally hurt you."

"I can believe that, but—"

"I wouldn't hurt you by asking you to believe such a tale if it weren't true."

"You believe it to be true," he said as gently as possible.

"I know what happened. I just don't know how it happened." She dropped her gaze to her clenched hands. "And I don't know how to get home," she added just above a whisper.

"Black Willow Grove can be your home."

She raised her eyes to his. "Even if the house *does* survive the flood, I can't live here."

"Why?"

"Because this society is obsessed with so much of what I can't stand. Prejudice, snobbery, and a total lack of opportunity for women and blacks. Where I'm from, we've come a long way in solving those problems. Oh, we haven't gotten there yet. We're still far too prejudiced against anything that is different than we are—no matter who 'we' is—and men and women are still fighting over gender roles. But as I see how backward this culture appears to me, I know we've come a long way."

"Randi, I don't know what to say. I can't change society."

She turned away, looking toward the blackness outside the window. "You know I'm terrified of the river. The idea of being caught in this flood scares me to death. And even if I thought we'd be safe here, I'd still miss my family. I'm so close to them, Jackson. I love my parents. I miss my brother and sister so much. If you knew them, you'd understand why. How can I leave them, especially when they have no idea what happened to me? I was all alone in the museum when I fell through the replica into the past. My car will still be in the parking lot. No one will know that I'm okay, that someone didn't break in, abduct me, rape me, or murder me. Can you imagine how worried my family will be when no trace of me is ever found?"

"Randi, I know you believe that you vanished from this museum, but that sort of thing is impossible."

"I would have said the same thing, except it happened to me." She looked back at him, a spark lighting her eyes. "Wait a minute! I know how I can prove to you I'm from the future." She pushed out of the chair and grabbed his hand. "Come with me."

"Randi, I'm hardly dressed for—".

"That doesn't matter. You've got to see my photos and driver's license."

"Your what?"

"Just come on, Jackson. Please."

He allowed her to pull him out of his bedroom, down the hall, and across the stair landing to the other side of the house. She was staying in the first bedroom on the right, sharing the same front view as his room.

"I hid my things under the bed so no one would find them and discover my secret. Now I want you to see what I came here with. You don't have anything like this in 1849."

She let go of his hand, leaving him to follow across the room. On the far side of the bed, near the window, she knelt down. "My fanny pack is right under here."

"Your what?"

"Fanny pack. It's like a thick belt. Don't you remember when I first showed up? You must have noticed it, but you didn't take it off me. When I woke up in this bed, it was still around my waist."

"I don't remember the details of that day. I was too angry when I saw you holding my daughter."

"Here it is!" She pulled out an odd-shaped leather bag with a belt on each end.

"You wear these when you want your hands free— when you don't want to wear a purse."

"A purse?"

"Yes. I'm sure you have some sort of word for it. It's a small bag that women carry things around in."

"A reticule."

"Okay." She pulled on a small object and an opening appeared. Jackson stepped closer, ready to see the nature of this strange bag.

He barely heard the sounds from outside the house. A prickle of unease made him stiffen, then stride to the window. He couldn't see anything but darkness and rain, but he heard the shouts.

"Something's wrong."

With a desperate prayer that all the levees still held, he rushed downstairs.

By mid-morning, enough weak sunlight leaked through the heavy rain clouds to show the extent of the damage. All around them, water covered the earth. Randi tried not to panic; at least with the windows closed and the rain coming down, the smell of the muddy river wasn't overwhelming.

If she didn't look outside, she could almost forget that she was surrounded by the life-threatening flood.

"Baby, what am I going to do?" she asked Rose, swaying back and forth to calm the infant. Rose seemed to have picked up on Randi's nervousness and the general disruption of the household. She was fretful, restless, and refusing to nurse.

Suzette was just as uneasy, pacing the other end of the nursery. "I feel so bad, Miss Randi," she said. "There's just nothin' I can do to help. Even the kitchen is filled with people."

"The only thing any of us can do is pray," Randi said, "unless we want to go outside with a shovel."

"The men took all the shovels over to the Crowder place," Suzette said, her voice rising and falling as she walked back and forth. "That silly man never did believe Mas'r Jackson. I know he didn't build his levees high enough or wide enough to hold back the water."

"How do you know that?"

"I heard Mr. Lebeau tell Mas'r Jackson that he'd talked to one of the drivers who delivered lumber to the Crowder place. He said they didn't put timber in the levees. Mr. Crowder said, wasn't any reason to spend the money on something that wasn't gonna come to pass."

"He was wrong," Randi whispered.

She wished she could look outside and see a whole

crew of strong men reinforcing the levee around the house. Today, only two watched for breaks. Most of the men were at Crowder's plantation, trying to mend the break, which Jackson had called a crevasse. She wasn't sure what good fixing the break would do now, since to her the entire Mississippi River appeared to be surrounding the house.

"I wish I knew if they were all safe."

"I imagine we'd hear if anything happened to Mas'r Jackson. You can bet Mas'r Crowder would be over here in a snap, even if he had to float."

"Why do you say that?"

"There ain't no one else to take over this place if something happened to Mas'r Jackson."

"Oh, my God," Randi whispered. The thought of Violet Crowder running this house, and of Thomas Crowder issuing orders to the staff made her blood chill. Surely that wouldn't happen. Surely Jackson had made arrangements in his will.

Randi turned and walked to where Suzette paced. "Take Rose, please. You just reminded me that there are some things I need to check on."

Suzette nodded, continuing her pacing with the baby.

Randi hurried downstairs, headed for Jackson's study. If she had to pry open the drawers, she was going to discover if he had a will, who would be guardian of Rose, and who would take over this plantation. Blinking back tears at the idea of Jackson not surviving this flood, she pushed open the door to his private sanctuary. If history was correct, someone else would be looking for his will very soon.

"Lebeau, I need your help."

Randi cornered the butler when he came into Jackson's study some time later. She wasn't sure how much time had passed; she'd been digging through papers in all the open drawers for what seemed like forever. With the rainy day and surrealistic experience of being an island in the middle of a flood, she could no longer tell if it was morning or afternoon.

"What are you doing?" Lebeau asked, each word emphatically pronounced in that deep, booming voice of his.

"Going through Jackson's things," she answered honestly. "I need to find his will."

"Why would you need to find his will?"

"Because when Suzette and I were talking, she told me that if something happens to Jackson, Thomas Crowder would probably take control of Black Willow Grove. Do you think she's right?"

Lebeau nodded, but looked skeptical. "You say you know what's going to happen. How?"

"You wouldn't believe me if I told you. I tried to tell Jackson, and even show him, but then the rider came . . . Darn it, where does he keep important papers?"

"There's a lawyer in Randolph. He might have a copy."

"We can't get to Randolph!"

"There's no reason to assume anything will happen to Jackson. The water is rising, but not that high."

"I don't know how it happens," Randi said as she shoved a drawer closed, "but history says that Jackson Durant and his daughter died in the flood in 1849."

"History? What are you talking about?"

She faced Lebeau with her hands on her hips. "Do you remember the day we drove to Franklin's plantation and I told you about what would happen in the future?"

"What you thought would happen."

"You sound just like Jackson," she said, feeling intensely frustrated. Helping save Black Willow Grove from Thomas Crowder was something constructive she could do while Jackson was off battling the flood, but not if she couldn't find any legal records.

"Why don't you discuss this with Jackson when he returns."

"I will, but I have to *do* something. I'm not sure when he'll die—today, tomorrow, or fifty years from now, if somehow I've changed history—but he's got to protect what he loves. That means making provisions for Rose and for his plantation."

"Jackson will take care of his own."

"He'll try, but he doesn't believe me."

"Can you blame him? You claim to have knowledge of events yet to happen."

"I do. I read all about the history of this place in a book."

"There are no books about Black Willow Grove."

"Not now, but there will be, a hundred and fifty years into the future."

Lebeau looked shocked, taking a step back.

"I'm not crazy. Look, I can prove it to you. Stay right here."

She hurried from the room, her footsteps pounding up the stairs. Again, she retrieved her fanny pack, then ran back downstairs.

"Look," she said to Lebeau, who had walked over to stand by the windows. She moved the lamp on the desk closer, then lay the purse flat on the mahogany. She unzipped the compartment and pulled out her wallet.

"What is that device?"

"A zipper. They haven't been invented yet, probably, but we use them for everything."

Over the next few minutes, Randi showed Lebeau her photos, driver's license, and each item in the fanny pack. He seemed fascinated, examining all the pieces with great curiosity. By the time they sat down to talk, he asked her what was going to happen.

Finally, someone believed her.

She told him what she remembered from high school history, although she still couldn't recall the exact dates. Lebeau seemed concerned about what would happen to the plantations and the people who lived and worked on them. She remembered criticizing him for not caring for "his people." She'd probably been way out of line, but she was encouraged that he no longer seemed so disconnected from the slaves and freemen in this society.

"If something happened to Jackson, what would happen to people like Birdie and Suzette?" she asked Lebeau.

"They'd be part of the estate, going to whomever inherited the plantation."

Randi shuddered. "So whoever inherited could do whatever they wanted with the people, the house, and the land?"

"Within the law. There are some constraints that are supposed to keep slave owners from mistreating their property," he answered, his tone and expression telling her he didn't believe those laws were regularly enforced.

"We've got to make sure that Jackson has made provisions for them. I can't stand the idea of Thomas Crowder selling people off. Suzette, especially. She's been through a lot in her young life. To think she could be abused by someone else . . ." Randi shuddered.

"She never told me anything about being abused."

Briefly, Randi told him about Suzette's former owner, the baby she'd given birth to and lost, and her mistrust of most men. "She needs someone to love," Randi told him, "not someone who will use her like that horrible man."

"Many slave owners use the women that way."

"I know, but that doesn't make it right." Randi leaned toward him, touching his hand. "You'll watch out for her, won't you, Lebeau? She needs someone to protect her."

"I'll do what I can, Miss Randi."

"You don't have to call me that."

The butler shrugged. "Everyone calls you that. In your case, it's a sign of affection and respect."

"You're sure it's not just a required title?"

"No."

"Then I'm very flattered. I know I'm different than what you're used to. I never did blend in very well."

"Your hair," Lebeau said, offering her a rare smile.

She smiled in return. "It's a dead giveaway." She kicked out her feet so her tennis shoes showed from beneath the hem of the skirt. "And my shoes. You don't have Keds in 1849."

Footsteps sounded in the hallway. Lebeau jumped up from the settee. At the same time, Micah entered the room holding a bucket of steaming water.

"Mas'r Jackson's just arrived. He's comin' in from the stable."

"I'll see to his meal."

Micah nodded and hurried out of the room.

"Can I do anything?" Randi asked.

"No, just give him some time before you talk to him. He's always more agreeable with a full stomach."

Chapter Twenty-three

Jackson finished his dinner, even though he was nearly too tired to eat. The crevasse at Crowder's Point was wider than he'd hoped—too large to mend without a pile-driving steamboat. They'd never get one upriver from New Orleans in this flood. He doubted they'd be able to get a boat or a rider downstream before the levee fell apart and the river flowed, rather than trickled, over their land. All they could do now was postpone the inevitable—or pray for a miracle.

Randi had been right when she'd said a flood was coming. But was it a lucky guess, a nightmare caused by her near-drowning as a child, or true knowledge from the future? He'd say a combination of luck and bad dreams caused her to believe so strongly in the impending disaster. That was all *he* could believe.

Of course, there was the unusual leather pouch she'd produced from under the bed. He hadn't remembered the item, but, as he'd told her, he'd been so angry to find a stranger inside his house, holding his daughter, that he'd been blinded to nearly everything else. He wished he'd had the opportunity to examine the items inside.

Micah had faithfully brought hot water for washing. Lebeau had brought a report of their provisions. Too bad they hadn't made it to Randolph. Now it would be days, maybe weeks, before they could get a wagon through.

Damn the flood! Jackson rubbed his eyes and wished with all his heart he could make the water go away. He needed time to explore his relationship with Randi, because even though he knew her story was absurd, he still wanted her in his life. He loved her. He hadn't been able to tell her so last night before she'd denied his proposal and asserted she was from the future.

He'd tell her now, if she were here. He wondered if he had the energy to go find her. His arms and legs felt leaden from wading through knee-deep water, carrying logs, straw, and mud to rebuild a levee that had never been more than poor at best.

As if his thoughts conjured her, Randi appeared in the doorway, holding his daughter. He smiled as well as he could.

"Jackson," Randi whispered, then hurried into the room. "You look terrible," she said, kneeling beside his chair.

"I'm happy to see you, too," he said, reaching out his hand. Rose grabbed one of his fingers and held on. His precious daughter. She didn't care that he was bone-weary and half-drowned.

"I was worried. You were gone so long."

"There's so much work."

"Then the break can be fixed?"

Jackson closed his eyes and shook his head. "I don't think so. Not without more equipment than we have available."

"Oh."

He opened his eyes. Randi still knelt in front of him, her expression one of concern and love. Rose wiggled to get down.

"I know you're tired," Randi said, "but there's something important I have to ask you."

"Go ahead."

"If something happened to you—something awful—who would become Rose's guardian? Who would take over Black Willow Grove?"

"More nightmares?"

"No, but please, Jackson, I need to know. I even went way over the line and looked for a will in your office. I'm sorry, but I was really worried. I still am."

"You looked through my papers?"

"Yes. Like I said, I'm sorry, but I had to. I told Lebeau what I was doing."

"And he allowed you to continue?" Where did the man's loyalty lie? With an old friend, or with a young woman who believed she was from another time?

"Yes. I talked him into it, so don't be angry with him. You know how I can be when I want something."

"Persistent," Jackson said, offering another weak smile.

"That's me. Now, back to the subject. Would Thomas Crowder get control of your plantation and Rose?"

"As her closest living relative, yes, he would."

"That's terrible! Do you want him raising your child?"

"No, but there is no one else."

"What about me? I could take her away from this flood, Jackson. Maybe you, too. Would you come away with me? I don't know if we can, but we could try."

"What are you talking about?"

"The sketch I made of the museum in my time. I got here through the replica of your house, so I thought maybe I could get back through a drawing of the replica in my time."

Jackson frowned. "You're not making any sense."

"I'm sorry. I know you're exhausted. I'm just so worried. According to the history books, you and Rose perish in the flood. I can't let that happen, Jackson. I love you both. I want you to come away with me. Come and be safe. I'll help you."

"There's no such thing as traveling through sketches into another time."

"You don't think it will work?"

"Randi, love, I don't even believe you're from another time. How can I believe you can return there?"

He closed his eyes against her hurt expression. He wanted nothing more than to curl up into his soft, comfortable bed with Randi and fall into a deep sleep. He could do nothing else tonight to save the levee. In the end, all he might have left were Randi, Rose, a waterlogged house, and flooded fields.

"Randi, I'm sorry I can't believe your story."

"I'm sorry, too," she whispered.

He felt her rise from the floor. Rose whimpered. "I'm going to take her up to bed."

"Come back," he said, opening his eyes to see his sleepy daughter snuggle next to Randi. "Come and stay with me. Nothing more."

He watched the confusion in her eyes before she turned and walked toward the door. "I'll come back," she said before she went out of the room.

Jackson closed his eyes again and let his head fall back against the chair. Randi was right about one thing: He couldn't let that puff-headed idiot Thomas Crowder gain control of Black Willow Grove or Rose. Jackson vowed he'd make other provisions, just in case . . .

Randi slipped back into Jackson's room after taking Rose up to Suzette. The conversation had been unsettling, to say the least. Suzette had overheard enough of an earlier conversation with Lebeau to pique her curiosity. She'd wanted to know if Randi knew powerful chants or carried strong magic in her bag. When she'd tried to explain that she didn't know how she'd arrived at Black Willow Grove, Suzette had looked skeptical. Randi had come away from the nursery with a feeling of unease, as though Suzette expected more answers than were available to any of them.

Randi didn't believe for a minute that Suzette would not give Rose the best care. She just seemed more interested in Randi's answers than the rest of the people here. Maybe she was more willing to believe because she needed some salvation in her life. Whatever the reason for Suzette's persistent questions about what was going to happen to all of them, she was not going to be easily convinced that Randi didn't have all the answers.

She closed the door, her eyes focusing on Jackson, still sitting in his chair by the fireplace, sound asleep. She walked toward him, hoping he'd wake naturally. He didn't.

"Jackson," she said after she knelt beside him, "you need to go to bed now."

He stirred, half-opening one eye. "Randi?"

"Yes."

"For just a moment, you sounded like my mother. Then I realized she wouldn't have called me Jackson."

"Why?" she asked, smoothing a lock of hair back from his eyes. "What would she have called you?"

"Jacques," he answered in a sleepy voice before closing his eye.

Randi frowned, resting her bottom on her heels. Jacques? He'd said the name so naturally, with a slight French inflection. Was that his mother's nickname for him? Perhaps she'd been French.

"Come on," Randi coaxed, lifting one of his arms. "Let's get you in bed."

"That's a nice offer," he mumbled, helping her by pushing out of the chair. He stumbled toward the bed

318

with her support under one of his shoulders.

"I don't remember ever being this tired."

"You ought to be tired. You worked at least ten hours for two days, then around the clock this last day. Did you eat?"

"Yes," he said, sitting heavily on the mattress. He smiled slightly in a strange way that made Randi think of the word goofy. "Violet brought me some sweet potato biscuits and slivered ham on a little silver tray."

"Violet! You're supposed to be out working your buns off to save this plantation, and *Violet* brings you sweet potato biscuits?" Randi knew she was nearly yelling, but couldn't stop the rush of red-hot anger that the bimbette's name evoked.

Jackson turned his head and looked up at her while he reached for his shoe. "You're jealous."

"I'm furious, that's what I am," she said with a huff. "I don't understand what you men see in women like her."

"I never said I saw anything about her that I liked. As a matter of fact, I thought this conversation about Miss Crowder was closed long ago." He pulled off the other shoe, then his socks.

"Believe me, she doesn't think the issue is closed if she braved the rain and mud to bring you dainty little biscuits on a silver tray."

"Randi," he said, reaching for her waist, pulling her between his spread knees, "I have no interest in Violet. I didn't love Pansy, and I sure don't love her little sister."

"Lebeau said you needed to marry someone from your class."

"Lebeau was telling you what he thought I wanted you to hear." Jackson sighed, resting his head against her stomach and pulling her closer. "And he knows better than anyone that in truth, the Crowders are as far removed from me in class as he is from the President of the United States."

"What are you talking about?"

"I'm so tired. Will you lie down with me and let me tell you a story of a boy who wanted very much to become wealthy and respected?"

"Jackson, what—"

He reached for the hooks at the back of her dress. "Just lie down with me and let me tell you. Then you'll understand why saving Black Willow Grove is so important to me."

With only the single candle burning on the mantle, she could barely see his face in the shadows of his canopied bed, his cheek pressed against her stomach. But she felt his warm fingers, steadily unfastening each hook, and she felt the cool air that eased into the opening when he separated the fabric.

When he finished with her dress, she pushed the robe and shirt from his shoulders, then pulled them from his arms. Silently, he unbuttoned his pants and pushed them down his hips. She watched with greedy eyes, noticing at once that despite his exhaustion and the cool night air, he was moderately aroused.

So much for just lying there and talking . . . not that she had any complaints.

Quickly, becoming chilled in the damp air, she finished undressing and slid beneath the covers. If they were going to lie side by side, they might as well be comfortable. And if she only had a short time with Jackson, she didn't want to spend it fighting over some woman Randi knew in her heart didn't have a chance with Jackson. He really was too smart to fall for Violet's transparent charms.

"You're cold," he said, slipping beneath the blankets behind her. He curled them together, spoon style, with her bottom fitting very nicely against his hips and thighs.

"You'd better start talking to me soon, Jackson, or

you're going to be a lot more tired than you were when you entered this bedroom."

He chuckled, the puff of air stirring the hair on her neck and sending shivers down her spine. "I'll talk. You need to understand that I've never told anyone about my past."

"I thought you said Lebeau knew."

"He does, but mostly because of where we met."

"Is that where the story starts?"

"Not really. I suppose the beginning of Jackson Durant occurred when a young boy was spit upon and thrown into the mud because he wasn't good enough to play with the children of the wealthy planters who passed through town on their way to church or market."

"You were poor."

"More than poor. We lived in a shack not far from the river, just out of New Orleans. My father worked, when he could, at the docks. He wasn't a healthy man, though, and his cure for his disposition was rum."

"He was an alcoholic."

"If that means he loved to drink, then you're right. My mother, God rest her soul, took in laundry and raised me and my brother with nothing but hand-me-downs and hope."

"She did a good job, then. You've succeeded."

Randi felt Jackson draw in a deep breath, his head restless on the pillow behind hers. "She never knew," he whispered. "I left home at the age of fourteen to make my fortune. She begged me not to go, but I told her I was going to make enough money to take all of them out of our shack and into a fine home. I promised her she'd have servants to do her laundry, and she'd never have to wash other people's clothes again."

"What happened?" Randi whispered.

"Less than a year after I left, a fire raged through the shacks. My family was killed, still lying in their beds as dry tinder and greased paper and oiled cloth burned around them."

"Oh, Jackson, I'm so sorry." She turned in his arms, smoothing her hands over his face, urging him to take whatever comfort he could find in her arms.

A shudder passed through his body as she held him. Then he was quiet and still, his breath warm on her neck.

"What did you do then?" she finally asked.

"I took the money I'd earned working along the river, from New Orleans to Louisville, and I learned to gamble."

"Gamble? You mean you were one of those slick riverboat gamblers like Brett Maverick?"

"Who?"

"Never mind. Go ahead with your story."

"I learned how to take money from dockworkers with monte, then I perfected my skill with chuck-a-luck on spectators to horse races. I shot craps with patrons of boxing matches. Before long, I was playing poker with deck passengers around the steamboats on the Mississippi. That's where I met Lebeau."

"He was a passenger?"

Jackson shifted, lying on his back and pulling Randi close to his side. "No, he was working at the docks in Baton Rouge. I was not yet twenty, but still a good-sized man. One of the players took offense at my card-playing abilities."

"He accused you of cheating," she clarified.

"Yes, he did. As he weighed considerably more than me and was at least ten years older, I was reluctant to test my luck in a fight. We were negotiating the terms of a rematch at cards when he became enraged and threw me off the ship. Lebeau happened to be the man I flattened in my fall."

"What a way to meet."

"Lebeau said something similar, only more colorful.

When he discovered I'd been thrown onto him and the other man was itching for a fight, he decided to help me out. He could have walked away, or defended himself with a length of chain, but he challenged the man himself."

"At cards?"

"No, at head butting."

"What in the world is that?"

"Two men square off, then run at each other. The one with the thickest skull and strongest neck usually wins."

"That's barbaric!"

"Lebeau was very good at the sport."

"Why would he do . . . Oh, never mind. That's probably a different story."

"Yes, it is. He can tell you some time if he'd like."

Randi seriously doubted she would be here to learn Lebeau's secrets, but she didn't want to remind Jackson of that. "Then what happened?"

"After Lebeau knocked the man out, we were asked to leave the docks. I didn't have anywhere else to go, since my clothes and personal items were aboard the ship, so I ended up camping with him at a shack not too different from where I'd grown up."

"That must have brought back memories."

"Ones I didn't welcome. Once Lebeau told me his story, I realized that I'd let the tragedy of my family's death harden me to life. Other people had overcome far more serious hurdles and succeeded. Lebeau and I decided to team up. He'd been raised as a house servant on a large, wealthy plantation, but had no use for the manners and taste he'd acquired. I'd grown up poor, but wanted to learn everything he knew. With his skills and the color of my skin, we did very well."

"What do you mean?"

"I played cards. He helped me buy clothes and personal items to make me look more the gentleman. He helped me with my speech, and reminded me of the importance of being well read—something my mother had also preached. In short, Lebeau turned me into Jackson Durant."

"You say that like you were a different person before."

"I was. You see, a poor Cajun has no chance to become a wealthy landowner who can mix freely with the white planters. I found that out after I acquired my first plantation, a smaller place near Monroe, Louisiana."

"What happened?"

"Although I had enough money to improve the land, refurbish the house, and bring in good crops, none of the planters wanted their daughters to associate with a Cajun who had pulled himself up by his bootstraps. In short, despite all the trappings of wealth, I lacked the one thing that they wanted: respectability."

"See, that's exactly the kind of prejudice I was talking about earlier." She stiffened, then turned on her side to face him. "But you understood that all along. Every time I said something about your past or made some assumption, you could have told me the truth."

"I didn't know you well enough to speak of my secrets."

"You could have at least told me you understood."

"Randi, if I had said those words, you would have asked me how I understood. I've found at times it's best to remain silent around you."

"That sounds pretty manipulative," she said as she relaxed he head on his shoulder. "I'm not mad, though. I understand how this must have been hard for you. You've been keeping the same kind of secret that I have."

"Yes, I suppose you're right."

"How did you get Black Willow Grove?"

"When I realized I would never be accepted into planter society in Louisiana, Lebeau and I discussed our options. I decided to change my name, my background—in short, I became a different man."

"Jackson Durant."

"Yes."

"Then who were you before?"

"I was born Jacques Bondurant," he said softly, "and I suppose that, inside, I'm still that poor Cajun boy who wants the whole world."

"You have what's important, no matter what happens. You have a wonderful daughter. You have the best friend I can imagine in Lebeau. And you have me."

"Rose is my reason for staying Jackson Durant, for putting up with the Thomas Crowders of the world. As long as no one knows my secret, she'll be safe from their jeers."

"What do you mean?"

"No one will ever call my daughter poor Cajun trash," he said fiercely. "I haven't gone through all this to lose the life I've built for her, for us."

"Will there be an us?"

He leaned over her, his palm resting against her cheek. "Yes, because I want you," he whispered, "and I need you." Then he took her lips in a deep, tender kiss that stole her breath and her heart.

She touched his chest, then slid her arms around his shoulders as he deepened the kiss. His skin burned like a furnace against hers, chest to chest, and she kicked at the cover. With a groan that came from deep in his soul, Jackson—Jacques—rolled her to her back.

He claimed her breasts with sure, loving hands, then a skillful, relentless mouth. Randi tangled her legs with his, wanting to be a part of him, of his life, of their future.

"Don't pull back this time," she whispered against his lips.

"What about—"

"Just don't. I want all of you, whatever may happen tomorrow or the day after. Just love me tonight."

"I do," he said softly, surging inside her with sure, strong strokes. "I do," he repeated, the vow ripped from deep inside as he quckened his pace.

She held tight, loving him, wanting him, and at last, joining him in an explosion of light and sensation. She held him so tight that she thought they'd be fused together as one. And indeed, they were, for he didn't leave her, but held her tight as they both drifted into an exhausted sleep.

Chapter Twenty-four

Randi knew she had only one choice left, and that was to help the man she loved try to save the plantation he'd worked so hard to possess. Everything in his life had led him to this point, where he could have the kind of place he'd dreamed of as a poor child, where his daughter could grow up in a society that offered her every advantage. Randi could understand his thinking, although she didn't agree with his idea of what would make him happy. She'd work on that later, though, once they got through this current crisis.

She didn't know what the future would hold for her. She didn't want to stay in the past, to live in this society. But she didn't want to leave Jackson and Rose either. She had to convince them to come away with her, if not into the future, then up north. Somewhere they'd be safe from the Civil War.

Jackson had bought and improved this plantation. He could do the same again. If he loved her. . . .

He said he did. Last night had been tender and special. She would never forget the feeling of completion when they joined together. She and Jackson had touched something special, something eternal, as rare as her travel back in time.

With a deep breath, she zipped her jeans, then pulled her striped velour shirt down over the waistband. She couldn't go out and work in the mud and rain in voluminous skirts and tight bodices. She couldn't face the rising water already weighted down with yards of soggy fabric. At least in her own clothes she'd feel as though she could get away from the water, run to the house if the levee broke.

Although the morning was nearly gone, daylight barely lightened the hallway as she rushed up the stairs to the third floor. More clouds, more rain. She wondered how many days this could keep up. How high could the water rise before all the levees broke and the land was completely covered for miles around?

"Suzette?" Randi entered the nursery to find the nurse with her fingers to her lips. She stepped out into the hallway so they wouldn't disturb the baby.

"Miss Rose just went to sleep. All this bad weather has her in a fretful way."

"I know. I'm edgy myself."

"Why are you dressed like that?" Suzette asked, walking around Randi and staring at her jeans and top.

"I'm going outside to work with Jackson. Since most of the workers are still at Crowder's Point, he needs all the help he can get."

"Women don't work like that around here," Suzette told her, as if she were talking to someone who was slow.

"Where I come from, women and men do whatever they can to save what they love. And Jackson loves this plantation."

"And you love Mas'r Jackson."

"Yes, I do. I'm going to try to help him, and I'm going to try to save him."

"From the water?"

"Yes, this darned flood. I'm so frightened of it that I can barely stand looking out the window. If I didn't know what was going to happen, I might not be so scared for him."

"What do you mean?"

Randi shook her head. "Never mind. I can't explain right now. All I can say is that we have to keep the water out. After that . . ." She didn't know what else to say. Suzette was looking at her suspiciously.

"I'm sorry. I'm doing what I can to make things right. Will you please watch very carefully over Rose? I might not get to come up to see her for a while. You know I love her too."

"Yes, Miz Randi."

"I'm just going to take a quick look before I go outside." She tiptoed into the nursery. The bassinet where Rose had once lay was now pushed aside for a larger crib. There were no colorful Winnie the Pooh sheets or bright shapes bobbing over her head in a mobile, but the baby seemed happy. She would be happy wherever they lived. In the future, or somewhere else in this time. Somewhere safe . . .

Randi kissed her fingertips, then touched the same spot to Rose's forehead. "I'm going to do whatever I can to save us," she whispered.

Tears burning at her eyes, Randi silently left the room. She walked down the back stairs, her feet heavy on the narrow treads. She didn't want to face the sight and smell of all that water, but she had no choice.

She was surprised to find that the rain no longer poured down. A few sprinkles were all that she felt as she slugged through the mud and muck toward the small crew that manned the levee around the house.

Jackson wielded a shovel with determination, packing clay against a new, taller timber that had been driven into the ground by two large men with sledge-hammers.

"Jackson."

He turned around, his face lined with sweat and dirt. Gone was the relaxed, tender lover from last night. This man was a warrior, out to protect his homeland from the invading flood. How could she not stand beside him, support him?

"What are you doing here? Why are you dressed like that?"

"I came to help. I know you're short of help since all the men are off at Crowder's break."

"I don't recruit women to do a man's work," he said, obviously trying to tell her gently to "get out of here."

"I know you think this is unusual, but I really can help. I'm strong and healthy. Just try to forget I'm a woman, okay?"

He shook his head, frowning. "You know I don't approve of those clothes."

"Long skirts aren't very practical for working in this muck."

"That's why this is men's work. Now please, go inside. Change clothes and stay dry. I'll be in later."

"Jackson, that's silly. I'm another pair of hands. I can help."

"Why don't you trust me to save my home?" he said, frustration and anger tensing his body. His white-knuckled grip on the shovel was all the evidence she needed that he was not going to listen.

"I trust you to do your best, but can't you see how unsure I am? The history book said you perished in this flood, Jackson. Right here, right now. How do you expect me to ignore what I read in black and white."

"You only *thought* you read that," he said, enunciating each word carefully. "You are not from the future. You don't know anything that's going to happen."

"Yes, I am from the future!" she shouted. "Why are you doing this to us?"

"I'm not the one who insists on such an absurd notion of traveling through time."

"It may be absurd, but it's the truth!"

"Randi," he said, grasping her shoulders, "you must face the fact that your fears and your dreams have mixed together. I don't know how or why you came into my house, but you did not tumble through some replica of this house. That's impossible. You walked up those stairs into Rose's nursery. Please, admit that fact. For me. For us."

She shook her head. "I didn't walk into your house. One minute I was in the museum, the next I was in her nursery."

Randi tore her gaze away from his set jaw and worried brow. Looking up to the third-floor corner nursery, she wished she could see inside right now. She felt drawn to Rose, worried about the baby more than usual. Perhaps she shouldn't have left her with Suzette.

She almost imagined she could hear the baby crying. That was ridiculous, of course. Suzette had the windows closed against the spring chill and dampness.

"I wish you'd look at my proof. With all the problems, and with you being gone, I forgot to show you my pictures and my driver's license. Once you see them, you'll understand."

"Randi, please don't persist in your claims. I cannot believe you."

"Jackson, if you truly loved me, you'd believe me."

"You ask too much. You've asked me to change how I feel about my life, my daughter, my own dreams. You ask me to ignore the flood and my responsibilities here. I cannot do that. I may have been raised poor, but one thing I learned was to live up to my role as a man."

"I'm not trying to make you less of a man! I'm trying

to help you save the home you love . . . and your daughter."

"We are not in any danger. This levee will protect the house. I will protect what I love!"

"Jackson, please—"

"No! I will not have my woman working like a common field hand, dressed in clothes that should have been taken away and burned. And I won't give in to your demands that I run away. I'm no coward! I'm the master of this plantation, and you will accept that fact!"

She stepped back, knowing she'd crossed the line of what Jackson could tolerate. He was a proud man, a man who had changed much in the last three weeks. Instead of focusing on those changes, she'd kept asking him to trust her to know what was right for him and Rose. But she'd wanted to save him. . . . to love him and Rose.

"I thought I was doing what was best, Jackson. Please understand."

"You're headstrong, Randi, and I understand that. But you ask too much."

"I can't give up on my hopes to save you."

"I can't run away from my responsibilities or my dreams."

Tears burned her eyes. The sun came out from behind a cloud, giving her an excuse for blinking and looking away. The air about them seemed charged by the welcome light. Even a few birds began to chirp and sing. The sound of water lapping against the levee sent a shiver of fear through her now that the rain and the shouting had stopped.

"Do you feel it?" she whispered.

"I feel tired and angry, Randi. What do you feel?"

"Like something is going to happen." She looked around, wondering if the water was going to break through. She was thinking it might rush over the top and engulf her in mud. Above the pounding of her heart, she heard Rose's faint cries.

"I have to go into the house," she said, her gaze darting to the upstairs window. "Do you hear her?"

"Hear what?"

"Rose. She's crying."

Jackson stilled, looking upstairs. "I don't hear anything but the usual sounds of spring."

"No, I can hear her. She needs me." Randi heard the panic in her voice, but couldn't control the rising fear.

"Randi, calm down. We'll go check on Rose. Then you can lie down. You're distraught."

"I'm not distraught. Women from 1999 do not get distraught. I'm scared to death!"

He took her arm. "Come along. This is why ladies shouldn't attempt heavy labor." He took a few steps toward the house, pulling her through the churned-up muck.

"That's the dumbest thing you've said since I got here," Randi said, jerking away from his grasp. "And I can't believe you don't hear Rose. She's your own daughter and she's crying." She took off on her own, her feet slipping and sliding.

"Let me help you."

"Why? You won't let me help you."

"Don't be ridiculous. You help in different ways."

"It's not enough!" Randi cried, throwing her hands over her ears. "Can't you understand that I have to make sure you and Rose are safe? And she won't stop crying!"

Slowly, Randi realized placing her hands over her ears hadn't stopped the sound of the baby's tears. A sense of déjà vu made her shiver. She'd heard the same thing in the museum, right before she'd reached inside and grabbed the little baby in the bassinet.

She dropped her hands, a stronger sense of panic making her look around for reassurance. Jackson stood in front of her, asking her a question. Beyond him, Lebeau stood at the back doorway, beneath the covered walkway. Birdie stepped out of the kitchen, an armload of folded linen in her hands.

Randi saw all that, but heard very little. Her senses seemed dulled. She even felt as though she was operating in slow motion as she reached inside the pocket of her jeans, to the irritating lump that pressed into her hip.

Her gaze locked with Jackson's, her fingers closed over the little plastic baby. She'd forgotten all about the doll.

"Look, Jackson," she said, although her words sounded hollow. "I didn't travel through time because of the replica. It was the baby. Always the baby . . ."

She saw a horrified look on his face, then her eyes shut against a bright blast of sunlight that seemed to throw her backwards to the ground. Her mind spun with a dizzying sensation of tumbling, then she landed.

Not in mud, she slowly realized. Her fingers connected with a hard wood floor on one side, a fuzzy, worn carpet on the other. She sucked in lungfuls of air, which weren't filled with the smell of the muddy river. Tentatively, she opened her eyes.

The overhead spotlight highlighted the white-boarded replica of Black Willow Grove, the plastic shield hanging from one nail.

"No," she whispered. "Jackson . . ."

She rolled to her side, then tried to stand. Her head spun so much she felt ill. "I have to find out," she whispered. "I have to know if they were safe." She tried to crawl toward the pedestal so she could stand up, walk to the gift shop. The history book would tell her if anything had changed.

But she couldn't pull herself to her feet. With a moan of frustration, Randi sank to the floor, her fingers closed around the little plastic baby as she fell into blackness.

Jackson staggered back from the spot where Randi had been just moments before. He'd watched her disappear in front of his eyes, but still couldn't believe what he'd seen. He reached out, swinging his arms wide, but she was gone.

With a cry from deep inside his soul, he tipped back his head and yelled, "Randi!"

The sound of birds, startled into flight, was his only answer. He felt so stunned that he couldn't function. Only when he felt a hand on his shoulder was he shaken from his stupor.

"Randi!" He turned, and found not the woman he loved, but his friend.

"She's gone," Lebeau said, his voice showing the wonder they shared over her disappearance.

"How could this happen?" Jackson asked, holding Lebeau's upper arms. He wanted to shake him, to make him give answers to all the questions that raced through his head.

"She was telling the truth," Lebeau said. "She really was from the future."

"She told you?"

"Yes, she told me many things. About the wonders of her time. About the war that is to come and tear the South apart."

Jackson shook his head. "It's so hard to believe. I've done enough slight-of-hand tricks to know the signs. I saw no tricks. She simply faded away, and then she was gone."

"What did she say before she left?"

"She heard Rose crying . . . Oh, God. Is Rose well? What if something happened to her? What if she's gone?"

Jackson fought the mud as he ran toward the house.

Ignoring the dirt and water he tracked across the marble floors, he ran up the stairs, two at a time. He vaguely heard Lebeau on his heels, but the pounding of his heart drove out all other reality.

"Suzette!" he yelled as he careened into the nursery.

"Mas'r Jackson!" Rose's nurse held the baby close to her chest. Suzette's eyes were wide with fear as she looked over his wild appearance.

"Is she well? Has she been crying?"

"No, sir. She just fed, and I was gettin' ready to put her down for a nap. Miz Randi said she might not be up for awhile."

"Randi," Jackson began, then swallowed the lump in his throat.

"Miss Randi is gone," Lebeau added.

"Gone? But where could she go in this flood? You don't mean she's . . . gone?"

Lebeau shook his head. "We don't know exactly where she went," he said gently, "but she's not coming back."

"How do you know?"

Jackson placed his hand on Rose's downy head. "I pushed her away. I didn't believe."

"Miz Randi said she had to go outside to save you."

Jackson nodded. "That's why she came here. To save us."

"Maybe to make us see the possibilities we wouldn't have understood unless she came into our lives."

"What to you mean, Mr. Lebeau?" Suzette asked.

"Things are going to change," he said, then turned and walked into the hallway.

Jackson placed a kiss on his daughter's forehead. "Take good care of her, Suzette. She's more precious to me than anything I have left on this earth."

He turned away from the nursery, his heart empty and sad despite Rose's health. For an instant, he'd thought perhaps his daughter had disappeared with

Randi. She'd been so concerned about what would happen to the baby if he'd died unexpectedly. He'd promised her that he would make provisions for Black Willow Grove and his daughter. He hadn't done that yet, but now he realized a true sign of caring was making those arrangements now, before anyone threatened the continued existence of his plantation or the happiness of his child.

Carrying out his promises was the least he could do out of respect for Randi. She had asked much of him, but he knew he was a better man for the changes she'd initiated. How could he have faulted her for caring enough to make him realize what was truly important? Instead of thanking her, their last moments together had been filled with anger and pain.

The knowledge that she'd taken away that image of him back to her time, to the family and culture she loved, filled him with sadness. He had to do something to honor her memory.

"Lebeau," Jackson said wearily, "would you come to the study, please? We have some things to discuss."

When Randi awoke, she was still alone in the museum. The night's silence weighed heavily around her, but she pushed off the floor with one hand and sat up. Just as when she'd gone back in time, she felt weak and dizzy. The feeling would fade, though. She knew the emptiness in her heart wouldn't.

She uncurled the fingers of her other hand, not surprised to find the plastic doll still pressed into her palm. Rose. The baby had found a special place in her heart. Not even the death of her own unborn child had affected her so deeply. She'd never hear Rose's squeals of delight, massage her gums, feel her snuggle up for a nap, or just walk around the beautiful old home with the baby.

She'd also never walk into Jackson's study and find

him sitting behind his huge desk, or slip into his bedroom for a night of passion. The loss of the man and the baby she loved filled her with such sadness that she didn't know how she'd go on.

This time when she tried to get up off the floor, her legs held her upright. She still felt dizzy, but she could walk. The first thing she needed to discover was if she'd changed history in any way.

With one hand on the wall, she slowly maneuvered down the hallway to the gift shop. By the time she reached the doorway, she was tired and out of breath, but had to go on. The stack of history books about the area were tucked beneath a shelf of Victorian postcards and colorful glass paperweights.

Randi sank to the floor, then slowly pulled out a book from the bottom of the stack—the one she'd "borrowed" to read up on the plantation. Sure enough, she could barely see the places where she'd turned the pages. Her breathing fast and shallow, she found the part about the people who had lived in the house. Her finger skimmed down the page, then stopped on the paragraph she sought.

"Jackson Durant and his infant daughter disappeared in the flood of 1849, their bodies never recovered once the water receded." Oh, God. She hadn't changed history. Despite her warnings, despite all her tries to get him to leave, they hadn't survived. Tears filled her eyes and she cried for the two loved ones she'd lost forever to time and the damned river.

After a few minutes, she pulled herself off the floor. She needed to know if she'd truly come back on the same night, so she made her way to Mrs. Williams's office on legs that felt encased in lead. Randi flipped on the light, then found the desk calendar on the museum director's desk.

Sure enough, it was turned to the same date as when she'd left. She glanced at the clock and found that she'd been gone only minutes, although she had been lying on the floor for some time. But she was sure it had been real—her jeans and shoes were still muddy and damp.

Her family hadn't been frantically searching for her. No one knew she'd gone back in time, fallen in love, or had her heart broken again.

All she wanted to do right now was go home, fall into bed, and sleep for the next twenty years or so. But there were things to do, she noticed as she stood in the doorway of the office and looked down the long, narrow dark hallway. She needed to fix the plastic shield and make sure all of her cleaning supplies were put up for the night. No need to alert the world to her unbelievable trip back to 1849.

As if they'd believe you, she told herself as she grabbed a hammer from the janitor's closet, then slowly walked back to the replica of the house where she'd once given her heart and her body to the man she loved.

When she stood in front of the house, though, she knew there was one thing she couldn't replace. The pink plastic baby. No way could she seal the tiny doll back up in the house, all alone. This baby was her only link to Rose, and Randi knew she'd treasure this keepsake always—her only link to the past.

She hadn't even been able to bring her drawings back. All the sketches she'd made of the house, then of Rose and Jackson, were still in her bedroom back at Black Willow Grove. Perhaps Jackson would find them and remember her. Fondly, she hoped. He'd been so angry when they'd parted.

She wanted to believe that was exhaustion and frustration talking, and not his true feelings. Jackson hadn't believed her, but he'd been honest about that always. She also believed that he loved her, in his own way. Maybe not like a man of this time, who had been raised in a society where men and women, black and white, were considered equals. But he had changed a lot in the three weeks she'd stayed in the past. When she'd first arrived, he wouldn't hold or acknowledge his daughter in public. He took every meal in the formal dining room. She wanted to believe that if by some miracle he survived, he would continue to be more open and loving to Rose.

And to any other children he might have with another wife. He'd always said he would remarry. Her hand strayed to her stomach. She'd asked him not to pull away the last time they'd made love. There was a chance, although a slim one, that she might be carrying Jackson's child.

If she was, she'd have an eternal, living reminder of him. If not, then she'd cherish the memories.

Finding the lost nail that she'd ripped out of the replica, she positioned it in the plastic and gently tapped it in. There. No one would ever know that she'd reached inside and gone back to the days when the real plantation house had stood on this ground.

As she straightened, a wave of dizziness reminded her that she was still suffering the effects of traveling through time. She needed to get home, go to bed, and try to mend her broken heart.

She put the hammer back in the closet, used some paper towels to clean up the mud she'd tracked around, then made her way carefully to the front door. Like so many nights, she looked around one last time before turning out the light. Everything looked so . . . normal.

With a sigh, she opened the door, then reached for her keys to lock the dead bolt before punching in the security code. Except her keys weren't there. They were still in her fanny pack, safely hidden in her bedroom in 1849.

Chapter Twenty-five

From a third-floor window, Jackson watched with pride as the levee around the house held back the Mississippi. Brewster had come back from Crowder's Point with news that almost miraculously, the break had been repaired enough to keep the gap from widening. The level of the river was going down already. Within two weeks, they'd have the cotton replanted. The crop would be slightly late this year, but they would have a harvest.

They were going to survive the flood.

Had Randi's insistence of danger played any part in his flood precautions? He imagined they had. Although he'd been cautioning the other planters about the possibility of flooding based upon reports from far upstream, he wouldn't have built the levee around the house. He'd provided extra surveillance of the levees because she was frightened of the river. Perhaps his efforts had at least saved the house from damage.

Randi had been gone a full day and already his future

stretched out bleak and lonely. He knew that no other woman would ever fill the gap she'd left. But would he try to find someone else? He told himself that he must, for the sake of Black Willow Grove. He needed a male heir, although the idea of making love to another woman left him feeling cold.

He wanted Randi back. She'd come to him through a replica of this plantation house, but he had nothing similar through which to contact her. She'd mentioned her sketches, but he doubted they would be powerful enough to carry a message through time.

He needed to try, though. With his affairs in order, the servants celebrating their fate with a fire pit outside, and the quietness of the afternoon pressing around him, he picked his daughter up from the quilt on the floor. Suzette had just fed her, then left to join the festivities.

"Let's go see what Miss Randi left in her room," he told Rose.

The baby babbled into his ear, tugged at his hair, and played with his collar as he carried her downstairs to the second floor. Despite his heavy heart, he smiled at her antics. She was much happier than she'd ever been before. A sad realization hit him: Rose would not remember her loving, unique governess.

"Maybe we can find a sketch of her," he said as they walked into Randi's bedroom. "I'll tell you about her when you're older."

He saw her drawings immediately, scattered haphazardly across the chair. After lowering Rose to the hooked rug, he sat down on the floor and started going through the pages.

He wasn't surprised to see Rose's likeness in many of the drawings. Randi had obviously spent many of her hours upstairs with pencil and paper, documenting the baby's play and rest. He also found several of himself. One was very odd, with curling lines and circles that appeared to look as though she'd swirled the pencil without thought or plan. Sketches of each room of his house did surprise him, since she hadn't talked about those. And he found one that he didn't recognize, which must be the museum where she worked.

The room's contents looked very similar to the furnishings he had around the house. The replica Randi had talked about stood in the center. Whoever had crafted the house had done a good job, because the proportions looked accurate.

He also found a sketch of another room he didn't recognize. It contained a plain bed with only a small headboard, a chest of drawers, several paintings on the walls, and several other objects he didn't recognize. He supposed this was Randi's bedroom, the place where she lay down each night and awoke each morning. With one finger, he traced the details of the drawings, trying to imagine Randi in the room. What he wouldn't give for her likeness instead of the lifeless paper with the lines she'd so painstakingly drawn.

Rose crawled to him, grabbing his knee. Jackson pushed the papers out of her reach, then lifted her into his lap.

"I miss her so much," he told the baby. "Why did she have to go away? She could have stayed here. We're safe now. The flood won't take the house."

Rose babbled as though she were answering all of Jackson's questions. But unfortunately, life wasn't as simple as a baby's first attempts at speech. What he really wanted to know was why Randi had been thrust into their lives, only to be taken back again. Was this a cruel trick of fate, or the vengeance of an angry God?

If he was being punished for his wrongs, he wondered which ones were the most offensive. His desertion of his family? His arrogance when he claimed he would gain great wealth? His luck—and his "skill"— with cards and dice?

Or perhaps the problem went deeper, he mused. Had he been so determined to succeed that he'd denied some of the most important lessons of his youth? When his family had no money, they'd shared stories and memories. Until Randi had come into his life, he'd been so sure that money and position would ensure Rose's happiness. If he just had enough money, he could do anything. If other planters chastised or shunned him, he would be able to destroy them through the economics of the cotton market. He'd bribe or buy out whatever broker or transport was necessary to break them.

That was not the way his mother had taught him to live his life.

And then there was Randi's deep aversion to slavery. He understood her feelings. He didn't like the reality of owning other people, but since he'd acquired his first plantation, he'd accepted the necessity of having slaves work his fields. He'd done his best to be a good owner, providing good-quality food and comfortable cabins. He'd supplied more than adequate clothing and shoes, and allowed church services despite sanctions against teaching slaves to read and write.

He recognized the hunger for learning in the eyes of the children. He knew it from his own poor upbringing, when books were cherished and rare.

Despite his efforts to make the best of a bad situation, Randi still condemned the practice of slavery. Had he forsaken his ethics to be accepted by planter society? Yes, he had. He'd sought the approval of people he neither liked nor respected simply because they were the ones who had money and power.

He'd worked hard for the past fifteen years to achieve all he wanted in life, only to realize that the two women he'd ever loved—his mother and Randi—could not accept the choices he'd made. He wasn't the man they wanted him to be.

And, he realized with a flash, he wasn't that proud of himself either.

"So where does that leave me?" he asked Rose, hugging her close. She squealed in protest, then settled back into his lap.

With a sigh, Jackson pushed himself up from the floor. The sun was setting. Embers from the fire pit, dug at the corner just inside the levee, glowed as brightly as the colors of sunset. The aroma of sizzling pork, sacrificed for the special occasion of surviving the flood, wafted through the air. The sounds of merriment and laughter helped fill the emptiness in his heart.

Randi would enjoy watching the happy event. If she were here, they could stand together with Rose at the window. Then they'd have supper together, put the baby to bed, and snuggle together beneath the sheets on his wide mattress. Making love would be sweet, so very sweet, like nothing they'd experienced before. If only he could have her back, he vowed he'd become the kind of man she wanted him to be. The kind of man he'd been raised to become.

"Can you hear me, Randi?" he whispered, hugging Rose close. "Come back to us. I'll listen to you now. I'll do whatever is necessary to make you happy. Just come home."

With watery eyes, he watched the sky for some sign. A shooting star, perhaps, or a special cloud. But he saw nothing that showed she'd received his message.

With a sigh of resignation, he turned away from the window, deposited Rose on the hooked rug once more, then lit a lamp. When a golden glow filled the room, he began searching for the rest of Randi's belongings. Perhaps something she'd left behind would be a key to reaching out to her.

She'd hidden the "fanny pack" under the bed, so he got on his hands and knees to locate the odd pouch. Sure enough, it was there, suspended between the bed

345

slats. He pulled it loose, then sat beside Rose and examined the item closely. He remembered a special closure, one he'd never seen before. She'd called it a zipper, he remembered. After fiddling with the small metal clasp for several moments, he managed to separate the edges of the pouch.

He pulled out a thick, folded leather wallet, knowing it was where Randi would have kept her treasures. He'd never seen a wallet such as this one, with shiny coverings like soft glass that showed the contents. Neatly printed documents with a painting of her that was so clear, so accurate, she appeared to be alive on the paper. With wonder, he carefully removed the item labeled TENNESSEE DRIVER'S LICENSE.'

"Randi," he whispered. Her smiling face stared back at him, so realistic that he touched her likeness again and again. His heart swelled with relief, because if he didn't have her, at least he had this. When Rose was older, he could show this likeness to her and tell the tale of the governess who had loved her, cared for her, and left her after a few short weeks.

He replaced the license, then turned to other colorful paintings of people. He supposed these were her family. Parents, looking happy and healthy. A family, probably her brother. A grinning child. What a marvelous time Randi must live in to produce such likenesses that could be carried with a person, pulled out to view and remember. How he would have loved to have such treasures from his family, but he knew the poor owned no grand portraits.

The sketch she'd made of him faced Rose's likeness in her wallet. She must have put them there just before she left. She wanted them to be a part of her family.

Jackson went through each item in the wallet, not recognizing some of them, but knowing they were important to Randi. The other things in the pouch were easier to identify. Keys, formed into strange shapes, dangled from some metal ornament called "Elvis."

Two tubes of face paint rested in the bottom of the pouch. These Randi had used to enhance her eyes and lips. He brought the lip paint to his nose and smelled the fragrance, then touched the smooth texture with his finger. He tasted the substance. The memory of a kiss came flooding back, and he closed his eyes against the pain. This is what she'd tasted like, another way he could remember Randi.

The sense of loss he felt overwhelmed him as he re-packed the pouch and placed it on the table beside the bed. He leaned down and picked up his daughter, hugging her, needing her warmth and affection now more than ever. She yawned, snuggling close under his neck.

She needed her rest, so he reluctantly left Randi's belongings on the bed and walked up to the nursery.

"Suzette?" Silence greeted him. The room was dark, the pale curtains billowing in the breeze. He looked in the small bedroom next to the nursery, but it was empty also.

"I'm not leaving you up here alone," he said to Rose. As he spoke she wet her diaper. Jackson held her away from his body and frowned. "I suppose I'll have to change you, won't I?"

He lit a candle on the chest beside the window, noticing that the revelry still continued. Suzette was no doubt enjoying the company of her friends, as relieved as everyone else the house had been spared.

Aided by the candlelight and Rose's sleepy state, Jackson was able to fasten a diaper around her with a minimum amount of difficulty. Proud of his accomplishment, he picked up his daughter again and went downstairs. He turned toward his bedroom, but then changed his mind and headed back to Randi's room.

"Let's rest here," he said softly. He needed to be close to Randi tonight. Where better to feel her presence than in the bed where she'd slept?

He blew out the lamp. The fire pit lit the night with a red glow. Taking a last look outside, he was surprised to see Lebeau's tall figure standing at the edge, as though reluctant to approach it. They'd talked earlier. Jackson understood that Randi had created a strong impression on Samson Lebeau, who had expressed a growing interest in both the people who worked the halls and fields of Black Willow Grove, and, in a larger way, the future of the South.

Perhaps his friend had decided to end his long, solitary journey. A good woman would help Lebeau heal from the painful loss of his family. Tonight would be a good opportunity for him to begin looking for someone to spend the rest of his life with. And since they'd signed the papers earlier, Lebeau would be assured the security few freeman could enjoy. He knew that if he found a woman he loved, Jackson would immediately sign her manumission papers.

Thinking about his friend's love life did little to relieve Jackson's pain over losing Randi. He turned away from the revelry below and pulled the window closed against the night's chill. "Go to sleep now," he whispered to his drowsy daughter.

A feeling of uneasy resignation weighed him down as he placed Rose on the bed, then lay curled around her small body. He pulled Randi's pillow close, inhaling her scent once again.

"Come back to me," he prayed as his eyes misted over once again. But the night was silent, and sleep was a long time coming.

"Mas'r Jackson! Mas'r Jackson!"

The sound of yelling woke him from sleep. He felt disoriented for a moment, unsure of where he was or with whom. Then he remembered; he'd fallen asleep in Randi's bed, snuggled next to Rose. His daughter slept deeply beside him.

But something was wrong. He rubbed his eyes, feeling the sting of the fire pit outside. Odd that the smell should be so strong inside the house. He'd shut the window against the chill.

"Mas'r Jackson!"

He rolled from the bed and walked to the door. "In here," he called out. The sound of footsteps running through the house sent a jolt of fear through his body. Had the levee broken after all? Was the flood upon them once more?

"Lebeau!" he yelled.

"Jackson!" He heard his friend's voice in the dark hallway, and soon he was there, breathing hard, a look of alarm evident even in the faint light.

"What's wrong?"

"The house is on fire. We can't stop the flames. You've got to get out now!"

"The house?" Jackson inhaled, knowing that he didn't smell the fire pit, but rather the aged wood, paper, and fabrics in his home.

"Where did it start?"

"Upstairs, in the nursery. But we didn't see Miss Rose there. Where is she?"

"With me, in here." Jackson spun and ran into the room, snatching up his sleeping daughter, then Randi's pouch and drawings. He couldn't carry everything, though, as Rose began to squirm.

"Take these," he said to Lebeau as he handed him the sketches. "Make sure they stay safe." He kept the pouch with him, unwilling to risk the precious portrait of Randi to anyone else.

They ran down the steps. Everywhere he looked, servants were carrying out furniture and books, his personal papers and the fine china. The clock in the hall was striking, again and again, as if to sound the death knell. The implication finally hit him: His house was burning down, and there was nothing he could do but salvage his most important possessions.

"Where's Suzette?"

"Probably working on the dining room. I saw her running in and out there before I came upstairs."

"Go ahead. Get what you can from the library. You know which papers to get out."

"I know. I'll take care of it. Go on, find her."

Jackson ran to the dining room, Rose squirming in his arms. She began to cry, but he didn't see Suzette. The smell of the fire was so much less here. He ran down the hall and outside to the front lawn. Pieces of furniture and the muddy ground were covered with dishes, books, and papers. The house staff and even field workers ran past him, carrying out his belongings.

"Suzette!" he yelled, but he couldn't find the baby's nurse so she could take Rose. She continued to cry as Jackson ran farther away from the house. He turned back and looked, shocked by the sight of yellow flames streaking from the upper floor, out the windows of the nursery, engulfing the cypress shingles of the roof.

Everything he'd worked for was going up in flames. His beloved plantation, flooded; his beautiful house, gutted by fire. On top of losing Randi . . . He staggered, feeling so desolate and alone that he couldn't go on.

But then Rose wiggled in his arms, her tears stopped now that she was fully awake and away from the noise and confusion of the house. She looked at the fire, her luminous eyes glowing from the dancing flames.

As long as his baby was safe, he knew he could go on. The house had been beautiful, but he could rebuild. The fields would be replanted as soon as the water receded. He would survive this disaster, but he didn't know if he would ever feel the same passion for living since he'd lost Randi. She was his life, far more than this plantation or the beautiful belongings in the house.

Suddenly, the words of the old crone, years before,

came back to haunt him. "Fire will destroy, but if you're honest and true, you'll escape to a new life." She'd been right, he realized with wonder, except he couldn't imagine a new life without Randi.

He heard the sound of crying, but when he looked at Rose, she was still staring in fascination at the house. Who else was around? He turned a full circle, looking for someone sitting or lying on the ground, but found no one. The sound increased. A strange feeling came over him as he remembered standing outside, very near this spot, with Randi. She'd said she heard Rose crying, even though the baby had been upstairs with the window shut.

The sound increased. Jackson listened carefully, finally realizing that he was hearing Randi's tears. He recognized the sobs from when she'd cried so hard at the levee after telling him about the baby she'd lost. Wherever she was, whatever was happening to her right now, she needed the same comfort.

"Randi, where are you?" he yelled into the glowing night sky. Sparks and embers drifted high overhead, blocking out the stars. "Randi!"

"Oh, Jackson," he thought he heard her sob.

He could stand to watch his house burn, his lands flood, but knowing Randi was someplace where he couldn't hold her close and dry her tears caused such gut-wrenching pain that he screamed his frustration aloud.

Rose became upset, and as he tried to calm her, he realized he held Randi's dearest possessions in his hand. The wallet . . .

He tore into the fanny pack, opening the wallet and tilting it so the fire illuminated the words and pictures. Carefully, he pulled out the document called a driver's license and stared at the portrait. Randi wasn't smiling any longer. He gently touched the shiny surface and felt a sheen of moisture. Confused, he brought his finger to his lips and tasted the salt of tears.

"Randi, where are you?" he whispered. "I need to find you, my love. We need each other far more than we need any of our possessions."

He watched the portrait seem to change before his eyes. No longer crying, she simply looked incredibly sad, and her mouth opened, as though she wanted to speak to him.

"Randi," he whispered once more.

A strange feeling of warmth crept over him. Holding Rose tight in his other arm, he looked up from the wallet. The flames, dancing so rapidly just moments ago, seemed to have slowed. Even the servants, who had been dashing about to save his belongings, appeared to be moving through deep mud or water. He saw Lebeau exit the door, then wave slowly at him. Jackson tipped his head to the side, trying to make sense of what he was seeing, but then the world blazed in a white light so bright he blinked. He spun around, holding tight to Rose and to Randi's possessions, frightened for both their safety. Then, with a jolt, his backside landed against a hard object.

Rose stopped crying, probably frightened as much as he. Gradually he began to see again, noticing not the glow of a fire, but the darkness of night. Even the air smelled different, not filled with smoke and embers, but the cool crispness of a spring night.

As his eyes focused, he began to see objects. In front of him stood an unfamiliar building. His eyes scanned downward, taking in the arched pediment about the door, the narrow columns on either side leading to a small porch.

And standing on the porch, her mouth gaping open, her fists rubbing her eyes, stood the woman he loved.

"Randi," he whispered, before the world began to spin and turn once more. He reached out his hand, he heard her answering cry, and then he felt himself sinking into darkness once more.

Randi had never run so fast in her life. She went from staring in disbelief at the man and baby leaning against her car to running toward them in the matter of a heartbeat. "Jackson!" she yelled as she saw him begin to faint.

She reached him in time to take Rose from his powerful grasp and sink to the pavement with him. Her body kept him from leaning sideways and hitting his head, but she was still worried.

"Darn time-travel aftershocks," she mumbled as she checked Rose for any problems. She looked as though she was sleeping, but then, so did Jackson at the moment. He leaned at an awkward angle against the front tire, his head kept fairly upright by the metal wheel well. She only hoped he didn't stay passed out too long, because she was going to have some explaining to do if Mrs. Williams drove up in a few hours to find an unconscious man and baby in her parking lot.

"You're worried about Mrs. Williams when you got the man you love right here?" she asked herself incredulously. The realization that he was really there finally hit. "You're here," she whispered, holding Rose tight with one hand, reaching out and touching Jackson's face with the other. Warm and alive, he'd found a way to come to her. She leaned close, placing a kiss on his relaxed and unresponsive lips.

That will change real soon, she vowed.

He smelled smoky, as though he'd been to a cookout. What had he been doing in the past? And how had he gotten here?

She eased Rose to a more comfortable position, then decided the baby could rest against her daddy for just a minute while Randi checked them both out. She arranged the baby into the crook of Jackson's arm.

Running her hands over both of them, she found no problems. Like her, they'd just become faint and disoriented. She'd gone through this twice, and remembered distinctly the awful feeling of weakness passing through time caused. In Jackson's hand, however, she was surprised to find her fanny pack and wallet. He still had a tight grip on the objects, as though he was afraid to lose them. How sweet. He'd been holding her stuff, looking through her photographs.

"That's what drew you here, isn't it?" she said in wonder. Her driver's license, especially, peeked above the plastic. With a smile, she realized that because of the object that had brought him through time, he'd come not only to her, but to her car.

She was still smiling when he opened his eyes and blinked up at her. "You're really here?" he asked.

"No," she said, smoothing her palm over his cheek. "*You're* really here."

"This is your time?"

"No, Jackson," she said, leaning down, her eyes filling with tears of joy, "this is *our* time."

Epilogue

Randi closed the textbook she'd been reading for the past half-hour while Rose napped. College was great, but Randi wished she could study only the courses she wanted. Math was okay. She'd taken a real interest in history, she thought with a smile, but economics—uck! She saw no reason why an architect needed to know about supply-and-demand curves.

With a sigh, she pushed herself out of the big wing chair that Jackson usually sat in each evening. He still enjoyed sitting by a fire, and she'd been hard-pressed to explain to him how furnaces worked. His first reaction to any cool weather was to build a nice roaring fire, she recalled with a smile. Then, of course, he'd wanted to snuggle in front of it. He'd become very attached to a certain quilt that Randi kept draped over the back of the chair, just in case he wanted to "snuggle" right there on the floor.

A familiar spot of pink caught her eye as she stood by the hearth. The little pink baby doll, never returned

355

to the museum, rested in a special tableau Darla had created from miniature furniture and tiny print fabric. Someday, Randi thought, she'd have a whole dollhouse. Rose would enjoy rearranging the furniture and using her imagination to create a family who lived inside—as long as she didn't go traveling through time!

Randi walked to one of the windows that looked out over their small front yard, the split rail fence, and gravel road that led across the property to their house on her Uncle Aaron's horse farm. Jackson should be home soon. She had a class that evening, but they always had enough time for a meal together before she drove to Memphis.

He'd insisted she quit work, not at all comfortable with a wife who made money when he was still struggling to learn the customs and technology of the time. She'd given in after compromising; she'd go to school, he'd work, and they'd both care for Rose.

For a bona fide nineteenth-century male chauvinist, Jackson was straightening up just fine, Randi thought affectionately. He retained the traditions most important to him, but had proved very flexible about learning new things. He had yet to take his driver's test, but he would, in time. He considered horses the best old-fashioned mode of transportation, just as he wanted a real fire instead of a modern furnace.

She sure didn't mind watching Jackson split logs he dragged in from her uncle's wooded acreage. He'd put on a little weight since arriving six months ago—all muscle. Working hard all day would have upset most wealthy landowners who arrived penniless in another century, but not her husband. He'd taken to manual labor as if he'd been born to exercise and train horses, fix up their cozy house, and care for the small garden he insisted every family should have.

Oh, and making love. He was quite good at that, too,

she thought with a widening smile as he walked up the fieldstone path to the front door.

"Hi," she said softly as she opened the door for him. He smelled of sunshine and horses, with a tang of autumn. "Rose is napping."

Jackson Bondurant smiled suggestively, bringing Randi close for a hug. "In that case, would you like to lie down yourself?"

"I have class tonight."

"Not for another," he paused and checked the modern wristwatch her parents had given him for Father's Day, "three hours."

"Aren't you hungry?"

"Just for you," he said, lowering his head and kissing her so thoroughly that her knees went weak.

She molded her arms around his back, pulling him closer, reveling in the solid feel of bone and muscle and warm flesh. At times like this, she still got misty-eyed. What a wonder that of all the people who had ever lived, she and Jackson had found each other. Time had been no barrier to their love.

He pulled back, his finger gently touching the corner of her eye and coming away damp. "Remembering again?" he whispered.

"Only good memories."

"The very best," he agreed.

She kissed him, lingering long enough to savor the taste and feel of him once more. When she pulled back, she looked into his dark eyes and asked, "Do you ever regret losing the plantation?"

"If I had to give up a hundred Black Willow Groves to have you and Rose, the answer would still be no. What I lost was only wood and dirt. What I gained was the world."

"Oh, Jackson, that is so sweet," she whispered, throwing her arms around him and hugging him close once more. She pushed away from his shoulders, although he held her tight at the waist. "But you don't mind that my sketches survived, and that they built the museum?"

"Of course not. Although I do find it amusing that you never thought those sketches were yours when you saw them in the history book." The lines around his eyes crinkled in amusement.

"How could I? I hadn't drawn them yet when I went back in time."

Jackson laughed. "I know, but allow me the irony of knowing my wife helped create the replica of the house she traveled back in time to see."

"Oh, no. I traveled in time for you and Rose, not for some old house."

"A house the history books still record as being destroyed by the flood."

Randi shrugged. "Who are *we* to correct history books? I suppose no one bothered to tell the complete story of Black Willow Grove. Or maybe the fire was left out by one of the authors. Who knows? The important fact—the one that I knew when I went back to your time—was that the plantation and house were destroyed."

"And that Rose and I perished in the flood."

"Yes." The memory of the devastating feelings still made her shudder, so she pushed the thoughts aside and smiled at Jackson. "Only you didn't. You just disappeared. Just like I disappeared from my time into yours."

"You haven't forgiven me for not believing you?" he asked, his teasing tone and expression telling her he knew very well she'd forgiven him for not initially buying her incredible story.

She rubbed his bulging biceps, up to his strong shoulders. "Just keep up the good work and I'll let you know in fifty years or so."

He swatted her on the bottom. "You still have to get in the last word, don't you?"

"Absolutely!"

They walked into the house. Jackson picked up the mail which had been delivered earlier that day. "What's this?"

"Oh, I almost forgot. It's a letter from Barbara Lebeau. I tracked her down on the Internet in computer lab at school. She's Samson Lebeau's great-great-granddaughter."

"Amazing," Jackson said, examining the Philadelphia postmarked envelope with awe. "Just think. If Lebeau had lost his wife and daughter now, there's a very good chance he could have found them quickly. After almost losing you, I understand the pain he must have gone through for all those years."

"But he ended up a happy man, according to the letter. Barbara never met him, of course, but she knew her great-grandfather, and he remembered his father very well."

"So Lebeau married."

"Yes, and you'll never believe who."

"Who?"

"Suzette. And they had seven children."

"Really?" Jackson chuckled and shook his head. "The rascal."

"He moved many of your former slaves to the North before the war. Some of them were involved in the Underground Railroad."

"What's that?"

"It was the way slaves escaped to the North, house to house, traveling with the help of sympathetic people of all colors."

"I have a feeling that if you had stayed in the past, that's exactly what you would have been doing." Jackson settled into his chair, then held out his arms for her to snuggle close.

"And you probably would have gladly helped. I'm still surprised you made provisions to give the land to Lebeau in your will, and that you'd freed so many of the people even before you knew you were going to leave."

Jackson shrugged. "I did what was right, and what would have made you happy, had you stayed in the past."

"I knew you were a good man. You obviously lived in the wrong time."

"I'm in the right place now," he said with a smile. "I'm glad Lebeau's life turned out happy, and I'm going to read that letter very carefully while you're at school tonight."

Randi settled on his lap, snuggling close. "Oh? And what are you going to do until then?"

"Show my wife," he said, punctuating his words with kisses on her brow and cheeks, "how happy I am that she fell through a dollhouse and into my life."

FOREVER & A DAY

VICTORIA CHANCELLOR

When Linda O'Rourke returns to her grandmother's South Carolina beach house, it is for a quiet summer of tying up loose ends. And although the lovely dwelling charms her, she can't help but remember the evil presence that threatened her there so many years ago. Plagued by her fear, and tormented by visions of a virile Englishman tempting her with his every caress, she is unprepared for reality in the form of the mysterious and handsome Gifford Knight. His kisses evoke memories of the man in her dreams, but his sensual demands are all too real. Linda longs to surrender to Giff's masterful touch, but is it a safe haven she finds in his arms, or the beginning of her worst nightmare?

__52063-X $5.50 US/$7.50 CAN

VICTORIA CHANCELLOR

Bestselling Author Of *Forever & A Day*

In the Wyoming Territory—a land both breathtaking and brutal—bitterroots grow every summer for a brief time. Therapist Rebecca Hartford has never seen such a plant—until she is swept back to the days of Indian medicine men, feuding ranchers, and her pioneer forebears. Nor has she ever known a man as dark, menacing, and devastatingly handsome as Sloan Travers. Sloan hides a tormented past, and Rebecca vows to use her professional skills to help the former Union soldier, even though she longs to succumb to personal desire. But when a mysterious shaman warns Rebecca that her sojourn in the Old West will last only as long as the bitterroot blooms, she can only pray that her love for Sloan is strong enough to span the ages....

_52087-7 $5.50 US/$7.50 CAN

DON'T MISS OTHER LOVE SPELL TIME-TRAVEL ROMANCES!

Tempest in Time by Eugenia Riley. When assertive, independent businesswoman Missy Monroe and timid Victorian virgin Melissa Montgomery accidentally trade places and partners on their wedding day, each finds herself in a bewildering new time, married to a husband she doesn't know. Now, each woman will have to decide whether she is part of an odd couple or a match made in heaven.
_52154-7 $5.50 US/$6.50 CAN

Miracle of Love by Victoria Chancellor. When Erina O'Shea's son is born too early, doctors tell the lovely immigrant there is little they can do to save young Colin's life. Not in 1896 Texas. But then she and Colin are hurtled one hundred years into the future and into the strong arms of Grant Kirby. He's handsome, powerful, wealthy, and doesn't believe a word of her story. However, united in their efforts to save the baby, Erina and Grant struggle to recognize that love is the greatest miracle of all.
_52144-X $5.50 US/$6.50 CAN

SANDRA HILL

Sweeter Savage Love. When a twist of fate casts Harriet Ginoza back in time to the Old South, the modern psychologist meets the object of her forbidden fantasies. Though she knows the dangerously handsome rogue is everything she should despise, she can't help but feel that within his arms she might attain a sweeter savage love.

___52212-8 $5.99 US/$6.99 CAN

Desperado. When a routine skydive goes awry, Major Helen Prescott and Rafe Santiago parachute straight into the 1850 California Gold Rush. Mistaken for a notorious bandit and his infamously sensuous mistress, they find themselves on the wrong side of the law. In a time and place where rules have no meaning, Helen finds herself all too willing to throw caution to the wind to spend every night in the arms of her very own desperado.

___52182-2 $5.99 US/$6.99 CAN

Dorchester Publishing Co., Inc.
P.O. Box 6640
Wayne, PA 19087-8640

Please add $1.75 for shipping and handling for the first book and $.50 for each book thereafter. NY, NYC, and PA residents, please add appropriate sales tax. No cash, stamps, or C.O.D.s. All orders shipped within 6 weeks via postal service book rate. Canadian orders require $2.00 extra postage and must be paid in U.S. dollars through a U.S. banking facility.

Name_____
Address_____
City_____ State_____ Zip_____
I have enclosed $_____ in payment for the checked book(s).
Payment <u>must</u> accompany all orders. ❏ Please send a free catalog.

Windmills In Time

Victoria Bruce

New Yorker Dierdre Brown is an independent modern-day woman. She doesn't need a man for anything; not love, not money—*not anything*. So when a twist of fate casts her back in time to the wild Nebraska plains, she is sure that with the fierce determination she learned on the city streets, she'll find her way back home. But when handsome cowboy Jesse Colburn takes her in his arms on the wide-open grassy plain, she feels an intensity in his embrace that she has not known in the men of her own time. And she begins to wonder if this is where she belongs: close to the earth, close to Jesse.

___52280-2 $5.50 US/$6.50 CAN

Dorchester Publishing Co., Inc.
P.O. Box 6640
Wayne, PA 19087-8640

Please add $1.75 for shipping and handling for the first book and $.50 for each book thereafter. NY, NYC, and PA residents, please add appropriate sales tax. No cash, stamps, or C.O.D.s. All orders shipped within 6 weeks via postal service book rate. Canadian orders require $2.00 extra postage and must be paid in U.S. dollars through a U.S. banking facility.

Name_____

Address_____

City_____State_____Zip_____

I have enclosed $_____ in payment for the checked book(s).

Payment <u>must</u> accompany all orders. ❑ Please send a free catalog.

CHECK OUT OUR WEBSITE! www.dorchesterpub.com

Love Just in Time
Flora Speer

After discovering her husband's infidelity, Clarissa Cummings thinks she will never trust another man. Then a freak accident sends her into another century—and the most handsome stranger imaginable saves her from drowning in the canal. But he is all wet if he thinks he has a lock on Clarissa's heart. After scandal forces Jack Martin to flee to the wilds of America, the dashing young Englishman has to give up the pleasures of a rake and earn his keep with a plow and a hoe. Yet to his surprise, he learns to enjoy the simple life of a farmer, and he yearns to take Clarissa as his bride. But after Jack has sown the seeds of desire, secrets from his past threaten to destroy his harvest of love.

___52289-6 $5.50 US/$6.50 CAN

Lady of the Night

Cordia Byers

Manacled to a stone wall is not the way Katharina Fergersen planned to spend her vacation. But a wrong turn in the right place and the haunted English castle she is touring is suddenly full of life—and so is the man who is bathing before her. As the frosty winter days melt into hot passionate nights, she realizes that there is more to Kane than just a well-filled pair of breeches. Katharina is determined not to let this man who has touched her soul escape her, even if it means giving up all to remain Sedgewick's lady of the night.

___4404-8 $5.99 US/$6.99 CAN